THE QUEEN WHO CAME IN FROM THE COLD

S. J. BENNETT

ZAFFRE

First published in the UK in 2025 by
ZAFFRE
An imprint of Bonnier Books UK
5th Floor, HYLO, 105 Bunhill Row,
London, EC1Y 8LZ

Copyright © S.J. Bennett, 2025

All rights reserved.
No part of this publication may be reproduced,
stored or transmitted in any form by any means, electronic,
mechanical, photocopying or otherwise, without the
prior written permission of the publisher.

The right of S.J. Bennett to be identified as Author of this
work has been asserted by her in accordance with the
Copyright, Designs and Patents Act, 1988.

This is a work of fiction. References to real people, events,
establishments, organizations, or locales are intended only to
provide a sense of authenticity and are used fictitiously. All other
characters, and all incidents and dialogue, are drawn from the
author's imagination and are not to be construed as real.

A CIP catalogue record for this book is
available from the British Library.

Hardback ISBN: 978-1-83877-770-8
Trade paperback ISBN: 978-1-83877-771-5

Also available as an ebook and an audiobook

3 5 7 9 10 8 6 4 2

Typeset by IDSUK (Data Connection) Ltd
Printed and bound by CPI (UK) Ltd, Croydon CR0 4YY

The authorised representative in the EEA is Bonnier Books
UK (Ireland) Limited.
Registered office address: Floor 3, Block 3, Miesian Plaza,
Dublin 2, D02 Y754, Ireland
compliance@bonnierbooks.ie
www.bonnierbooks.co.uk

For Ben, who wanted a mystery set on a train

Character List

Royal family

Queen Elizabeth II
Prince Philip, Duke of Edinburgh, her husband
Princess Margaret, her sister
Anthony Armstrong-Jones, Margaret's new husband
Queen Elizabeth, the Queen Mother

Royal household

Sir Hugh Masson, Private Secretary (PS)
Major Miles Urquhart, Deputy Private Secretary (DPS)
Dominic Stonor, Press Secretary
Joan McGraw, Assistant Private Secretary (APS)
Rear Admiral Nick Cotterill, Master of the Household
Hattie Cowell, maid
Sandra Pole, temporary lady in waiting to Princess Margaret

Murder case

Pavel Michalowski, photographer
Henry Coxon, journalist, friend of Michalowski
Josiah Thorburn, landowner
Tracy Thorburn, his daughter

Police

Chief Superintendent George Venables, Murder Squad
Chief Inspector Fred Darbishire, Murder Squad
Chief Inspector Jim Weatherby, Staffordshire County Police

Others

Stanley Hill, Coal Board advisor
Peter Vernon, BBC
Major Hector Ross, Head of D branch, MI5
Madeleine Simon, officer, MI5
Rear Admiral John Marlow, Commanding Officer, *HMY Britannia*
Commander Peter Attwell, Executive Officer, *HMY Britannia*
Commander Trefor Kinnock, Supply Officer, *HMY Britannia*
Paul Schwartz, bookseller
Doctor Tatiana Sokolova, scientist

THE QUEEN WHO CAME IN FROM THE COLD

S.J. Bennett was born in Yorkshire and travelled the world as an army child. She had a varied career before her first novel was published when she was 42. Since then, her books have won awards, been optioned for TV, and have been translated into over 20 languages.

She was once asked to interview for the role of Assistant Private Secretary to the Queen and still considers it the job that got away. A curious royal watcher for many years, she lives in London, where she can often be found haunting its palaces, museums, galleries and libraries. She currently writes the 'Her Majesty the Queen Investigates' series.

You can find her on Instagram @sophiabennett_writer and on X @sophiabennett.

To receive Royal Correspondence about the Her Majesty The Queen Investigates series – including royal family trivia and more – sign up at bit.ly/SJBennett

Also by S.J. Bennett

The Windsor Knot
A Three Dog Problem
Murder Most Royal
A Death in Diamonds

In the long history of the world, only a few generations have been granted the role of defending freedom in its hour of maximum danger. I do not shrink from this responsibility – I welcome it. I do not believe that any of us would exchange places with any other people or any other generation. The energy, the faith, the devotion which we bring to this endeavor will light our country and all who serve it – and the glow from that fire can truly light the world.

President John F Kennedy, Inaugural address,
20 January 1961

Prologue

'Isn't Mrs Jones vile? I loathe her. I just hate her to the depths of my being and want awful, disgusting things to happen to her. Is that terrible of me? I have visions of her stripped of that gaudy dress and dragged through the streets. You should have been there, Pav. I'll have her rendition of 'Let's Fall in Love' going through my head for a week. She deserves rich punishment for that, at the very least.'

Pavel Michalowski listened to the disembodied voice coming from the speaker he had rigged up to the telephone receiver in his basement flat. Pavel was good with wires and technology; he had been building radios since childhood. The speaker, combined with a microphone 'borrowed' from the BBC, was a neat little technological solution to the problem of staying in touch with loquacious friends and demanding clients while getting on with the task in hand. He still had work to do tonight.

'You love her, admit it,' he said, picking up a stack of bills and glancing through them. 'You're just jealous.'

'Of Tony? Are you joking? The man is *tiny*. And *outrageous*. And so *bourgeois*.'

The voice, rich and resonant, belonged to Pavel's friend Henry Coxon, a journalist and *bon viveur*. He was talking about Princess Margaret, nicknamed 'Mrs Jones' by Henry since her recent marriage to their mutual friend, Tony Armstrong-Jones.

'So are you – bourgeois at least,' Pavel pointed out. 'So am I. At least Tony's talented. As is Margaret, admit it. I heard her sing once. She should do it professionally. It would do her good to try hard at something.'

'Did you say she was *good*?' Henry asked. 'I can hardly hear you, Pav. Have you got me echoing round your house again? I hate it when you put me on that speaker contraption of yours.'

'Then don't call me when I'm catching up on work after a long day.'

Henry was upset. 'When else can I call, if not after a party? It's the only time I have anything to say.'

'You have nothing to say. You're a bigger bitch than Her Highness.'

His friend was only bitter because he'd had visions of squiring the princess himself. When her last engagement had gone wrong, Henry had honestly thought he was in with a chance. He wasn't, and her amused indifference baffled him. Then she ran off with their mutual friend, who was short and limped as a result of childhood polio, and he was astonished.

'Oh, that's mean!' he complained. 'And it's Her *Royal* Highness. You wouldn't know that, being foreign.'

'I'm not foreign,' Pavel reminded his friend, equably.

'With a name like Michalowski?'

Pavel ignored this remark. He thought back to the song he'd once heard the princess sing at a soirée, adapting the lyrics as she went along.

Birds do it, bees do it, They say the navy overseas do it . . .

He hummed to himself as he turned to his over-stacked dining table, which served as his office desk, picking up a black and white print that had been sent to him in the post. It was like Pavel's own stock in trade: a girl with shiny hair, head turned three-quarters to the camera, body in a black polo-neck sweater that paid testament to the structural quality of her underwear. This particular subject wasn't a girl, more of a proper woman, with a younger version of herself sitting beside her, hair neatly brushed and caught in a clip, staring blankly at the viewer.

The print was one of a set, and the quality of the image wasn't great. Frowning, Pavel checked it with a magnifying lens for imperfections. He shot his cuffs and ran his fingers through his hair. He was tired. He'd look at it again later.

Henry was still going. 'Of course, I'll have to say something nice in my column on Friday. God, I hate the way we have to grovel, don't you? It's so outdated. They're humans, these royals. Why can't we just say so?'

Pavel grunted a non-committal reply.

Henry lowered his voice, but its plummy tones, rendered raspy by a forty-a-day cigarette habit, still filled the room.

'You know, I was rather outspoken at The Ivy a couple of nights ago, after the second bottle of claret. I could swear someone started following me afterwards. The dark forces of the Establishment, out to stifle the gentlemen of the press.' He paused. 'Can you hear me? Are you even listening?'

'I'm listening,' Pavel assured him. 'But I don't know why. You're so full of shit. Go to bed, Henry.'

'You love my shit, Pav darling! You do! And you know I adore *madame la princesse* really, the minx. We're supposed to feel sorry for her, giving up the love of her life for the sake of her so-called duty – when what she really wanted was the chance to keep us all bobbing and bowing, and to carry on at Kensington Palace. Doesn't it drive you *mad*? But that waist, that hair, those . . . I know you don't like it when I refer to the royal bosoms, but they were spectacular tonight. I wonder if she's preggers. Of course, you like 'em boyish . . .'

Pavel went into the hall to fetch a batch of enlargements he'd made in his darkroom earlier. He wanted to see if any might be worth including in a small show that he and some friends were thinking of putting together. When he came back, Henry was saying,

'. . . but of course I couldn't, because the duchess would have killed me. Talking of which, a bird threw herself at me last week. Proper totty. Forgot to tell you. You think I don't still have it in me, Pav, but I assure you, this one was a stunner. Legs all the way till Christmas. Couldn't get enough of me . . .'

Pavel listened with one ear while he examined the prints. He'd been at a pub in Chalk Farm last night, trying to capture the energy of a new guitar band through a haze of smoke. The blow-ups were certainly more arresting than the posed portraits he did to make a living, but he'd misjudged the depth of field. He preferred a casual snap of the blonde with the French-looking hair, cut very short, like Jean Seberg, whom he'd encountered at the bar.

'Look, someone's at the door,' Henry said. 'I'll be back in a moment. If I'm not, call the police. *I'm coming, I'm coming!*'

His voice faded away, and Pavel's thoughts remained with the blonde, who had slipped out of his flat this morning leaving a tangle of sheets imbued with her smell. Before going, she'd borrowed his camera to take a post-coital picture of him and, more by luck than judgement, she'd done a decent enough job. He examined his face impartially in the resulting images, noting the lack of symmetry between the eyes, the angularity of the nose. He was neutral about his looks, but they got the job done, as witnessed by the rumpled sheets. He thought of them as another tool of his trade, like the hands that were so good with wires and switches.

Pavel wondered in passing how Henry had got on with the 'proper totty' he'd just mentioned. Henry wasn't usually successful with women, unless they happened to have a thing for tweed jackets and cord trousers. He still clung to the uniform they'd worn at prep school together aged seven. Which probably explained a lot.

Pavel looked round. Something was off. Behind him, the flat had gone very quiet. Where was the raspy, plummy voice?

'Hello?' he called out.

Silence.

Hadn't Henry mentioned being followed, after a trip to The Ivy? Pavel had automatically ignored his friend's mentions of 'dark forces of the Establishment'. Still, Henry was very good at making enemies, and apparently he'd trash-talked the Queen's sister in a public restaurant. Pavel felt a prickle of unease.

'Coxon?' He reverted to schooldays, where the boys were all called by their surnames . . . except for him. 'Michalowski' had been too 'exotic' and so Pavel was 'Michaels' to the masters, 'Mikes' to his friends. He walked over to the microphone, which sat on a teetering stack of unreturned library books. 'Henry?'

There was a strange, muffled sound through the speaker.

'All present and correct,' Henry said, through a mouthful of crumbs. 'I just had to go to the cake tin for a little something. Fruit cake. Wedding last weekend. Whisky makes me peckish. And Mrs Jones was very miserly with the canapés. What was I saying?'

'Someone was at your door.'

'Oh yes. The mad old bat downstairs wanted to tell me off for dancing around in hobnail boots. By which she means tiptoeing in stockinged feet across my own floorboards. What was I saying before that?'

'The stunner. Legs till Christmas.'

'I'll tell you all about it later. I think I'm onto something there. But, God, tonight's cabaret. Bloody Cole Porter again. I'll have to put something in my column on Friday. The usual slurry. "Charming', "gracious", "tuneful", grovel grovel . . . "Her Royal Highness, in sparkling form, accompanied herself on the piano with the skill of a seasoned performer . . . The blooming cheek of a fresh young bride . . ." Blooming cheek indeed. God, I hate myself. I said, *I hate myself*, Pav! Are you there?'

But this time, it was Pavel who was busy answering a knock at his own front door. His flat in Primrose Hill was relatively central, and it wasn't unusual for friends who'd been tipped out of pubs and clubs to show up at his place in need of an overnight stay on his sofa. However, to his surprise, two men in overalls and shirtsleeves stood outside, slightly shivering. The younger of the two held a toolbox by the handle.

'Sorry to bother you, sir,' the older one said. 'The young lady above's had a leak in the kitchen pipe. Water everywhere and we can't find the stopcock. You don't happen to know where it is, do you?'

Pavel was impressed to see plumbers out at this time of night. He knew that the lovely young Mrs Hughes upstairs had a baby to worry about. The last thing she needed was a flooded kitchen.

'Well, mine's in a cupboard in the bathroom,' he told them. 'It's an odd place, I grant you. Hard to reach.'

'We've looked there. D'you mind showing us yours? Maybe we missed it?'

Pavel waved them in, just as Henry's voice boomed from behind him,

'Pav! Honestly! I don't think I can do it. I need another job. D'you think the *Socialist Worker* will hire me?'

The older man hovered on the threshold, looking embarrassed. 'You have company? Sorry, sir, we don't want to disturb you.'

'No, no,' Pavel assured him. 'Come through.'

He led the way from the narrow hallway into the living room.

'You're not listening. I'm hanging up!' Henry threatened. 'Honestly, all you do is *berate* me anyway, when I'm just speaking for the common man.'

They all looked towards the speaker and the plumbers' eyes lit up with recognition. The younger one grinned and gave Pavel the thumbs up. The older one went over to the phone, as if to examine the set-up. But to Pavel's surprise he depressed the exposed hook switch with his finger, cutting Henry off mid-flow.

'Hey!' Pavel called out.

Turning back, the man took two athletic strides towards him and caught him on the jaw with an upper cut so powerful that he heard his brain rattle in his skull.

The pain was secondary to the shock. Pavel's legs gave way, and he began to fall. His scrabbling hands clutched at thin air.

So, it had happened after all. He should have been paying attention. At the first sight of them, he should have realised – but he'd been thinking about Mrs Hughes upstairs. Her baby, her flooded kitchen . . . This must be how they did it.

As he hit the ground, he felt someone grip his forearm, and the sharp jab of a needle through the crisp cotton of his shirt. His vision was blurred and the two men seemed to swim above him, as through water. He said a prayer, but no words came out of his mouth.

'Nice speaker set-up,' the younger man observed, in Russian.

'Shut up,' the older one told him.

Seconds later, the world faded to a pinprick and turned black.

PART ONE
BLOOD AND CUSTARD

Chapter 1

Sunday, 26 March 1961

The Queen sat in the back of the Daimler, with Prince Philip beside her, and her sister and new husband following in the car behind. The journey from Buckingham Palace to Euston wasn't long, but it gave Elizabeth a chance to catch up on some paperwork.

This morning, her boxes had contained a note from her assistant private secretary that she particularly wanted to read. It was a briefing about the Kennedys, who'd be coming for dinner in several weeks' time. The new American president and his wife were making all the headlines these days. There was an aura of enchantment about them that reminded Elizabeth a bit of her own days as a fresh head of state. But whereas she already knew quite a lot about the president – his father had been ambassador to the United Kingdom, after all – she was less familiar with his wife beyond the newspaper headlines, which she never trusted.

She was aware that Jackie Kennedy, née Bouvier, was beautiful and glamorous, but what was she like as a person? Was she intelligent, curious, friendly? Did she (oh, the Queen hoped so) have a great fondness for dogs, for example? Was she an Anglophile? It was important that their visit went well, so she diligently got down to her homework, while the car travelled up Grosvenor Place at a stately pace.

Joan McGraw, the assistant private secretary, had put a decent amount of material together in the file. The Queen was surprised to read that the First Lady had studied at the Sorbonne, during a year out from her college course at Vassar. She had won a competition to work for *Vogue* magazine in New York – an offer that she had declined for some reason – and had ended up writing for the *Washington Times-Herald*. Goodness. A woman of letters. Intelligent, without doubt and curious, certainly. The Queen read on. What sort of thing did Miss Bouvier write?

She gave such a sudden start that Philip looked up from his own briefing papers in alarm.

'Everything all right, Cabbage?'

'Perfectly,' she said, staring straight ahead.

'It clearly isn't. What're you reading?'

'Just a little thing about Mrs Kennedy. It's very . . . interesting.'

Philip smiled. 'Ah! Jackie! Well, I suppose I should read that too, don't you think? What does it say?'

He leaned over and she reluctantly handed the open file to him. He quickly scanned the first paragraphs, nodding and raising an eyebrow. Then he exploded.

'Bloody hell! Is this right? Her very first published article was . . .' He prodded the paper. "Is Princess Elizabeth as pretty as her picture?" What in heaven's name?'

'It was in '51, during our first visit to Washington.'

'I saw that. What utter drivel! I thought she was supposed to be a literary scholar. You'd never get a man writing that guff, by God.'

'You'd never get a man being asked to,' the Queen pointed out. She had spent more time with press barons than she cared to remember. This was just the sort of thing they wanted a woman to write.

'And were you?' Philip asked.

'What?'

'As pretty? According to the article.'

'Joan didn't include it. She says she couldn't find it, only the headline in an index.'

Philip nodded. 'Mmm. Very prudent.' He went back to the file. 'Ah! Here Jackie is again, writing about the coronation. Miss Bouvier came over to London especially. She has a thing for you, Lilibet. Oh, look, she got a couple of exclusives, too, according to Joan. Apparently, your attendants had to get up at three in the morning to have their hair and tiaras done in time for a dawn start. Is that true?'

'It was rather early, I seem to remember.'

'And that bit about the crown. Someone told her about them marking it secretly, so the archbishop didn't put it on back to front, like he did for your father. Ha! She had good sources, whoever they were. It's accurate drivel, at least.'

The Queen had a vague recollection of one of her ladies-in-waiting inviting a couple of young Americans to stay at her townhouse in Mayfair. Henriette had told her they'd had a ball in London, going to all the best coronation parties and dances. Which she, personally, hadn't been able to do because she was too busy rehearsing for the big day. Was that Jackie? How extraordinary.

'What did she do next?' she asked Philip, who was still looking through the file.

'She got engaged to the future president of the United States, got married and started a family. You were the beginning and end of her journalistic career, my dear.'

He gave her a satisfied smile and handed the file back.

After some heavy traffic at Hyde Park Corner, the car turned onto Piccadilly. They passed the address where Elizabeth had lived happily as a little girl. From that lovely Georgian house, she used to wave across Green Park to the king, 'Grandpa England', as she called him, in Buckingham Palace.

But her childhood home had been flattened in the Blitz and was still a bomb site when Jacqueline Bouvier came to report on the coronation. The Queen thought of all those years of privation and sacrifice. Thank goodness for the Americans, who came to the rescue in the end (unlike Mr Kennedy Senior, one couldn't help recalling, who had moved out of London when the bombing began and didn't seem particularly keen on defeating the Germans). However, the country would be paying them back for decades.

Was Philip right to look so satisfied? she wondered. When 'Grandpa England' was king, London had felt like the centre of the world. *Britannia* ruled the waves, and every foreign nation bowed to her supremacy. Not so now. When

President Kennedy came to visit, it would be as the vigorous ally everyone looked up to, with the economy, the industry, the technical and financial supremacy all other countries dreamed of. And he'd be doing it with his fashionable wife, the ex-Vassar student and sometime royal correspondent, at his side.

It was going to be quite a visit in June. The Queen *hoped* Jackie Kennedy liked dogs.

Chapter 2

There was a time in Joan McGraw's life – between the end of the war and about four years ago – when a ride up the west coast on the royal train would have been an event, a highlight. Something to look forward to.

But today, as she waited at Euston station, the Queen's assistant private secretary reflected that plane journey from Kathmandu to Tehran was an event. An elephant ride through Bombay was a highlight. A few days' sailing in the Mediterranean on the Royal Yacht *Britannia* was something to look forward to. The royal train was now merely a convenient means of transport. And what had Joan become? Spoiled, certainly. Busy. Happier than she had any right to expect.

The tall, exceptionally good-looking man standing on the platform beside her leaned down to mutter in her ear.

'What are you doing next Tuesday, because I—?'

'Shh.'

The Queen had just appeared in the Great Hall entrance, followed by her husband, her sister Margaret with a pair of white terriers on leads and, bringing up the rear, the intriguing figure of Margaret's new husband, Anthony Armstrong-Jones.

It was teatime on the Sunday afternoon before Easter, near the spring equinox. Afternoon light flooded through the hall's high windows, illuminating the Greek columns that gave it the air of a temple to Victorian railway gods. Soon the building was to be ruined – swept away to make place for something more practical and modern. The man beside Joan had the look of a Greek god about him, she thought ruefully. It wouldn't be hard to imagine a statue to him.

The Queen flashed them a smile as she strode past. Prince Philip looked as if his mind was elsewhere. Behind him, Margaret kept frowning and glancing behind her as if looking for someone, while Tony Armstrong-Jones walked head down, hands behind his back, uncomfortable with the attention. They continued towards the platform where the royal train was waiting.

As they shook hands and chatted with the station manager, Joan cast her eye briefly along the train itself. Between the engine and the brake, there were eight carriages today – saloons, as they were known – including the couchette near the front where she would be sleeping. They were travelling to Lancashire, where the Queen was due to address a coal mining convention tomorrow. Meanwhile, Princess Margaret and her husband would take a couple of the carriages on to Glasgow for a quick official visit, and then Balmoral for a slightly longer break.

'I say, it's a bit of a mishmash, isn't it?' said the Greek god, otherwise known as Dominic Stonor, the Queen's press secretary.

'What is?'

'The train. I mean, bits of it look terribly smart in their dark red livery and all that, but you'd think they'd borrowed some of the carriages from Noah.'

'Didn't he specialise in arks?'

'That era, though. Pre-war, anyway. First World War, by the look of it. Is the ride horribly uncomfortable? It's my first time.'

'It's surprisingly smooth, actually,' Joan reassured him.

'What's smooth?' another, gruffer, voice asked.

This one belonged to Miles Urquhart, the Queen's long-standing deputy private secretary. He bore himself with the stiff importance of a man whose job was to be in the presence of greatness.

'The ride, apparently' Dominic said with a cheerful absence of stiff importance. 'I say, look at that smoke from the engine. Very romantic, don't you think?'

'Romantic?' Miles Urquhart peered at the sooty steam.

'I mean . . . "the royal train" and all that. Sleeping cars.' Dominic grinned. 'It reminds me of that Auden poem, you know. "This is the night train, crossing the border, diddly-pom diddly-pom, postal order". Not that we will be. Crossing the border, I mean. By the way, who's the corker?'

Urquhart frowned. 'To whom do you refer?' he asked, archly.

Joan suppressed a smile. Staff never referred to women in the royal party as "corkers".

'The woman in the mink,' Dominic explained, looking back towards the hall. 'Heading our way. Ash blonde hair, body of a mannequin, soft, peachy lips . . .'

They all stared at the new arrival, who walked with a sway to her hips reminiscent of Marilyn Monroe. A porter trailed behind her with a trolley stacked with bags.

Urquhart stared hard at her, and Joan could see he wasn't pleased.

'That's Sandra Pole. But surely . . . ?'

'Oh, gosh! She has quite the reputation.' Dominic grinned happily. 'Is *she* coming aboard with us? Glorious!'

'She's batty as a fruitcake,' Urquhart muttered. 'Totally unreliable. Go and find out what she's doing here will you, Joan?'

Joan hurried over.

'Excuse me,' she said, stopping her mid-stride, 'are you Sandra Pole?'

The woman in mink looked Joan up and down. Her eyes glittered. 'Guilty. Who on earth are you?'

'Her Majesty's assistant private secretary,' Joan explained.

A perfectly plucked eyebrow rose by half an inch. 'Ah, the secretary. I can see that.'

Joan hid her irritation. A few years ago, she was regularly mistaken for the typist she had once been. Nowadays, more people understood that she, too, held a senior position in the private office. In fact, she was one of the Queen's closest confidantes.

'I hate to be rude, but . . . Why are you here?'

'Well, for someone who hates to be rude you're doing a marvellous job,' Sandra drawled. 'I'm Princess Margaret's lady-in-waiting.'

'I don't think so.'

A second eyebrow rose to join the first. 'I beg your pardon?'

'The princess has two ladies-in-waiting,' Joan explained. 'I know them both.'

'Lucky you,' Sandra responded coolly. 'But for the purposes of this trip I'm it, and I'd appreciate a bit of respect.'

However, she glanced over Joan's shoulder at the small, select number of people on the platform, and realised that Joan was quite possibly closer to the Queen than she'd realised.

'If you must know,' she relented, 'Lady Muriel forgot about the clocks going forward last night, and when she saw she was running late this afternoon she must have dashed around her house like a headless chicken, because she fell down the stairs and broke her silly collarbone. Lady Jane was stuck in the country and the princess needed someone who could pack like the wind and step in at the last minute for when she gets to Glasgow. She asked me and . . . *voilà*. So, you're stuck with me, I'm afraid. And Major Urquhart can stop glowering at me like I'm something the cat dragged in. Here.'

She'd been carrying what Joan had assumed to be a pale fur muff with the animal head still attached, but it turned out to be a small dog, very much alive, who was now plonked in Joan's arms, wriggling furiously.

'You're good with dogs, I assume.'

'I prefer cats,' Joan said, unsuccessfully trying to hand it back.

'Oh dear!' Sandra folded her arms. 'My mother says you can only trust a dog person. What's your name?'

'Joan McGraw.'

'Well, you don't look trustworthy at all, Joan. You look like someone I wouldn't want to give evidence against me in a court of law. Look, I'm late already. The princess is calling me. Her name's Conchita.'

'Princess Margaret?'

'No, you fool. My chihuahua. She's a darling, but she's quite upset and she needs the little girls' room.'

At which point, the driver let off a long hoot of steam, and Joan felt a warm stain slowly penetrate her jacket and her new silk blouse. The dog glared at her, unrepentant. Joan watched as Sandra sashayed on down the platform with the porter in her wake.

Chapter 3

'So who on earth,' Hattie Cowell asked, as the train pulled out of the station, 'is that dolly bird in the mink?'

Hattie was one of the Queen's maids, and was sharing a sleeping compartment with Joan in the second carriage, behind the staff dining car.

'Her name's Sandra Pole and she's here to help Princess Margaret.'

Joan was busy changing her outfit while the chihuahua quietly growled at her from the blanket of her top bunk. She explained to Hattie about the clocks, the broken collarbone, the last-minute call for help.

'And the dog?'

'I think they're a package.'

Hattie narrowed her eyes. Royal dogs were welcome everywhere, even when they bit you, but other canines were generally frowned upon.

'She'd better watch out. I don't like her already.'

'Conchita?' Joan asked.

'Yes. She has a nasty look in her eye. Anyway, thanks for the scuttlebutt about Sandra Pole. They're going to love me in the dining car.'

Joan was glad to be of service. Gossip was the greatest form of currency in the royal court: like cigarettes in prisons, as she had once been reliably informed by a wayward young aristocrat with experience of both.

'I'm not sure about Mrs Pole either,' Hattie added.

'Why?'

'The shape of her skirt.'

Joan laughed as she smoothed her suspenders and zipped herself into a slim tweed skirt of her own, which was a copy of a recent Chanel design. 'It's not so very different from mine.'

Hattie shook her head. 'Oh, but it is. I got a good peek as she handed her coat to the porter. A smidge too tight on the thighs, and an inch and a half too short. You could see her kneecaps. Even Jackie Kennedy wouldn't go that far.'

Joan sighed. Everyone wanted to be the new First Lady these days. Joan had had Mrs Kennedy in mind when she commissioned this outfit from her aunt who was a seamstress . . . But with almost all sexiness removed for the sake of decorum.

'Mrs Pole looked very good in it,' she admitted.

'That's the point,' Hattie said. 'Too good. It'll get her into trouble. Just watch.'

The fourth carriage along was the private office saloon. Miles Urquhart settled down at his desk in the day compartment, and listened as the train puffed its way up the incline at Camden Bank. Perhaps Dominic was right: there was something a little bit romantic about the clickety-clack of the wheels on the tracks; the sense of the smoking engine guiding them on their journey like a living, fire-breathing creature; the promise of a safe and quiet night in a simple bed.

Still, Miles would miss the sense of being rocked to sleep that he usually got on the night train to Balmoral. This journey was shorter, and in just a few hours they would be parked up for the night in a quiet siding east of Liverpool. It wasn't terrifically far, but travelling this way meant Her Majesty could have a working dinner on the move, before arriving in Lancashire fresh as a daisy in the morning.

It also meant that the deputy private secretary could carry on with his working day while passing through the British countryside. The compartment was wide and comfortable, simply decorated and furnished with enough chairs for an office meeting, and a desk worthy of a senior courtier.

Normally, the man who sat here was Sir Hugh Masson, the private secretary. However, last weekend Sir Hugh had suffered an unusual art-related accident on holiday – falling from a tricky perch while trying to render an Alpine scene in watercolour – and done something funny to his neck. He was currently in Harley Street, trying to get it fixed. One of the duties of the royal household was to ensure that his desktop was always identical to the way Sir Hugh left it in his office at Buckingham Palace, regardless of where he happened to be travelling. Today, as Miles was in charge, *his* desktop was replicated here, with his in-tray and partially completed out-tray at eleven o'clock and one o'clock respectively, his blotter and reading materials in front and to his left, his ink-well to the right, his favourite carriage clock angled just so, beside the telephone. The latter only worked when the train was in a station or sidings, but quite honestly, it was nice to be incommunicado while it was in transit. It enabled one to think.

And Miles's thoughts inevitably strayed to Sandra Pole. Surely Joan McGraw had got it wrong about her role? Joan tended to be on the money about such things, Miles knew, but this was outrageous. Princess Margaret needed someone level-headed and experienced to attend her. Sandra was known for being flighty, silly and criminally unreliable. Her parents were solid, country people from Sussex, friends of his parents, and Miles had been shooting with them many times. Sandra's father was rich as Croesus actually, but that didn't stop the girl from being a kleptomaniac who was frequently on the watch lists of Harrods, Fortnum's and Dickins & Jones. She used to ride to hounds like a demon until she married, when her husband banned her from the field for her own safety, in case she broke her neck. Her Mercedes roadster had been in accidents in every road in Knightsbridge, as far as Miles could tell. If the princess got through the next twenty-four hours without some disaster prompted by her so-called lady-in-waiting, it would be a miracle.

Grunting, Miles reached for the folder at the top of his in-tray. He liked to think he carried the weight of office lightly on his shoulders, but it wasn't easy being the chief adviser – for now, at least – to the woman whose father had inherited the largest empire in history. These were trying times. To the west and the east, America and Russia were flexing their muscles. In Africa, countries were queueing up for independence, and one wanted to be sure they didn't turn to the communists for support. At home, a humiliating spy scandal was brewing behind closed doors. It took great minds to tread nimbly through such stony ground. (Could minds tread nimbly? Miles felt his could.)

The thing was, Miles was aware that he carried an extra responsibility. Ever since the business of the Chelsea murders a few years ago – around the time Joan had joined the private office, actually – people had looked up to him with new respect. He wasn't sure exactly what he'd done, but something about him inspired confidence from the police and MI5. They told him their secrets, and he guarded them wisely. His mother told him the Queen was very lucky to have him, and while he was too modest to go that far, he had to admit, things had worked out well.

If anything *did* go wrong today, Her Majesty could rely on him to fix it. He prayed that nothing would.

In his sleeping compartment next door, Dominic Stonor sat in the narrow armchair beside his bed, feeling guilty. Household staff were expected to sing for their supper, and as the afternoon sun shone on the outskirts of the city beyond the window, he was supposed to be helping play host to a couple of guests in the third carriage. But the young press secretary was halfway through a very exciting novel and it called to him like a drug.

Just a few pages more, to ensure the hero survived to the end of the chapter. Dominic flicked through them faster than he really wanted, and had just got to a terrifically exciting cliffhanger when there was a knock on his door.

He opened it to find a flurry of blonde hair and two shining eyes staring at him from the corridor. It was the corker from earlier, with the soft, peachy lips. She gave him a warm smile which almost certainly made him blush, and he felt something hard between them.

'Oh hello, what's that?' he asked, glancing down.

'My new camera. D'you like it?' She lifted it up to show him. 'It's a Japanese single-lens reflex. I don't know what that is, but it's much cleverer than me. I'm Sandra, by the way.' She held out a hand for him to shake.

'Dominic,' he said.

'Hello, Dominic. You're official, aren't you? D'you think the Queen would mind if I took a few photographs? This train's extraordinary. I was expecting red velvet and gilding everywhere, but it's actually like being in a rather bland hotel.'

'I wouldn't tell Her Majesty that,' he advised. 'I think the gilding and red velvet went out with Queen Victoria. Her Majesty likes to keep things simple.'

'For a personal train.'

'For a personal train,' he agreed. 'And she would, by the way.'

'Would what?'

'Mind. About the photographs.'

'Would she?'

The peachy lips grew, if anything, softer. Were the eyes blue or slightly grey? It was hard to tell in this light. Dominic was tempted to say yes to anything she wanted, but that was not what the hero of his novel would do. James Bond was hardened to beautiful women – even the lovely Domino, no doubt.

'I'm afraid so.'

'Dash it.' Sandra shrugged. 'Oh well. You couldn't show me the way to Princess Margaret's carriage, could you? It's deadly dull in mine. One man tried to engage me in conversation about daylight saving and the other literally asked me if I thought the world was about to end. I mean, in his company, I'd want it to.'

'Oh, you're sharing with the guests, are you?'

'Not if I can help it,' she said. 'Right now, I'd like to show Tony my little friend.' She tapped the self-loading reflex.

'Has the princess said you can join them?' Dominic asked. 'We're supposed to get together for drinks at seven. It's only . . .' he looked at his watch '. . . half past five.'

'Yes, she said to join her as soon as possible,' Sandra said, her blue-grey eyes limpid pools of honesty.

'Well, this way, then.' He motioned towards the rear of the train, just as female footsteps sounded rapidly behind them. He looked round to see Joan approaching from the direction of the engine with a small animal under one arm.

'I've been looking for you,' Joan said to Sandra. 'Here's Conchita.'

'But I thought you'd—'

'I'm busy, I'm afraid. We all are.'

Sandra frowned. 'Isn't there a footman or someone who can—?'

'Perhaps you can ask.'

Dominic wondered why Joan was being so peremptory. It wasn't like her. Then he noticed that she was now wearing green tweed with her pearls, not the blue from earlier, and she and the animal clearly had an awkward relationship. He correctly surmised that little Conchita had disgraced herself. He grinned sympathetically.

'Come on. I'll take Conchita.' He indicated the way again. 'Sandra, after you.'

Chapter 4

In her carriage at the rear of the train, the Queen got on with her paperwork, oblivious to the world outside. The workspace in her day compartment was small and functional, with space for a few papers and a telephone. Philip had once said approvingly that it reminded him of a naval officer's desk on a frigate. Nothing like her private secretary's desk, or her Chippendale at Buckingham Palace, which was a wonderland of papers, books and photographs of favourite family members, dogs and horses. There, she could be expansive. Here, she liked to be concise.

She had put the Kennedy file aside for more urgent matters. Today's red box was full of debriefs from the British High Commission about the recent visit to India and Nepal, and questions from the embassy in Rome about her upcoming trip to Italy (she was very much looking forward to that one), along with a query from Norman Hartnell about the length of veil she would wear to meet the Pope. Underneath those, the Minister for Technology was asking for more money for research into unmanned space flight, attached to a long note from the Treasury explaining why he wouldn't get it. Finally, there was the briefing note for tomorrow's visit to Preston, where the great and the good were meeting to discuss the future of the coal industry.

The Queen read the note twice, and felt her eyes swim. It was written in very dense prose by someone in the Cabinet Office, full of talk of deficits and decentralisation, strikes and influenza, and a general shortage of men. She didn't blame them: why go down a dangerous and dirty mine when you could work in a clean and comfortable factory? The coal industry was tremendously important, of course. It had powered the nation through the Industrial Revolution and onwards into the twentieth century. It was powering this very train. One was grateful for its contribution – but Elizabeth's recent visit to India had taken her to hydroelectric dams and some of those futuristic factories. In the age of the space rocket, coal mining suddenly felt more like the past than the future. (*What length of veil was appropriate, in this day and age, for a visit to the Pope? Should the United Kingdom invest in unmanned space flight when by definition it meant not putting a British man in space?*) She was just closing the box, at last, when the footman outside her door knocked and announced the Duke of Edinburgh.

Philip strode into her sitting room.

'Good, Lilibet, you've finished. Anything fun?'

'An update on coal and steel production.'

'Illustrated with dancing girls?'

'Very much not.'

Philip squeezed her shoulders.

'Chin up, sausage. Drinks in twenty minutes. D'you know who the corker friend of Margaret's is, by the way?' he asked. 'Sandra something, she was introduced to me as.'

'Sandra Pole. Margaret's stand-in lady-in-waiting. She married Nigel.'

'That blighter from the RAF? I thought the name rang a bell. She's been showing us all her nice new camera. It has Japanese technology, apparently. Tony was all over it. I have a strong feeling he might get one of his own.'

'Doesn't Tony have enough cameras?'

'A professional photographer never has enough cameras,' Philip said confidently. 'It's like you having enough racehorses. Extraordinary legs the girl has.'

'Does she?' There were times, very occasionally, when her husband forgot the Queen was a woman. One liked to think one's own legs weren't horrific.

'Skirt far too short,' he added, more as an observation than a criticism. 'Very nice knees. Terrible dog, though. It keeps terrorising the Sealyhams, even though it's half their size.'

'Little ones are often the worst,' she said. 'Wait, Sandra brought her dog on board?'

'Apparently, she thought the damn creature would like a holiday in Scotland. Wouldn't we all?'

Well, quite. Lucky Margaret and Tony. The stay at Balmoral after their visit to Glasgow tomorrow would be a bit of a second honeymoon for them. Lucky Sandra, too, tagging along.

'Shouldn't she be helping to entertain the guests?' she asked.

'Apparently your man from the Coal Board is a first-class bore and the BBC johnny is a doom merchant of the first order. Sandra said she fled to Margaret's cabin, seeking asylum. Funny girl. I like her.'

The Queen smiled, but her mind was still on the knees. Her mother, who had met Sandra several times, said she 'had the perfect legs for emerging from a sports car . . . and the perfect brain for crashing one'. The brain was clearly not in perfect working order because, if nothing else, Sandra had married Wing Commander Nigel Pole, one of the most supercilious men of his generation. She was twenty-one at the time, and very beautiful, the Queen remembered. She must be at least thirty now, and he at least forty-five. Poor woman. Despite the knees, the Queen was predisposed to be kind.

In the absence of Sandra and the novel-reading press secretary, it had fallen to Joan and the Queen's lady-in-waiting, Lady Sarah, to entertain the guests in the third carriage while the royals were busy. The men in question had been invited along by the injured, absent Sir Hugh to be 'informative' and 'entertaining', respectively, and perhaps in their natural habitat, they were. But the poor man from the Coal Board had succumbed to a common affliction of people about to meet the Queen, which was extreme nerves, resulting in an inability to form coherent sentences. And the BBC man's nerves seemed to be working in the opposite way. He was a young television producer called Peter Vernon, and he was almost aggressively confident.

'Those are clerestory windows, aren't they?' Vernon said to Lady Sarah.

She and Joan frowned politely.

'Those high windows round the top. My father's a train buff, you see,' he went on. 'Carriage made of teak. Used by Her Majesty's great-grandfather. Quite the museum piece.'

'Gosh, aren't you clever?' Lady Sarah said. 'We call it the semi-royal saloon. We like it because it's nice and wide, and good for circulating with drinks. Would you like another cup of tea, by the way?'

'No thanks. Of course, in a few years' time, we'll all be travelling by vactrain and maglev.'

'I'm sorry?'

'Vacuum and electromagnetic technology,' Vernon asserted. 'It's quite advanced already. Carriages like this will be good for firewood.'

'Oh dear.'

'We'll probably end up ditching the whole rail network, to be honest. *If* we make it that far.'

'Yes, you mentioned that earlier,' Lady Sarah said tightly.

Vernon nodded. 'I mean, the whole world's dangling by a thread, isn't it? Have you read *On the Beach*?'

Joan, who had, pretended she hadn't. The Coal Board man shook his head. Lady Sarah gulped.

'I don't think so.'

'Scary stuff. It's about surviving nuclear war, or rather, not surviving it. Or *Two Hours to Doom*?'

'Um, no.'

'Same sort of idea, but more strategic. It's about a US Air Force general who goes rogue and manages to start a war all on his own, despite everyone trying to stop it. Terrifyingly realistic.'

Lady Sarah, who was made of strong stuff, heroically tried to change the subject by telling them all a long and surprisingly funny story about the time she was arrested during an attempted coup in Asia.

Joan, who had heard the story several times before, gratefully allowed her mind to wander. She found herself affected by a sudden, unexpected wave of nostalgia. It was something about the green and brown view from beyond the window, and she realised that this stretch of the line through the Chiltern Hills was one she used to know intimately. It was the route of the milk train from Euston to Bletchley Park in the war – the one they all took back to their digs after a weekend of dinner and dancing in London, if the bombing let them, exhausted, elated and grateful to be alive.

Peter Vernon thought he knew about war, but it was an intellectual exercise for him. He must have been a child during the last one. Joan had been a young officer in the Wrens, and the intense emotions of those days came flooding back: being surrounded by friends, working hard on something desperately important, not knowing if she would survive the night, the week or the year.

Before the war, she'd been a motherless college porter's girl from Cambridge, with rampant red hair, a fondness for crosswords and a facility for languages – all of which counted against her with the students of the day. At nineteen, she'd had no future at all. Then suddenly, at twenty-two, she was a girl in uniform with a beloved boyfriend in the RAF and a job working on solving the mysteries of the Enigma code at the most secret facility in the country. Her life had unfolded at a rapid pace, much as the countryside was doing now. No wonder the scenery took her back.

In the months that followed Bletchley, Joan had been moved and promoted to a couple more top secret locations, then found her career whipped out from under her by a bitter superior. Her boyfriend, like so many others, was shot down over France. A dozen years on, single and just about scraping a living in London, she had been lucky to get a typing job at Buckingham Palace. Then one day she'd helped the Queen retrieve a lost speech . . . And now, here she was.

Lady Sarah reached the end of her story about the coup. The BBC man turned to ask Joan if anything similarly interesting had happened to her.

'Oh no,' she said, with a smile and a shake of her head. 'Sadly nothing at all. But tell me, what is it you do at White City? You must have all sorts of tales from television.'

Finally, in the nick of time, Dominic Stonor arrived.

By five to seven, the Queen had changed into a suitable evening frock and run a brush through her hair. In order to give staff the space and freedom to set up the dining car, cocktails were being served in the semi-royal saloon. Gathering Margaret, Tony and Sandra Pole on the way, the royal party headed down through the dining car and the private office saloon to reach it.

Miles Urquhart led them in, and the Queen found herself facing two ashen-faced men in black tie, one tall and bearded, one short, frizzy-haired and bespectacled, along with Joan, Dominic and Lady Sarah. The taller man looked as if he were about to face a firing squad, while the short one looked like someone who might be on one.

The Queen walked over to the tall one, and Lady Sarah said, 'May I introduce Stanley Hill, ma'am, adviser to the Coal Board? I know you've been looking forward to meeting him.'

She was about to say something welcoming and reassuring, but Margaret leaped in, with a wicked glint in her eye.

'Oh, the Coal Board, how *wonderful*!' she exclaimed. We're *fascinated* by coal. Do tell us everything.'

Mr Hill shot her a look of pure terror and started babbling statistics about steel production, gripping his handkerchief with white knuckles, until someone arrived with a tray of martinis.

With a nudge of a gloved elbow into her sister's ribs, the Queen assured him they'd have plenty of time to talk about all of that at dinner, and asked instead about the poor man's hobbies. It turned out that he was a great fan of the ballet, where his daughter was a dancer. He and Margaret were in the middle of a lively discussion about the forthcoming visit of the Kirov to Paris, when the rear door of the compartment opened, and the Queen's page appeared with a white Sealyham terrier in his arms.

Everyone turned to stare.

'Pippin!' Margaret yelped. 'Arthur, what's happened?'

'Nothing too serious, ma'am,' the page said. 'He's been bitten. There was a bit of a fight.'

'Oh my God. Where?'

'In your carriage.'

'I mean, where's he been bitten? You poor creature.' This last was to the dog, not the page.

'On his ear, ma'am.' Arthur indicated a graze. 'I'm afraid he came off the worse for it. I've put Johnnie in your bedroom ma'am, for safety.'

'For safety?'

'Just in case the lady's chihuahua goes at it again.' He nodded towards Sandra, standing between Prince Philip and Dominic, clutching a martini glass in a manicured hand and looking as wide-eyed as anyone.

Margaret glared at her and turned back to Arthur. 'Where are you taking him?'

'I was just off to the staff dining car, ma'am. There'll be a first-aider there with access to iodine and whatnot.'

'And who's in charge of Conchita meanwhile?'

He shifted from foot to foot. 'No one, ma'am. I'm afraid everyone's rather busy right this minute.'

'I see.' Margaret looked daggers at Sandra again. 'Go and see to your bitch and sort her out,' she hissed. 'I did *tell* you not to bring her.'

'But she'll be good as gold in Scotland!' Sandra protested. 'She *loves* tartan.'

'Now,' Margaret insisted.

The page went in the direction of the engine with the terrier, while Sandra headed back the way he had come.

For those who were left, the shock of Arthur's entry, and Margaret's visible fury, rather put the kybosh on light conversation. To the Queen's relief, Dominic Stonor stepped in to lighten the mood.

'I say, I'm in the middle of a terribly exciting spy novel,' he told the assembled group.

'Oh, what?' the Queen asked.

'It's called *Thunderball*. It's the new James Bond. Out next week. I was lucky enough to get an early copy because my sister works at Jonathan Cape. It's terribly good.'

'I hope it's better than *Dr No*,' Miles Urquhart muttered. 'Utter hogwash.'

'Didn't Kennedy say he was a fan of Fleming's?' Stonor noted in the author's defence.

'Did he?'

'Last week.'

'How extraordinary that the President of the United States reads spy novels,' Lady Sarah said. 'What's it about?'

Stonor took the floor with a confident smile. It didn't hurt that he looked more than a little like a young Errol Flynn, the Queen thought.

'There's a man called Emilio Largo who's stolen a nuclear bomb,' he explained. 'Two, in fact, and he's hiding them on his yacht in the Bahamas so he can—'

'Hiding *bombs* on a *yacht*?'

Stonor frowned, cut off in mid-flow. The Queen turned to see who had done it, and it was the short, bespectacled producer from the BBC. Sir Hugh had assured her he was 'clever and fun', but quibbling about the details of a popular novel was neither, in Elizabeth's opinion. Lady Sarah was watching him nervously. Sandra Pole had called him a 'doom merchant', hadn't she? Oh dear.

'Where on earth would you put them?' the doom merchant persisted.

'Well, I think it's supposed to be quite a big—'

'*Nuclear* bombs? That's the thing with some of these pulp writers, isn't it?' Vernon shrugged dramatically. 'We're at serious risk of Armageddon – forgive me, Your Majesty – and they turn it into common entertainment.'

'I must say, I was rather looking forward to some entertainment,' she muttered, but she was drowned out by the rich baritone of her deputy private secretary.

'Ah, but just think. The Bahamas are a boat-ride from Cuba. Imagine if President Castro acquired some nuclear missiles on America's doorstep,' Urquhart said. 'Perhaps Mr Fleming knows something we don't!'

'Kennedy's got enough problems with Castro already, without bringing nuclear weapons into it,' Philip chimed in. 'I'm surprised he's put up with it this long. Eisenhower certainly wouldn't have.'

The Queen tried to catch her husband's eye, because politics before dinner was always a disaster, but Philip was having too much fun with his fellow men, and they seemed convinced the world was about to end unless the new president put down his novels and did something about it.

'The trouble is, where do *we* stand?' the doom merchant asked. 'In the UK, I mean. We've got some excellent brains, but we'll become also-rans if we don't heavily invest in new technologies.'

'Missiles, or moon rockets?' Dominic asked.

'Well, isn't that precisely the question?' the doom merchant said, and the Queen, who wasn't sure *what* the question was, reluctantly gave up on hearing any more about James Bond's adventures in the Bahamas, which had been just the sort of thing she wanted to know at this point in the evening.

She caught Tony Armstrong-Jones's eye, and he winked. Which was unusual. Not many men did that in her direction. But he seemed to know what she was thinking. He walked over to her side and said, *sotto voce*, 'If we're not all dead by Easter, I know a revue that's coming to London, ma'am. I saw it in a fringe show at Edinburgh last summer. They talk about Armageddon, but in a funny way. You have to laugh, or you'd cry. Oh, look who's back. I hope Conchita is suitably chastised.'

Sandra Pole gave them a breezy look and accepted a cocktail from the footman's tray.

'How's the Mexican Monster?' Tony asked her.

Sandra glanced across at Princess Margaret, who had very deliberately turned her back on her. She downed the cocktail in a couple of gulps.

'If you mean Conchita, she's asleep, actually,' she said to Tony. 'Like the sweet little girl she is. I've settled her in my compartment, and I'm not at all sure she was the culprit. She's a very gentle soul, and those Sealyhams are enormous. Yes, I'd love another one, thank you.' She nodded to the footman and reached out a hand for a fresh martini. 'What were you all talking about?'

'The end of the world,' Tony said.

'Gosh, how awful.' Sandra threw a glance at the doom merchant. 'I didn't miss anything, then.'

At that moment, the dinner gong was sounded and the Queen led the way back towards the royal dining car.

Chapter 5

Outside, the sun was no longer visible above the horizon, and the sky was turning a dark shade of lavender. Wall lamps gave the dining compartment a warm and welcoming light, while candles flickered among flowers on the table. The crisp and efficient sounds of plating up came from the kitchen next door.

The table was set for ten, with the Queen sitting at one end and Philip at the other. Men alternated with women, and senior staff were sprinkled among family and guests – all except for Dominic Stonor, for whom there wasn't room tonight. The Queen was disappointed. After his showing just now, she felt his presence would be missed.

Instead, Mr Hill from the Coal Board was seated on her left, so she could talk to him properly. That was why he was here, after all. Joan sat on his other side, next to Tony Armstrong-Jones, with Lady Sarah next to Philip at the far end. Across from them, Margaret sat on Philip's left, next to the doom merchant from the BBC (poor Margaret). Sandra Pole sat between him and Miles Urquhart, who was positioned to the Queen's right.

Etiquette demanded that the Queen talk to the man on her left first, so, as little plates of salmon mousse were placed in front of them, she duly turned to Mr Hill. He was a bit more relaxed now, and for five minutes he held forth with reasonable eloquence on the main topics of tomorrow's big convention.

To her right, she was aware of her deputy private secretary politely asking after Sandra's husband, and being loudly told that he planned to divorce her. Oh dear. Sandra had overdone the martinis. Further down, the man from the BBC was talking to Margaret about intercontinental ballistic missiles. When she got home, the Queen would have a word with Sir Hugh about him.

Stanley Hill told the Queen a bit more about deep shaft mining. She tried to concentrate, but Mr Hill himself seemed distracted by Miles Urquhart and Sandra Pole. Miles had a naturally loud voice, and Sandra's was unnaturally bright this evening. To the Queen's relief, at least they had somehow shifted their conversation to the recent royal visit to India. Sandra was asking all about it. The Queen caught the odd phrase from Miles about the glory of the Taj Mahal in Agra, and the technicolour confusion of Varanasi.

Then Mr Hill stopped in the middle of one of his own sentences. He was staring across the table at Sandra and his frown of concern caused the Queen to look, too. Sandra had a glassy look in her eye. Her wine glass was already empty and a footman was stepping forward to refill it.

'I know!' she said to Miles, pressing a finger into his dinner jacket. 'Wasn't it you who dispatched the second tiger?'

'The second tiger?'

The Queen felt Miles stiffen in his seat. She could almost see his moustache bristling.

Sandra ignored the signals, took a sip from her freshly filled glass and carried on blithely. 'Oh, my father was talking about it last weekend. He said the Duke—' she glanced to the end of the table where Prince Philip sat '—shot a tiger in India while you were on tour. All very well and all that, but hardly sporting as the poor thing had already been practically tied to a post.'

'We do not discuss the tigers,' Miles enunciated quietly, through clenched teeth.

Oh no, the Queen thought, not the tigers. Even politics and divorce were probably better topics.

But Sandra carried on as if Miles hadn't spoken.

'And then the Duke was supposed to shoot another one in Nepal. But hadn't he just been made president of the World Wildlife Fund?'

'Not exactly,' Miles grunted. 'It was the UK branch.'

'And so, tell me about the problems with manpower,' the Queen said to Mr Hill.

But while he answered, she was thinking back to their stay as guests of King Mahendra in Kathmandu. God, what a diplomatic nightmare that tiger hunt had been. It seemed quite natural to the Nepalese to propose an event that was once a highlight of any major visit. Her grandfather had personally shot twenty-one tigers in Nepal without issue, but that was decades ago, and times had changed – certainly in the West – and Philip was keen to lead efforts to manage wildlife conservation. It was one of his most heartfelt causes. But how to say no when dozens of elephants were already corralling the animal into place?

The Queen risked a glance to her right again. Poor Miles looked like a cornered tiger himself. The Queen sensed he quite honestly wanted to kill Sandra.

'The shooting parties were arranged at great effort by our hosts,' she heard him explain, through a jaw tight with clenching. 'It would have been disastrous to refuse the king after he'd gone to all that effort.'

'Oh I know,' Sandra agreed. 'But as my father said, if you're a top dog in the WWF, to shoot one tiger may look like misfortune, but to shoot two looks like carelessness. Ha! Except, according to the news reports, in Nepal . . .' Sandra paused for another sip '. . . the Duke had an injured trigger finger.'

'That's correct.'

The Queen could almost feel Miles's desperate horror. The salmon mousse had been cleared away and by now other people around the table were abandoning their own conversations and listening in.

'So he couldn't participate.' Sandra was in her stride, oblivious to the ice practically frosting the windows of the saloon. 'Papa thought you managed it brilliantly. Go along with the first shoot in India, take a jolly nice picture, then second time, injured finger, very sorry, what can you do? Give the Duke's gun to the Foreign Secretary. Except he can't shoot for toffee, and in the end you did it, Miles, didn't you? You were the hero! Congratulations! Poor tiger, though.'

By now all other chatter had stopped and even the servants were staring. The Queen glanced warily at her husband across the length of the table. Philip was dangerously quiet.

He had obviously heard every word. He placed his water glass down with great precision and Sandra, who had finally noticed what she'd done, sat back in her chair, bracing herself. She looked like a frightened child.

'You might tell your father,' Philip said to a silent room, enunciating each word with great care, 'that he can keep his thoughts on my shooting activities to himself. I don't accompany my wife on royal tours of foreign countries in order to provide him with funny stories for his house parties.'

'But I—' Sandra's face had drained of blood. She looked stricken. 'I'm sorry, sir,' she muttered. 'I didn't think.'

'You don't, do you?' Philip snapped.

She pushed back her chair and stood up – something else that wasn't done while the royal couple were still seated.

'I think I'm rather chilly,' she said. 'I-I'll go and get a wrap, if you'll excuse me.'

She left the dining car at speed and didn't return for over ten minutes, during which time the next course was served, the direction of conversation changed, and the man from the BBC was left twiddling his thumbs with no one to talk to.

The Queen looked round the table and assessed the damage.

Philip, who had been in a good mood earlier, remained a rumbling volcano. Joan and Lady Sarah had the rictus smiles of women who just wanted the earth to swallow them up. Margaret waved her wine away and looked annoyed and unwell. Tony Armstrong-Jones was torn between shock and amusement, while the man from the Coal Board looked as if someone had just hit him with a cricket bat. The television man on Sandra's other side was clearly taking mental notes for future anecdotes of his own.

It was Miles's turn to address the Queen. He was very apologetic about the whole thing.

'The woman's a walking disaster, ma'am. Believe me, I tried to head her off at the pass, but there was nothing I could do. It's as if she's possessed. No wonder her husband's had enough.'

'Oh dear,' the Queen said. 'Is that why . . . ?'

'Gosh yes. I hear it on good authority—' Miles lowered his voice and leaned towards her '—that Nigel's regretfully discussed the idea of putting her in an institution. As a kindness, you understand. I wouldn't have said she's *that* bad, but . . .' He coughed and cut himself off.

Sandra had finally returned – to a congealing plate of beef wellington. As she sat stiffly in her chair it was obvious she had been crying, and she had forgotten to bring the wrap.

Dessert was a strained affair. The harder Miles Urquhart tried not to refer back to the second tiger, the more he couldn't help himself.

'Whatever *some people* say, the villagers who were being terrorised by the beast were grateful. We had to be polite to our hosts. King Mahendra felt honour was served. I was only doing my duty. I—'

Desperate to get off the subject once and for all, the Queen cut across him.

'Thank God we're off to Italy next. Don't you think, Miles? At least nobody's going to ask you to dispatch the Pope.'

*

'How did it go?' Dominic asked Joan, when she popped her head round his compartment door twenty minutes later. He'd been quite pleased there wasn't space for him at the dining table, and actually he had been happy to read his book, accompanied by an excellent ham sandwich from the kitchen and a couple of Benson & Hedges from one of the cigarette boxes in the semi-royal saloon.

'It was bloody. Worse than I anticipated.' Joan looked gloomy.

'What? Why?'

'The tiger,' she told him grimly.

'Bloody hell. Not Sandra?'

'Of course, Sandra. I think she thought it was funny. Until the Duke explained otherwise.'

'Oh Lord.'

Dominic thought back to Nepal with a shudder. The Tiger Incident had been his first trial by fire as the new press secretary. He had fielded journalistic questions for weeks.

'You handled it very well, I thought,' Joan said. 'How's James Bond getting on, by the way?'

Dominic was conflicted. 'The lovely girl is being tortured for information. I'm not sure I like how much Mr Fleming enjoys inflicting pain on people. But I think Mr Bond might come to the rescue.'

'You amaze me. Anyway, come and join us for port and brandy. It's just us, Miles and the man from the BBC. The royals are safe in their carriages and everyone else is off to bed.'

'Including Sandra?'

'Especially Sandra. She got tight and looked whacked. No after-dinner drinks for Mrs Pole.'

'Oh my goodness.'

As he stubbed out his cigarette, there was a long hiss and a decline in the rhythm of the wheels on the track. Dominic's curtains were already closed against the darkness, but they felt the train slow and finally shudder to a stop. It had safely reached the sidings and all would be quiet for the night.

Chapter 6

A steam locomotive is a creature that needs attention. It must be put to bed gently and the boiler tended through the night. A shed man arrived for the purpose so the driver and fireman could sleep. At his hands, the engine gave the odd reassuring puff of steam. Underneath the carriages, the ice packs that provided the air conditioning gave the occasional crack as they slowly melted.

Inside the train, the maids and footmen, chefs and butlers bunked up in the staff couchette, while the guests and dressers, the valets and ladies-in-waiting made themselves comfortable in small sleeping compartments of their own. Joan and Hattie caught up on the highlights of the evening, whispering and giggling together. Miles Urquhart relaxed in a comfortable bath, unwinding the muscles that had clenched tightly during the dinner. Pippin, the Sealyham terrier, dreamed of terrible revenge against the overconfident Conchita. Prince Philip wondered which Ian Fleming novel he should read, so he could have an informed conversation with Mr Kennedy if the occasion arose. The Queen sensed that something had been wrong at dinner – beyond Armageddon and Sandra Pole's unfortunate choices of conversation topic – and couldn't sleep for wondering what it could have been.

Along the sidings, a small phalanx of police officers quietly patrolled the tracks. It was a clear night, almost cloudless, not a bad time to be out earning overtime. Around them, nothing stirred, beyond the odd bat and feral cat. Slowly, the waxing gibbous moon tracked its way across the starlit sky.

Chapter 7

Joan woke with a start, unsure of where she was or why there was a wall beside her pillow. For a moment, she thought she was in a guest room in Pakistan or Gujarat, until she remembered it was a train in sidings outside Warrington. It was still stationary, but the snores of Hattie Cowell in the lower bunk were fit to power the engine all by themselves.

Joan risked opening the curtain just enough to check her watch, which told her it was approaching five. Technically, she had another hour of sleep, but she knew she wouldn't find it again with Hattie's symphonic breathing, so she grabbed her green silk kimono and slipped to the floor. Then she quietly padded down the corridor in search of a cup of tea.

At that time in the morning, she expected the staff dining compartment to be empty. But it wasn't. One person sat alone at a table for four to the right of the aisle. Her head was bowed, her face lost in the gloom, but it was obvious from the blonde hair and the padded peach satin dressing gown that it was Sandra.

'Hello,' she said, warily.

Sandra looked up with a frown. 'Damn. I was hoping you'd be Dominic.'

Joan saw how pale she was, even taking into account the dim light of early morning. 'Sorry to disappoint you. Are you all right?' she asked. 'Has something happened?'

Sandra shook her head hard. 'No, I'm not all right. I haven't slept.' She eyed Joan speculatively. 'Perhaps you'll do. I suppose I can trust you.'

'You told me yesterday that I was the sort of person you *couldn't* trust.'

'Did I?' Sandra asked disingenuously. 'I might have said you didn't look trustworthy. But I meant you look like someone who'll always do the right thing, even when it's wrong. You look . . .' she searched for the right word '. . . *unpersuadable*. Right now, that's what I need. People are going to tell you I'm mad, but you mustn't believe them.'

'What *I* need,' Joan said firmly, 'is tea. I'll be back in a minute.'

'Get me one,' Sandra ordered. 'With sugar. They say it's good for shock.'

In the kitchen compartment, a sleepy chef did as requested. Joan came back with a linen-lined tray bearing a pot, silver strainer, milk, sugar pot, extra hot water, two crested teacups on saucers and a plate of home-made ginger biscuits. Even at five in the morning, royal servants never did things by halves.

She watched as Sandra, thin as a beanpole, put three fat sugar lumps in her tea.

'You said people are going to tell me you're mad,' Joan prompted.

Sandra stirred her tea, winced at the first sweet sip, then took another. 'They are,' she said at last.

'Why would they do that?'

'Because I saw a murder last night.'

There was silence. Joan was lost for words. Sandra drained her teacup and poured herself another.

'A *murder*?' Joan said eventually. 'Here on the train? You don't mean Conchita, do you? Did one of the Sealyhams get to her?'

'No I don't mean Conchita! I mean a man. And not on the train. Out there . . .' Sandra waved a bony hand to indicate the shadows outside.

'A *murder*?'

'Yes! I told you!'

'On the sidings? Is the body still there?

'No, of course not!' Sandra said crossly. 'It was miles back. Before we stopped here for the night. I happened to be looking out of the window as we passed near a lake or some ponds or something like that, and the water was pinkish in the sun, and then we went through a cutting, and as we came out the land fell away, and there was a gap in the trees and I saw two men at the far end of a field . . . No, *three* of them . . . And they had another man between them, one at his head and two at his feet. They were holding him by the arms and legs, and swinging him, like a skipping rope. They let go, and he sailed through the air, and disappeared towards a compost heap . . .' She trailed off and stared at Joan defiantly.

'When was this?' Joan asked, caught between the vividness of the skipping rope and the hallucinatory quality of the rest.

'Last night, as I said. After dinner.'

'Wasn't it dark by then?' Joan wondered. 'We were at the table until nine, at least.'

'I suppose we were.' Sandra looked down and faltered a little. 'But with the clocks going forward it was only eight, really. It was quite light, if you remember.'

'I don't think so,' Joan said, frowning. 'As we walked to the dining car, I remember thinking how gloomy it was outside already. I could hardly see anything. I don't see how—'

'*Dammit!*' Sandra banged a fist on the table. Joan was surprised to see her eyes suddenly glistening with tears. 'You have to believe me!'

This was not what Joan had been expecting at five o'clock in the morning. It was quite an act. Had Sandra been watching Hitchcock?

'I'm sorry,' she persisted gently. 'It doesn't make sense.'

'It wasn't . . . it wasn't exactly *after* dinner, you're right,' Sandra amended. 'When I went back to get my wrap, after . . . After Prince Philip . . .' She bit her lip and her eyes glistened harder. 'After the tiger story . . . I'd been a bit, oh I don't know . . . I said the wrong thing and I-I wasn't feeling well. Once I got to my compartment, I went to rest my head against the window . . . And there they were.' She blinked and her eyes bored into Joan's. 'You have to believe me.'

But even with the clocks changing and the slight change of time, the story didn't hold water.

'Did you have the light on in your compartment?'

Sandra hesitated fractionally. 'No, no I didn't.'

'Why not?' Joan asked.

'Because . . . my head was hurting. I felt sick, I told you, I was unwell.'

At least that made sense. With the light on, it would have been impossible to see anything.

'And how far away would you say the men were?'

'Oh, I don't know!' Sandra waved hand. 'I'm terrible with distances. A hundred yards? Fifty? How long is a field? That long.'

'And there were three of them? Men, I mean?'

'Yes. With the body between them.'

'Are you sure it was a body? It could have been, oh, I don't know, a sack of potatoes. In that light . . .'

Sandra shook her head. 'It was a human body! It was murder! I swear it!'

'If you thought it was murder,' Joan persisted, 'then why didn't you say something when you came back?'

Sandra looked panicked. She pressed her palms to her temples.

'I should have. But I simply couldn't believe it!' She looked pleadingly at Joan. 'I-I didn't want to interrupt everyone at supper, so I tried to tell myself it hadn't happened. But it did! I've been thinking about it all night. I feel as if the man is calling to me from wherever he is – the skipping rope man. He needs me. He needs me to be brave, d'you understand?

For the sake of his family, or *something*, I don't know. And then I thought, they'll never believe me. Me, of all people!'

Joan noticed that Sandra continued to hold her gaze. Up until now, she had glanced away briefly several times after she finished speaking. It was a common habit of liars to avoid watching the reception of the lie. Joan had learned this during her war service, where she had interrogated Nazi officers at a secret location called Trent Park. Sandra had been displaying classic behaviours of dissimulation, but not this time. She *had* seen something. Or thought she had.

'So why tell me today?'

'Because he's lying there in that . . . that heap or hedge, or whatever it is, and he wants to be found. He *needs* it. He needs *you*.' Sandra reached across the table and grabbed hold of Joan's arm. 'You believe me, don't you?'

Joan gently prised Sandra's fingers off her dressing gown sleeve.

The last part was true, but the rest was unconvincing. Sandra's story had too many details, and they didn't add up. Besides, it was as if she was starring in a West End play. If she had been, she'd have got a round of applause a few years ago, Joan decided. Nowadays, audiences tended to prefer more realism.

'Let me see if I've got this right,' she said. 'You were in your compartment after feeling unwell at dinner . . .'

'Getting my wrap,' Sandra agreed.

'Which you didn't bring back,' Joan pointed out.

'Exactly! I-I was so distracted. The last thing I was thinking about was wraps.'

'Which would make it eight o'clock, more or less,' Joan continued. 'Seven forty-five at the earliest. Despite the dark, after the train passed a pond of some sort and went through a cutting, you spotted these men a full field away, through a gap in the trees beside the track.'

'It wasn't *that* dark. And a rather large gap, yes,'

'They were swinging something between them . . .'

'Definitely a man.'

'And just at that moment, they released him?'

'I know! Isn't it extraordinary? Maybe they saw the steam of the engine, or heard it, suddenly, as we came out of the cutting, and that sort of startled them.'

'Did you see their faces? Would you recognise them again?'

Sandra frowned. 'No-o. It was dark-*ish*,' she admitted. 'And they were quite far away. But anyway, I was thinking about the skipping rope man.'

'And you think he was dead? How can you be sure?'

'Because he was naked, and he was being thrown in the air, and he wasn't trying to resist, and his face! Oh my God. His face!' Sandra's mouth formed a perfect 'o'. She stared at Joan one last time and collapsed forward with a groan. Her shoulders heaved.

The show was over. Joan went to get help.

Chapter 8

'She saw what?'

Joan tried not to concentrate on the fact that the deputy private secretary was standing at his compartment door in a tartan dressing gown and bare feet, displaying unexpectedly hairy toes.

'A naked man being thrown onto a heap of some sort,' Joan reported.

'Dear Lord preserve us!' Miles Urquhart said. 'How many martinis did she have before dinner?'

'I'll find out.'

'I was being rhetorical. I saw her down them with my own eyes.' Urquhart belted his dressing gown more tightly. 'And he was dead, this individual? She knows this how, exactly?'

'Something about his face.'

'*Something about his face.* I see.' Urquhart's own face was deeply unimpressed. 'Were there flying devils? Was the Queen there? Was anybody else naked in this dream of hers?'

Joan knew what he meant, but she stood her ground. 'I don't think it was just a dream, Miles. I couldn't say exactly what she saw, but she's convinced it was real.' It was the way Sandra had looked at her when trying to explain why she hadn't said anything at the time. Something had seriously shocked her. 'She says it happened at around eight, when she went for her wrap. Perhaps the driver saw it, too?'

'And said nothing?' Urquhart grunted. 'I know Howard Shaw. He's a good man, been with British Rail since it started. That woman. There's always *something* with her. Husband's a saint. I'm not surprised he's divorcing her. Surprised he lasted as long as he did. Hmm. All right, go and get dressed. Then come with me and we'll ask a few questions. Oh, and meanwhile, put Mrs Pole back in her cabin with her extremely irritating animal and if possible, lock the door.'

Joan nodded. She had already asked Hattie to keep Sandra company. The maid was with her now, in Sandra's sleeping compartment, attempting to pacify her with more tea and a tot of brandy. Hopefully that would fulfil the main aim of stopping her from talking to anyone else, until they'd found out what had really happened last night.

As Urquhart had anticipated, Howard Shaw, the driver, was adamant.

'I don't know what the lady's talking about. Eight p.m., you say? That would be between Crewe and Runcorn. There aren't any ponds or lakes around there. Anyway, it was dark by then. Maybe not totally black, but with the light on in the cab I could only see silhouettes outside. And I couldn't see much beyond the tracks anyway, because of the cuttings. Nor could she, I doubt. Three men, you say, and a sack or some sort?'

'Something like that, we can't be entirely sure,' Urquhart said smoothly, sharing the train driver's sceptical expression.

'I'm afraid you'll have to humour me.' He'd told Joan he didn't want talk of naked bodies glimpsed by the royal party. It was bad enough as it was.

The deputy private secretary was fully dressed and neatly shaved now, and Joan sensed he liked to think of himself just a little bit like Hercule Poirot, with an equally impressive moustache. He sat in one of the armchairs in his office compartment, while she took notes in another chair, and each witness in turn sat in a third to say their piece.

'How far away were they?' Shaw asked.

Urquhart looked across to Joan, who said, 'The witness wasn't sure exactly. About a field away.'

'A field? To see as far as that – even if you could make anything out in that light, which I doubt – you'd have to be able to get a decent view through the trees and hedges,' Shaw said. 'As I say, the track is mostly wooded and high-sided cuttings between Crewe and Runcorn. You can't see more than a few yards, and nothing through the trees. Then it's industrial as you get closer to Liverpool. Flat, with sheds and yards, and a bit of scrubland. Not fields.'

Shaw stole a quick look at his watch and both Joan and Urquhart sensed his need to get on. The fireman was looking after the engine, but the driver needed to take charge if Her Majesty was going to stick to her schedule.

'I must let you go, Mr Shaw,' Urquhart said. 'If anything strikes you, any sudden memory or idea, please let me know.'

It was the same with the maids, the footmen, the butlers and the kitchen staff. Between seven forty-five and eight fifteen last night, which amply covered the time Sandra had been missing from the royal table, everyone had been busy preparing food, serving it, eating it in the staff dining car or going about their other evening tasks – which in the case of two of the maids involved tending to a slightly injured dog. All agreed that it was dark outside by then anyway, or so gloomy they hadn't made out much beyond the windows at all.

Prince Philip's valet and the Queen's lady-in-waiting were seen individually, as befitted their status. The valet had been dining at the front end of the train with the other staff before the royal dinner, and then had returned to tend to the Duke's wardrobe for the following day. He had been bulling shoes and brushing coats, and didn't remember even glancing out of the window. Lady Sarah had been at the dinner table and agreed that, given the lamps and candlelight, it was almost impossible to see anything outside by then.

Dominic Stonor had nothing to add. The press secretary had dark circles under his eyes. He'd been up late, drinking whisky and finishing his novel, which had seemed a good idea at the time, but which he now rather regretted. He'd closed his cabin curtains when he got in after the drinks, and was sorry he couldn't be more helpful, but there it was.

The two guests, who were outsiders and therefore couldn't be trusted to keep this – as Urquhart called it – 'nonsense' to themselves, were asked about anything unusual they might have seen during dinner, in the vaguest possible terms. Unsurprisingly, they, likewise, had seen nothing. Or rather, Stanley Hill from the Coal Board had seen an owl, possibly a barn owl, white and majestic in the moonlight, but that had been much later, and probably wasn't what Major Urquhart had been thinking of? It was not. The man from the BBC said he had been too wrapped up in the tiger story, which was quite simply the last thing Urquhart needed to hear.

Only four people remained, and they were still asleep.

'I think we can safely assume,' Urquhart said to Joan and Dominic when they were alone, 'that Her Majesty, the Duke, Princess Margaret and her husband were too busy entertaining to notice anything beyond the window. You and I, Joan, were with them the whole time.'

'Were the curtains closed in the dining car?' Dominic asked.

'Not until dessert, as I recall. But if any of them had seen a naked man with a face so hideous the witness can't describe it being thrown around a field in the distance . . .'

'They might have mentioned it,' Dominic agreed.

'We won't disturb them with the story. I'll have a very quiet word with the Duke and Mr Armstrong-Jones, at some suitable moment. I won't go into detail. Needless to say, the Queen mustn't hear of this.' Urquhart turned to Joan. 'I know you and she chat about things, as women, but the last thing Her Majesty needs is the thought of her sister's companion having some sort of . . . episode. She has a very busy day ahead.'

The Queen would hear of it, Joan thought. Lady Sarah, or somebody, would tell her: the Queen loved gossip as much as anyone. Then she'd ask for details and Joan, who had the full account, would oblige as requested.

'Yes, of course,' she said.

Chapter 9

In fact, it was Princess Margaret who passed on the news, rushing to her carriage to impart it while the Queen was sitting up in bed with a cup of tea.

The Queen waited until she was up and dressed, and Joan arrived with the morning schedule, to find out what was really going on.

'Good morning, Joan. My sister tells me that according to her maid, Sandra Pole saw a dead man last night. Or claims she did. What on earth did she mean?'

Joan curtsied. 'I'm not sure what Mrs Pole saw, but she'd like us to think it was a body, Your Majesty.'

'Whose, exactly? When?'

Joan described her conversation with Sandra in full, including the bit about the skipping rope, and the timings at dinner that didn't add up.

'Was she in earnest?'

Joan hesitated. 'Some of the time, yes. She was also quite evasive. But something had rattled her.'

'Did anyone else see anything?'

'Not at all, ma'am.'

Joan gave a quick summary of Urquhart's investigations, including the fact that the train didn't go past ponds and open fields, or the sort of landscape Sandra had described, at the time she gave.'

'Perhaps she got the time wrong,' the Queen suggested.

'I don't think so. Mrs Pole said it was when she went to get her wrap while we were at dinner, which narrows it down a lot.'

'She was pretty pickled by then.' The Queen sighed. 'But you say something rattled her. I wonder if it was farmhands, mucking about with sacking, stuffed with hay.' She twiddled her pen thoughtfully. 'Like they used to use for bayonet practice. That might look like a body, especially in near-darkness.'

'It might, ma'am.'

'It always intrigues me, the games young men play,' the Queen ruminated. 'But in that case, what did she mean about the face? Did she give you *any* details?'

'No, ma'am. She found it too upsetting.'

This time, it was the Queen's turn to be irritated by Sandra.

'She told you she needs your help, Joan. But if she won't explain, what can we do?'

They turned to the schedule, which listed the Queen's activities in five-minute intervals. But she was still thinking about Sandra.

'Perhaps Miles can get a message to the local police and ask them to check that section of the track anyway?' she instructed. 'If there *are* any fields with hedgerows, they can examine them. It can't do any harm. Thank you, Joan.'

Chapter 10

A small team of constables from the Cheshire police force spent several grim hours that Monday afternoon and evening, tramping up and down a series of sheds and allotments beside the tracks. The general feeling was that they all had worthier places to be and better things to do. The details given had been sparse, and the officers didn't even know exactly what they were looking for, merely that somebody from the royal train – a toff, presumably – had seen something unusual as the carriages sped by the night before. Apparently, they were worried about an injured person.

'Found any casualties yet?' the super asked, on a flying visit to show willing, given where the original call had come from.

The grumpy, damp detective sergeant in charge merely extended an arm to indicate the landscape of semi-industrial buildings and backyards.

'It's hardly teeming with bleeding corpses,' he observed. He glanced down the track, where the claret-coloured carriages of the royal train would have passed in the gathering gloom. 'I suspect an overactive imagination. P'raps they were thinking of that boy in *The Railway Children*.'

The super smiled. 'I read that one to my boys. He was a hare, wasn't he, leaving a paper trail? Didn't they rescue him from a tunnel?'

'That's the one. But no hares here. No tunnel, either. So far, the haul is two abandoned bedsteads, half a bicycle and a suitcase of old trousers. Flea-ridden, the lot of 'em. I doubt they're from Buckingham Palace. Who called this one in anyway?'

'Gent called Major Urquhart. He's a high-up with Her Majesty.'

'Well, Her Majesty, God save her, can come out here in her own mackintosh and wellingtons on a wet Monday afternoon, and damn well search for whatever it is herself.'

The super knew he should tick the DS off for a lack of suitable deference to the Crown, but they were all equally wet and cold, and they were patently on a wild goose chase. For the sake of a quiet life, he promised that there would be decent sandwiches waiting for the team when they got in.

'No mention of this to the press,' he added. 'Major Urquhart was very firm about that. We don't want trouble from the palace.'

'Oh, certainly, sir,' the DS retorted. 'I'll rein in the fierce temptation to tell the hacks from the *Herald* about the bedsteads.'

But he did tell them, as it went, because his brother-in-law worked for the paper and he thought he deserved a royal scoop, even if it was a very damp squib. Dominic Stonor had to work hard on his return to London to prevent the story going out, with promises of lots of pictures of the family with the corgis next week to make up for it.

It was the private secretary, Sir Hugh Masson, still sporting a neck brace after his accident in the Tyrol, who relayed the news to the Queen at Buckingham Palace that evening. She sat by lamplight at the crowded Chippendale desk in her study. Murder seemed light years away.

'Apparently nothing of interest was found, ma'am,' he said. 'I'm still kicking myself that I couldn't be there to support you at the time. The news must have been incredibly distressing.'

'Oh, I managed,' the Queen said, wishing for the umpteenth time that her staff wouldn't try and wrap her up in cotton wool. Comforting friends, family and young officers during the war, who had lost loved ones in the most appalling circumstances, had hardened her well enough. She had weathered the death of her own father in her twenties, and countless barbs and setbacks since. Being told of the possible death of a stranger was not the sort of thing to knock one off course. Especially when it increasingly seemed that it must have been a mirage.

The Queen knew that Joan thought it was more than that, and she trusted Joan's opinion. What *had* really happened that evening? Why had Sandra Pole invested so much energy in spinning a tale that was so easy to disprove?

She knew, too, that she herself had spotted a problem during that awful dinner on the royal train. Something was off, but she still couldn't for the life of her work out exactly what. It would come to her eventually, but for now all she could do was wait.

'Thank you, Hugh,' she added. 'You'll tell me if anything crops up later, won't you?'

'Certainly, ma'am,' Sir Hugh said, with a distracted smile that suggested he probably wouldn't.

He bowed stiffly and left her to her evening paperwork. The Queen thought back to the doom merchant from the train, and his talk of Armageddon. Was that what had alarmed her? Despite everything, she thought not. It had been something far more human and personal than that.

Chapter 11

There was something rather wonderful about Primrose Hill, Henry Coxon thought, trudging up from Chalk Farm tube station to Pavel Michalowski's flat the following morning. To an old cynic like Henry, the name 'Primrose' promised endless bleak acres of urban grime, but in fact there really was a park with flowers, a popular one, where he and Pav would often walk on Sundays. You could mosey up the hill, by day or night, and see London spread out below you like something out of Dick Whittington, with the dome of St Paul's one way and the Houses of Parliament the other, and Regent's Park below you in the foreground, extravagantly green, separated by the narrow, hidden waters of the Regent's Canal.

Behind the hill, the streets were contained by the sweeping curve of the railway; below it, the squares were jolly, the little restaurants on street corners were rather good, the pubs did a thriving trade, and interesting people lived there. Young people from all over, who thought about life, and wrote poetry about it, made jokes, made food and music. When he had time, Pav took pictures of them at it. Henry wrote about them in one of his magazine columns occasionally, and cadged cigarettes off them in the course of long, boozy evenings, when they redesigned the world in a haze of alcohol and smoke.

Something was brewing here, he felt, and it wasn't just pale ale. It was an egalitarianism based on talent and a refusal to be hidebound by anything old fashioned. Why Primrose Hill, exactly? Henry wasn't sure. He wanted to sound out his theory with Pav when he roused him. But mostly, he wanted to talk about a girl.

Chalcot Square was a bouquet of colourful villas: square and Victorian, designed with a lightness of touch that gave them an Italianate look. Pav's flat took up the basement of one of the pink ones. Henry had already tried his studio down the road, and now here he was, banging on Pav's door for the second time in three days, hoping to God the man hadn't succumbed to sudden 'flu, or gin, or worse.

'Hi, Pav, it's me!'

He knocked hard. Two days ago, when he'd done it for the first time, he had given up quite quickly. Pav's motorbike was parked in the street outside, but he was known for suddenly taking off for Paris or Saint Tropez, when in funds, and if a sexy bird was waiting. Yesterday, convinced that even the sexiest bird must have done her worst by now, he had tried Pav on the telephone several times, with no joy.

Henry wasn't a man to worry unduly, but last night, he couldn't sleep. He hadn't spoken to his friend for over a week, and nor had anyone he knew. Pav was supposed to have gone to lunch with a mutual friend the day after their last phone call, and Henry himself the day after that, but he'd let them both down. Meanwhile, he had a show to put together, and several society women to photograph for their mothers.

Something was wrong, Henry could feel it in his water. He'd even found himself calling at a police station to report a missing person – and they couldn't possibly have been less interested. A plod assured him that his friend would return soon, they always did. But they didn't always, did they? Henry's water was worryingly reliable. Where *was* the man?

'Pav, look, if you don't put her down and come to the door, I'm going to break it down, I warn you.'

Henry hadn't realised he was going to shout this. But he found himself eyeing up the door, which was down a narrow set of concrete steps from the street. If he rushed at it, he might be able to splinter it, possibly. But then, who would pay for the repair? Nevertheless, summoning all his power, Henry put his shoulder to the panelling and did his best. It wouldn't budge. He took what little run-up he could and tried again, giving his shoulder a thump like the recoil from a shotgun. Still no joy. Feeling sorry for himself, he slumped down on the doorstep.

'I'm frightened, old man,' he muttered. 'I need you. I need your advice. There was this gorgeous girl – d'you remember, the one I told you about the last time we spoke? And now she won't see me. What have I done, Pav? Why don't I understand women? What did I *do*?'

'Are you all right down there?'

A young woman was staring down at him through the railing. She had a nice blue woollen coat, a fringe that curled in different directions, and a friendly face. Her accent had a twang of American.

'Absolutely fine,' Henry assured her, sniffing and standing up.

'Are you locked out?'

'In a manner of speaking.'

'So, you know the owner?'

'Of course I do,' he said. 'It's my friend Pav. He's disappeared and the police don't care. Nobody cares.'

The friendly face looked concerned. 'Are you Henry?'

'Yes! How did you know?'

'It was your pants.'

'What?'

'Your trousers. Pav talks a lot about you. Look, I care. I live upstairs and I've got his spare keys somewhere. Keep an eye on the baby carriage and I'll find them. We can check the place out together.'

This must be the Mrs Hughes Pav had sometimes talked about, Henry realised. She disappeared for several minutes, while Henry fixed his eyes on the large, hooded perambulator he had only just noticed beyond the railings. Presumably there was a child inside. Henry wasn't good with children. He found their moods confusing and they never seemed to know what they wanted. Much like women. Men like Pav were so much easier.

Eventually, she returned triumphant, with a set of keys on a ring.

'Help me,' she said, and he did his best to help manhandle the heavy pram down the steps, bumping the wheels on each one as they went.

She peered under the hood.

'She's sleeping. We can leave her here. She'll be fine.'

Close up, Henry was sure her fringe looked familiar. They'd met in a smoke-filled party kitchen somewhere. He racked his brain for her first name.

'Cynthia, isn't it?'

'Sylvia.'

'Yes, of course. I don't suppose you've seen Pav recently?'

She put the largest key in the lock and wiggled it until it turned.

'No, I haven't. He was going to babysit for me last week, but he never showed up. I assume he had a girl.'

'So did I.'

'But . . .'

She stopped, staring down at a heap of envelopes, grown so large that made it difficult to push the door open. When she looked back at him, Henry sensed that she could feel it in her water too.

'He didn't have any unwelcome visitors that you're aware of?' he asked. 'Men in suits demanding money with menaces, that sort of thing?'

'No.'

She stepped gingerly over the mail and walked on ahead of him down the hallway.

'Any angry husbands?'

'Not that I'm aware.'

Henry joined her in the living room, where Sylvia was opening the curtains. Daylight shone onto an untidy space. This was normal for Pav. There were columns of books and papers on the floor, on tables and some of the chairs.

A wooden chess set rested on a teetering pile of magazines; a pair of black stockings hung over a lamp. Nothing looked particularly out of place. Henry's eye caught the telephone, which had been his last form of communication with his friend. The receiver was in place, with Pavel's pad of scribbled notes beside it.

'Nothing here,' Sylvia called out.

She had gone into the bedroom next door. Henry joined her in the doorway.

'Except evidence of sex,' she observed drily, nodding towards the bed.

Henry coloured beetroot, taking in the pulled-back sheets, the indented pillows, the blankets on the floor. Two coffee cups sat on tea chests used as bedside tables. He walked over and picked one up. The dregs were dry.

'What's that?'

Sylvia was pointing to a door in the inside wall, opposite the window. It looked like a built-in wardrobe, squeezed into a gap behind the bathroom.

'Who locks their clothes up with a padlock?'

'Pav has very nice clothes,' Henry said. 'He gets his shirts from Jermyn Street. God knows how he affords them. What are you doing?'

She was lifting knick-knacks and peering in drawers. 'Looking for a key,' she said.

'Why?'

'Because you're concerned, and now so am I. And I don't like locked things in the houses of missing people.'

'What about the keys he gave you?'

'He surely wouldn't . . .'

She rummaged in her pocket and held up the bunch of keys again.

'Worth a try,' Henry said.

The smallest key fitted the padlock. If Pav didn't mind Sylvia having charge of it, Henry assumed he didn't keep anything ultra-secret in there. Anyway, she was already undoing the padlock and opening the door.

'Golly,' she said. 'What on earth is that for?'

Henry went cold.

'I think I know,' he said. 'I need to make a telephone call.'

Chapter 12

Six days after the train ride, Margaret was back from her visit to Glasgow ('A bore! The rain! So *dreich*, as Mummy would say.'), followed by a brief but pleasant sojourn at Balmoral.

March had given way to April, and the family were at Windsor for the Easter weekend. The Queen would shortly be taking her two eldest children to a local point-to-point, but she had time for a quick dog walk with her sister and her mother after breakfast. Despite the Queen Mother's façade of gaiety, her daughters sensed her lingering loneliness. She still missed the late king, and perhaps even more, her own position at the centre of palace life. In between meetings, paperwork and visits, one cheered her up as well as one could.

It was a cold day, made colder by a biting easterly wind. The three women walked head down past regimented rose beds, silk scarves fluttering in the breeze like flags.

'Margaret tells me the hyacinths were out at Balmoral,' the elder Elizabeth said wistfully. She had grown up at Glamis Castle, the home of Macbeth, and her heart remained in Scotland.

'How lovely.'

'And primulas everywhere,' Margaret added, 'like a yellow carpet. The bluebells will be out quite soon. You'd love them, Mummy.'

'I would,' their mother agreed sadly. This wasn't helping.

'What did Tony do while you were there?' the Queen asked her sister. 'I was worried he might be bored.'

'Why?' Margaret asked warily.

'Well, as you say, you have such an active life in London.' The bohemian photographer hadn't struck Elizabeth as a much of a nature lover.

'He *loved* it!' Margaret was firm. 'He took a hundred pictures of me with turrets in the background. And we went for some gorgeous rides. He looks very sexy on a horse, you know. He wears all the wrong clothes, and sunglasses, and just . . .' She made a vague hand gesture and went pink under her headscarf.

'I hope you were careful on horseback,' their mother said.

Margaret instinctively put a hand on her stomach. 'Not really. Not yet. I think this little one will be a horseman anyway. He'll have to be, if he's one of us. But I did cut back on the wine. It makes me woozy, which is annoying.' She broke off, to deter her white-haired terriers from going too close to a filthy-looking puddle. 'Anyway, poor Sandra Pole drank enough for all of us. She didn't really work out as a lady-in-waiting. She was sick on the shoes of the Duke of Buccleuch. You know how smooth he is, but even he looked rather startled.'

The Queen Mother shook her head. 'Poor, dear Sandra. I'm very fond of her mother, but she was always a handful. One can understand that sort of behaviour in a man, but she was a headstrong—'

'Oh! I've just remembered,' Margaret interrupted. 'She told me the funniest story. Guess where she was when she saw this so-called murder that didn't happen?'

The Queen frowned. 'On the train. She said so.'

'Ah, but *where* on the train?'

'In her carriage.'

'No!' Margaret paused dramatically. 'In yours!'

The Queen stopped dead, and her sister was forced to come to a halt beside her.

'Surely not? Is this an April fool?'

'Scout's honour!' Margaret said, doing the three-fingered salute.

The Queen was appalled. Nobody was allowed inside her carriage without her permission, even Philip. Its entrance was manned night and day by a footman or a page, with a brace of policemen hovering nearby. The thing was literally bulletproof, because her father had had it built that way in the war.

'And even worse,' Margaret added, 'she was in your bathroom! Taking pictures! Like that *Vogue* girl – what's her name?'

'What?'

'I *know*!' Margaret said. 'Sandra was sozzled when she told me. She made me *promise* not to pass it on, so don't let on that I did. Anyway, she has this thing about your bathtub. The idea of having one on a train – she thought it awfully glamorous. And she was reminded of this Lisa woman . . . What *is* her name? Baker? Butcher? Miller! Lee Miller. That's it. Friend of her mother's in Sussex. Lee's another . . . Well, let's say she likes a snifter or two. Anyway, Lee took a picture of herself in Hitler's bathtub—'

'What?' The Queen was very confused. 'Adolf Hitler?'

'Of course, Adolf Hitler. Is there another one?'

'I don't think—'

'Don't you remember? In '44,' Margaret persisted, as they resumed their route. 'We saw the photograph in *Vogue*. Apparently, it turned out to be the day he committed suicide, Sandra told me, although Lee didn't know that at the time.'

'Hitler's bathtub?' the Queen Mother joined in. 'What does that have to do with anything?'

'Lee was visiting Hitler's old apartment in Munich, according to Sandra,' Margaret explained. 'She had just been to Dachau, that very day. She had the ashes of it on her boots when she took the picture. Except, she was sitting in the tub, so I suppose somebody else actually took it.'

'*Hitler's bathtub?*' the Queen Mother repeated faintly. '*Vogue?*'

'Yes. She took a lot of war pictures for them. Didn't you see them at the time, Mummy?'

'I really don't . . . *Hitler's bathtub?*'

'Oh, honestly, Mummy. Yes. And when Sandra heard about it, she thought that was the bravest, most extraordinary image, making fun of Hitler that way, putting all his kitschiest ornaments in the background, wiping the dirt of the concentration camps off on his very bathmat, proclaiming victory by simply being there, and a woman, too. And on the train – our train – that day, Sandra suddenly had this overwhelming urge to take her own picture in a bathtub – yours, Lilibet. Except, she couldn't really get a decent shot of herself, so she ended up doing it of Conchita, which wasn't—'

'Excuse me,' the Queen said. Her voice was shaking with the effort of taking it all in. 'You're telling me that your friend took a picture of her *chihuahua* in my bathtub, because it reminded her of Adolf Hitler?'

'Not Hitler, Lee Miller, the photographer. She was a model, you know. I wouldn't be too offended by it.'

'My bathtub? On the train?'

'Well, I know,' Margaret said, somewhat piqued. 'You're not the only person with a bathtub on the train. Sandra could have used mine.' She turned to her mother in appeal at the unfairness of primogeniture. 'It's perfectly nice. But she wanted it to be Lilibet's tub because Lilibet's . . .'

'Lilibet,' her mother finished for her. She waved a hand and smiled, as if that explained everything.

But the Queen's sense of humour had deserted her. It had never crossed her mind that her travelling tub could be some sort of trophy image; one of her most private, intimate spaces being used for photography by a woman acting like some cheap tourist.

'*How?*' she asked.

This was what really worried her. If Sandra Pole, the drunk, could do it with a chihuahua, then what about a determined assassin? Or a madman with a gun?

'It was just quick thinking and luck,' Margaret said. 'And that bloody dog. That's what started it. You remember the fight Conchita had with Pippin and Johnnie?'

'Vividly.'

'Well, when Sandra passed through the royal dining car to get to her dog, she saw your protection officers in the kitchen, scoffing some sandwiches, so she realised they weren't outside your door at the back of the train, and all the footmen except Arthur were hands-on-deck serving drinks or getting ready to serve dinner, so they weren't there either. Arthur was supposed to be on door duty, but he was nobly helping out with Pippin right at the other end. And, I mean, you weren't inside, so I suppose they weren't worried.'

'They should have been!' the Queen protested.

'Oh, Lilibet. Well, anyway, they weren't. Sandra had the idea suddenly. She'd left her newfangled camera in my carriage, so she grabbed it and Conchita, and nipped along through Philip's carriage to yours. She found your bathroom and took a couple of snaps of Conchita in the tub. Except, she said they came out all blurry in the end and she might as well not have bothered. Oh, don't look so cross, Lilibet. Sandra's a bit forward, but she's not *dangerous*.'

The Queen pursed her lips and folded her arms.

'Anyway,' Margaret continued, 'she'd pulled back the curtain to get a bit more light, and when she went to close it again . . . That's when she saw the men with the body. Through that top little pane, you know.'

'So, she saw them from my bathroom window?'

'Except of course she didn't,' Margaret corrected her, 'because you said the police checked afterwards, and they didn't find anything. Goodness knows *what* she thought she saw.'

'I don't suppose she took a picture?' the Queen inquired.

'Of what?'

'The naked man being used like a skipping rope!'

'Is that how she described it? Goodness. She never told me *that*.' Margaret shrugged. 'I suppose she didn't. If she'd had a picture, somebody might have believed her.' She stopped and looked round. 'Where's Mummy?'

They both turned back to find their mother standing stock-still again, a couple of yards behind them.

'Are you all right, Mummy?' the Queen asked.

'*A naked man being used like a skipping rope?*' the Queen Mother echoed, faintly.

'Don't worry, it's just Sandra's vivid imagination,' Margaret reassured her. 'Miles Urquhart asked everyone on the train about it and nobody saw anything.'

'I'm glad to hear it,' the older Elizabeth said. 'I think we should get back inside, don't you?'

A trio again, they headed back up to the relative warmth of the castle, with the dogs leading the way.

Chapter 13

'This changes everything.'

The Queen managed to find five minutes to talk to Joan in her study at Windsor, between the return from the point-to-point and drinks with the gathering weekend guests. Margaret seemed to have missed the point of her own anecdote entirely, but Joan saw exactly what the Queen had seen.

'It explains the level of daylight, ma'am', Joan agreed. 'We gathered for drinks at seven and Arthur appeared with the terrier about ten minutes later. Sandra was back with us by seven thirty to go into dinner. Allowing for the time for her to collect Conchita, sneak into your carriage and take the photos, she could have been looking out of the window as early as twenty past seven. That's forty minutes earlier than she said. I checked, and sunset was around seven thirty. She could just have made out facial features then.'

'And the ponds and general landscape, too,' the Queen said. 'I gather the driver was adamant there was nothing like them beside the track at eight, but what about twenty past seven?'

'I'll check with him, ma'am.'

The Queen realised what had been bothering her from the night on the train. From what she herself had observed, Sandra had been drinking sociably to start with. She only started downing cocktails in earnest when she came back from the visit to Margaret's carriage after the dog fight. If she *had* just seen a murder, or its aftermath, then it was hardly surprising. That explained her over-bright behaviour at the table, causing a scene as she tried to distract herself. It all made sense now, but . . .

'It still doesn't explain why nobody else saw anything,' she sighed.

'It might do, ma'am,' Joan said. 'Most people on the train were busy at that point. You were entertaining, and the servants were getting the meal ready, or eating dinner themselves in the staff dining car. If they looked out of a window at all, it was probably just a glance. They might have missed it, especially if Mrs Pole saw it through a gap in the trees.'

'It would explain why Sandra kept correcting herself when she spoke to you,' the Queen said thoughtfully.

'Yes, ma'am, if she was telling the truth and just trying to fudge which carriage she was in at the time, and therefore when it happened.'

The Queen was still not fully convinced. 'Surely, though, she'd realise that meant we would never find the body she was so worried about? If the train was forty minutes back down the track?'

'Perhaps she just talked herself into a hole,' Joan said.

'But didn't she say she wanted to do the man justice?'

'She said he needed her to be brave.'

'Then, perhaps she wasn't brave enough,' the Queen suggested, grimly.

'Until she found herself in a more relaxed state with Princess Margaret.'

'You're very diplomatic, Joan. "Relaxed" is one word for it.' The Queen was busy thinking. 'Look, I know you said you'd talk to the driver, but if they *do* find anything, he'll realise who was asking. I have another idea about how to do it.'

'Who should I visit, ma'am?'

'No one for now,' the Queen told her. 'Leave this one with me.'

Chapter 14

Easter Sunday was completely packed with activities. No matter how urgently one wanted to do something, every minute was accounted for with children, meals, the service in St George's Chapel, greeting the many people who contributed to it, entertaining guests and checking that they were being suitably looked after. Normally, the Queen loved the busyness of the day, the beauty of the liturgy, and the happy company of family and friends. Easter at Windsor was a joy. But today there was also the skipping rope man to think of, and she would have been grateful for some private time to pay attention to him.

On Easter Monday, she got up an hour early and made her way, alone, down the hill to the Lower Ward, where Horseshoe Cloister sat tucked between the castle wall and the chapel. The latter's magnificent late gothic architecture made it look and feel more like a cathedral, really. The brick and timber buildings of its cloister were very different. They were much more humble in scale and looked as if they might be a Victorian fancy, but in fact they, too, dated back to the fifteenth century and had been used ever since to house the lay clerks who sang with the chapel choir, and some of the clergy who helped run chapel life.

The longest-serving resident in the cloister was a canon called Maurice Vaughan, whom the Queen had known since she was a princess. He was responsible for looking after the fabric of the chapel buildings and sometimes sang with the choir. He had a warm and confident bass voice that matched his bear-like exterior, which occasionally reminded the Queen of Winnie-the-Pooh, after a particularly generous pot of honey.

'Good morning, Your Majesty,' he said, opening his front door to her. 'I gather you wanted to see me. I've made you a nice pot of tea.'

His small and colourful front room was dominated by a Bechstein baby grand piano, squeezed in as if it was holding up its skirts, which just about left space for a couple of bentwood chairs and a spindly side table, set with tea for two. Canon Vaughan was far too polite to ask her why she was there, but after half a cup of Darjeeling and several pleasantries about his health and the difficulty of finding decent stonemason apprentices, she explained that she had a question for him on the completely different subject of railways.

He beamed. 'What an honour, ma'am. What made you think of me?'

'Well, you have reputation at Windsor as something of a train buff.'

'Do I?' He grinned shyly at her.

'This room, for example,' she said, indicating the surprising combination of cream walls and crimson woodwork.

'I remember somebody once telling me that the colour scheme was "Blood and Custard".'

'Ah, yes! The first livery of British Railways passenger carrying coaches. I couldn't resist. Though I'm also partial to the Plum and Spilt Milk of the London and North Western Railway. Neither is as impressive as the claret of the royal train, of course.'

'I'm glad you like it,' she said.

'I have a model of that train that I'd love to show you, if you have the time.'

The Queen smiled, but she was thinking that she probably *didn't* have the time. They had a lot to talk about, and she needed to be back for breakfast.

'Am I right that you're familiar with all the railway lines of England, and the timetables and so on?'

That shy grin again. 'You could say so, ma'am.'

'Excellent. But, Maurice, once I've gone, this conversation never happened. You may read things in the newspapers, or hear gossip perhaps . . . but you mustn't put two and two together. I'm here today, because I know I can trust you.'

'The Seal of the Confessional,' he promised her. 'Nothing goes beyond these four walls. Now, what can I do for you?'

The Queen carefully described the journey of the royal train on the afternoon and evening of the twenty-sixth. It took longer than she'd anticipated, because she had to keep stopping to explain which locomotive had been used (she wasn't sure), who the driver was (Howard Shaw; 'Of course, ma'am, one of the regulars, I should have known'), which saloons were being used ('Was the semi-royal saloon in the configuration? It was? I always have a particular fondness for that one, ma'am, practically a museum piece, you might say'), what the décor of the royal dining car was like ('I hate to ask, but I've always been fascinated to know'), and how smooth the train felt on taking corners (she hadn't noticed, which probably meant it was).

Eventually, she managed to outline the journey from Euston to Crewe. After that point, she was fairly certain it didn't matter because Mr Shaw had said it was too dark to see and the countryside didn't fit the description of the fields and waterways.

'What I want to know,' she said, 'is whether it's possible that our witness was right when she described ponds, a railway cutting, a field, and men who were visible at a distance. And if so, we need to narrow down as much as we can where exactly we might have been.'

'Of course, ma'am.'

'I'm afraid I can't explain exactly why.'

Maurice Vaughan waved a hand. 'You don't need to. Somebody thinks they've seen a murder, don't they? Or possibly the stashing of bullion after a robbery, but I haven't read about one of those recently.' He smiled. 'Don't worry, ma'am, as I say, the Seal of the Confessional applies. You can't ask Mr Shaw, because he might tell somebody you did the asking, but you can certainly ask me. If you don't mind going next door, I think I have everything we need.'

He led her through to a room at the back of the house, similar in size to the first, and similarly stuffed with furniture not really made for modest Tudor interiors.

'Oh, how wonderful!' she said, stepping through the door.

She hadn't been in this room before. In between the bookshelves and the desk, most of the space was devoted to an intricate model railway and several sets of Hornby trains. The railway was arranged at waist height, on solid boards, big enough to contain a hill, a tunnel, a town, two villages and substantial sidings with sheds and a turntable. It was the masculine equivalent, she felt, of the doll's house made for Queen Mary, which was one of the treasures of the castle.

'You must be delighted with it.'

'I am,' he agreed. 'Though I probably shouldn't be. Earthly pride, and all that. But it gives pleasure to lots of people, not just me.'

'Is it somewhere in particular?'

Vaughan nodded. 'I grew up near Shrewsbury in Shropshire, ma'am. Isn't there exactly, but it gives a sense of the place. Would you like me to run a couple of the trains for you?'

The Queen pictured the engines racing round the track, disappearing into the tunnel and stopping at the little stations. She wondered what noise they would make. Prince Charles, and probably Anne too, would adore them.

'I'd love to, another time. I need to be back home in half an hour.'

He shook his head and sighed.

'So be it. To work. We're going to need this . . .' He searched along one of the shelves in front of them and pulled out a slim volume. 'A rail atlas. For precision on distances and timings. And an almanac for sunrise and sunset the week before last, which would be . . .' He scanned the shelves for no more than a second. 'Here. Yes.' He arranged the papers on the desk. 'Right, ma'am. Let's get to work.'

First, they established that sunset was at seven thirty-two that day, and that twilight – when it was dark enough for the stars to be visible in the sky – came twenty-five minutes later. After a glance at the atlas, Canon Vaughan got going. The Queen noted that he didn't need to refer to the printed timetables. He seemed to have them all in his head.

'Now, ma'am, you say you left Euston at five past five. You would have done, to avoid clashing with the five o'clock to Liverpool, and the five twenty-five to Glasgow, which goes at a decent lick. Then there's the six forty-four from Rugby to Crewe, which slips in behind the Liverpool train. I wonder if you went ahead of it, or after. It's only seven minutes after the through train, so I imagine . . . Yes, Mr Shaw would have adjusted speed to slot in after the Rugby service, then sped up a bit after Crewe. By then, as he said, it would have been shortly after eight p.m., and quite dark.'

'I see.'

'You started drinks at seven and you say the witness couldn't have seen anything before seven twenty. By my calculation, you would have been in this area . . . Let me show you on the atlas . . . Here . . . South of Stoke-on-Trent, where the track bends east-west. Potteries country, ma'am, where you get your Wedgwood from. Wait a minute, I just need . . .'

He stood straight and his eye rapidly scanned the bookshelf to their left, which was lined with cream and orange folded Ordnance Survey maps. He pulled out one of them and opened it up.

'Number 119, for Stafford. It's an inch to the mile. Good enough for our purposes, with cuttings and waterways. I know the line well, anyway, of course. It's the route of the *Royal Highlander*, one of my favourites. I used to offer to mark exams in Scotland, just for the pleasure of travelling on her. Dinner in Crewe and breakfast on the way to Inverness, if you're lucky to go that far. I'm surprised people travel any other way. Of course, you have a yacht, ma'am . . .'

'I do.'

He shook his head again. 'Now, where was I? Ah, yes. By my calculation, at seven twenty or thereabouts you would still have been a few miles east of Stafford. There's lots of water round there because the line runs close to the Staffordshire and Worcestershire canal, and later, a river, the Trent, I believe . . . Ah no, I see it's the Sow. Not a name I'm familiar with, I admit. And if we look closely, there are only a couple of places where the water becomes significant enough to be what I might call ponds, or a little lake. There's one here, but no cutting nearby. And another, here. Look, *there's* the cutting you mentioned, and it's definitely near fields, unless they've been built on in the last year or two, which seems most unlikely. I know that stretch of the line well, ma'am. It's very beautiful. Sheep may safely graze and so on. Or rather, it's next to Cannock Chase, which I believe your ancestor, William the Conqueror, had created as a hunting forest. More, "deer had better look out", I suppose.'

'What's that?' the Queen asked, pointing to a large building about an inch away on the map.

The canon peered down. 'That's a place called Heatherwick Hall, ma'am. I don't know it, do you? There are several great houses in that area.' He looked up. 'Does that help?'

'It does. Tremendously.'

'The other thing is,' he said, glancing down again, 'Mr Shaw might have been going slightly slower than usual, in order to leave a decent gap after the Rugby train to Crewe. That would be just the place.'

'Thank you Maurice. I'm glad I asked.'

'The pleasure was all mine.'

He was busy putting the papers away as the Queen scanned his bookshelves.

'Oh, gosh,' she said, noticing a collection of little volumes at the end of one of them. 'I recognise those. That's *Thomas the Tank Engine*, isn't it? Charles used to love them. I would have thought they were a bit beneath you, though, surely?'

Canon Vaughan looked up. 'Not at all, ma'am. They're by a fellow clergyman, of course. Wilbert Awdry knows his stuff. Do you really have them, too? I must tell him.'

'What is it about railways and clergymen?' she asked. 'If I think about it, almost every vicar or bishop I know is a train buff or a cricket fanatic.'

'Or both,' he said, smiling. 'I've often wondered that myself. The dean likes to say that God is in the details, so He's to be found in the delightful precision of steam engines and timetables. I disagree. In my opinion, ma'am, the order and predictability of railways is very different from the human world one often finds oneself in, where people do and say the oddest, most unpredictable things. Especially parishioners and schoolboys. *They* are where God is to be found, I believe, but they can be very exhausting. Trains tend to run on time, and go where you expect.' He paused to consider. 'Unlike your train, to an extent, I suppose. I mean, it goes where *you* expect, ma'am, but not everyone's expecting it. That must be rather exciting for trainspotters. However, it does travel at consistent speeds in predictable directions, so I feel pretty confident about when it passed the ponds near Heatherwick Hall. It would have been within five or ten minutes of sunset. Any later, and the witness wouldn't have seen much at all.'

'You've been hugely helpful,' she reiterated, and once again, he batted away the compliment.

'Next time you come, we must play trains, ma'am' he suggested.

'I'd be delighted,' she said. And meant it. Then she hurried back to her private apartments – feeling rather sad that they lacked a model railway of their own.

Chapter 15

On Tuesday morning, the Queen was back at her desk at Buckingham Palace, and Joan had managed to make sure she was the one to collect the royal boxes.

'Did you have any luck yesterday, ma'am?' she wondered.

'I did. Canon Vaughan kindly narrowed it down to a small stretch of track near Stafford, a few miles south of Stoke-on-Trent. This time, it fits Sandra's description in all points: the water, the fields, the time the train would have been passing, which would have been around seven twenty-five, a few minutes before sunset.'

Joan grinned. 'Congratulations!'

The Queen felt there was little to celebrate.

'Is there a problem, ma'am?

'A very big one. Because if Sandra didn't make up the time and place, she probably didn't make up what she saw there. In fact, she's turned into a surprisingly accurate witness. Certainly as far as the landscape goes.'

The Queen was quiet for a moment, glancing out of the big bow window that overlooked Green Park, working out how to proceed diplomatically. When one officially didn't solve crimes, solving crimes could be complicated.

She turned back to Joan. 'I'd like you to visit Sandra, privately. The police are going to want to talk to her, and I think it would be better if she were to go to them first. I'd rather she didn't tell the world how easy it was to get into my carriage unchallenged. It might give people ideas. But she can easily say she was in my sister's. It's only two carriages down and she had every right to be there.'

Joan frowned.

'What is it?'

'Sorry, ma'am, I was just thinking, she could so easily have said that the first time, to me.'

'She could have,' the Queen agreed. 'Perhaps she should have. But I think the illicitness of what she'd really been up to made her want to pretend she'd been as far from my bathroom as possible. And seeing the body on top of it all – if there *was* a body – made her lose her head.'

Joan clucked in annoyance. 'Did she really just come back and join us for cocktails?'

'I suppose so,' the Queen said. 'Shock can do strange things to people. In Sandra's case, it seems as though she drowned her sorrows, got distracted and said things she regretted about tigers.'

Joan gave a wry grin. 'Then the next day, when she panicked and told me she was in her own carriage, she talked herself into a corner.'

'And now, she needs to talk herself out of it,' the Queen said firmly. 'But if she *does* say it was Margaret's carriage, she'll need to give a reason for not having originally said she was where she was perfectly entitled to be.'

They both thought about it.

'She was doing it to protect the princess?' Joan suggested. 'A bit like she'd be protecting you, really, ma'am. She "wanted to keep Princess Margaret's name out of it"; that sort of thing.'

The Queen considered it. 'That might work. Perhaps you can persuade her not to mention Conchita, either. For her own sake. It doesn't do her credibility any good. D'you think she can manage it?'

'I really don't know,' Joan said, honestly. 'Sandra isn't a great actress.'

'Well, if the worst comes to the worst, she must say what really happened.'

The Queen didn't like the idea, but murder was murder. If there *was* a murder.

'I'm not sure anyone would believe that either,' Joan said. 'That's Sandra's problem. But I'll talk her through it as well as I can.'

The Queen sighed. 'The important thing is to focus on the new time. It shouldn't be hard for the police to triangulate it with the landscape, the way Canon Vaughan did. Then it's in their hands. Who knows? It was over a week ago. I can't imagine there will be anything there, but at least we've tried.'

After Joan left, the Queen wondered whether anyone would believe the witness, or whether the damage was done. As Joan said, the woman had a reputation. Even Margaret admitted it: the poor Duke of Buccleuch, and his shoes.

She realised she wasn't sure what she wanted to happen next. If Sandra was wrong, or simply not believed, it was going to be hard for her. But if they found *something*, well what then?

'*The face*,' she had said to Joan, with a look of horror.

The Queen shuddered. She called one of the corgis to her for a cuddle.

PART TWO

THE SKIPPING ROPE MAN

Chapter 16

'I say, Joan?'

Dominic Stonor poked his head round Joan's office door. 'Oh, good, you're back. D'you know, the most extraordinary thing's just happened.'

'Has it?' Joan asked, slightly out of breath. 'Do come in.'

'D'you remember the Pole woman, the corker from the train who made our lives hell?' he said, perching his long frame against a windowsill.

'Naturally.'

'She's changed her whole story. She rang me half an hour ago and asked me to help with the press side of things, assuming it leaks, which it will.'

'Oh really?'

'Yes, out of nowhere, she's had a change of heart. Now, she's saying she saw the whole "body in a field" thing during cocktail hour, when she left us to tend to that damn dog of hers. D'you remember?'

'I do.' Joan affected a light, casual air. 'Did she explain why she didn't say so in the first place?'

Dominic shrugged. 'Something about trying to protect Princess Margaret, whose carriage she was really in. She didn't want that splashed all over the press. But she can't live with herself and she's going to the police as we speak.'

'My goodness!'

Dominic looked exasperated. 'Who knows what will happen now? I tried to talk her out of it, but she insists on doing her public duty, or something.'

'Does she?' Joan asked innocently. Her breath was calmer now. Hopefully there was little sign that she had recently run from Sandra's flat in Chelsea to the nearest corner where she could find a cab.

'I think someone's been having a word with her,' Dominic said. 'I tested out the story, the new one, the second one, and she actually sounded almost plausible this time. She was very certain about light levels, waterways, distances, how much she'd had to drink by then, which wasn't too much, all that sort of thing.'

'Oh good. Lovely. Right.' Joan smiled brightly.

'Only, I thought you'd want to know because she told you that cock and bull story the first time. What d'you think? Might there be something in it?'

Joan adopted a look of vague hopefulness. 'I suppose there might. So, whatever it was, she saw it earlier, did she?'

'Yes, around sunset or just before.'

'That sounds plausible, then, doesn't it? It was always the light levels that made no sense to me.'

'That, and the fact the woman's one sandwich short of a picnic,' Dominic muttered. 'I did like her, though, despite the whole tiger disaster at dinner. The thing is, I bet she was just trying to make conversation. So was I, with my chat about my novel earlier, and that touched off a whole world of Armageddon.'

'It did a bit.'

'But nobody really minded,' he went on. 'I sort of got away with it. Whereas poor Sandra . . . I mean, she didn't help herself with the martinis. But if she'd just seen a body being chucked around a field . . .'

'So, are you going to help her?'

Dominic picked up a pencil from a pot on her desk and twiddled it around his fingers.

'Noblesse oblige, and all that. After all, if she *did* see something, the police ought to know the real story. And then it'll get out, because it always does. It's going to be hard work to persuade the gentlemen of the press that Princess Margaret doesn't travel around with crackpots – especially when she does – but I'll see what I can do. I might at least be able to keep the princess's carriage out of it. By the way, talking of martinis, are you sure I can't persuade you to come to the Ritz with me later this week? They do things to gin with lemon peel and olives there that are positively erotic.'

Joan gave a start and smiled apologetically. 'Gosh, sorry. I'm afraid I'm booked up this week.'

'Don't tell me you're washing your hair. What *do* you do with your spare time, Joan?'

'A lady never tells.'

Poor Dominic. He was part Greek Adonis and part Labrador puppy. If that were her type, she would go to the Ritz with him in a heartbeat. But Joan had met her type, and she smiled even more to herself at the thought that he was neither of those things, even remotely. Her type would be cooking for her this evening and, as a matter of fact, she did have a plan to wash her hair for him. He could do things to gin with lemon peel and olives that were positively erotic, too.

Chapter 17

Three days passed, in which the 'ROYAL TRAIN WITNESS MYSTERY' made regular headlines. Dominic Stonor had worked his magic, and neither the nature of the carriage the witness was in at the time, nor her 'crackpot' tendencies, were mentioned in the press. Privately, the police weren't convinced about her reliability, but she had travelled by train with Her Majesty, so something had to be done.

On Friday, 7th April, Chief Superintendent George Venables looked round his office at Scotland Yard with a sense of satisfaction. He'd been angling for a job at the venerable Murder Squad for a couple of years and, as usual, the gods had been kind and the thing he really wanted had recently landed in his lap.

What Venables liked about the Murder Squad was that its tentacles spread around the country. It enabled its officers to be useful not just in London, but wherever a local force felt out of its depth. If they'd gone more than twenty-four hours without nabbing a suspect, they could call on the squad – *his* squad – and, wherever they were, they'd get the wisdom, the resources and over half a century of experience from the best in the business.

Venables stretched his aching spine and felt the tingling finger of age starting to creep up on him. He was aware that, young as he was for his high position, he didn't have forever to make the mark he intended. He'd been a shining star at the Met for a while, it was true, but his patch had become a bit parochial for his taste. They knew him across London from east to west, but did they know him in Yorkshire? Could he bring his special leadership qualities to bear in Dorset? What about those dinners for the great and the good in Birmingham, or Manchester, where his mother's family was from, for example? Wouldn't his grandfather – a proud man, but hard to please – be happy to say casually to his friends at the golf club that his grandson was responsible for the 'X' case, where a local hardman was brought to justice? Rather than it always being 'those soft lads down south' who were incarcerated? Not that Venables would have called the foot soldiers of the East End gangs particularly soft.

What he needed – apart from a comfortable cushion to sit on – was something juicy, something that would make the papers. He looked at the memorandum that had recently arrived on his desk, in answer to a query, and wondered whether this could be it. His fingers had actually tingled when he first ran them down the page. Venables knew the ingredients of success and all the elements were potentially here: a mutilated body (if it could be found); a missing person; a strange veil of secrecy; and, last but not least, a royal connection. If the gentlemen of the press loved one thing more than secrecy, it was royalty. Yes, he could hear the front pages calling.

The chief superintendent picked up the telephone to his secretary.

'Jilly, check if DCI Darbishire's gone to lunch yet. If not, call him in.'

Fred Darbishire was less happy than Venables about their joint move to the Murder Squad. He preferred the friendship and familiarity of his old team at the CID. He'd always found the Murder Squad men a bit ambitious and self-satisfied. Not that Fred wasn't ambitious, and his wife had been delighted when he'd told her about the move. But he felt he'd been doing all right before, on his old beat at Chelsea, where he knew every officer and every street, good and bad. However, Venables had asked for him personally, and what the chief superintendent wanted, the chief superintendent got.

'Jilly said you needed me, sir.'

Darbishire noted how quickly Venables had made himself at home in his new office, with all his framed certificates on the wall and his awards lined up on an empty bookshelf behind his head.

'I did. I do. Take a seat, Fred. I need you to take a little trip.'

Darbishire's heart sank. Tomorrow was Saturday, and his elder daughter's birthday. He had a lot of plans.

'What's the story?'

Venables tapped the file in front of him.

'The Staffordshire county force are looking for a body. The one that woman claims she saw from the royal train.'

'Wasn't that a while ago, sir?'

Venables nodded. 'She says she saw the incident on the twenty-sixth – twelve days ago – but she got her knickers in a twist and couldn't pinpoint the location to start with.'

'I read that,' Darbishire said. 'Don't understand it.'

Venables shrugged. 'The impression I get is that she was drunk, or upset, or some combination. Cocktails were consumed.'

'Ah, I see, sir.'

Venables and Darbishire shared the look of men who rarely consumed cocktails, never in moving vehicles, and only dimly understood the lives of those who did.

'Anyway, the Staffordshire force have been on the case for a couple of days,' Venables continued. 'The dog team seem to think they've found something near a place called Heatherwick Hall, but they're not sure.'

'Not sure how?'

'Well, they seem convinced there's something there, or at least, one dog does, but the officers can't find any traces. It's in a muck midden at the top of a field that leads down to the railway track. They went through the midden again yesterday, but definitely no corpse. They might have been tempted to give up, but the dog's not happy. And the tip-off came from the palace after all. D'you know Benson?'

Darbishire frowned. 'No, sir.'

'David Benson, Staffordshire's chief constable. He's a man with his eyes on the prize. He doesn't want to let this one slip away if he can help it.'

It takes one to know one, Darbishire thought.

'Has he asked around for likely missing people?'

'He has, Fred,' Venables said. 'A white male, almost certainly. Missing for at least eleven days as of yesterday, possibly more. One of the clerks at the Yard found a couple of reports that matched here in London, but what's interesting is that his search triggered something in the system . . . and this morning I received this very interesting note.'

Venables tapped the memorandum in the open file in front of him.

'From someone in the Government, sir?' Fred asked, recognising the Civil Service crown on the letterhead.

'You could say that. Calls himself Major Ross. Home Office, he says. But we know what that means.'

'Do we?'

'Come on, Fred. Security services, reading between the lines. MI5 or MI6. Five, I assume. The thing is, they'd already taken an interest in one of those missing people, a professional photographer called . . .' Venables glanced down at the typescript '. . . Michalowski. A British citizen. Father was a fighter pilot in the war, a Pole who didn't survive it. Michalowski is a bit of a peacock, apparently.'

'Sir?'

'A social butterfly. What they used to call a dandy. He could be anywhere, and this Major Ross would very much like to establish his whereabouts because they found 'certain items of concern' in his flat. Of great concern, given that Ross had a runner come over to hand-deliver me this note.'

'Can I ask what items?'

'You can, Fred, but I can't tell you, because I don't know. Major Ross fails to mention what they are, and you might think, not a problem, we'll just ask at the local station in Chalk Farm near where Michalowski lives, because they'll have been the ones to check out the flat when he went missing. But they didn't. Major Ross's outfit seems to have checked it out for themselves before we had the chance. Michalowski had been reported missing at the station a couple of days before, but Chalk Farm hadn't followed up yet. The first they knew about the "items of concern" was when I told them.'

'Ah.'

'"Ah" indeed. Someone, possibly the same concerned friend, must have told Ross's outfit, too. Very uncivil of them to keep us in the dark about their visit. But now Ross thinks the new lead in Staffordshire is promising, and he'd appreciate our help. His outfit is retrieving items of clothing from the missing man's flat as we speak, to give the dogs something to go on. Someone's popping round with a bag, and I want you to take it up to the Midlands as soon as possible. You can catch the fast train to Crewe after lunch. Someone will meet you at Stafford station and take you to the farm where they found the midden.'

'Today, sir? Isn't that something a sergeant can take care of?' Darbishire took care to sound extra-polite, but honestly – he hadn't recently been promoted to detective chief inspector so he could ferry dirty underpants up and down the country.

'No, it isn't. Not this time, Fred. You can buy a toothbrush in Staffordshire.' The head of the Murder Squad twisted his neck and eased his uncomfortable spine. 'The palace can't afford to be kept waiting. And I need someone up there who can make decisions and take control. Do whatever you need to. We at the Murder Squad need to show our mettle. And Fred . . .'

'Yes, sir?'

'Don't take any nonsense from the Staffordshire lot. Got it?'

'Yes, sir.'

'Good.'

Chapter 18

Later that afternoon, Darbishire sat in the passenger seat of a pale blue Morris Minor, feeling car sick as a local sergeant navigated winding Staffordshire roads. A leather bag containing a selection of shoes, shirts and dirty underwear sat at his feet. His wife, when he'd called her from the Yard, had been less than pleased.

'You do this sort of thing often?' the sergeant asked from the driver's seat beside him.

'Not really.'

'It must be interesting, down in London.'

'It is,' Darbishire agreed, picturing his daughter's birthday party, which was probably not what the sergeant meant. 'Nice countryside,' he offered.

It was. Green and rolling grazing land, criss-crossed with hedgerows, dotted with sheep, and fringed with copses of birch, elm and other trees Darbishire couldn't exactly name. Having lived in Chelsea half his life, he wouldn't claim to be an expert on anything greener than a bay tree in a pot.

'Tell me about your boss,' he said to the sergeant.

'DCI Weatherby? He's a Stoke man, Potteries born and bred. Takes care of his men, if you know what I mean.

Knows everyone worth knowing round these parts. If there's anything there, he'll find it.'

'How does he know he's looking in the right place?'

The sergeant shrugged. 'He can't be certain, but the witness on the train said she saw the body being chucked about at the back of a field near ponds or lakes or some such, near a cutting, through a gap in the trees by the railway. If you put all of that together, assuming it was a field that wasn't overlooked by houses, there's not many locations round this way that fit. And Hero doesn't think much of the others.'

'Is Hero another detective?' Darbishire hadn't come across that name in the briefing notes he'd got from Scotland Yard.

'In a way,' the sergeant said. 'She's one of the dogs. She's a different breed from the rest. Not literally, she's a springer, but in talent, I s'pose. She's got a sixth sense about her, that mutt has. She's trained in finding corpses. If she thinks there was a body in that field, then you can bet there was one, even if it's not there now.'

'Right.'

'Honestly, if you'd just lost a loved one and you thought they were out there, she'd be your go-to canine.'

'I'll bear that in mind,' Darbishire said drily.

'Here we are.'

The sergeant turned off the road and took them half a mile down a bumpy track. He parked the car at the edge of a field, next to a Land Rover, a police van and a mud-spattered Rover. They both got out, and the sergeant took charge of the leather bag.

He grinned. 'Just wait till you see Hero at it.'

Darbishire liked the officer's touching belief in his force's star animal, but he had little faith, personally, in the power of dirty underpants against the lush landscape that spread out below them, past one green field to another, ending in the railway line that he could just make out through a gap in a slim row of trees.

Hero was a black and white spaniel, who seemed to vibrate with energy from the minute she was let out of the van. She took the most interest in a white cotton shirt from Darbishire's bag. Her phlegmatic handler, Sergeant Blackshaw, said the armpits were what did it.

'Sweat, sir. Loaded with scent.'

The shirt in question looked pristine to Darbishire: Michalowski was indeed (had been?) a 'peacock', and this garment was smarter than anything Fred ever wore.

Anyway, after burying her nose in the fabric, the dog set off beside Blackshaw down a route made by several sets of tractor tracks that led down the field towards a gap in the hedge. Fred jogged along, keeping up as best he could. The lower field was mostly grass, but off to the right was a large, muddy area contained by a low stone wall, with a shack roofed in corrugated iron at the back. To their left, beside the hedge, was a series of ripe-smelling heaps of muck and straw.

'That's the midden,' Blackshaw explained. 'Or it was, until we took it apart yesterday. The farmer wants it put back in a big pile, so he can use it for fertiliser, but he can do that hims—'

He was interrupted by Hero's furious barking. She'd positioned herself beside one of the heaps and stood stock-still, legs planted, howling at Blackshaw to pay attention.

'She's louder than yesterday,' he said. 'After sniffing that shirt. He was definitely here, your man. Michaels-whatsit?'

'Michalowski.'

Had been a peacock, then, Darbishire thought. God rest his soul. Whoever had been drinking cocktails on that train had seen more than they bargained for.

A couple of men in plain clothes and trilbies were walking up from the direction of the railway. One stepped forward to introduce himself.

'I'm DCI Weatherby. Jim,' he said, extending a hand. 'This is my sergeant, Ferris. I'm the senior investigating officer. Except I'm not now, I suppose?' he added. 'If the Murder Squad is here.'

Darbishire made reassuring noises, but he knew the boss wouldn't want to let go of this one; Venables was like Hero that way. He turned and squinted past Weatherby's shoulder at the railway. From where they stood, near the midden, he could make out the individual branches of the trees beside the track. There was a substantial gap between them, where a few were reduced to stumps. Someone looking out of that train window would be able to glimpse the midden briefly, but clearly. So why . . . ?

Just as he was pursuing the thought, a train emerged from a cutting hidden by trees and clattered past, heading north-west for Crewe. It was a diesel locomotive, so there was no swoosh of steam to accompany the sight. Behind the engine, half a dozen carriages followed on, their windows rendered blank and anonymous by the reflected light from the sky.

'Does that happen often?' Fred asked. 'The train?'

'I'd say so,' Weatherby answered. 'I've seen quite a few since we've been here. It's a busy line.'

Darbishire wondered who would be stupid enough to dispose of a body somewhere they could be overlooked by strangers at any minute. Perhaps they had underestimated the chance of it happening. But who would take that risk?

Hero had been given a treat that kept her quiet, but she seemed keen to carry on, shifting from paw to paw and looking up at her handler with fierce intensity while she waited for new instructions. Blackshaw led her around the perimeter of the field, into the muddy area with the shack, and back to the gap in the hedge where they'd entered. She merely sniffed until she reached the turning point of the tractor tracks, when she barked again, her body shivering.

'She did this yesterday,' DCI Weatherby explained. 'So, he was here, your man, but he must have been taken away by tractor. God knows where they put him. We had her search the field above and all the way along the lane, but she wasn't interested, and the body could be anywhere. We even had her search near the ponds, half a mile away. That's where I'd have put it. Still can't swear it's not there, of course. We could try and get divers, I suppose. But Hero wasn't interested there either.'

'Who owns the land?' Darbishire asked.

'Chap called Thorburn. He lives at Heatherwick Hall.'

They started to walk across the upper field together.

'What's he like?'

'He's popular enough,' Weatherby said. 'Bought the land a few years ago and enlarged the Hall a fair bit. He employs a decent number of locals, despite everything that's happened on the land. He runs a shoot and owns three farms – arable and grazing. Made his money in holiday camps and car parks, would you believe, but he's quite the country gentleman now. Likes to ride with the hunt. A proper squire.'

'Where's the Hall?' Darbishire asked.

'The other side of the railway. Thorburn owns land both sides of the track. You can see it from further down the lane – I'll show you. Impressive place. Wouldn't mind living there myself. Not that you'd get to do that on a policeman's wage, hey?'

Weatherby treated Darbishire to his friendly smile. Fred wasn't sure about the smiling. It was supposed to make him feel warmly included, respected, even – but he found it odd. The man should be resentful. He would have been.

They got into their vehicles and drove slowly back down the track for a few hundred yards, while Hero trotted along behind them, showing no great interest in the hedgerows. Then Weatherby's Rover stopped next to a five-bar gate and the sergeant brought the Morris Minor to a halt behind it. Weatherby and Sergeant Ferris led Darbishire through the gate, pointing out a wooded area down to their left, beyond a couple of fields of crops. Trees and a small embankment masked the railway track at the bottom.

'That's where the ponds are,' Weatherby explained. 'You can't really see 'em from here, but the witness mentioned them. And over there . . .' he pointed beyond the brow of the hill opposite '. . . you can make out the chimneys of Heatherwick Hall. Thorburn owns just about all the land you can see from this spot. He farms wheat and—'

'What's that?' Darbishire asked, moving off rapidly down the hill.

'Just a scarecrow,' Sergeant Ferris said, jogging after him. 'You get lots of them in these parts. The birds are terrible round—'

'What's it wearing?'

'Some sort of shirt,' Weatherby puffed. 'That's quite normal. Sometimes it's a coat, but shirts are good because they catch the light and flap like billy-o.'

They reached the scarecrow.

'I recognise this shirt,' Darbishire said.

He'd had a feeling about it from a distance. Up close, he was certain. It was white and smart, with double cuffs and a modern cut to the collar. Not exactly farmers' gear, but the kind a 'peacock' would wear. He had brought its twin up from London.

'Don't touch it!' he shouted, as the others ran through ankle-high stalks towards him.

They all stood and waited for Blackshaw and Hero to catch up with them. As soon as the dog got within fifty yards, she raced towards the scarecrow, barking hard. She agreed with Darbishire, no question. Weatherby gave instructions for the shirt to be extracted carefully, but Darbishire overruled him.

'This is for forensics.'

Weatherby glanced over at the horizon. 'It's getting dark,' he said. 'They won't be able to see anything by the time they get here.'

'They can bring torches. Somebody needs to go and make a call.'

Weatherby reluctantly dispatched the sergeant who had acted as Darbishire's chauffeur. While they waited, Blackshaw let Hero take him where she wanted. Nose to the earth, she ran in zigzags halfway down the field, checking, losing, finding, pulling her handler on. Five minutes later, she'd unearthed a filthy but well-made, lightweight woollen jacket stuffed into a rabbit hole. Her satisfaction at the find rippled through her body. Darbishire wondered what it would be like if his daughters ever encountered a dog like this. He strongly suspected it would be total love, forever.

There were tractor tracks around the edge of this field, too. They finished near the bottom, where Hero seemed to pick up the scent again, pulling at her lead as she turned along the drystone wall that marked the bottom boundary.

Darbishire noted that there were no neighbours, here, not even a cottage. Given the embankment and the trees beside the railway, further down, this part of the field was only overlooked by the chimneys of the distant Hall.

'Surely they'd not be stupid enough to take the body from the tractor and drag it along the ground to the next location?' Sergeant Ferris asked.

'Never underestimate the stupidity of your average villain,' Weatherby told him.

Ferris looked perplexed. 'We had the dogs here yesterday. None of them were that interested. Not like Hero today.'

'Perhaps they didn't have enough of a scent to go on yesterday,' Darbishire said. 'But now Hero knows exactly what she's looking for.'

He was already working on a theory. Had the naked body been wrapped in a tarpaulin, perhaps, to ease transportation? It might have made the scent harder to detect, until Hero was given the exact match by the contents of the bag he'd delivered earlier.

Whatever she was doing, Hero had reached her destination, which was in the far corner of the field. She planted her feet again and barked over a rectangular metal panel set into the earth and marked with a rusty iron ring. One of the sergeants leaned in to heave the panel up. They all looked in.

'Bingo,' Weatherby muttered.

They were looking down on a disused water tank made out of a large steel drum. The naked body of a man lay curled at the bottom, its legs bent at an angle to fit it into the space. A dirty tarpaulin was stuffed at his feet. The body was in good condition, given that the man had probably been dead for at least two weeks, but it still wasn't a pretty sight. It had suffered the indignities of the midden, leaving scrapes, scratches and patches of dried manure on the limbs. The stomach was distended. The face was turned away, but even so it was plain that both it and the tips of the shoulders were a deep reddish-purple, as if a statue's head of porphyry stone had been attached to the torso.

'Never seen that before.' Weatherby glanced away momentarily.

'I have, but on backs and legs,' Darbishire said, leaning in. 'Never a head.'

Weatherby's sergeant peered in closely. 'Hands are in place, sir. Fingertips look OK.' He frowned.

'You seem disappointed,' his boss observed.

'It's just . . . They go to all this trouble to hide the body, but they make him pretty easy to identify if he *does* get discovered.'

'I don't know,' Weatherby countered. 'Prints only matter if we have something to match them to.'

'What if the prints *were* on file, sir?'

'Perhaps they assumed they wouldn't be, Ferris. After all, if he's Inspector Darbishire's London gent, like it seems, I doubt he'd have been arrested at any point.'

'It's a big assumption, isn't it?' the sergeant persisted. 'For them, I mean.'

Weatherby grinned, showing a perfect set of teeth. 'Ours is not to reason why, Ferris. Like I say, never underestimate the stupidity of a villain.'

Darbishire felt it was very much theirs to reason why. In his view, the water tank must have been a temporary resting place. The killers had been disrupted before they could move the body on. Perhaps they were going to deal with fingerprints later. He said nothing, but his sympathies increasingly lay with the curious sergeant, not the affable inspector.

Meanwhile, whatever forensics might come up with, Hero had already done most of the work. The jacket she'd found in the rabbit hole was handmade, with the tailor's mark, and tomorrow, the tailor in question would no doubt confirm who his client had been. The chances of it not being Michalowski, and of the body not being the photographer, seemed vanishingly small.

Darbishire looked at his watch. Six forty-five. It had taken the Murder Squad less than eight hours to identify the corpse. Or that's how Venables would tell the story anyway. Meanwhile, Fred made sure to thank Blackshaw for Hero's service.

'I'll make sure she gets a good write-up.'

'Oh, she doesn't need it,' the handler said. 'She knows how good she is. She loves the work.'

'How are they? Spaniels?' Fred asked. 'Do they make good family dogs?'

'The best, if you train them properly.'

'I got my daughter a bike,' he said, ruminatively.

'I'm sorry?'

'Oh, nothing.'

Then, with a sigh, he reflected that Hero's job was over for the day, but his wasn't.

What stupid idiots had tried to dispose of a body within sight of a busy train track, and then in dry storage a couple of fields away? Why, if the victim came from London, had they travelled halfway up the country to do this terrible, half-cocked job of getting rid of him? What, if anything, had the victim done to incur their wrath in the first place – and would the 'man from the Home Office' ever let him find out? Darbishire had experience of being held up in his investigations by men from the ministry with ulterior motives. Glancing across at Weatherby, hands thrust deep in his pockets, chatting with his sergeant, Fred wondered if the obstacles would come from both directions this time.

He put up his coat collar and got back to the tank.

Chapter 19

In his Mayfair office, a brisk five-minute walk from the Ritz (not that he ever went there), the 'man from the ministry' would have smiled wryly if he'd known that Darbishire was worrying about obstacles.

Hector Ross himself had been one of those very obstacles four years ago. Back then, it had been in his organisation's interest for Darbishire not to investigate certain witnesses in a delicate murder case. The policeman had investigated them anyway, but fortunately it had all turned out for the best. This time, Ross dearly hoped for Darbishire's success, but had very low expectations of him achieving it.

Would the bet on Pavel Michalowski work? Ross was staying late, waiting for an update from the Midlands. However, if Michalowski had been killed by the people Ross was starting to suspect, it was incredibly unlikely that his body would have ended up halfway to Scotland, and almost impossible that they'd have been stupid enough to try and dispose of it near a railway line.

Hector was in the middle of preparing a report for the palace. No such report had been requested, but the witness had been travelling with the Queen at the time, and the men in her private office had an uncanny way of finding out what was relevant to Her Majesty, and asking for details. If such an instruction came, he wanted to be ready. While he waited for the telephone to ring, he looked over his notes.

A week ago, two members of the public, concerned about Michalowski's recent disappearance, had found unusual photographic equipment hidden in a cupboard in his flat. Most of his supplies were kept in his studio and darkroom down the road, but the cupboard's contents were specific and concerning. They consisted of a camera loaded with very fine-grain film, more rolls of the same film in reserve, a range of interesting stationery items, several pairs of tweezers, a pile of chess magazines, and a powerful lamp.

The cupboard had been cleverly wired up so the electric supply for the lamp wouldn't show from outside. However, the door was fastened with a crudely attached padlock. The concerned friends had opened the lock without difficulty and one of them turned out to be a journalist who'd recognised the set-up as one that could be used for making microdots.

The journalist had immediately informed a friend of his, who happened to be one of Hector's colleagues at MI5 (because as Chief Superintendent Venables had correctly guessed, that was the organisation he worked for), who had passed on the information to Hector himself. One of Hector's teams was at the flat within the hour.

The Michalowski case was intriguing and strange. The missing man had set himself up to send and receive secret messages, but they were not so secret that he had gone to enormous lengths to hide the fact he was doing it. After all, it took a friend and a neighbour five minutes, armed with a spare key, to discover the truth.

MI5 and the CIA had been busy unmasking various Russian spy rings in recent months, and this was not how they operated. As head of D Branch, Hector was responsible for several successful counter-espionage investigations. *Those* spies had elaborate false identities, false passports and radios carefully concealed in spaces behind false walls. By contrast, Michalowski made no attempt to hide who he was. The journalist who reported the equipment had known him since his schooldays. His attempts to disguise what he was doing were slapdash. Either he was an amateur, playing at spies, or he wasn't unduly concerned about what would happen if he were discovered. So, not a proper spy, then. Not a traitor. But someone who was communicating with one, perhaps. He wasn't concerned for *his* safety, but for theirs.

This had been Hector's first hypothesis, and he had met various contacts in the Soviet dissident community in London to sound out what the photographer might have been up to. Was he seen as a threat, a friend? Did they know about him at all?

It turned out that a couple of men had heard rumours of 'the Pole', who had helped two distinguished physicists escape from East Germany via Scandinavia last year. In their circles, 'the Pole' was spoken of with reverence. The scientists in question had gone on to universities in America, so were of more interest to MI6 than MI5. Hector had known of their journey, but not that a 'Pole' from London had supposedly helped them. Was this Michalowski? Hector was waiting to hear back from them.

He had spent the last few days doing more research, and meanwhile putting out feelers for any missing men who might meet the photographer's description. The news from the Midlands was promising, but he had little hope of such an easy win.

In his lamplit office, the telephone rang. He rubbed his eyes and answered it.

'Ross here. You're sure? In a disused water tank? My God. And what condition was the body—?Really?'

According to Chief Superintendent Venables, who was calling in person, the body was indeed Michalowski, almost certainly. So far, there was no obvious cause of death. Beyond the post-mortem scrapes and scratches there was very little damage. No gunshot wounds, knife wounds, telltale bruises or the half-expected signs of a ligature. Apart from some unusual blood pooling, it was surprisingly unmarked, in fact. The local forensic pathologist would get to work on it properly tomorrow.

'Listen, I'm sure they're very good up in Staffordshire and all that,' Hector said, 'but can you talk to a man at Guy's Hospital in London, who I think should be involved? . . . That's right, Mallory, the expert on poisoning . . . I'm afraid I can't answer that question, Chief Superintendent. I'm sorry.'

Despite Hector's reluctance to confirm the head of the Murder Squad's hunch of potential Soviet involvement, Venables promised to make the necessary arrangements and keep him updated.

Hector put the phone down, equal parts elated and confused. It seemed he'd found his man after all, but if his emerging theory about the KGB was right, then he'd been expecting signs of torture, should the body ever emerge, and certainly a bloody death, at least. So, perhaps his theory was wrong after all.

If not, then Michalowski must have given up his secrets easily, or he had died before he could. Which was probably a blessing, though it wouldn't have seemed so at the time.

Chapter 20

'Have you seen the newspapers?' Philip asked the Queen on Saturday morning at Windsor Castle, looking up from his kippers as she joined him for breakfast.

'Not yet. I went to the nursery to say hello to the children. We're busy this evening and we won't have time to—'

'Forget the nursery. They've bloody found Sandra Pole's body!'

'Sandra Pole's body? Oh God!'

'No, no, not *her* body, the one she claimed she saw from the train. Well, it turns out she actually did see it.'

'The skipping rope man!' the Queen murmured.

'What?'

'Oh, nothing. So, they found it? Where?'

'Exactly where she said, eventually, by the sound of things,' Philip told her. 'Somewhere in Staffordshire. Man called Michalowski.'

'They know his name already?'

'Oh yes, the whole thing's tied up with a bow. But I have a bone to pick with you, Lilibet.' Philip pointed at her with the butter knife.

'What is it?'

'I have it from my valet this morning that according to the gossip from Kensington Palace, Sandra told Margaret that she wasn't in *her* carriage – Margaret's, that is – when she saw the man from the window . . . she was in yours!'

'Oh, ah.'

It was still quite early and the Queen's head was still full of babies and cuddles and promises of pony rides. She wasn't fully on her game. Philip pounced.

'It *was* your carriage! Why didn't you tell me?'

'I meant to,' she said. She had, but somehow work and family life had got in the way, and she'd known her husband would be furious if he found out, and so the incentive to tell the full story had never quite been strong enough make her do it.

Philip brandished the butter knife.

'This is bloody outrageous! A woman, a practical stranger, armed with a dog and a camera, so the gossip goes, was taking pictures in your private bathroom, in your private saloon, on your private bloody train!'

'Well, yes, the circumstances were unfortunate.'

'Un-bloody-fortunate? She could have done anything! What were your bloody protection officers doing when they should have been outside your door? Tucking away canapés in the dining car?'

'Um, well, yes, I think so.'

Philip thumped the table so hard the crockery jumped an inch and two spoons clattered off the table, to be whisked off the carpet by a footman who quickly backed away.

'You're the damn Queen! You should be safe at all times, by God. If an Englishman's train carriage isn't his castle, I don't know what is. Yes, all right, this castle. But goodness knows how safe Windsor is, for crying out loud, if your protection officers are going to lounge around snacking when they should be looking after you. I want to see them in my office this morning, both of 'em, so I can give them a damn good bollocking. And then sack 'em.'

'They're currently on restricted duties,' the Queen said, truthfully. Philip wasn't the only person who could be furious, and take action. She had done so the day after Margaret told her about Sandra's little escapade.

'Cleaning latrines, I hope,' Philip thundered. 'Or mucking out the stables. Like Achilles, or whoever it was. Hercules! That's the bugger. Like him.'

She had a feeling their new assignment wasn't a bed of roses. But whatever it was, they were probably grateful that they wouldn't be on the end of a Philip tongue-lashing.

'Sir Hugh has assured me that all the security protocols have been reviewed, and it won't happen again,' she assured him.

'It better bloody hadn't.'

For the sake of her husband's blood pressure, she decided to steer him away from the subject.

'What did you say the man's name was? The dead man, I mean.'

'Michalowski. He went missing in London, apparently,' Philip said. 'According to *The Times*, Venables is in charge. From the Yard. Good man. I've come across him before. He solved the Chelsea Murders, d'you remember?'

'Oh, did he?' she asked absently.

'Highly efficient. According to the paper, Michalowski was a society snapper. A bit like Tony.'

'I wish you wouldn't call Tony that.'

Philip shrugged. 'Shouldn't be a society snapper then. I wonder if he knew this Michalowski chap. No doubt we'll find out. The gossip channels are alive this morning.'

'What else does it say in *The Times*?'

'No idea. I haven't had a chance to read it yet.'

'Then don't let me disturb you.'

The breakfast room was quiet, as the Duke perused the paper and the Queen wondered privately if Margaret knew the man in question. If so, how absolutely awful for her. She must call today, when she had a moment, and find out how her sister was getting on.

But how very strange that the victim's body had ended up in Staffordshire, when according to *The Times* he'd disappeared in London. Had Michalowski been a guest of someone there, perhaps? Or working on a job, like Tony Armstrong-Jones did sometimes? Margaret had first met her husband at a wedding where he took the photographs. Perhaps this man had taken a picture of something he wasn't supposed to. If so, there would be a fearful symmetry between Sandra's fateful camera and his own.

He must have been staying or working there, she thought, because no one would simply drive randomly from London to Staffordshire with a corpse in the boot and turf it out in the nearest field. But wherever the poor man died, honestly, what *idiot* would try and dispose of a body near a railway track, when a train could come by at any minute? Something Canon Vaughan had said when they were narrowing down the location prodded at her brain. She tried to think exactly what it was . . .

'How's the *Racing Post*?' Philip asked, raising his eyes from his newspaper.

She realised that she'd been staring at the front page of her own chosen paper, but hadn't taken in a word.

'Oh, you know . . .' she said.

She'd lost her train of thought. But it probably didn't matter. Once they knew where to look, the police seemed to be on the skipping rope man case with remarkable speed. Her own view of Chief Superintendent Venables was not quite as rosy as Philip's. She wondered if he still worked with the trusty Inspector Darbishire, from the Chelsea CID. If so, she sincerely hoped they would come up trumps this time, as they had before. Albeit with a little help.

Chapter 21

'I'm sorry, Chief Inspector, I don't think I can be of assistance.'

It was early on Saturday afternoon at Heatherwick Hall, and the sun shone on the forests and fields of Staffordshire. Josiah Thorburn, a solid, middle-aged man who would have been good looking if he hadn't indulged quite so much in the pleasures of the table, sat facing Fred Darbishire in a large wicker chair on the terrace, flanked by his gamekeeper and farm manager.

Thorburn raised his hands as if defeated by the strangeness of the thing. 'It's confounding. None of us can make sense of it at all. I can only imagine a bunch of dumb gangsters took a joyride to the country with their victim. God knows how they chose one of my farms. Sheer bad damn luck, I suppose. Hopefully you'll find them, you and Chief Inspector Weatherby. Anything I can do to assist, of course . . . Always happy to help the boys in blue. I'm a big donor to the Police Orphans Fund, you know. Not for the glory, none of that bullshit – I just know what you men go through. Your families, too. Excuse me while I . . .' He indicated the large porcelain teapot in front of him and reached forward to pour himself a second cup. 'You sure you won't join me?'

Darbishire was quite sure. He wanted this to be an interview, not a tea party with a side helping of charitable self-congratulation. He wasn't so easily bought.

'I gather you were away on the twenty-sixth of last month, when the body was seen from the railway,' he said. After an hour or so at the pub last night, he'd been up late, reading Weatherby's notes, which were both copious and unenlightening.

'That's right. Le Touquet,' Thorburn elaborated. 'I doubt the gang would have dared use my land if I'd been here.'

'How would they have known?'

'Good point, good point. Anyway, my wife and I went down to France for the weekend and flew back on the Monday with a friend. He has a landing strip a few miles from here.' Thorburn gestured expansively across the valley. 'He keeps a little Cessna for popping down for the races. My wife likes a flutter on the gee-gees. Got to keep the old girl happy.'

Thorburn was bluff and avuncular and relaxed, and didn't fool Darbishire for a minute. You didn't get to be as rich as he was, from the humble Stoke roots he came from, without being a shrewd businessman, good at detail, aware of what was at stake. He might like to give the impression of 'hail fellow, well met' and all that, but his sharp eyes missed nothing.

Thorburn was dressed in riding gear, having explained that he was going out with the lady wife and a family friend later 'for a hack'. The two men either side of him were as lean and lithe as he was broad-beamed and well-upholstered. Both had donned their Sunday-best suits to meet the inspector from London, and looked about as comfortable in them as Darbishire would have felt in plus fours and a tweed flat cap.

'But you were here, Mr Fishburne,' he said to the gamekeeper.

'Arr, I wuss.'

'Talk properly, man,' Thorburn joshed him.

The gamekeeper did his best. 'I wuss out on the banks, fixing fences, then down in the cut till tay. I were 'ome by six and spent the evening with mar missus, like I told Mr Weatherby. After tay, we listened to the radio. *My Word!*. 'Er favourite.'

Darbishire noted the precise naming of the radio show. Fishburne's wife had said the same thing to Weatherby when questioned, also mentioning that it was her favourite programme. Their stories neatly matched in all particulars. No chinks at all.

The farm manager repeated his alibi for the same day – a busy one – but the details shifted a little. Darbishire was inclined to believe him, given the unreliability of memory. The gamekeeper's certainty, by contrast, was more interesting.

'And Mr Riley, who runs the farm in question . . .'

'Off sick,' Thorburn said, raising his hands again. 'Sick as a dog, I'm afraid. Some sort of virus, or a flare-up of farmer's lung. He'll be able to see you in a day or two, I should think. The farmhands are out in the fields, but we can send someone to fetch them, if required. You can use one of the empty garages to question them.'

'That would be helpful,' Darbishire said.

'It's not ideal, because they're very busy – more so, what with Mr Riley being in his sickbed – but if needs must . . .'

'They do,' Darbishire insisted gently. 'Because these visiting gangsters, or whoever they were, they must have been in contact with at least one of your men, don't you think, sir? Or how would they have known about the midden?'

Thorburn glanced at the men who flanked him in their chairs. All three shrugged – the gamekeeper minimally, the manager in some bemusement, Thorburn theatrically.

'*Did* they know?' the latter queried. 'My guess is that they were just looking for somewhere to get rid of the corpse, and found the midden by chance. They hadn't realised it was near a railway line, and as soon as a train came by – that must have been quite a shock for them, by the way – they moved it to the next place they could find . . .'

'Which just happened to be a hidden water tank,' Darbishire pointed out. 'Several fields away. How did they manage that, do you think?'

'Well, it's just a theory, Chief Inspector – you're the policeman, after all – but my guess is that one of them came from farming, originally, and he knew about water tanks, and they kept looking until they found one.'

'In the dark?'

Thorburn raised his hands again. 'As I say, you're the policeman.'

Darbishire was, and as such had considered that if strangers to the area really had been suddenly interrupted in nefarious activities, the last thing they'd have done was scour the land in near-darkness for as long as it took until they happened upon such a specific hiding place. They'd have scarpered, surely? Besides, there was a similar tank in the first field, as he'd discovered this morning, but it was half-full of water. City gangsters wouldn't mind polluting the supply with a dead body, but locals might.

'What was normally housed in the first field, can I ask?'

'Hmm?'

'The one with the midden. There was some sort of animal shelter,' Darbishire said. 'A stone enclosure and a lean-to with a corrugated roof.'

Thorburn looked bemused. 'I'm afraid I couldn't say. Sheep, probably. We have a lot of sheep.'

The farm manager leaned forward. 'You mean the shippen,' he said. 'Pigs, until recently.'

'What happened to them?' Darbishire asked.

'The finishers went off to slaughter. We moved the sows across the valley.'

'When was this?'

The farm manager was about to answer, but he caught the merest hint of a shake of the head from Thorburn, and turned his breath into a sigh and another shrug.

'I couldn't say exactly. You'll have to ask Mr Riley. When he's better.'

Darbishire turned to the gamekeeper. 'Are you familiar with that field?'

'Not really,' Fishburne replied. 'It's not used for the shoots, nor the 'unt. I've no cause to go there.'

'You don't help out Mr Riley, for example?'

Fishburne narrowed his eyes. 'No. Why would I?'

'You're not friends?'

'By no means.' The ice-cold look Fishburne threw Darbishire suggested the question was ridiculous.

Darbishire nodded, but he was thinking back to his conversation with the barmaid last night, who had said that Riley and the gamekeeper were regular drinkers there together. He'd given Fishburne a nice opportunity to admit to this unobjectionable fact, and it was interesting that he hadn't done so.

Nor was it mentioned in Weatherby's report. Weatherby, it turned out, was married to Thorburn's housekeeper's cousin, who was a sister of the barmaid herself.

'And no nicer brother-in-law you could hope for. He'd do anything for you, would Jim. He's a lovely uncle to my boys.'

This was a story, Darbishire thought, not of London thugs so much as hard-working country folk, who helped each other out. They were helping each other now, and forming a barrier to the truth as complete and intricate as a drystone wall. You had to admire it, really.

Thorburn looked restless. He glanced behind him and said, 'Do we have anything more to discuss? I hate to rush, but I can hear that my friend's arrived, and I hate to keep him waiting. As I say, I'm sorry we can't be of more assistance. The whole thing's a mystery.'

'Don't worry, we'll solve it for you, sir,' Darbishire assured him, rising and offering his hand. 'The chief constable's taking a personal interest. So's my boss in London. The last thing you need is strangers roaming your land, taking advantage of local hiding places. I'd hate to think of what it must be doing to your lady wife. I'll have a team working on it night and day.'

Thorburn shook his hand. 'Thank you. That's very reassuring,' he said with a thin smile.

They were joined on the terrace by another man in brand-new jodhpurs and a smart tweed jacket. This must be the friend Thorburn had discussed. He thrust his hand out at Darbishire.

'Dennis Wilson,' he said. 'Nice to meet you. And you are . . . ?'

Darbishire introduced himself, noting that Josiah Thorburn didn't seem particularly delighted about his friend's appearance in their midst, despite what he'd said before.

'Are you a regular visitor?' Fred asked.

'Not at all, not at all,' Wilson replied. 'This is my first time. But I've been looking forward to it. Beautiful here, isn't it? Fit for a king.' He grinned as he took in the view.

Thorburn smiled thinly again.

'Thank you very much for your visit, Chief Inspector. One of my staff will see you out. As I say, I'm so sorry we can't help you at all.'

Chapter 22

On Monday, Sandra Pole surveyed the results of her latest shopping trip to Peter Jones. Her flat on Cadogan Square was well placed between the department store on Sloane Square and Harrods, a gentle ten-minute amble to the north.

Sandra liked Peter Jones best because she found the staff quite rude. Firstly, she enjoyed the frisson of watching their snooty, bored faces as they were forced to serve her (what was it about her that put them off? she wondered) and second, it gave her a greater sense of vindication when she was a little bit naughty, like this morning, when she had managed to slip three packets of gossamer-fine nude nylons amongst her legitimate purchases of silk cushions, silk nightdresses and a promising summer hat.

The cushions had looked better in the shop than they did on her favourite sofa, which now seemed overcrowded. She would have to take them back, along with the hat, which she had only bought to hide the nylons. The nightdresses were perfectly fine and would be better when she'd got her little woman in Fulham to take up the hems by a couple of inches. Sandra had been told, more than once, that she had the best legs in London. Nigel wouldn't notice, of course. He rarely spent time in Cadogan Square.

Right now, her husband was probably with his mistress in Kensington. Veronica, she was called. Sandra rather pitied Veronica: she was no doubt preparing to become the second Mrs Pole after the divorce, but Sandra had learned the hard way that Nigel married for money, and Veronica was a taker, not a giver. Ironically, it was Sandra's own contribution to the family coffers that was funding the 'secret' flat in Kensington. She liked to think of it as a charitable cause, if not one she would have personally chosen. At least the divorce would give her control of her own finances for the first time – or what Nigel would allow her to keep of the vast fortune she had brought with her, which he ardently thought of as his own. Nigel was not, on the whole, a passionate man, but when it came to her money, he positively smouldered, guarding it with a sometimes violent intensity. Why did she still dress for him? Habit. A refusal to be beaten. Not metaphorically, anyway.

The nylons, on the other hand, were an out and out success. Nigel had terrible taste in lingerie and only appreciated fishnet stockings. These new ones would look as if she was wearing nothing at all. She had taken them for her own pleasure, which was enhanced tenfold by having walked out with them under the snooty noses of at least six shopgirls.

Sandra went to the large refrigerator in the pristine kitchen of her lonely flat, and found a half-finished bottle of champagne. She poured herself a glass to celebrate.

Why did she get such a kick out of it after all these years? She still didn't know why she did it, really. Her father had paid for the most expensive therapists, but Sandra thought it was probably because she was just a terrible person. Her mother agreed. You couldn't rationalise something like that. You could get awfully nice stockings out of it, though.

She was about to pour a second glass when the phone rang, and a man with a plummy voice introduced himself as Henry Coxon. She knew the name from his articles in a couple of her mother's magazines.

'I know this is awfully odd,' he said, 'but I understand that you were the witness on the royal train who saw the . . . Well, anyway, it was thanks to you they found the body. It's just that—'

'I assure you, I have nothing to say on the matter.'

Their sentences crossed, and Coxon waited for Sandra to finish hers.

'I'm sorry,' he went on. 'It's just that, I knew Pav. I mean Mr Michalowski, the man you saw. Anyway . . .' He coughed. He sounded quite emotional to Sandra, which was a surprise. 'I just wanted to say . . . I know this sounds strange, given everything that's happened, but I just wanted to say thank you. Look, can I come round? I know it's the oddest thing, and absolutely inappropriate, and of course you can say no, and you should, but I just . . . You're a friend of the princess, so you probably knew Pav a bit, too, and I just . . .'

Sandra had let him rattle on while she finished her second glass. She'd never heard anything quite so extraordinary. All that emotion, in those plummy tones. Hadn't it been beaten out of him at boarding school, as with most of the men she knew? It had from Nigel, certainly, except when it came to money.

But Henry was right. Sandra had known Pavel Michalowski a little bit. She'd met him once at Kensington Palace and another time at a party in a flat somewhere in Shoreditch, and she'd thought he was a total dish. There was something magnetic and charismatic about him, with those eyes, and that smile, and the cigarette held so nonchalantly between those fingers. In fact, if Sandra hadn't been a married woman, she would have joined the queue for his attention. So, when the identity of the victim was announced, she had been devastated and confused and simply dismayed to think that she had seen, spoken to, and liked very much that face that was so horrifically disfigured on the skipping rope man. Nobody until Mr Coxon had thought to consider this possibility, and she didn't have anyone she could bear to confide in. It was too strange.

'I'm sorry. Are you there?' Henry asked.

Sandra realised she must have been silent for a while.

'Come over now,' she told him. 'Do you know where I live?'

'Yes, it's in the telephone directory. I can be there in half an hour if you—'

'I'll be waiting,' she said.

Chapter 23

In the North Wing of Buckingham Palace, Sir Hugh Masson strode towards his office, free of the neck brace he'd worn since his painting accident, feeling taller and more loose-limbed than he had for weeks.

Miles Urquhart greeted the private secretary halfway down the corridor.

'You're looking chipper, Hugh. Neck on the mend at last?'

'I think so,' Sir Hugh acknowledged, inclining his head gingerly. 'I feel all right, as long as I'm careful. Just saw a new osteopath. Man's a miracle worker. Stephen Ward, d'you know him?'

The deputy private secretary shook his head.

'Everyone's going to him these days,' Sir Hugh said. 'Which is why it wasn't such a surprise when . . .' He glanced around and lowered his voice. 'Why don't we go into my office, Miles? I've got something to . . . Oh, Joan!' He saw the APS approach from the lift to the Queen's apartments. 'Come and join us.'

The private secretary's sanctum was as well-lit and comfortable as any decent-sized Georgian sitting room should be. Near the marble fireplace, it contained a pleasant seating area for Sir Hugh, Miles and Joan to take an armchair each. The two men, with their pinstripe suits and neat moustaches, and Joan in her heels and pearls, made an impressive trio, Sir Hugh liked to think. He moved his head around carefully, testing his neck ligaments again.

'Definitely better. As I say, Stephen Ward's the best in the business. But listen, who should I meet coming out of Ward's practice door, just as I was going in, but George Venables, the man who runs the Murder Squad!'

'Really? He's looking into the Michalowski business, isn't he?' Urquhart asked. 'That's going smoothly, I think.

'Not as smoothly as he'd like, actually,' Sir Hugh corrected him. 'They've met a few bumps in the road. But more to the point—' he leaned forward '—the Murder Squad are not the only ones investigating.'

'Oh?' Urquhart leaned forward too.

'I was early for my appointment this morning, and I had a bit of time,' Sir Hugh went on, 'so Venables and I took a stroll up to Regent's Park. On the way, he asked me how MI5 were getting on.'

'MI5?'

'Well, exactly. And I asked what about them, and Venables said he thought we already knew. Anyway, it turns out that for reasons they won't explain, Five are interested in Michalowski too.'

'Oh Lord,' Urquhart groaned. 'Who's in charge? Anyone we know? That's the last thing we need. It's that bloody Pole woman, I tell you. Everything she touches turns to—'

'Hector Ross,' Sir Hugh said emphatically. He turned to Joan. 'Are you all right? D'you need some water?'

'Something caught in my throat,' she said, swallowing and smiling. 'Ross, did you say?'

Sir Hugh nodded. 'Director of D Branch, MI5. You knew him, didn't you, Joan? He was your landlord at Dolphin Square. What happened about the flat in the end?'

'I'm still in Dolphin Square,' Joan said. 'It's very convenient for work.'

'Is Ross still the landlord?' Urquhart asked.

'I think so. I mean, his name's on the bills.'

'D'you still see anything of him?'

'A little.'

Hugh tutted impatiently. 'Anyway. I don't know what he's got on Michalowski, but I mean to find out. I'll ask Major Ross for a report this afternoon. Not a word to Her Majesty, by the way. The last thing she needs on her mind, with Italy coming up, is her sister being involved in spy shenanigans.'

'Major Ross isn't holding back the police, is he?' Joan asked.

'Not as far as I know,' Sir Hugh said. 'The body itself is, though, a bit. Michalowski had no visible fatal injuries. Venables is getting a very good toxicologist from London to do a second post-mortem on the body – not popular with the locals, apparently – but he expects interesting results, he said. He's going to send me a summary.'

'Were those the bumps in the road you mentioned?' Joan asked. 'For the Murder Squad?'

'Ah, no.' Sir Hugh leaned back in his armchair and steepled his fingers. 'The tricky thing right now is making the link between Primrose Hill and Staffordshire. Venables suspects the landowner, man called Thorburn, of orchestrating the disposal of the body. Everyone in the frame has an alibi and nobody's talking. The police think the plan was to feed the body to the farmer's pigs – I know, doesn't bear thinking about, but very effective, I gather – but the pigs had recently gone to slaughter. There must have been some communications screw-up. The thing is, how and why did the killers even think of pigs in Staffordshire? Michalowski didn't know the place. Never been there as far as they know. And nobody from Thorburn's outfit went to London apart from the farm manager, the week before, and he only took a briefcase with him on the train – hardly room for a body. What's the connection? How does it work?'

'Hmm,' Urquhart said. 'Presumably they're checking telephone records?'

'Oh yes, all of that. And bank accounts. They're doing their job, but it's time-consuming, and it would help if somebody had the decency to confess.'

Urquhart laughed. 'The Tudors had the right idea. Lock them up in the Tower with a rack and some fire tongs. That would do it.'

In her armchair, Joan stiffened. 'Then they'd tell you whatever you wanted to know.'

'Well, yes!'

'Whether it was true or not.'

Urquhart frowned at her. He seemed to think she was spoiling the atmosphere. 'Come on, Joan, you know the drill.'

Joan looked at him coldly. He was almost certainly referring to her secret war work at Trent Park, where she was posted after Bletchley. This was where she'd interrogated the captured Nazi officers. The operation had been very successful, but they hadn't used thumb screws and hot pokers . . . quite the opposite. Instead, the interrogations had been fake. The German officers had withstood much of the questioning that was thrown at them in the cells where it happened, and gone back to the comfortable rooms they shared, where they crowed to each other about how well they'd resisted – especially if the interrogator was a young woman. *This* was where they'd spilled their secrets, treated like the superior beings they assumed themselves to be, unaware that every square inch, inside and out, was bugged.

Joan was a fan of psychology, not torture. Otherwise, what made you any different from them?

But Scotland Yard didn't employ either technique, and the chances of an unprompted confession from Thorburn and his men seemed slim. What *was* the connection between London and Staffordshire? she wondered. Meanwhile, she had a lot to tell Her Majesty.

Chapter 24

Sandra put on one of her new pairs of nylons under a nice little Mary Quant day dress, and placed a fresh bottle of champagne to chill in the fridge. She could always make tea at a pinch, but she hoped Henry Coxon wouldn't be boring. And she felt their conversation would probably require some lubrication. It would be hard.

Thirty minutes later, she buzzed him up to the flat and he stood at the door in tweed and mustard corduroy, clutching a bunch of carnations and looking, she thought, like an overgrown ten-year-old child.

He thrust the carnations towards her.

'These are damnable, I'm sorry, but I didn't know what to get you. Hello, I'm Henry.'

'I'm Sandra. I hate carnations with a passion, don't you? Let's leave them on the doorstep.'

He put them down with relief, readily accepted a glass of 'something refreshing' and plonked himself next to a sleeping Conchita on the sofa. The chihuahua woke up briefly and accepted a little nuzzle from Henry's free hand – the one that wasn't holding the stem of a champagne flute. Sandra was pleased.

'She likes you. She never does that.'

Henry looked down. 'Really? Oh, I'm good with dogs. Bad with women and children.'

'Me too.'

They made small talk for a couple of minutes – it turned out they had several friends and parental friends in common – but Henry soon broke off.

'Look, I realise I've come here to talk about something awful, and just tell me to stop if it's too bad. I can't really sleep for thinking about it.'

'I want to talk about the awful thing,' she assured him. 'The photographer, Pavel, was your friend?'

'My best friend, since prep school. We told each other everything.' Henry paused. 'That's not true, actually. I told *him* everything. I'm not sure how much he told me. The broad strokes of things, I suppose. He used to tease me endlessly.'

He stopped. Sandra realised it was because he'd said 'used to'.

'I know what you mean. I hardly knew him at all, and it doesn't seem real to me. Pavel seemed like such an interesting man. I can't believe the last time—'

Then she stopped, too, because she was about to talk about the last time she'd seen him, in that field at sunset, and she couldn't do it, even now.

'I say, d'you might if I light up?' Henry asked.

Sandra didn't mind at all, moving an ashtray so it was closer to him on the coffee table. He extracted a half-full packet of Player's and lit one for each of them.

'The thing is, though,' he said, after a deep and much-needed drag, 'you were looking. That evening, you were looking out of the window at the exact moment you needed to be looking. You saw what nobody else saw. I feel as if Pav . . . He must have been dead by then. Dear God, I hope so . . .'

'He was. I'm sure of it.'

'But I feel as if it was his spirit, reaching out to you.'

'Do you? So do I!' she exclaimed. 'That's exactly what I said the next day, to Joan.'

'Who's Joan?'

'Oh, this woman I met on the train. Conchita peed on her.'

Henry grinned. 'Conchita, you rascal.' The dog eyed him sleepily and gave him her tummy to tickle. 'Anyway, I'm eternally grateful, you know. It was terribly brave of you to say something. You must have been so frightened, but I couldn't have borne it if he'd been out there forever. It's bad enough as it is, but that makes it a tiny bit more bearable.'

Sandra drew on her own cigarette.

'What I don't understand, is how they knew it was him. I mean he was naked.' Her voice broke a little. 'And . . .' She still couldn't talk about the head.

'Well, I might have helped there a bit,' Henry said. 'I'd reported him missing.'

'That was you?'

'And there was some suspicious stuff in his flat and—'

'What kind of stuff?'

'I can't really discuss it,' he said. 'Nothing sordid, don't worry, but it got certain people interested.'

Sandra smiled. She reached out a hand to squeeze his for a moment.

'So you were part of it, too. Finding him, I mean.'

'I suppose we're two parts of a puzzle,' Henry said. 'I've been thinking about it. Perhaps that's why . . . I wanted to ask you something, Mrs Pole.'

'Sandra.'

'Sandra. You don't know me from Adam, but I wanted to get your opinion. Do you mind?'

'Ask me anything.'

'There's this girl, you see.' He gave a deep sigh.

'A girl?'

Oh dear, she didn't want to talk about relationship problems at this point, but he'd been so nice to her that she could hardly say no.

'A rather lovely, beautiful girl called Tracy,' he elaborated.

'Tracy? That's an unusual name.'

'Isn't it? She was named after Tracy Lord in *The Philadelphia Story*. You know it? The one they made into *High Society*? It really doesn't matter, except that's what we talked about, Tracy and me, when we met last month. You wouldn't think it was that interesting, the relative merits of Katharine Hepburn over Grace Kelly, but she was all over me.'

Sandra nodded, and started to feel bored, and hid it with another drag of the cigarette in her fingers.

'We were at some club or other,' Henry went on. 'Pavel had been with me, but he'd gone home by then. However, Tracy asked me about him a couple of times, wanted to know if we were friends, that sort of thing. Anyway, she gave me her telephone number and I have to admit, girls don't do that very often. Not beautiful, leggy young blondes like Tracy. Not most women, to be strictly accurate.'

'I'm sure you're a killer on the dance floor,' Sandra said politely.

'I assure you I'm not. Anyway, Tracy said she went riding in Hyde Park sometimes, and did I want to join her one morning, and so I did, and we had a nice chat and went out to a coffee bar afterwards, and she asked me some more about Pav that time, too, like whether he had a steady girlfriend, and did he have house guests? She even asked about the neighbours.'

This wasn't what Sandra had been expecting. 'How bizarre.'

'Well, exactly,' Henry said. 'Isn't it? We talked about all sorts of other things, and plans we were going to make together, and she made it all seem quite natural, somehow. She asked about other friends of mine, too, but she didn't seem particularly interested in the answers.'

'What reason did she give?'

'I honestly can't remember,' Henry said. 'I was too busy imagining our honeymoon in Paris. Don't laugh at me, I know I'm ridiculous.'

'You aren't at all,' she promised.

'A hopeless romantic. A silly fool. I was also busy planning what I'd tell Pav the next time I saw him, about this gorgeous young bird who couldn't get enough of me. Anyway, she *could* get enough of me. A couple of days later, I tried to call, and she said I must have the wrong number. I happened to see her on the street in Knightsbridge, and she looked right through me. She'd obviously changed her mind, I thought, but she *could* have been kinder about it.'

Sandra agreed. 'Was that what you wanted to ask me?'

'Oh, no!' he said. 'Not that at all. No, I was an idiot on all fronts. Deserved whatever I had coming. The thing is, her name was Tracy Thorburn, and I happened to notice in one of the articles about Pav that the landowner of the field where his body was found . . . where you saw him, Sandra . . . was this man called Josiah Thorburn. I looked Thorburn up in our magazine archives and Josiah – unusual name – has a daughter called Tracy – unusual name – who rides.' He took a last gulp of champagne and stared at Sandra belligerently. 'And I think that's very odd, don't you?'

'Gosh,' Sandra said, taking it all in. She felt for a moment as if she could feel that spirit in the room again, the one she'd felt when she saw the skipping rope man, which she'd put down to shock, but couldn't shake off. It had haunted her all that night.

Henry was agitated. He finished his champagne and absent-mindedly stroked Conchita so hard that she woke up and nearly bit him, before scooting off the sofa. 'I'm sorry,' he said. 'I know I'm probably overreacting. I mean, it's *possible* Tracy just went off me. Perhaps she wanted to go out with Pav and she was using me. But the timing is just so . . . Tell me I'm being paranoid. Pav was always telling me I was paranoid, and I found it quite reassuring, actually. I just need a sane human to tell me what to do.'

Sandra laughed. 'No one's ever called me a sane human before.'

'Honestly, what d'you think?'

'Honestly,' she said, 'I'd love to tell you this Tracy woman was just trying to get into those natty cord trousers of yours, but I have a nasty feeling she may be a scheming villain of some description. What do they call them?'

'*Femmes fatales*,' Henry said gloomily. 'That's what I've been thinking. Except, look at me. Am I *femme fatale* material?'

'You're very sweet,' Sandra announced. She liked watching Henry blush, and blush harder when she leaned across again to rest a hand on his corduroy knee. 'It can't do any harm to tell someone.'

'I know a man at MI5,' he said. 'I spoke to him about Pav's flat. But the trouble is, well, I did *talk* to the Tracy girl. I told her things, about Pav's movements. Things I regret, looking back. Obviously, I didn't know anything at the time, but I don't want a black mark against me by that lot. God knows what I could get blacklisted from, especially with my job.'

'I know someone reliable,' Sandra said. 'She'll give good advice. And she won't talk.'

'A *woman*?'

'Don't be so surprised. Women can be reliable.'

'I see,' he said. 'Yes, OK, I suppose. If you're sure.'

'I am.'

'Is she well connected?'

'Very.'

'Tell her, then. Let me know what she says.' He sat back. 'Gosh, that feels better. Thank you, Sandra. I knew you'd be a brick. I felt it in my waters. I say, are you hungry?'

'Ravenous.'

'We ought to eat something to soak up the bubbles. Can I take you somewhere for lunch?'

'How about Rowley's?' She saw the look on his face. 'I'm paying.'

'I can't let you do that.'

'Then we can't be friends.'

After a minute of tussling, he gave in. While he went outside to try and hail a taxi, Sandra called Buckingham Palace and asked to speak to Joan.

Chapter 25

The Queen was out at dinner in the City of London on Monday night, and her diary for Tuesday was full. When Joan arrived first thing that morning to go over the schedule, Elizabeth could tell that her APS had something to tell her, but they only had two minutes before she needed to be somewhere else.

'Why don't we discuss it in the car?' she asked.

Joan would be accompanying the Queen on an official visit later, which should give them at least half an hour to talk. But the APS shook her head.

'Too public, ma'am.'

Oh dear. This was something that even one's utterly discreet chauffeur and protection officer couldn't hear. It must be either the Michalowski case, or something political, secret and unpleasant. The Queen hoped it was the former.

'Why don't I read about it, then?' she suggested.

Joan thought for a moment, and nodded. 'Thank you, ma'am. I'll get the paperwork ready.'

At five to twelve, they settled themselves in the back of the Daimler. Joan opened the briefcase she'd brought with her and handed the Queen a file. The first page was a note

Joan had prepared, explaining what was underneath. It *was* the Michalowski case, the Queen was relieved to see. There was a memo addressed to Sir Hugh from Chief Superintendent Venables at the Murder Squad (Oh good, they'd made further progress); a post-mortem report; a note from MI5 (What? MI5? Really?); and a summary from Joan herself of a conversation she'd had yesterday with Sandra Pole. Gosh, that woman didn't go away, did she?

The Queen began with Venables' memo, which made some faux-modest observations about how 'fortunate' the Murder Squad had been to find the body 'within hours of being called upon to help'. It referenced the post-mortem report, and she remembered Joan describing the look of horror on Sandra Pole's face as she had pictured the 'skipping rope man'. As she turned to it, she steeled herself for some nasty details.

The post-mortem had been conducted on Saturday. The pathologist found it easier than expected, because despite having been dead for at least two weeks by then, the body had been stored in cool and watertight places. *They might as well have used a mortuary drawer*, he said.

Honestly, who *were* these people? Were they stupid, unlucky, or was this really some very clever plan that just *looked* idiotic? Given Sandra's reaction, the Queen had expected a long list of horrible injuries, but there were almost none, and she frowned in surprise and sighed with relief. Joan raised a questioning eyebrow, and the Queen pointed to the bit she'd got to. Joan nodded.

'I was amazed, too.'

The red face was simply a thing called 'livor mortis', apparently. Horrible, but not unusual – except for its location on the body. The pathologist suspected it might have happened during transit: he suggested the body might have slipped, and the head and shoulders fallen below the rest, so the blood had pooled there. Poor Mr Michalowski. At least he was dead by then.

But how?

They weren't sure, but carpet fibres in the hair suggested he had been attacked at home. A bruise on the arm was evidence of an injection, and Venables had called in a very clever expert on poisons. The resulting toxicology report could take weeks, but the lack of ligature marks or defensive wounds led the police to believe that once down, the victim had not risen again.

Venables' current thinking was that Michalowski had died soon after the attack, and the body had been stored somewhere else for a day or two, head down, before being transported to the midden in Staffordshire, for reasons the report didn't explain. From there, it had been moved to the water tank where it was found by a police dog. The original idea had probably been to feed it to pigs. (Pigs! No! Really?) In Venables' opinion, the water tank was just a temporary hiding place. Something had disrupted the killers before they could finish the job.

And who were those killers? The Queen assumed one of the London gangs . . . but Venables seemed to take great satisfaction in suggesting the KGB. She frowned at this, but remembered that the next report was from the head of D Branch, MI5. That might explain it.

Before moving on, she said quietly to Joan, 'You might tell Sandra about the face. I think it might reassure her.'

Joan nodded again. 'I will, ma'am. It must have been awful, to see it so briefly.'

'Simply dreadful. She was spot on, though, wasn't she?'

'Yes, ma'am, she was.'

The report from Major Ross at MI5 was detailed and well written, despite Sir Hugh only asking for it yesterday, according to Joan's note. It was almost as if Ross had been expecting the request. Anyway, it explained about the unusual equipment found at Michalowski's flat. No wonder MI5 were interested. A Russian spy, surely? But Ross thought otherwise.

He had discovered that there was an attractive young man known simply as 'Pav', who liked to play chess with some of the old men at the Polish Club. 'Pav' didn't talk much, but he was always curious about what he called 'the home country' and wanted to hear tales of what it had been like before the war, before the German invasion, the massacres, and the Soviets. This man seemed opposed to Stalin and all he stood for. It seemed increasingly possible that 'Pav' was Pavel Michalowski, and that he was also the man known simply as 'the Pole', who had helped two persecuted scientists escape from behind the Iron Curtain last year. Some materials found at his flat, such as odd diary entries and guidebooks, supported the theory. Ross suspected that he had been communicating through microdots hidden in chess magazines. Microdots? Gosh.

If so, his persona as a society photographer – a 'snapper' as Philip called them – was an excellent cover. Reading the note, the Queen was reminded of Charles Darnay in *A Tale of Two Cities*, or, even more, Sir Percy Blakeney in *The Scarlet Pimpernel*. He, too, had been busy smuggling out victims of a revolution gone bad. The Russian one had been a long time ago, but the Queen saw a straight line between its excesses and what was happening in the Soviet Union now. When people deposed their monarchs, they always did so with the best of intentions (and good reason, sometimes, if one was being strictly honest), but then . . . things had a habit of going wrong.

Had Michalowski been discovered by Soviet spies in London? Was that why he was killed? The Queen looked up from the note for a moment. In the tinderbox environment of the Cold War, states couldn't be seen to interfere in each other's business, so it seemed that it was often left to extremely brave individuals to save lives where they could. These people lived in constant danger, their efforts unrecognised. If things went wrong, they couldn't share their grief. Successes, too, remained private. Tragic deaths went unexplained.

She saw Pavel Michalowski in a whole new light. If Ross was right, he could be an unsung hero. Who knew? The scientists who owed their freedom to him might be busy, even now, helping the West defeat the forces of communism.

She hadn't met the man, but she'd spoken to Tony Armstrong-Jones on Sunday, and according to her brother-in-law, Michalowski sounded huge fun: sociable, popular, arty, interesting. Tony said he thought 'Pav' had a great future in photography. Not the boring 'girls in pearls' stuff he usually did . . . Oh dear. Every single one of the Queen's friends had sat for that kind of portrait, as she had herself. Were they passé now? . . . Anyway, not that, apparently, but 'candid photography'. In the Queen's experience, that was a bank of cameramen with flashbulbs, taking pictures of you when you were trying to walk out of a building, or step out of a car. She wasn't a natural fan, but she loved taking photographs herself and they certainly weren't posed (horses didn't pose, and neither did children, usually), so perhaps she had more in common with Michalowski than she thought.

And now he was in a mortuary in Staffordshire, while his innards were investigated for poison. If the KGB really were involved, was it revenge for the defections last year, or was it to prevent more? Ross wanted to know if there were any rumours of other people coming through. The report said his contacts hadn't heard anything so far, but they were asking discreetly.

Why did the body end up where it did? Like Venables, Ross had no idea, and unlike Venables, he said so in so many words. Both were working on it without success so far.

Beside the Queen, Joan was looking out of the car window. The Queen tapped her elbow and pointed at Ross's report.

'Have you spoken to him about this?'

Joan shook her head primly. The Queen inclined her own. She knew the two had known each other for a while. Of course, they *shouldn't* speak about secrets, but people didn't always do as they were told, did they?

The last note in the file was Joan's account of her conversation with Sandra Pole yesterday evening, after work. It talked about Tracy Thoburn's pursuit and then rejection of

Henry Coxon. If true, then here was the link between Josiah Thorburn in Staffordshire and Pavel in London. But how on earth did the KGB fit in? Perhaps they didn't, after all.

Coxon had been reluctant to share his story, but Joan had advised him to do it anyway. He wanted assurances that he would be 'safe', and Joan, quite rightly, couldn't give them. If the police or MI5 decided he had done something unlawful, then she couldn't help him.

The Queen turned to her and said softly, without naming names in front of the chauffeur, 'Being pursued by a pretty girl is not a capital offence.'

'He shared details about his friend,' Joan said. 'That was his worry.'

'They were hardly state secrets. If that's all he did, then he's perfectly safe. I'm afraid the powers that be are far too busy to concern themselves with his conversations in coffee bars, whatever he might like to think.'

'He might be disappointed to hear it.'

'Then you must disappoint him. The girl's identity is too important to keep to himself. Lives may depend on it. Tell him that.'

'Yes, ma'am.'

'He should follow Mrs Pole's example. And if he can't be persuaded, tell the right people anyway. They need whatever help they can get.'

Joan agreed and the Queen closed the file.

All in all, she was impressed that so much progress had been made within a week of Sandra's admission to the police of what time she really saw the skipping rope man.

Michalowski's family would have a body to bury, which would be some consolation. The investigation had gone in directions Elizabeth certainly hadn't expected, though. Russians, defections, microdots . . . Goodness. James Bond would be in his element.

Chapter 26

The following day, on the twelfth of April, the Queen was woken by Hattie Cowell with her usual a cup of tea. Normally, Hattie whisked in and out with a simple 'Good morning, Your Majesty,' but today, she couldn't help adding, as she walked over to the nearest window, 'I don't suppose you've heard the news, ma'am. It's ever so exciting.'

The Queen sat up against the pillows.

'It's not about my sister, is it?'

Pray God the press hadn't found out about Margaret's pregnancy. The family were trying to keep it private for as long as they could.

'The Russians have put a man in space!' Hattie swished the curtains back and light flooded the room.

'Goodness!'

'He's up there now, ma'am, flying right over our heads. They've put it on the television in Moscow. Everyone's cheering in the streets. The Moscow ones, I mean.'

'Is he all right?' the Queen asked anxiously. She still thought about Laika, the poor dog who hadn't survived.

'Right as rain so far,' Hattie told her. 'He's doing an orbit, the BBC said. He should be down after breakfast.' She curtsied and withdrew.

The Queen got out of bed and went to the window. Of course she wouldn't be able to see him, wherever he was, but she wondered how many other people around the world were looking up to the sky, just like she was – and wishing him well, even if he happened to be on the opposing team.

The first man in space. That was quite something.

'Name's Gagarin,' Philip said at breakfast. 'A flight major, apparently. Twenty-seven years old. Nobody'd heard of him till this morning. They played a short clip of his voice from the capsule, and he sounded confident, happy, even. He said the earth was beautiful.'

'I'm glad to hear it,' the Queen said.

'Shame he's a Ruski. I wouldn't mind talking to the man one day. If he makes it down alive, of course.'

'So would I,' the Queen agreed. She'd only known of his existence for an hour or so, but already she liked the sound of him. Anyone brave enough to go up into orbit in a tiny metal capsule, and who pointed out the planet's beauty, rather than crowing about sides and victories, sounded like someone she'd like to meet very much.

'The PM would never allow it, though.' Philip crunched on a piece of toast. 'They're the enemy, after all. Which reminds me . . .'

He threw her a look very similar to the one he'd given when he was threatening to sack her protection officers. She braced for the hand grenade.

'Yes?'

'Talking of communists, my equerry tells me that your deputy private secretary happened to mention in passing that Sir Hugh told him Venables at the Yard suggested a couple of days ago that this Michalowski fellow might be mixed up with the KGB.'

That was a bit left-field. Goodness, news travelled fast in Buckingham Palace. The Queen tried to look innocent, but her momentary flicker of exasperation at Miles Urquhart's indiscretion showed Philip that he was onto something.

'Dammit, Lilibet! Don't tell me Tony Armstrong-Jones brought a spy into our midst.'

'I'm afraid I can't say.'

'Can't, or won't?'

'Won't,' the Queen admitted.

'Please, in God's name, tell me he wasn't the next Burgess or Maclean.'

She sighed, then decided to answer honestly. 'I think it's safe to say he almost certainly wasn't.'

It wasn't her habit to tell her husband state secrets. But Philip was alarmed, and she didn't want him suspecting his own brother-in-law of harbouring Russian spies when, from what she'd discovered, MI5 seemed to think the opposite.

She looked at him meaningfully. He grunted.

'Ah. Good. So, spying for us, then. Fine. I'll keep schtum. Poor bugger.' Philip was calming down again, as he always did. 'Poor Tony,' he added. 'Fellow snapper, and all that. He admired him, apparently.'

'Well, yes, exactly.'

'Must be hard to hear we sped past the man's body being thrown into a pit. What did your sister say?'

'Margaret's taken it badly. She knew him and liked him. It's all a bit surreal. It seemed a bit of a game to her when it was just a stranger. Now it's different . . .' The Queen paused. 'By the way, talking of spies, d'you know how to make a microdot?'

Philip frowned at her. 'Yes. Why?'

'Oh, nothing. I just wondered.'

'Well it's pretty easy.' Philip's face lit up, as it usually did when he talked about technology. 'I had a go with my equerry a last year. He's chums with a chap from MI6. I mean, this is a simplified version, but you type your message on white paper and put it on a dark background, or stick up a diagram or stolen paperwork or whatever it is. You shine a light on it to maximise the contrast, take a picture with your camera, then you stick up the negative, or several, and take a picture of *those*. Instantly a fraction of the size, see? Then you cut out the bit from the second negative showing the first negative in micro, and hide it where you like. Some of the real spies mess around with magnifying glasses and make the dots so small you need to pick them up with a syringe. Obviously, they need to a powerful lens to read them at the other end, but that's where fine-grain film comes in. Or no grain at all, ideally. Did I mention that?'

'I don't think so.'

'Anyway, you need it to capture the detail.'

'Fascinating.'

'Isn't it? Bloody straightforward, really. They just needed to invent the right film to make it possible. God knows what's winging its way through the postal system these days.

You could get half the plans for a missile base on the bottom of a question mark.'

There was a knock at the breakfast room door, and a note was passed to one of the footmen, who walked over to the radio set on the sideboard next to the dog station.

'Ahem, your private secretary says you might like to listen to the Home Service, ma'am,' he said.

A BBC announcer was busy explaining that Flight Major Yuri Gagarin had landed safely at an undisclosed location in the Soviet Union, and was being hailed as a national hero. The Americans would be furious, but the Queen couldn't help sharing Hattie Cowell's excitement. What a day for everyone. To be the ones who were alive when the first man on earth went into space.

She also spared a thought for Major Gagarin personally. She knew better than anyone what it was like to be twenty-seven and very, very famous. She hoped he was ready to cope with what was about to happen. His life would never be the same.

Chapter 27

'Ave you seen the pictures? 'E's terribly good looking. Not a bruise on 'im. And 'e's been where literally no other person's gone. Amazing, isn't it? Up in the nowhere, like 'e's 'alfway to the moon.'

Joan agreed with her hairdresser, who was doing extraordinary things of her own with curlers, a brush and a gold can of Elnett hairspray.

'Although,' the hairdresser continued, 'my old man says it would be terribly smelly up there. Haha! One man sweating like hell, no room to swing a cat and no windows in 'is rocket!'

'I doubt he minded,' Joan said.

'Set for life now, isn't 'e? Yuri Gagarin . . . Everyone knows 'is name now. I wonder if there's a Mrs Gagarin . . .'

Joan happened to know there was, because she'd been following the news coverage closely over the last few days. Like the rest of the world, Mrs Gagarin didn't have a clue what her husband was about to do until it was announced that he was entering the earth's orbit. How thrilling was that? How extraordinary. How Mrs Gagarin must have worried herself sick for a hundred and eight minutes, until he got back down to earth safely. How proud she must be now . . .

Joan found herself thinking about brave people, and the people they left behind, a lot these days. It had been happening ever since the train journey with Sandra Pole, and to start with she'd thought it was something to do with that ridiculous, over-the-top (but, as it turned out, quite accurate) story of the skipping rope man. But lately, she'd realised that it wasn't that at all.

It had started the evening before, when the train was travelling through the Chiltern hills. She'd been thinking about the milk train to Bletchley, and the person she was then. The codebreaker. The Wren in uniform. The young woman whose sweetheart taught her how to fire a gun in case she ever needed to defend herself. The one who listened to the terrifying pop-pop motorbike sound of the V-bombs falling on London, not knowing if she'd be alive in five minutes.

She missed that girl.

Yes, even now, when her daily job involved planning the agenda of Queen Elizabeth II, Joan missed that girl.

She wanted to do something about it, hence the hair. A quick shampoo and set at home wouldn't do today. And after the hairdresser, she planned to visit the chemist to get a proper little bottle of olive oil, because everything had to be the best if this evening was going to work.

She thought back to Martha, a friend from Bletchley Park days, whom she'd met in a coffee house near the Tate Gallery last weekend. Joan had known her for nearly twenty years, and they'd shared a hut and digs together, but they had never spoken about it since, not even once.

Like Joan, Martha hadn't married. Joan strongly suspected that she worked for someone high up in MI6 these days. The office near St James's Park that she was uncharacteristically vague about suggested as much. Normally they didn't refer to their work lives at all, but Joan was feeling restless, and had found herself asking Martha general questions. Was her job interesting? Was it enjoyable?

'Oh, you know,' Martha said, playing with her coffee spoon. 'It's all right. A bit frantic sometimes. We're horribly understaffed. Isn't everyone, though?'

Without prompting, Martha had looked at Joan and said, 'They'd love you, with all your experience. Your mother, you know . . . But of course you're so busy. It must be *wonderful* to be at the palace. Tell me, is it true that Princess Margaret might be expecting?'

At which point, Joan was absolutely convinced that Martha worked in intelligence, because that was exactly the sort of deflection you were taught to do. She was good at it herself: she'd responded by wondering instead whether Elizabeth Taylor might be pregnant, and Martha had caught her at it and merely smiled.

The reference to Joan's late mother was about her facility for languages. Mrs McGraw had French and German heritage, and Joan spoke both fluently. Meanwhile, her Irish father had given her a love for crosswords and puzzles generally. Martha was right: Joan was *good* at this stuff. In the last few days, she'd been following MI5's progress in the

Michalowski case, and even contributing to it by passing on to them what Sandra Pole had said about Henry Coxon and Tracy Thorburn, but she couldn't *do* anything. Not directly, not personally.

She'd been hoping the Queen would get her teeth into the case and they could work on it together – but Her Majesty had too much on her plate. Besides, the Queen preferred to leave it to those around her to solve problems where possible, and in this case the man in question was a certain Major Ross, whom she trusted. That was probably a good thing, but Joan wasn't satisfied.

'Ooh, you do look lovely, Miss McGraw, if I say so myself. Like a proper Maureen O'Hara.'

The hairdresser stood back to admire her handiwork, and Joan had to agree that the style somehow brought out the red in her hair. The new hairspray let it fall more loosely than it used to. The result was . . . sexy. Yes, there were no two ways about it.

Maureen O'Hara? Or Mata Hari? She would see what she could do.

At seven o'clock, Hector Ross came home to the riverside flat in Dolphin Square after another very busy day in Curzon Street. The Americans had just royally messed up an attempt to help a group of exiles retake Cuba from Castro. So far, Kennedy's forces were being given a bloody nose. There was nothing Hector could do about it, but the jungle drums were alive with commentary from both sides and he needed to listen, on top of managing a couple of recent spy scandals and the Michalowski business, which still took up a lot of his time.

Joan greeted him in the hallway with a kiss. He stood back and eyed her carefully.

'My goodness, Miss McGraw. There's something about you. Have you done something to your hair?'

'I might have.'

'And can I smell chipped potatoes?'

'Possibly.'

'To what do I owe the honour?'

'Don't worry about it,' she told him. 'Come through and relax.'

Officially, Hector now lived in a different flat, two floors up, but in practice he had shared this place with Joan since shortly after she first moved in as an accidental room-mate, four years ago. Since his recent divorce from his wife, who had run off with the family doctor long before he met Joan, Hector had started to wonder if he should do something about their situation. But Joan had one of the most interesting jobs in the world and he couldn't bring himself to take it away from her.

Hector loved Joan for her quick mind, her courage, her unending ability to surprise him, and the fact that, in his personal opinion, she had the most beautiful face and body of any woman he'd ever met. However, her cookery skills did not rank high on the list: if either of them cooked for the other, he tended to be the one who took charge of the kitchen, usually something Italian. Joan's only star dish was the herb omelette her French mother had taught her, accompanied by chipped potatoes (very hard to burn or boil to death) and a simple salad. Thanks to growing up in a Cambridge college, where her father was head porter, she was also good at choosing wine.

The table, he noticed was set with a nicely dressed green salad, while a rather good bottle of burgundy sat breathing next to fresh candles in their smartest candlesticks. She wanted something. He smiled to himself as he wondered what.

Joan quickly whipped up the omelette and cooked it in a thick foam of butter, while he took off his jacket, lit the candles and poured the wine.

'So come on, hit me with it,' he said, as she emerged from the kitchen with the plates. 'Anything you like, as long as it's not about the Bay of Pigs.'

'Not remotely,' she promised him, and for a couple of minutes they ate in silence, apart from his moan of pleasure at the lightness of the omelette, and an 'ah' in appreciation of the wine.

Then she took her ability to surprise him to a whole new level.

'It's about the Michalowski case.'

He had a forkful of omelette in his mouth, so his eyebrows merely formed two quizzical arches. But what on earth . . . ? The Michalowski case was *sub rosa*. The files were marked 'Top Secret'. This wasn't done.

Joan carried on quickly. 'Sir Hugh likes me to be up to speed, so I know about Primrose Hill. I know Michalowski probably helped the physicists who got to America. And I know that Henry Coxon made the link with a girl called

Tracy Thorburn, because Sandra Pole told me, and I wrote the note and passed it on to you.' She swallowed nervously.

Hector gestured with his fork. 'Have some omelette. You're a magician, you really are.' His eyebrows still hadn't lost their quizzical shape.

Joan took a couple of mouthfuls and put her fork down. She obviously wasn't hungry. Hector, who listened for a living, carried on doing so while he ate.

'What I mean is,' she said, 'I've been reading your work at my desk for days, and sometimes you read my work at your desk, and we both have top security clearance, but we don't talk shop. We never say a thing. We pretend it hasn't happened. I even suggested as much to the Queen a few days ago.'

'I think that's rather sensible, don't you?' he observed.

'Oh, it probably is.' She took a large gulp of wine. 'But I had coffee with a friend recently . . .'

'Martha Riley, I know.'

'You *would* know. And she gave me the strong impression that her outfit is short-staffed and overstretched. Given your hours, and what the Cabinet papers say about funding the Civil Service, I'm sure yours is, too. Martha said they need women like me, with languages and – oh for God's sake – Bletchley experience, dammit. You know what I did.'

He took a sip from his own glass. 'I do.'

'And I think I could help,' she said, leaning forward earnestly, so the candlelight caught the russet tints in her hair. 'I *want* to help. I was in on this Michalowski business from the start. I was the person Sandra originally told about the body . . .'

'I know that, too. But I don't see how—'

'In your reports, you make clear that you need to know what Michalowski was doing with those microdots. You're checking all the London post offices for clues as to what he was sending and receiving, and going through everything in his flat. I know how desperately painstaking that must be. You're looking for clues and . . . I think I could help find them. I've got French and German, and a smattering of Spanish and Italian. I know how codes and ciphers work, and I practically live with the royals, so if there's anything connected to them, I could spot it long before—'

'My darling, do you want me to *recruit* you?' Hector asked.

Joan took another gulp of burgundy. 'Yes, I do, rather.'

'Officially?'

'No.'

He grinned at her through the candles. 'How interesting.'

'It's just . . . You look so tired, Hector. You've been working through the night, sometimes. If there's anything I can—'

He raised a hand. 'Don't tell me this is all about me,' he said, his faint Scottish brogue softening the hard truth of what he was saying. 'This is about you, isn't it? Don't tell me you're bored, my love? You've just got back from India and Iran, and soon you're off to Italy. Next year it will be the "J"s.'

'Not bored, exactly . . .' She pushed her plate aside and looked him deep in the eyes. Hers were grey, and glittered with intelligence and sincerity. 'You trust me, don't you?'

'With my body, soul and life,' he said, spearing a chip. 'You know that.'

'Do you trust me with secrets?'

Hector ate the chip while he thought about it. She glared at him, offended.

'Of course, *naturally* I do,' he said. 'I was just asking myself if I do officially.' He sighed. 'Given your access to Her Majesty and all her briefing papers, if you *are* working for the KGB, God help us all.' He paused and speared a lettuce leaf. 'Although, it has been known.'

'Not in her private office.'

'Not there, no.'

'What I mean is,' Joan said, 'I get the impression you're a bit stuck at the moment. You think Michalowski was trying to get someone out from behind the Iron Curtain. You think that's probably why he died. But you don't know who, or how, or when, and if I could just—'

'You look extremely lovely in the candlelight,' he interrupted, softly. 'I like very much whatever it is with your hair. This wine is excellent. I couldn't possibly let you into Michalowski's flat, though. Much as I'd love to. I'm sorry.'

But Joan was nothing if not persevering.

'There's something wrong about the padlock on his cupboard door,' she said, referring to the description in his first report. 'It doesn't fit with everything else in the flat.'

'The man was slapdash. The place was a mess.'

'But he wired his phone to use a radio speaker. He wired the lamp into the cupboard . . .'

Hector was amused. 'You *have* been reading carefully.'

'It's what I do. He wired in the lamp so the lead wouldn't show, but stuck a bloody great padlock on the door, like a sign.'

'We've been wondering about that, don't worry.'

She changed tack.

'Tony Armstrong-Jones mentioned that Pavel taught himself Russian, as well as the Polish and French he already knew. But the scientists he helped escape were German, so unless they spoke English or Russian very well, he might have needed a translator, and—'

Hector's smile of amusement faded.

'I found the translator this morning. He's an antiquarian bookseller who used to play chess with Michalowski.'

'Oh,' Joan said. She looked disappointed She obviously had a plan for finding him herself. She was grasping at straws, and he didn't blame her. Without seeing the flat, it was hard.

'But I'm very interested in what you say about Mr Armstrong-Jones,' he said.

Princess Margaret's husband had known Michalowski better than many, both socially and professionally. But Sir Hugh Masson and his ilk had told Hector the new royal couldn't be approached at any price.

'I'd like to know his thoughts very much. Did he mention anything else?'

Joan looked as if she was about to say something, then stopped herself. 'I couldn't possibly comment.'

'Come on, dammit! Tell me!'

'Well, I could,' Joan said, with a smile, 'but the thing is, it works both ways.'

He shook his head sadly. 'Does it? I don't think it does, you know.'

He finished his meal, which had been delicious, and topped up both their glasses with the excellent wine. Joan sat very still, meanwhile, like an alabaster statue. There was a sort of shimmer about her, which happened when she was angry or frustrated and refused to admit defeat. For the first time, he properly noticed the dress she'd put on, which was a little black shift of a clever design that she'd probably got her aunt to make specially. It was of course vitally important not to give in to feminine wiles, and no man would give up national secrets for an omelette and a frock . . . But he loved her, and she was right: if she weren't already doing a job of national significance, and if he wasn't sharing a bed with her, he would have happily hired her to work for him. Imagine if they *could* talk about these things. He knew of a few, select couples – ambassadors and their wives, for example – who did. He'd always envied them.

'All right,' he said, wondering if he was making a huge mistake. 'I'll trade. You'll read it in my report tomorrow anyway, but I'll give you a first exclusive: my meeting yesterday with the man who knows what Michalowski was up to, in return for whatever Mr Armstrong-Jones and Princess Margaret have said. Do we have a deal?'

Joan nodded, and he could see she had to bite her lip to stop herself from smiling.

'You first,' she said.

Hector told her about Paul Schwartz, a German-speaking Hungarian bookseller in St Martin's Lane, who was an active part of the dissident community in London. Schwartz would meet Michalowski at a Soho restaurant called the Gay Hussar, and afterwards they would play chess together. Last year, Schwartz had acted as translator for a couple of important messages between the photographer and the defecting East German physicists. As he told it, the escape was supposed to be a one-off. Then Michalowski was persuaded to attempt another one in Berlin, which had gone very badly. Schwartz had assumed he wouldn't try again, but one day in January, the young photographer had invited him back to Primrose Hill and, standing on the hill itself, in the darkness, looking up at the night sky, he had said 'someone special' was coming.

'That was all he said, at the time,' Hector said to Joan. '"Someone very special", to be precise. Schwartz didn't ask for details, and Michalowski didn't offer them. But a few weeks later, at their favourite table at the restaurant, they were talking with a fellow diner about the Russian space programme. The other man mentioned something about the Chief Engineer, as they call him – the man in charge of the whole programme – and Michalowski said, "Wouldn't you like to know who that was?" According to Schwartz, he had the same look in his eye as when he was winning at chess and he'd seen mate in five.'

Now it was Joan's turn to look quizzical. 'He was helping the Chief Engineer to escape?'

'No no, not that. I'm sure he's staying put. The man has almost godlike status in the Soviet Union. His real identity is a closely guarded secret. It's so secret in fact that even to find out who he is would be a major coup, especially for the Brits, if we could do it. We're falling so far behind the Americans. We need all the leverage we can get.'

'And the bookseller thinks Michalowski's contact could have told you?'

'That was the strong impression he gave.' Hector took another sip of wine, savouring it for a moment. 'The thing is, this Chief Engineer is much more than the director of an organisation. There's something talismanic about him. When you see what the Soviets have given him to work with . . . His space rockets are practically held together with sealing wax and string, the Yanks say. He has a fraction of the money and technology of the West, and I wouldn't trust one of those capsules to keep me safe for five minutes. But whatever alchemy he's using, he's created a hero like Yuri Gagarin, and we haven't. Somehow, we're always on the back foot.'

'What would we do if we knew who he was?' Joan asked warily.

'Don't worry.' Hector caught her meaning and shook his head. 'We wouldn't try to kill him. We wouldn't get close, anyway. But we could learn what made him so good. Repeat those lessons, if we could.' He looked at his empty plate and gave a satisfied sigh. 'Thank you, my darling.'

Joan got up to clear the plates, replacing them with a fruit bowl. Then she watched as he took an apple and peeled it in one smooth spiral with a switchblade from his pocket. He cored it, cut it into quarters and gave two of them to her. Their fingers touched with the inevitable jolt of electricity.

'Did Schwartz say when he's coming – this contact who knows the identity?' she asked.

'No. He has no clue. It's possible the man works at a base called Star City in the Moscow Oblast, where the cosmonauts train. It's a very long way to travel. It would take meticulous planning.'

'Do MI6 have people there who can look into it?'

Hector's face hardened. 'They might. This is not something I'm sharing at the moment.' He sighed deeply.

Relations between the two agencies oscillated between strained and frosty. They had never been close, even in the war, and now MI6 turned out to have produced an alarming number of double agents. First there were Burgess and Maclean. Now, a man called George Blake was about to go on trial at the Old Bailey. So many lives had already been lost. Frankly, James Bond was just as likely to be working for Khruschev as the fictional 'M' these days. Hector couldn't risk it.

'I suppose the Russians will have got to him first anyway,' Joan said sadly.

This had been Hector's original assumption, too. But several details had led him to question the idea. He leaned back to grab a silver box of cigarettes from a nearby side table and lit one, relishing the hit of nicotine to accompany the wine.

'Ah, well it's just possible they didn't,' he said.

She looked surprised. 'Oh?'

'The men who took Michalowski were working quickly. If they were searching for details of a plan, they might have missed them.'

'How d'you know?'

Hector thought back. There had been a few things. On the whole, the flat looked untouched, as if they'd tried to cover their tracks. But there was an enlargement of a photograph taken of Michalowski by a lover on the morning of his disappearance, for example. It showed that the poster behind the bed had since been moved. There were books put back on the shelves in the wrong order. Michalowski was a sloven in some ways, but he was particular about his library of travel guides, which were shelved in alphabetical order of country, apart from those relating to Russia, Finland, Sweden and Norway, which were out of place and upside down. The top of the bathroom cabinet was covered in a thick layer of dust, suggesting they hadn't looked there at all.

He told her about the books and the bathroom cabinet.

'What do you think happened?' she asked.

'They were rushing. They might have been spooked by someone knocking at the door, or the telephone ringing – it could have been anything. But I wonder if perhaps they'd realised they'd given Michalowski too much of the knockout drug. Or he was allergic to it.'

'D'you think that's what killed him?'

'It seems likely. Perhaps he was behaving oddly – fitting, or something. They might have decided they needed to get him quickly to someone who could help.'

'Only, it was too late,' Joan said.

'Yes. Luckily for him, given what they'd have had in mind for him next. Of course, they *might* have found what they wanted in the meantime, but my sources at the embassy are telling me they're in a bit of a panic. They're desperately contacting their own networks, trying to find out what he was up to.'

'Can Tracy Thorburn help?'

'She's playing dumb. She told Special Branch that she was hoping to go out with Michalowski, but nothing came of it. I'm having her followed.'

'Coffee?' Joan suggested.

This was another of Hector's areas of expertise, and he made it for them both with a little steel espresso machine on the hob.

When he came back with two steaming cups, she asked, 'Have you checked the client appointments in his diary?'

'Michalowski's? Yes. Why?'

'I assume there aren't any big gaps, or you'd have spotted them.'

'True, there aren't. He was busy until late June.'

She blew on her coffee and took a sip.

'I spend a lot of time with diaries. Maybe he wasn't always as stupid as the man who puts a padlock on a secret cupboard. Maybe there are fake bookings for days when he might be otherwise occupied. He could make real bookings with restaurants and hotels and cancel them easily enough, but not with clients. If he did so with them, his name would be mud quite fast.'

'He used fake names and addresses, you mean? We checked for those.'

'Real names, but people who don't have the appointment in *their* diaries.'

Hector smacked his forehead.

'What a bloody idiot!' he muttered. 'We checked back over the days of the Scandinavian escape, and he'd simply put in that he was vacationing in Sweden. We assumed he hadn't learned.'

Joan took another sip of coffee.

'People do learn, sometimes.'

'I don't, apparently. *Damn!*'

'You're short staffed,' she said sympathetically. 'I understand. You've got a lot going on . . .'

Hector held up his hands in surrender. 'All right, all right! You win. Not a visit to the flat, though, that's impossible. I love you, Joan McGraw. I'll see what I can do.'

Chapter 28

Hector merely laughed when Joan fulfilled her side of the bargain. Tony Armstrong-Jones had said nothing of use about his friend beyond the languages he spoke. Princess Margaret, too, had said little, except how attractive Pavel was, and how attentive he'd been at lighting her cigarettes. However, Joan had already earned her reward.

It took twenty-four hours for Hector to sort it out. She wouldn't get access to the flat on Chalcot Square, but when his team had gone through it, they had photographed and logged every paper and object that might be useful, now or in the future. The images were held in filing boxes in the basement of his office on Curzon Street, and he arranged for her to have access to them for one evening only, to see if she could use her codebreaking experience and familiarity with the royal family – or something else, anything – to spot a detail they hadn't seen.

Joan walked there from work on a Thursday evening, enjoying the sunshine in Green Park, and the sense of spring in the air. The royal family had gone to Badminton House, to stay with the Duke of Beaufort and watch the horse trials.

It was the Queen's birthday tomorrow and she had lots of plans for the weekend, none of which involved Joan.

Curzon Street was a quiet road off Piccadilly, between the red-light district of Shepherd Market and the bright lights of the Ritz. The address Hector gave Joan was one of the shabbiest houses on the street, which didn't surprise her. She knew that MI5's teams were scattered across cheap offices all over London, chosen not to stand out.

A porter opened the door and asked her name. Like the building, he'd made an effort to look anonymous and unprepossessing. At his desk, he telephoned to someone to come and meet her.

Joan lingered in the hall, which was long and narrow, badly lit and poorly furnished, with cracked linoleum on the floor and a series of framed, old-fashioned sketches on the walls. Eventually, a woman in her forties came down the sagging wooden staircase, clutching a pink card file.

'Hello, I'm Madeleine,' she said. 'Major Ross asked me to look after you. Sorry to drag you here on such a nice evening.'

Madeleine had an open, intelligent face, hair swept back into a tidy bun, sensible cardigan, sensible shoes. She was staring hard at Joan, who still thought of herself as looking quite similar, but Joan remembered that her own uniform of pearls and heels and fashionable skirts was very different these days. However, what she had gained in glamour, she had lost in the thrill of the chase. This sagging, sweaty building, with all its secrets, felt like home.

She reached out a hand. 'Delighted to meet you. I'm Joan.'

Madeleine smiled. 'Let me show you the way.'

She took Joan down the hall to another, positively dangerous, staircase and through two doors in the basement that had to be opened with a key. A short corridor lay ahead of them. Madeleine opened the second door on the right, and flicked a switch to turn on two bright strip lights above a couple of flimsy tables set back-to-back. There was one chair and no window. The place smelled of mould and whatever cleaning fluid they had unsuccessfully used to try and get rid of it.

'Welcome to Chateau Curzon,' Madeleine said. 'Make yourself at home.'

Joan grinned.

'All the images from the Michalowski case are in these boxes,' Madeleine explained. She indicated a series of identical cardboard boxes sitting in rows on a set of open shelves against two of the walls. 'They're labelled on the front as to where in the flat they came from. You can look at them on the table, and take notes as you need to with the pad and pen provided. I'll look after your coat and handbag for you. Just leave the enlargements in piles when you've finished with them, and I'll make sure they're filed again.'

'Have you made any progress since I spoke to Major Ross?' Joan asked.

Madeleine's expression suggested that she was wondering under what circumstances the well-dressed redhead in front of her had spoken to the Director of D Branch – and coming to a pretty good guess, Joan thought. It wasn't an unfriendly look, though.

'We have, actually, Miss McGraw. You were right about the diary. There were four entries in mid-May for photo shoots with clients who knew nothing about it. And a booking at a hotel in St Tropez which, as you say, Michalowski could've easily cancelled. Unless he was really going there to recover, or prepare.'

'Mid-May? That's only three or four weeks away.'

'It doesn't give us long. From what we've learned, he had a wide correspondence. Mostly to America, but to Russia and Poland, too. He used a lot of different post offices for his chess magazines and letters, so we think he was trying to cover his tracks. We could easily have missed one.'

'How did he even know people in those places?' Joan asked. 'Russia and Poland, I mean?'

'Mostly through the chess clubs and correspondence,' Madeleine said. 'In Poland, he knew some people through his family, and others through members of the Polish Club here in London. No doubt his letters and cards were read by the censor, but they got through anyway, and vice versa.'

'And Russia?' Joan asked.

'Again, chess. Also, he'd been there on a trip in '51, and he'd stayed in touch with the organiser, for example. A man called Grigovski who works in a machine tool factory near St Petersburg. Their correspondence is here.' Madeleine tapped the box in question.

'He'd been to Russia?'

'Oh yes,' Madeleine said. 'A lot of people have. Our unions like to arrange trips, and the communists like to show off their factories and farms, and they can be genuinely friendly. Funny, isn't it?'

'Was Michalowski in a union?'

'No. When his parents died, he was semi-taken in by a Quaker family, and the Quakers organise these trips too. Or at least, they did back in '51. He wasn't a practising Quaker or anything, but I think he wanted to practise his Russian. He was desperate to find out what had happened to the world his family came from. Trying to reach out to the ordinary people being oppressed by their own governments. That's how he saw it anyway, from what the family say.'

'It must be very hard for them,' Joan said.

'It's awful. They adored him. They said he was a special person, with so much promise.'

That word 'special' again. Michalowski himself had used it to describe the person he was helping. What did it mean, exactly?

Madeleine explained how the box filing system worked, covering each area and piece of furniture in the flat and Michalowski's dark room and studio down the road, with images collated according to shelf, pile, stack or drawer.

'I'll be back in an hour to see how you're doing,' she promised. 'There's a telephone on the wall that rings through to my desk. Good luck.'

She said it as if Joan was going to need it. There were dozens of boxes, but Joan was hopeful. Somewhere in this haystack there was a needle, and she intended to find it.

By the end of the first hour, she'd learned the folly of her ambition. If anything, she'd gone backwards. She was driving herself mad trying to spot clues in completed crosswords, checking for codes in chess magazines and trying to recreate the chess game in progress on the board.

'This doesn't make any sense,' she said to Madeleine on her return, indicating the image of the game as it was found. 'The queen shouldn't be there, and there's a pawn missing.'

'We found that on the carpet,' Madeleine said. 'We think the KGB officers moved the pieces when they lifted the board to look underneath.'

'Oh.'

'Major Ross probably told you, they were a bit slapdash.'

'He did.'

'Would you like a cup of tea? There's a kitchenette down the corridor.'

Joan would indeed. She was grateful for a couple of custard creams, too. Then it was back to work for another hour, during which she drove herself just as mad. And then another.

'I assume you saw the folded page corners in the guidebook to Vienna?' she asked Madeleine, over their third cup of tea. The custard creams had run out.

'We did. I know, it's difficult, isn't it?'

'I was interested in the portrait photographs that were found in a plain envelope. They were in Pavel's style, but he didn't take them, did he? The lighting was slightly different.'

'Yes. The three-quarter profiles of a woman in a black jumper, one with a little girl, too. We found a note to say they'd come from a photographer in Belgium who admired Michalowski's technique. He was asking him for tips.'

'I saw that,' Joan said. 'I notice you'd filed them with the copy of a different image from the bedroom.'

'Yes, the snapshot. We found that in the lining of a lid of a cufflink box.'

'The young woman in the snapshot looked a bit like the little girl in the portrait photo. Is that what you thought, too?'

'Well, we did,' Madeleine agreed. 'But it's impossible to be sure it isn't just coincidence. They can't be the same person – the portrait photograph is recent and the girl in it can't be more than ten.'

'Could it be the older woman in the portrait?'

Madeleine shrugged. 'Personally, I think they do look alike, but apparently not. There's something wrong about the nose and the distance between the eyes, according to our chap who examines these things. I mean, all three look quite similar and it's tempting to read a lot into it, but that snapshot is very poor.'

'And we don't know who it is?'

'No. Or where or when it was taken. It was cut from a bigger picture and there are no clues in the background.' Madeleine grinned. 'Fun, isn't it?'

'I admire your dedication,' Joan said, sincerely. The team had only had a few days to work on hundreds and hundreds of these papers and objects, and they seemed to have spotted anything of interest already. Perhaps Hector was just being kind in inviting her to help. She wasn't trained in this method of investigation, and so far, she wasn't any good at it.

The fourth hour was just as bad, and she felt a nasty headache coming on, until she decided to stop concentrating so hard, searching for patterns where there weren't any. She was there in part because she knew about aspects of Michalowski's world that Madeleine and her colleagues didn't. She needed to relax, step back and just absorb the information. Let the patterns come to her.

In the middle of the fifth hour, Joan jerked her head up, looked back down again, flipped two or three images back and forth in her hands, and glanced across at the telephone. But she didn't pick it up. She spent the next fifteen minutes going through the box in question – labelled 'SITTING ROOM 9: TELEPHONE JOTTING PAD, DRAWERS 11 AND 12 CONTENTS, DIARY' – image by image. At one point, she almost made a note on the pad beside her, but thought the better of it.

By half-past midnight, she had been through all the boxes she could manage and was exhausted and ready to go home. Madeleine had gone home herself by then, so it was a young, sandy-haired man who gave Joan back her handbag and asked if she had found anything useful.

'Sadly not,' she said, indicating the empty pad of paper.

Nobody had asked if she had a photographic memory.

Back in Dolphin Square, Hector was waiting for her with a saucepan of hot chocolate, an open bottle of whisky and a line of kisses along her neck, under her hair.

'How did it go?' he asked.

She looked him in the eyes and shook her head. 'I'm sorry.'

'You look exhausted, my poor darling.'

'I am,' she admitted. 'It was worth trying.'

He helped her out of her coat.

'Really, nothing?'

'You've done so well already, Hector. I'm sure your team will find what you're looking for.'

He smiled with resignation. 'As you say, it was worth a try.'

Chapter 29

Friday, the twenty-first of April dawned grey and drizzly. If not quite 'dreich', as her Scottish mother called it, it was not far off. Still, the Queen didn't mind the weather, because she was going to be out in it. As long as one was dressed for the elements, it didn't really matter what they were. And goodness knows, she needed a day outside.

Today she turned thirty-five, halfway through her three score years and ten, and she couldn't think of a nicer way of spending it. No paperwork or meetings. Badminton was about to play host to some of the best horses in Europe, and it would just be friends, family and animals for most of the day, followed by a party back at Windsor Castle. It would take her mind off . . . everything. Not only her looming state visit, but the unfolding disaster of the Bay of Pigs in Cuba, the threat of Armageddon, the body in the water tank, and the Russians who seemed to be practically on one's doorstep, drugging men at will.

'D'you remember what we were doing ten years ago?' Philip asked her, as they descended the stairs for breakfast at Badminton House.

'My twenty-fifth? We were in Rome,' she said, relaxing at the thought of it. 'You were playing polo.'

She was a princess then, with a certain amount of freedom. Philip was a busy naval officer and the most glamorous man in Europe. She might have been biased, but only slightly. Her father was still alive then, just.

Philip grinned. 'They gave you a party in Hadrian's Villa. Fit for an emperor.'

'Slightly ruined.'

'The party?'

'The villa. I liked the party.'

'I didn't,' he said. 'Given that you share your birthday with the city itself, we assumed that the cream of the Roman aristocracy would be there, but half of them had hightailed it to the hills, so they wouldn't have to meet you.'

'Oh yes!' She had forgotten. 'Wasn't that extraordinary? I know we'd been at war a few years before, but I assumed they wouldn't hold it against me, personally.'

'Ha! Well, they did. They're going to look pretty silly next week, when you go back as . . . *you*. I imagine they'll be falling over themselves to be nice to you.'

'And I shall be perfectly nice to them,' she said, nodding to the Duke of Beaufort's footmen and surveying the generous buffet table in the breakfast room. 'One doesn't hold grudges.'

'You don't, I do,' Philip said, crisply. 'I'm sure you'll permit me the odd pertinent comment.'

'Absolutely not!'

'Whatever you say, sausage.' He smiled quietly to himself.

They finished a lavish cooked breakfast, and once they'd gathered the children and travelled to the grounds, it was lovely to become members of the public for a while, wandering around the tents, looking at hard hats and saddle soap for sale, buying a few horsey toys for Charles and Anne, and joining the 'grandstand' – which was a stationary cart, borrowed from the farm – to watch the cross-country event.

Her daughter was in her element. Princess Anne was ten, utterly fearless, and already an accomplished rider herself. The grandstand cart was nicely positioned near one of the water jumps, and she was transfixed by each horse's take-off and landing, subconsciously mirroring their movements with hers, not breathing until they'd got through safely.

'Can I do that?' she asked, turning round to her mother briefly as a mud-spattered man in tight breeches wheeled his horse out of the water and up the hill to the next section of the course.

'Not for a little while,' the Queen said, considering that her daughter's feet wouldn't even reach the stirrups across one of these animals yet.

'I mean, one day,' Anne said. 'Oh look!'

She was pointing at the next rider, an experienced eventer called Shirley Grey, who stood a good chance of winning this year. Shirley crouched forward over her mount and sailed over the obstacle without a second's hesitation.

Anne clapped and looked back, grinning. 'I want to do it in the Olympics one day.'

The Queen smiled at her. She admired her daughter's rock-solid confidence, but this might just be an overstretch. Getting a place on an Olympic team demanded a lifetime of dedication, and even someone as brilliant as Shirley couldn't do it, because she was a woman. However, here at Badminton, anything was possible for someone who was good enough.

The next two contestants made it comfortably over the fence in front of the water, but when the third arrived, her elegant bay refused, and she had to turn him round to have another go. The Queen trained her binoculars on the horse. She liked the look of him, with powerful shoulders and fire in his eyes. She was sure she'd seen him before somewhere. His rider leaned down to pat his flank and ready him for the next attempt. She was almost facing the royal party at this point, and the Queen noticed how young she was, and how attractive. The girl's face was familiar, too, though it was hard to place her under the mud spatter and the hard hat. The Queen scanned the programme for the third combination after Shirley and her horse. Aha! This one was called Sirocco.

Just as she read his name, his rider squeezed her legs for the new attempt. But she was more unlucky the second time. Sirocco caught the fence with one of his forelegs and they both went down in the water. Everyone zoomed in on them, but both rider and horse stood quickly. The girl took her helmet off briefly to wipe some of the mud from her face, and a blonde lock of her hair fell loose as she reached for Sirocco's bridle.

The Queen found herself looking into the eyes of the twenty year-old she'd seen in a photograph a few weeks ago in the pages of *Horse & Hound*, standing beside her horse. She remembered being struck by how very pale the girl's hair was in the photograph, almost like one of Margaret's

Sealyhams. She glanced back down to her programme for the name.

It was Tracy Thorburn.

For several moments, the Queen didn't hear the roar of the crowd. She watched intently as the girl replaced her hat, remounted and rode away. So *this* was the young woman who had thrown her cap at poor Henry Coxon. One could see why he'd fallen under her spell.

But there was something else. The Queen remembered the other person in that magazine photograph. He had been standing at the other side of Sirocco, with his hand on the horse's neck, looking proud as punch, in a cravat, tweed jacket and yellow waistcoat – like Toad of Toad Hall, she'd thought at the time. She knew him very slightly, and it was hard to forget that waistcoat. She had seen him once or twice at race meets and knew him as Bill Douglas, a successful businessman from New Zealand.

However, it had recently turned out that he wasn't from New Zealand at all. He wasn't called Bill Douglas. After a tip-off from the CIA a few weeks ago, MI5 had uncovered him as Sergei Steklyar, a Russian from Gorky Oblast. He had been running at least two spy rings in London and the Home Counties, and was currently being held in an MI5 safe house, undergoing questioning.

The next rider took the obstacle comfortably. Charles said he was hungry and went off with his protection officer to get a snack. The Queen looked exactly as she had before, as though she was following the action on the course with Anne. But really, she was thinking that surely the spooks at MI5 would have already made the connection between Douglas/Steklyar and the Thorburns?

But would they? Steklyar was under lock and key now, so if they were tracking the Thorburns, they wouldn't catch them together. Meanwhile, presumably they were combing through all Steklyar's many friends and acquaintances to look for suspicious activity, but he'd been operating in the UK for years and that operation was bound to take some time. Would they know that a picture of him in the diary pages of *Horse & Hound* was important? Would they even know it existed? If he co-owned Sirocco with Tracy's father, presumably there would be a record of it somewhere, but perhaps he didn't. It could have been a loan.

However, the Queen *had* seen the picture. And now she knew that Tracy Thorburn, who was connected to a Russian agent, had spent time with Henry Coxon finding out about Pavel Michalowski's living arrangements, shortly before the photographer disappeared. His dead body then showed up on one of her father's farms.

If that was a coincidence, then she was the Queen of Sheba.

She needed to talk to Joan.

Chapter 30

The Queen noticed that when her APS arrived from London at Windsor Castle on Saturday morning, Joan looked very pale. Having partied well last night herself, she knew the feeling.

'Thank you for coming at short notice,' she said. 'I thought we could go for a walk outside. It looks as if we both need the air.'

They went down to the Dog Door that led to the castle terrace, but for once the Queen decided not to take the corgis with her. She needed to concentrate on what she had to say.

'I made a discovery yesterday,' she began, glancing down the misty, tree-lined Long Walk that led through the Great Park. It was a heart-stoppingly beautiful view. She remembered Canon Vaughan telling her that the place where Sandra Pole saw the body from the train was near an old hunting ground made for William the Conqueror. The Great Park was once one, too.

But a thousand years had gone by since then. She gathered herself and explained about Tracy Thorburn, her remarkable horse and the Russian agent who seemed to be its owner.

'I knew Bill Douglas – as I thought of him – very slightly,' she said. 'He moved in horsey circles. He rode to hounds whenever he could. He was a very good natural businessman, I gather. After he was arrested, they said he was probably the richest man who'd ever worked for the KGB.'

'And you think he knew Tracy?' Joan asked.

'I'm sure of it. If someone researches the ownership of Sirocco, they'll find the connection.'

'So that's how he knew about the farm in Staffordshire.'

Sadly, it wasn't that simple.

'There are links in the chain that we don't know,' the Queen said, 'because Steklyar was in an MI5 holding cell by the time Michalowski went missing, but he must have introduced someone else to the Thorburns – someone who arranged for Tracy to find out about Michalowski's schedule, and later, for her father to help dispose of the body.'

'Are we sure Thorburn *did* help dispose of it, ma'am? Tracy could always just have told her contact about the farm.'

The Queen shook her head. 'The thing is, the train.'

'The train, ma'am?'

'Yes. The fact that they were trying to dispose of a body so close to a busy track. The police report suggests that the men in question might have been London-based, so didn't understand about the trains being there at all, but Canon Vaughan pointed out to me that they'd have seen the Rugby to Crewe train going by only five minutes before. Anyone else would have waited for dark, surely? I think someone knew the timetable very well: *too well*, because he assumed that they had a good few minutes clear before the next train came by. He didn't expect us, because we weren't part of the timetable. I imagine he assumed we were a freight train, then saw that we weren't and panicked – but it was too late.'

Joan nodded grimly. She still looked pale.

'Do you want me to tell Major Ross?' she asked.

Ah, she was 'telling Major Ross', not 'informing MI5' these days. The Queen noted that with interest.

'Absolutely not,' she said. 'The horse world is not in your orbit, Joan. He'll instantly know the news really came from me.'

'I suppose so.'

The Queen smiled. '*You* can't tell him,' she said, 'but someone else can.'

Joan considered this. 'Someone he already knows,' she said. She raised an eyebrow. 'Someone horsey, who likes to talk; who might have heard of the connection through anyone at the palace.'

'Exactly,' the Queen said crisply. 'Our *eminence grise*.' She and Joan exchanged a smile. 'It's a role he fulfils very nicely.'

Neither of them had said the man's name, but they both knew who they meant. They pictured a thick moustache bristling with satisfaction.

'Major Ross is an intelligent man,' Joan said. 'He may well see through the subterfuge.'

'I know,' the Queen acknowledged. 'But he wouldn't be able to prove it, and actually, I doubt he'd want to. Plausible deniability, that's what we need.'

'Plausible deniability, ma'am. I'll see to it.'

Elizabeth was pleased that the conversation was over, and they didn't need to take up any more time on a Saturday filled with family plans. She was sorry that Michalowski had met his awful end, grateful that the body had been found, and hopeful that the Russian connection could soon be resolved. Meanwhile, the castle was crammed with VIPs from last night's party who needed her attention. She put on a turn of speed to get back inside, but her APS hesitated.

'Was there something else?' she asked.

Joan looked positively miserable.

'Is it to do with this case?'

Joan nodded.

The Queen glanced up at the castle. 'Can you perhaps leave it to Major Ross or DCI Darbishire? They both seem very capable?'

Joan shook her head. 'Not unless you want me to, ma'am.'

'Oh? And why wouldn't I?' Elizabeth didn't like the sound of this. 'Do we need to take another turn around the terrace?'

'I think we should.'

Joan briefly explained the background of her trip to Curzon Street. So, things *had* changed between her and Major Ross. The Queen wondered if Joan expected her to disapprove, but she didn't. If anything, she was surprised it had taken them this long.

'What did you find?' she asked.

'Something I didn't tell him. But it was there for everyone to see, so they can work it out for themselves if they want to.'

Joan jutted out her chin, as if she might be challenged.

'Go on,' the Queen said, cautiously.

Joan described how the images were filed.

'One set of photographs showed the pad Michalowski kept next to the phone for taking notes.'

'I see . . .'

'He had a very busy life, so he was constantly jotting down names, dates, addresses, sometimes for clients, often for parties or trips with friends, often using initials and acronyms. He was an infrequent visitor to Kensington Palace and "KP" appeared a couple of times, for example.'

The Queen nodded. 'I assume MI5 could work that out for themselves.'

'Of course. Anyway, halfway down, one of the pages had the letters "RYB" written in pencil, under various notes in ink.' Joan paused, as if this was significant. 'That's how I refer to the Royal Yacht *Britannia* in my own notes.'

The Queen turned to face her. What on earth? *'Britannia?'*

Joan's pallor started to make sense. The Queen glanced at her watch. She was supposed to be at breakfast. The whole schedule could be in jeopardy if she wasn't careful.

'Lots of things could be RYB, surely?' she suggested.

'Absolutely,' Joan agreed. 'I've just learned that it also stands for "red, yellow, blue", which is a model for the use of colour in design. Artists refer to it a lot. I think the team at MI5 assumed that's what Michalowski meant, because they didn't ask me about it.'

'And you didn't tell them.'

Joan shifted uneasily. 'No.'

'Because . . . ?'

'Because in the bottom corner of the next page, in the same pencil, was the number 29 in a little circle,' she said.

'The twenty-ninth?'

'I think so, ma'am.'

'But that's when---'

'Yes. And on the following page, another note in ink quite clearly said, "C Genov 1 p.m.".'

The Queen frowned. "C Genov" doesn't mean anything to me. Is that a person?'

Joan sighed. She crossed her arms, as if she didn't want to be saying what had to be said.

'It might be,' she agreed. 'But an old friend of mine married a naval officer who's an attaché to NATO in Naples. We haven't seen each other for years, and she proposed to catch up with me very briefly in Cagliari on the twenty-ninth, the day we arrive to join *Britannia*.'

The Queen felt an icy sense of dread, like cold water seeping up one's clothes from a wintry river.

'Go on.'

'I have a similar note in my diary, ma'am – "Caffè Genov" in my case – for the twenty-ninth of April, at 3 p.m. Of course, it's possible that and "RYB" is a design thing. Twenty-nine needn't be a date, and "C Genov" could be a café somewhere else, or it *is* a person after all, or it's something else entirely. But . . .' Joan shrugged unhappily '. . . as soon as I saw it, it screamed out to me. It's not even in code. Over those three pages, there's a date and a meeting place and a time. It's in April, not May, which is when MI5 think Michalowski scheduled the defection, but other than that, it's exactly what Major Ross's team have been looking for.'

'By the time *Britannia* gets back to Portsmouth it will be May,' the Queen murmured. 'Presumably the number stood out to them, too?'

'It don't think it did. There are so many other numbers in the phone pad and this one was overlaid by a scribbled list of dark room supplies. As far as I know, they're working on the assumption that "Genov" is a person in the Eastern Bloc, and trying to work that out.'

'They haven't made the connection with us,' the Queen said, more to herself than anyone.

'No, ma'am. Not yet. But I looked at the images they took of Michalowski's diary, and there's a "B" with a dot against the thirteenth of May, when *Britannia*'s due to dock in Portsmouth.'

The Queen's head throbbed. 'Do you realise what this means? I thought we were done with this whole damn business.'

She very rarely swore in front of staff, but *honestly*. Her father, under similar circumstances, would have thrown a rock across the terrace. His language could be very ripe.

'I know, ma'am. I'm so sorry.'

'I hope you're wrong. But if you're right, this puts me at the heart of it.'

PART THREE

BRITANNIA RULES THE WAVES

Chapter 31

The next few hours were excruciating. Following her birthday, the day was packed. There were departing relatives to say goodbye to, presents to open, and earnest conversations to be had with members of staff who wanted to wish the Queen a belated happy birthday. Someone had arranged a surprise cine film viewing of last year's horses winning races. The Prime Minster rang with birthday greetings of his own. It was all very thoughtful and heartfelt, but each kind gesture only reminded Elizabeth what was at stake if her APS had really discovered a plot to use the royal yacht for a political defection, made by a man who had quite possibly been killed by the KGB.

Finally, she declared a sudden, blinding headache, and managed to escape to the library, so she could get a few more minutes in a quiet room alone with Joan. She left strict instructions not to be disturbed.

By the time Joan arrived, the Queen was already on the far side of the room, examining a globe. It was a substantial piece of furniture – a sphere about two feet in diameter, supported on a mahogany frame that moved on brass wheels. The Queen pushed it near to a window to catch the light.

'Before we do anything else,' she said, 'I want to see why on earth Michalowski would choose Cagliari to try and fix an escape, of all places. Berlin I could understand, or somewhere on the East German border. Finland even. But Italy?'

The globe was covered in a detailed and colourful map, marking out the old British Empire in pink against the vast blue of the oceans. It was a few decades old and what it didn't do was show the extent of the Soviet Union, which would have been helpful at this point. However, the Queen was good at geography. She knew where all the modern borders were.

She quickly scanned the globe for Italy. There was Sardinia, the large island to the west of Naples, opposite the shin of Italy's boot. She pointed to the island's southern edge.

'The port of Cagliari is here, yes?'

Joan, who was intimately acquainted with every location on the upcoming royal visit, agreed that it was.

'And Tunis is there.' The Queen shifted her finger down to the African capital directly south of Cagliari across the Mediterranean Sea, and closer than Naples, now that they looked. 'My mother will be there in, what? Three days? Four? Assuming we haven't all been vapourised by then. But what really matters is what's up here.' She spun the globe until she found a black dot in the land mass north of the Black Sea, almost exactly due east of Edinburgh. 'Moscow. Major Ross seems to think our scientist might work nearby.'

It was a very long way from London and if anything, even further from Sardinia, down to the south-west. They were three points of an enormous triangle, like a slice of cake. The Queen frowned. 'It doesn't make sense.'

'Not if you start from Moscow,' Joan agreed. 'Perhaps he's starting from somewhere else. Hungary, possibly? Except . . .'

'What?'

'Major Ross's contact was Hungarian, but that didn't come up. No, it definitely sounded as though the defector was Russian. And that's where Michalowski went in '51.'

The Queen peered at the globe. 'He could have been trying to use Scandinavia again, but that doesn't fit at all. What about Austria? It's neutral. Soviets do visit.' She stepped back, recalculating the distances. 'From there, it might be easier for the man to go south, to Italy, rather than north, to England. But still, once in Austria, why not just ask for asylum there?'

Joan joined her in looking at the country's location on the map. To the east, it bordered Czechoslovakia and Hungary, behind the Iron Curtain. To the south, across the Alps, there was Yugoslavia, which was also communist. A small southern border with Italy ran through the mountains. There had been terrorist activity there recently, and it, too, was tightly controlled.

'He wouldn't just be able to go to the local authorities,' Joan said. He'd have to get to an embassy in Vienna and claim asylum. If he's a highly prized scientist, they'd be watching him like a hawk. Perhaps he thinks he can go south because they won't be expecting it. There are trains that cross the Alps.'

The Queen wasn't convinced. 'Even so, let's say he did go south to Trieste or somewhere. Couldn't he try to get to England in the boot of a car? It's how some defectors do it, isn't it? And if he *must* be smuggled aboard a boat, why not any one of the thousands of craft that line the Italian coast?' She glowered at the coastline. 'Why mine?'

She saw Joan struggling to suppress a smile. Her APS knew how much *Britannia* meant to her. But her indignation was understandable, surely? There were few things in life that the Queen guarded jealously. Her family life was one of them, her rare moments of privacy another. As she travelled the world, *Britannia* was vital to them both.

'And why join the yacht at the start of my visit?' she went on. 'If anyone *did* get aboard, they'd have to hide there for days and days. Why not wait until we got to Venice? That's practically next to Trieste, on the border with Yugoslavia.'

'I don't know.' Joan shrugged. 'Perhaps Michalowski was improvising. He used whatever levers he could pull to get the defectors out of East Germany. Their route through Scandinavia worked because he had friends there. He only worked with people he trusted. He might have known someone on board *Britannia*, who suggested Cagliari for some reason.'

'A naval officer? They'd know a hundred other people with boats.' The Queen was still seething.

'But Pavel wouldn't know them personally,' Joan suggested. 'I'm just hypothesising.'

The Queen calmed a little. 'Perhaps you're right. But if that's the case, he'd need to know someone aboard who could hide the man for two weeks – long enough for me to do the state visit and for *Britannia* to return to Portsmouth – without anyone else getting a hint of him at any point. The ship is crawling with sailors. Even the officers' cabins are tiny.'

'There are the stores, though,' Joan said. 'I've been down there, and there's space. They'd be packed full for a trip to the Pacific, but perhaps not so much for a few days in the Mediterranean.'

The Queen sighed and took the frame of the globe in both hands, pushing it back where it belonged.

'Think of the risk! If it *was* the plan, it's ridiculous. It would never have worked.'

'No, ma'am.'

'Whoever Michalowski was working with would have to be very junior and very stupid, or very senior and positively out of his mind.'

'I agree.'

They regarded each other across the room. The Queen hesitated for a while, wrestling with her conscience.

'In fact, it's so ridiculous,' she said eventually, with a brittle edge to her voice, 'that I don't think we need to bother MI5 with it just yet. Yes?'

Joan nodded soberly. She had obviously seen this coming.

'I can keep it to myself,' she said. 'For as long as you need, ma'am. Meanwhile, I'll get to work on the Tracy Thorburn business.'

The Queen pursed her lips.

'Thank you, Joan.'

Chapter 32

Miles Urquhart was having a quiet moment in his apartment at Windsor Castle, catching up with the cricket on the BBC, when Joan knocked and asked if she could have a word.

He'd already heard that she'd been summoned from London.

'What did Her Majesty need you here for so urgently?' he asked.

'She wanted some reading material before her trip to Venice.'

'I could have done that.'

'I'd already pulled some things together. I was happy to bring them,' Joan said. 'The thing is, I have a big favour to ask you.'

'Oh?'

Miles realised the poor girl was still standing on the apartment doorstep. He invited her in, poured a drink and made her comfortable in one of the armchairs in his sitting room overlooking the Round Tower. Somewhat reluctantly, he turned off *Test Match Special* on the radio.

'How can I help?'

Joan, it turned out, had just bumped into an officer from the Royal Horse Guards, the regiment that was currently guarding the castle – she wouldn't say who, exactly, because he's spoken to her in confidence – and the man had told her the most extraordinary story. Apparently, he knew the daughter of the landowner whose farm the body of Michalowski had been found on (Miles got the impression that they had dated a few times, which was typical of the Blues), and he'd unearthed a link from her to, of all people, a recently unmasked Russian agent! The girl, Tracy, was an eventer (Miles loved girls on horses, something about them . . .) and, before this unmasking, this Russian had given or sold her a rather magnificent horse . . . A horse the officer in the Blues had had his own eye on, which was why he remembered.

'So, if he's right, there's a link between the Thorburn family and the KGB,' Joan said. 'I know the police and MI5 have been looking for one. I thought I ought to tell them, but it all feels a bit tenuous.'

Miles took a thoughtful sip of the snifter at his elbow. 'Hmm. I see what you mean.'

The story was fascinating, but it did sound a bit iffy, coming from a girl like Joan, who knew nothing about horses and was really rather junior. One could imagine the likes of the head of D Branch at MI5 and Chief Superintendent Venables of the Murder Squad not taking her entirely seriously.

'And I think if I told one of them, they'd probably keep it secret from the other, and they should both know,' Joan added.

223

'I think I *can* help,' Miles said kindly. 'I'm seeing the director, D Branch on Wednesday, as it happens. I could bring the meeting forward and invite Venables along. Make it more formal, you know . . . Give it a bit of gravitas.'

Joan's eyes widened. '*Would* you?'

'Do you want me to? I'd hate to step on your toes.'

'You wouldn't at all, Miles. I'd be very grateful. Gravitas is exactly what it needs, if you think there's something in it. I mean, it's just this little anecdote, really.'

'You never know.' He took another sip of pink gin. 'But there is one thing.' He put his glass down and felt gravitas infusing him by the minute. 'The Queen is very fond of horses. She's enmeshed in their world.'

Joan looked worried. 'Ye-es?'

'So we must keep her away from this completely. It's a sordid affair, if true. We don't want Her Majesty being the slightest way involved in it.'

Joan nodded earnestly. 'I couldn't agree with you more, Miles.'

'Mum's the word, yes? You let me take care of it.'

'Mum's the word.' Joan drew a finger across her lips. 'I can't thank you enough, Miles, honestly. I knew I could count on you.'

The Queen hoped that Joan was having fun with her deputy private secretary, but meanwhile she lingered in the library far longer than she should. Philip had got a game of hide-and-seek going on in the castle and normally she'd have joined in with glee, but now she left instructions that even the children mustn't disturb her.

Hide-and-seek was the last thing she needed. It didn't often happen, but she was thoroughly fed up.

Britannia?

The escape plan that they had just imagined at the globe was fantastical, geographically nonsensical, pragmatically impossible, and quite frankly, politically outrageous. It was also, very personal. Elizabeth felt a fury she rarely knew.

What would happen if the Queen of the United Kingdom and her other realms were found, in the middle of the Cold War, when the Americans were trying to help mount a coup against the communists in Cuba, to be smuggling a Soviet defector across the Mediterranean and the Bay of Biscay, into England, on her personal yacht?

Goodness, the very idea of it made her skin crawl so much that she had to pace the room. It wouldn't happen, of course, it couldn't. The plan almost certainly didn't exist, and if it did it was doomed to failure. The defector would be discovered coming aboard, or once ensconced inside, and some sort of diplomatic solution would be engineered to return him whence he came. To what? The Queen didn't know, and it didn't bear thinking about, but the implications of not returning him were worse.

The West was strengthened by its alliances, and whether she liked it or not (as it happened, she did), part of her role was to maintain these by visiting those allies, as she'd been doing all year and would continue to do. The Queen saw her yacht as a statesman's tool. If such tools helped keep a fragile peace, then they saved lives, too. In the midst of her fury, she stopped to ask herself if she was simply being selfish to take it all so personally. What did God think? Perhaps it *was* selfish, in part, but protecting her diplomatic usefulness seemed an important thing to do.

She shuddered. If this got out, no one would ever trust her again, not completely. All this, to get the potential identity of a man who was currently winning the space race – and who might keep winning it, whether one knew who he was or not.

She had worked so very hard all her life to be above the ebb and flow of day-to-day politics, to be a steady hand, utterly dependable, a beacon of integrity. Every day there were little compromises, and sometimes big ones, that had to be made, unsavoury people one had to be polite to, public gestures one wanted to make, but couldn't. But those were things that her ministers required her do, never things she did on her own and kept secret from them. And even though this wasn't her plan in the slightest – quite the opposite – it would be seen that way.

Her ship, her responsibility.

The trouble was, if she told MI5 about even the merest chance that such a thing might happen, so they could stop it, the idea that it *could* have happened would always be there. Some people might see it as heroic, but others would condemn it as idiotic, and the taint would never leave. And if the KGB found out? What then?

She thought back to her conversation with Margaret about the royal train. At that point, Sandra Pole and her chihuahua seemed the biggest threat to her personal safety. Ha! She laughed aloud in the empty room.

Oh, it was personal, and she *was* being selfish. She knew that, too. The royal train was useful and she was grateful to have it, but as she travelled the world, *Britannia* was her home from home. Her father had died just as the new royal yacht was finally ordered, and she and Philip had stepped in to update the design of the interior together, so it was exactly the way they wanted it. Not gilt-edged and florid as proposed, but quite plain and pared back, as befitting those times of austerity. Anyway, comfortable simplicity and family-friendliness suited them both.

In fact, their shared vision for the project had made her realise more deeply than ever how well suited she and Philip were for each other. He loved *Britannia* as much as she did. Unlike most of her predecessors, they hadn't built any castles, palaces or fortresses together. *Britannia* was it, and they had spent their happiest times on the ship, from the high seas of the Pacific to the icy waters of the North Sea. In the middle of a gruelling royal tour on the far side of the world, having the safe, familiar routine of the royal yacht to return to was what made it possible.

It wasn't just the yacht. The officers, around twenty of them at any time, ran the ship with exceptional British efficiency, which was the envy of any port they visited. And then there was the crew, the two hundred loyal 'yotties' drawn from the Royal Navy, who often worked there for years, and had become one's friends.

All of that, all of it, would go if anyone got a hint of Joan's little theory. Because if anyone did, it would be around the Government in seconds. It would make the headlines. The Queen knew how these things worked.

And right now, a little theory was all that it was. Just a series of coincidences on a few pieces of paper on a jotting pad.

The Queen rubbed her arms through her cardigan sleeves. Outside, it had started to rain. Nevertheless, she felt a strong need to be out in the elements again. She slipped down to the Dog Door using passages normally reserved for the servants. She hoped to calm her brain as she walked, but it didn't work. In fact, she got crosser.

Elizabeth didn't often envy her multiple-great ancestor, Charles I, who had lost his head at Whitehall, but back then, the monarch could say what he thought and do what he liked. Since Parliament got involved, one had been put very much in one's place. For the last six hundred years there had been an unspoken understanding that, step out of line by as much as half an inch, and the future of the monarchy would be in doubt. There was no divine right of kings, the Constitution (not that it actually existed, except as a series of habits and conventions) was what mattered, and one had jolly well better look out.

At the Dog Door, she slipped on her coat and hat, and walked, head down, into the drizzle.

Well, she had looked out. She did look out. She did it every day, and toed the line, and only poked her nose in where it was wanted, and said the most unobjectionable things to the most objectionable people to keep her ministers happy, and today, she just wanted to go for a very long ride, or stand here on the terrace and scream. But she didn't. Instead, she had an inkling of an idea about what to do next.

Right now, *Britannia* was alongside at Gibraltar for a day, on the way to Tunisia with the Queen Mother on board. No doubt some would see the visit as a jolly, but her mother would quite frankly rather be at Clarence House, given the choice. The royal widow's visit to the revolutionary President Bourguiba was a diplomatic mission. She was there to wave the British flag as hard as possible before Bourguiba was received by the President and Mrs Kennedy in Washington in a couple of weeks.

From there, the yacht and its crew would sail to Italy, where the Queen would fly out to meet them in Sardinia. On the twenty-ninth of the month. At a port that contained a well-known café called the Genovese.

Of course, the correct thing to do would be for her to tell Joan to raise her concerns with her lover at MI5, to expose Michalowski's plan, and to live with the consequences. But those consequences were big. Before pressing the button, the Queen needed to know if the plan was real.

If it *was*, then some poor Soviet dissident was risking his life, relying on a harebrained scheme that could never work. Her first thought had been that they would have killed him by now anyway, if they had killed Michalowski, but apparently Major Ross at MI5 thought they hadn't yet worked out who he was.

Whoever Michalowski's contact was on *Britannia*, she needed to talk to him first, and warn him to put the assignation off, and ideally change the plan altogether. As it was, she felt that the poor man (the dissident, not the yottie, for whom she felt nothing but fury) was walking into a trap. He would be assuming safe passage, and instead, he'd be in the heart of a potential political time bomb.

The Queen had an idea that her mother might be able to help without alerting all and sundry, and as it happened, she was briefly contactable this afternoon, while *Britannia* was in port. To prepare, Elizabeth needed to talk to an experienced naval officer – the Master of the Household would do – and tell him a convincing string of lies.

Honestly, it wasn't ideal, but it wouldn't be the first time. She spent a significant part of her life pretending not to know things she *did* know, and not to care about things she cared about very much. What was it about her that meant she so often found herself solving problems she wasn't supposed to? she wondered.

The Queen knew the answer, really, and it lay in her red boxes, and in those damask-hung rooms where she entertained. She had sight of state secrets, and the private lives of the rich and famous (and more to the point, the rich and infamous), and if you had any intelligence at all, you couldn't help putting two and two together occasionally, even if it wasn't officially your job. She had thought to make her life easier by getting Joan to help her, but her APS was just as bad. Joan had the same level of curiosity as the Queen and was just as susceptible to finding out information that could do her more harm than good.

What was the solution?

As she was pondering that existential question, the Dog Door opened again and Whisky and Sugar, the two senior corgis, padded over to her across the terrace, as if this was a perfectly normal time for a walk. Their cheerful wagginess turned out to be just what the doctor ordered. She crouched down to greet them, and as she did so, she remembered the wise words of her grandmother, Queen Mary. *It's not about you, it's about the job, so don't take yourself too seriously. You must simply do what's possible and carry on.*

She petted the dogs and stood up again, breathing in the damp air and looking down at the plane trees and horse chestnuts lining the Long Walk, which lifted her spirits a little. And in a week's time, she reminded herself, thanks to *Britannia* she and Philip would be sailing the Aeolian Islands off Sicily together. She tried to ignore the near future and focus on that instead.

Feeling better, she spent the next five minutes working out exactly what tissue of lies to spin to the Master of the Household in a few minutes in order to find out who on board her yacht might be capable of hiding away something as large and unmissable as a human being, without the poor man having the slightest clue what she was talking about.

If one was going to lie so shamelessly, one had better do it well.

Chapter 33

Shortly before tea, Rear Admiral Nick Cotterill arrived at the Queen's study feeling cheerful. There were times in the running of the royal palaces when life was strained for the Master of the Household – but this wasn't one of them. All was rosy, and soon his large team would have the castle and Buckingham Palace to themselves, while the royal couple went on tour to Italy. They would use the time to catch up, deep clean, take a breath and get ready for a busy summer. He was looking forward to it.

The Queen seemed a little more tetchy than usual, and he put it down to hunger or some feminine ailment. Nevertheless, she was inquiring and polite. She asked after his daughter, who was hoping to go to university in September, his son, who was a demon bowler for the school cricket team, and the dogs and guinea pigs, of whom there were many – all of them on top form.

'I have a question for you, Master,' she said. 'I know you were fond of your time on HMS *Aurora*.'

'Absolutely, ma'am,' he agreed. 'She was a happy ship. Those were golden days.'

'Yes, so I gathered. You know the navy better than anyone.'

'Oh, I wouldn't say that, ma'am. I—'

'And you served on *Britannia*, of course.'

'For my sins. Those trips to the Western Isles were always a pleasure.'

The Queen nodded. 'It helps that you know the ship so well. The thing is, I want to do something rather difficult.'

'Oh?' There wasn't much that was difficult for Her Majesty. Her staff – men like him – were there to make sure of that.

'I'm getting Prince Philip something rather unusual from Venice, while we're away,' she explained. 'It's for his birthday in June, and it's rather large, and I need somewhere to store it on *Britannia* without him finding out. It has to be a surprise.'

The Master threw his mind back to his *Britannia* days. The royals themselves had decent-sized rooms on board, but crew cabins were small and snug. Working areas, too, were tightly managed and immaculately kept. However, there was stowage for everything from Her Majesty's Rolls-Royce to the fresh flowers that could be kept in chilled storage to last for weeks. A decent-sized nook or cranny could undoubtedly be found.

'Oh, but that's easy, ma'am,' he assured her. 'I'm sure anyone on the crew would help you. You need only say the word . . .'

She raised a hand. 'You'd think so, Master, wouldn't you? But the trouble is, there's a bet.'

She explained that the Duke of Edinburgh strongly suspected her birthday surprise, and had made a significant wager that she wouldn't be able to keep it secret for more than twenty-four hours. He'd be doing whatever he could to find out.

'I want to know who, of the crew, is best placed to stash it somewhere secretly for me. Just one man, ideally. I always find the fewer people who know, the less chance of anything going wrong.'

'The Commanding Officer, ma'am . . . Admiral Marlow.' *Britannia* was not a large ship by naval standards, but as she contained the Queen, she had to be captained by one of the most senior men in the navy. Marlow was one of the best.

'I'm sure he'd love to help me if he could, Master,' she said, 'but he's too far removed from the gubbins of the ship, if you know what I mean. Admiral Marlow would look very out of place sneaking around in the stores. People might talk.'

'He could arrange for it to be done for you though.'

'True.' The Queen looked mildly annoyed. She had obviously thought of this already.

'You mean, who would *he* ask to help you?'

'I do.'

Cotterill gave it some thought. 'I see what you mean, ma'am. Any yottie could bring something aboard, but he'd need help putting it somewhere, and he'd have to ask permission. Secrecy would be problematic.'

'What about the head chef, for example?' she asked. 'I know he gets in large supplies when the ship's alongside. I imagine others do, too.'

'True, ma'am.' Cotterill considered the idea. 'But you say you want just one man, and the difficulty is putting the package somewhere that other seamen wouldn't trip over it. They'd pick up if it was something unusual, especially if primed to look by the Duke. If your man wanted to keep it secret, he'd have to find a spot out of the way, and square it with the supply officer.' He smiled. 'In fact, *he'd* be the man you're looking for.'

'The supply officer? That's Commander Kinnock, I believe' the Queen said. 'I remember talking to him last summer.'

'I don't know the man. But he'll have his eye on all the supplies – anything that comes on board that isn't a man or a weapon – and he's in charge of where they go. He could put something aside for you, ma'am. He knows where there's space, and his orders wouldn't be questioned.'

'That's very helpful, Master.'

Cotterill had another thought.

'Or there's the executive officer, I suppose. Commander Attwell, I believe it is at the moment. He reports to the CO, but he runs the ship on a day-to-day basis, so it wouldn't seem odd to find him checking a storeroom or a cabin, or asking a yottie to cart something around and keep schtum. I doubt anyone except the supply officer or Admiral Marlow would dare challenge him. Does that help, ma'am?'

'It does, Master. Very much.'

'And of course, Attwell is the new press secretary's uncle, so he'd definitely be the one to go for.'

The Queen looked startled. 'Is he?'

'Didn't you know? Yes, Stonor's mother's brother. Dominic must have mentioned it.'

'He hasn't, actually.'

The Master was impressed by the young man's restraint. 'Good man. Doesn't want to hang on family coat-tails. Attwell's a decent chap, too, I understand. Very by the book, but I'm sure he'd make an exception for your little surprise, ma'am. Or not so little.' He gave the Queen a conspiratorial smile.

'That's just what I needed to know,' she said. 'Thank you.'

'A pleasure. And your secret's safe with me, ma'am.'

He tapped his nose. The Master was pretty sure he'd already guessed what the surprise would be. Who would go to Venice and not bring back some decent Murano glass? Her Majesty probably had her eye on a chandelier or a large Venetian mirror of some sort.

He wondered how much the wager was. Knowing the Queen and her husband, it was probably who would do the washing up after a barbecue in the summer. It wouldn't matter a jot to anyone else, but if they'd bet on it, it would matter very much to them.

Chapter 34

An hour later, the Queen Mother returned to *Britannia*, at anchor in Gibraltar, after a pleasant little trip ashore, and discovered that her daughter would like to speak to her as soon as possible. A telephone line had been hooked up to the royal apartments. When she was ready, it was patched through to her bedroom aboard.

'Hello, Lilibet,' she said. 'Has something awful happened? Is Charles all right? How are the dogs?'

'They're perfectly fine,' the Queen told her. 'How's the journey so far?'

'The Bay of Biscay was flat as glass. Picture that! The band have learned some new dance tunes, which I'm very much enjoying. I've written you a letter. It'll get to you eventually.'

'I know you've got bit more time at sea coming up,' the Queen said. 'Could you find a moment to have a word with a couple of people on board, individually, and call me again as soon as you get to Tunis to tell me what they said?'

'Of course, darling. Who shall I talk to?'

With the Master's unwitting help, Elizabeth had narrowed the suspects down to two senior officers. Now she needed to discover which of them was responsible for the assignation in

Cagliari. If indeed there *was* an assignation. Assuming Joan's insight was right, and not just a series of coincidences after all.

Without explaining the background, she outlined her plan. What she loved about her mother – one of the many things – was that the older Elizabeth didn't question it for a moment, however odd it was, and even though it would involve her lying, too.

'Commander Kinnock and Commander Attwell? Is that right?' the Queen Mother checked.

'Yes, Mummy.'

'And to look out for the one who looks appalled? I assure you, darling, nobody looks appalled when I ask them to do something. It's in the job description not to.'

'It won't be obvious,' the Queen suggested. 'But you'll spot it.'

'How exciting!' Her mother's delight was audible down the phone. 'Are we in the middle of some huge spy drama? I do hope so.'

The Queen laughed at the very idea, as if it was the furthest thing from her mind.

Two days of anxious waiting passed, while *Britannia* sailed along the north coast of Africa

On Sunday, back in Windsor, there was a celebratory service for the Queen's birthday in St George's Chapel, full of pomp and circumstance and gothic grandeur. It was absolutely beautiful, but Elizabeth's mind was entirely elsewhere. She only just managed to return Canon Vaughan's smile when he grinned at her from the choir.

Monday, the twenty-fourth of April came and went without news, while the Queen and Prince Philip returned to London. Despite a howling gale at sea, *Britannia* safely docked in Tunis on the twenty-fifth, and before disembarking, the Queen Mother arranged to speak to her daughter at the palace as soon as a phoneline could be established.

She sounded excited.

'It was just as you said, Lilibet. Quite astonishing. I spoke to the executive officer, the *lovely* Commander Attwell, first of all. He really is the most attentive, charming man. He's Dominic Stonor's uncle, did you know?'

'Yes, Mummy.'

'A very attractive chap. It runs in the family. And I told him I'd had this idea that I really wanted to explore the port in Cagliari when we got there after this visit – although why I would, darling, I honestly can't imagine. There are many ports I'd love to explore but Cagliari isn't one of them. It was bombed to pieces in the war. Anyway, I said I knew he'd be busy on the twenty-ninth, what with you arriving and everything, but I was sure he had all that under control and it would be an enormous personal favour to me if he could spare an hour to accompany me on a little tour of the place . . . And the man was utterly delighted. Really, Lilibet, his whole face lit up, and I feel awful for letting him down when I change my mind later.'

'What about the supply officer?' the Queen asked. Trefor Kinnock was in charge of the logistics of furnishing the ship with everything from fuel to food and feather pillows. He was a bluff Welshman who'd been in post for nearly two years and was popular with the crew.

'That was the astonishing thing,' her mother said. 'I told Commander Kinnock the same story, and his face dropped like a stone the moment I mentioned Cagliari. Normally he's so cheery. And when I said I wanted him to come with me ... Well, I might as well have shot him. I said of course he would be very busy, and he said yes, ma'am, extremely, and under any other circumstances he'd be honoured to accompany me but ... Well, frankly darling, he said no. Nobody does that.'

'Do you think he *was* just worried about being busy that day?' the Queen asked.

'It's true, he would be, although anyone else would just delegate and get on with it. That's what they do on *Britannia*, isn't it? They work miracles. That's why it's so lovely here. But he looked really quite unwell.'

'Thank you, Mummy.'

'Does that answer your question?'

'I'm afraid it does.'

'Has he done something awful?'

'Quite possibly.'

'Should I say something to him?'

'Definitely not, Mummy. Be extra charming, if anything. Don't worry, I'll deal with it.'

'Very well, Lilibet. I must go now. President Bourgiba is waiting to receive me in his palace. It'll cause a diplomatic incident if I'm not there.'

'Good luck,' the Queen said. 'You'll be wonderful.'

'Thank you. Give my love to the children. I'll see you very soon, my darling.'

And that was the problem. She would. They'd be meeting in Cagliari in a matter of days. And everything had to be sorted out by then.

The Queen knew who her man was now. It seemed Joan was right all along. Could they stop him? She could only hope.

Chapter 35

Two confidential telegrams had been prepared over the weekend: one for *Britannia's* executive officer and one for the chief supply officer. After the Queen's phone call, one was sent to Commander Kinnock aboard *Britannia*, saying simply:

> *The plan for Cagliari has been discovered. An alternative is essential. Send an order for twenty boxes of asparagus from Sandringham to show that you have received this message.*

At Buckingham Palace, Joan checked with her source in the Royal Household who monitored the royal yacht's communications for orders of anything they might need to bring out with them on the flight from London. But no request for asparagus came. There was no response at all for the next three days, while the Queen Mother carried out her official visit.

Meanwhile, the Queen's days were packed with visits from diplomats, audiences with ministers, formal events and last-minute dress fittings. She made time each evening to be with the children, who were more clamorous than usual for her attention, knowing they'd soon be without it for a week.

There wasn't time to think about much else, but she used what little time she had to reassure herself that Joan had been *wrong* about Cagliari, or that Commander Kinnock was playing a more sophisticated game than she would have given the man credit for. Perhaps her mother had misread his horrified reaction to her tour proposal for the twenty-ninth, and he had ignored the anonymous ultimatum because he had no idea what the message was talking about. If so, she had never been more pleased to have been mistaken. Alternatively, he must have made other arrangements without choosing to announce the fact, which was also a relief.

Either way, there were other things to occupy her mind. In the skies above Cape Canaveral, an unmanned rocket ship had survived a misfire from one of its boosters – but it didn't bode well for the Americans' proposed attempt to launch their own man into space. In Africa, Sierra Leone became the latest nation to declare its independence from Great Britain, making friendship with countries like Tunisia all the more vital. The Queen knew her mother would be beaming her way through the visit, but she would be working hard.

Meanwhile, in London, it rained so much that even the ducks began to be sick of it.

Philip, a sailor at heart, was eager to be at sea again on the royal yacht. They'd managed to arrange it so that they had a couple of free days aboard *Britannia* before the official visit started. He happily watched the days tick by. As they headed for the plane on the twenty-ninth, the Queen told herself that *Britannia* was safe, and everything would be all right.

It went wrong almost immediately.

In amongst the paperwork in her boxes, which she didn't have a chance to look at until she was in the air, the Queen found a note from Joan, who saw her pick it up and gave her an anxious look from her seat at the rear of the plane. It said that one of Hector Ross's sources in Vienna had heard rumours that a visiting Russian chess player had gone missing in the city two days ago. The Russians were trying to keep it quiet, but they were desperately searching. A defection, it seemed, was underway. And from exactly where she'd feared it might happen.

There were a couple of unexpected details. The chess player was a woman, called Tatiana Sokolova. And she'd gone missing with a child, believed to be a girl. Major Ross was travelling out personally to see if he could find them, though by now he held out little hope.

'Are you all right, Cabbage?' Philip asked. 'You look like you've seen a ghost.'

'Oh, just the Russians,' she said.

'Ah. No bombs actually in the air, I hope?'

'Not yet.'

'They haven't put another man in space already, have they?'

'Not that, either.'

Later, leaning to look out of the window as the plane came in to land, Philip barked out, 'Bloody hell. More rain.'

The Queen had to inspect the guard of honour on the airfield from under a big umbrella. Her spirits lifted slightly when she met up with her mother, who had come ashore to greet them. Together, they drove to the harbour where *Britannia* looked magnificent as ever, sitting a little way offshore, blue paint gleaming, the ship's company lining the decks immaculately, flags fluttering in the breeze.

'You'll want to see Commander Kinnock for whatever business you have together,' the older Elizabeth said quietly, on the way out to the yacht. 'I've told him I don't need him after all, but that you wanted to have a few words. He looked perfectly cheerful, darling. I'm sure he has no idea what's coming.'

But it was impossible to do that straightaway. The yotties were delighted to have the royal couple back again, and Philip was in his element. There were officers and seamen to congratulate on marriages, babies, promotions and sporting achievements. There were upgrades to the navigational equipment to admire. Everyone was happy and relaxed, as if they had all the time in the world. In fact, it was already eleven thirty, and the Queen needed to be certain that by one o'clock, nobody would be heading to the Caffè Genovese to cause a diplomatic incident. At eleven forty-five, she said she needed to see the supply officer very briefly in her private sitting room.

He arrived with an amiable smile on his face.

'Your Majesty, what an absolute joy to have you back again.'

'Thank you, Commander Kinnock.'

Kinnock was a short and broad man, with a warm baritone voice, and a weatherbeaten face made entirely of horizontals. A cauliflower ear was the result of a rugby injury. His eyes were small and bright, and friendly. He glanced at one of the armchairs in her office, but she didn't ask him to sit down. The Queen remained standing, too. Meetings were quicker this way.

'It's been wonderful to have Her Majesty aboard,' he said, referring to the Queen Mother. 'I hope she enjoyed the trip. I think she did.' He was beginning to look slightly nervous. 'Music nights are always special when she's—'

'Commander, did you get my message?' the Queen cut in.

The blood drained from his face. 'Ma'am? I don't think so. A special message from you? I'm sorry it must have—'

'An anonymous message,' she said. 'Telling you to order asparagus. You didn't answer.'

His eyes shot wide open. 'That was from you? I thought it was a mistake. I don't understand. I'm not sure what I'm supposed to have—'

'You're supposed to have been in contact with a Russian defector,' she said. There wasn't time to muck about. 'She recently escaped in Vienna, apparently.'

'No, ma'am! What?' he spluttered. 'I mean . . .' He shook his head and laughed. 'I don't know what anyone's been telling you, but I assure you . . .'

She pursed her lips. 'I hope you took me seriously, Commander. And stop denying it so ridiculously, I haven't got time. Whatever happens, you're not going to the Caffè Genovese.'

'No!'

Finally, Kinnock had fully realised what trouble he was in. The naval officer glanced back at the chair and sank into it without permission. His legs had stopped working.

'Do you have any idea how much danger you're exposing the whole ship's company to?' she hissed. 'And me? The Duke? *Britannia*?'

He groaned quietly.

'Tell me you've made alternative arrangements,' she insisted. 'I've given you long enough. You had some sort of code you could send this woman from Tunis, surely?'

Kinnock looked as if he was about to be sick. When he looked up at her, his eyes were full of fear.

'No other plans,' he said dully. 'No point. Doctor Sokolova was uncontactable once she left Moscow for Vienna. And anyway, I could only contact her through a man called Michalowski, and he's dead.'

'So, she's still on her way here, to Cagliari? What will she do when you don't meet her?'

Kinnock shook his head and stared at the carpet. 'I don't know, ma'am. I can't imagine. I don't know if she even got out of Vienna safely.' He glanced up again. 'I have to be at the café.'

There was desperate supplication in his eyes. It wasn't what the Queen was used to on the face of her naval officers. When someone knocked at the door, she shouted at them that she was busy. *God, I sound like Philip*, she thought. But this was too important for niceties.

'I mean it,' she said. 'What will happen to her?'

Kinnock stared into the middle distance. 'Doctor Sokolova doesn't speak Italian. Her English is patchy. She has no money, no friends – apart from me. No identity documents to get her into England. I have those for her. They'll track her down very fast, I imagine. And kill her, probably.'

'And what about the girl?' the Queen asked. She was appalled beyond measure at this whole sorry mess. She had honestly convinced herself that she'd been imagining things.

Kinnock looked terrified.

'What girl?'

Chapter 36

The Queen needed time to think. She called for tea, and told the footman outside the door that Commander Kinnock had had some awful news, and please could someone tell her mother and husband that she would be a little bit delayed. Everyone would have to wait until she was ready. There were occasional advantages to being Queen.

'Oh,' she added, 'and can you tell Joan I need her?'

She sat down, finally.

'How did this happen?' she said furiously to Kinnock. 'Sokolova was in Vienna with a child, and you didn't even know?'

He told her of a conversation he'd had with Pavel Michalowski in London a couple of months ago, when he was on shore leave. They'd known each other since Kinnock's naval college days, when he would occasionally come up to town for parties and Michalowski seemed to be at most of them.

'Pav and I often chatted about my trips. He loved to travel; he wanted to know every detail. I'd told him we'd be docking in Venice in early May. At the time, he was just envious, ma'am, but afterwards he had this wild and crazy idea ... He needed help getting something out of Italy.

It matched so nicely with my trip to the Med. He said it was a package, but nothing shifty, ma'am – just something precious and important that he could only entrust to me. He couldn't believe that the timing would be so perfect. Then he admitted it was a person, not a package, and he said the timing wasn't totally perfect. They would have to hide for a few days . . .'

'And you didn't mind that your friend was asking you to smuggle someone out of the country, aboard my yacht?' the Queen demanded.

'I thought it was outrageous, ma'am. I thought he'd lost his mind, and I told him. The answer was no, obviously. And then he said it was a woman, and she had secrets about the Russian space programme, and this was a one-off opportunity to get hold of them. By a miracle, she'd been sent to Vienna, where she could escape if they managed it perfectly. And her life depended on safe passage at a crucial time . . .'

'And you said yes.'

'It wasn't quite that simple.'

But really, it was. Kinnock struggled to make excuses, but his bright eyes told the true story. His friend's 'wild and crazy idea' involved Kinnock playing James Bond to rescue a woman from behind the Iron Curtain and affect the space race. All he had to do was get her on board *Britannia* in Italy, and off again in England, and stop her from starving in the meantime. He'd stopped thinking of the bigger picture as he'd started to plan out the details.

'We couldn't pick her up in Venice, like Pav wanted,' Kinnock said, 'because she'd have to wait in Trieste, which was dangerous, and *Britannia* would be sitting off St Mark's Square then, like a shining star, with the whole world watching. So, it made more sense to do it here, in Cagliari, before your visit officially started, ma'am. Doctor Sokolova just had to get from the border at Trieste to Sardinia – no papers required – and I told Pav I'd meet her at the port with nobody watching. There's a storeroom I've set aside. There was the question of . . . minor sanitary issues. It doesn't have access to the heads. But with a bucket and a—'

'I'm sure you solved the minor sanitary issues,' the Queen told him sharply. 'But you didn't solve the major diplomatic nightmare of getting caught with a Russian on board my yacht.'

'I had it under control, ma'am. I—'

'You didn't, Mr Kinnock. I found out about it. And as you say, Michalowski's dead. There's a child he didn't tell you about. Goodness knows how she fits in. Come in!'

The knock at the door presaged a tea tray laden with fruit and cucumber sandwiches alongside the pot. It was brought in by Joan who had guessed what was happening and offered to take it off the steward who was delivering it from the galley.

'Sit down, Joan,' the Queen instructed. She poured tea for herself and Kinnock – who needed it, much as he didn't deserve it – and brought Joan quickly up to speed.

'There is no plan B,' she finished. 'Either someone from *Britannia* meets Doctor Sokolova and the girl at the café, or in all probability the KGB will kill her. If she isn't dead already. I think that's about the size of it. Sugar, Commander?'

'Yes, ma'am.'

'Cucumber sandwich?'

He could tell she was being scathing, and looked down at his shiny shoes.

'I can go,' Joan offered. 'I'm going to be there anyway.'

'And if you did, what then?' the Queen asked. 'Where do you take them?'

'I'm sure my friend would help,' Joan suggested. 'Her husband's attached to NATO.'

The Queen was trying to work out how they could quickly and safely get a NATO officer in Naples to take charge of a Russian defector with a child and poor English, when Kinnock said, 'It has to be me, ma'am. She'll only talk to me.'

They stared at him.

'Why?' Joan asked.

'Because Pavel had an escape that went wrong last year. He told me about it. The man got as far as a post office in West Berlin, but he mistook the contact and talked to the wrong person. He was dead by nightfall. I mean, I suppose Doctor Sokolova might trust another officer in British naval uniform at the café, but she's been told only to talk to me. I have everything ready. But I need to be there in . . .' He looked at his watch.

'Fifty minutes,' the Queen said. She was acutely aware of the time. 'And you don't have everything ready, Commander. What about the girl?'

'I can manage that,' he said. 'But I just can't . . .' He looked from her face to Joan's, desperate and pleading again. 'I can't leave them there.'

There wasn't time to find a better solution.

'Go,' the Queen said. 'We'll sort this out later.'

'I'll offer you my resignation in the—'

'Go!'

A few minutes afterwards, she bumped into her mother on her way to her bedroom to sort out her hair and regain some composure.

'Lilibet!' her mother said. 'I thought something terrible had happened!'

'It has,' the Queen assured her.

'Nobody's dead, I hope?'

'Not yet. Not as far as we know.'

And *Britannia*, which usually felt like the safest place in the world, suddenly offered no comfort at all.

Chapter 37

Joan sat at a table for two by the window of the Caffè Genovese, watching the door and scanning the people who walked by outside.

It was ten past five in the afternoon and the weather had cleared. Bustling Italians ordered pastries at the bar and guarded their shopping at nearby tables, pausing to stare briefly at the attractive redhead with the pale skin and very smart jacket, who stood out like a sore thumb.

Joan's friend had left an hour ago, after a stilted conversation. She could tell that Joan had a lot on her mind and put it down to working for Her Majesty at the start of a busy trip. She'd been sympathetic, and Joan didn't contradict her.

Kinnock had left the café when she got there, two hours after the original meeting time. He had simply shaken his head: no sign of Sokolova or the girl, and he was already very late to return to supervising the storage of everything they had brought with them from London, as well as the supplies he'd ordered to be delivered to the port.

Joan thought back to the image of the double portrait photograph she'd seen in Curzon Street: a woman with short dark hair, a broad brow and high cheekbones, like the girl beside her, and a look of great purpose in her eyes, a bit like those communist propaganda ads. Was this Sokolova after all? She kept checking every female face under every scarf, and the owner of every skinny pair of little girl's legs.

The barman had turned off the coffee machines and was starting to wipe down the counters. The café would be closing soon.

Had Sokolova gone to a hotel? Was she waiting somewhere else, nearby? Had she misread the message, or had she spotted a KGB agent lurking outside, keeping her at bay? Joan scanned the street for men who could be him. But she knew that if they were any good, they would blend in as well as any local. She pictured Hector in that position, on the lookout for someone in London. He would be such a part of the furniture that no one would notice him at all.

At twenty to six, the barman became surly and made gestures for her to leave. There was no point in lingering nearby: she wasn't what Sokolova was looking for, and if Kinnock was right, Sokolova wouldn't trust her anyway. Joan had hoped to keep her at the café long enough to explain the situation. Out in the street, she wouldn't have a chance.

A telephone rang at the back of the bar and the barman turned away to answer it. Joan was picking up her handbag when she heard him call out, 'Kinn-otch.' He was glaring in her direction. She stood up and raced over.

'Is you?' he asked. 'English, *si*?'

Joan nodded. He handed her the receiver.

'Commander Kinnock?' a thickly accented woman's voice asked.

'I work with him. I've been waiting for you,' Joan said. It seemed the quickest way to gain her trust, if she could. There was silence for a moment. 'He had to go back to the ship,' she added.

'Say to him . . .' A pause. The voice was low and sounded stressed and upset. 'Say to him I have trouble at the border. My girl is sick. Same time tomorrow.'

'We won't be here then,' Joan said urgently. 'We leave tonight.'

Another pause. 'Eleven. I be there at eleven morning. Tomorrow.'

'I'm sorry, we can't stay. Can I arrange to talk to you somehow? We can arrange a different meeting. I just need to—'

There was a click, a dull buzz, and the line fell silent. The barman saw the look on Joan's face and shrugged.

'*Gettoni*. Tokens. Finish.'

The line didn't ring again. Joan wondered if the lack of fresh tokens had just sounded two death sentences.

Across the harbour, *Britannia*'s flags waved gaily against pale pink clouds in a pale blue sky. In the street outside, men and women called out evening greetings to each other. The air smelled of salt and frying fish and dimly of diesel oil. Joan gathered up her things and headed back to the dock where a little launch would take her back to the yacht.

Chapter 38

'God, it's good to be back,' Philip said, wandering through the connecting door from his bedroom into the Queen's as he untied his bow tie.

She smiled briefly at him in her dressing table mirror and carried on removing the sapphires she'd worn at supper.

'You were very quiet, though, Cabbage. Busy week?'

'Very.'

He came to rest his hands on her shoulders.

'This is exactly what we need. Two whole days with nothing to worry about, except which island to sail to and what to have for lunch. Apparently, there were some hairy moments getting into port in Tunis with your mother. Boats in the welcoming flotilla sailed practically under the bow. The executive officer was telling me about it. He's invited me to join him in the wardroom with the other officers. You don't mind, do you? I won't be long.'

'Not at all,' the Queen said. 'I need to see the admiral anyway, about tomorrow.'

'I'll see you later, then.' He bent to kiss her cheek. '*A plus tard.*'

The Queen pursed her lips as she watched him go. Since saying goodbye to her mother, she'd had a few hours to think about this little meeting with the admiral. In fact, she'd thought of little else.

After Joan told her about the failed assignation and the phone call, her first reaction had been one of certainty, dim relief and great regret. There was nothing anyone could do; the royal yacht would be spared any hint of diplomatic danger; but two lives might well be lost. They were probably as good as lost already. A woman and a young girl were being hunted down by the KGB in a foreign country. In a day or two, news of their demise would probably appear in the Italian papers. What an awful tragedy.

Then uncertainty had crept in. *Was* there really nothing anyone could do? The relief had faded; the regret became altogether different. Now, she sighed deeply as she thought about what she had decided. But she knew she wouldn't change her mind.

The thing was, little Princess Anne, at home, was ten. The Queen wasn't sure she could love her brave, determined daughter more. And there was a little girl out there tonight, who had nowhere to go except *Britannia* in the morning. It made it real. It made it personal. Would she feel this way if the defector had been a man, alone? She couldn't say.

The rear of the ship contained the bedrooms and entertaining spaces for the royal family and their household. The front half was for the yotties and the administration of the ship. As she made her way down the familiar passages unaccompanied, the Queen took in the carpeted quiet and the very faint smell of fresh paint. Everything here was always impeccable and immaculate – unlike Buckingham Palace, which was practically falling down in various places, and Windsor, which was a thousand years old, and like the Forth Bridge in its constant need of redecoration and repairs.

The commanding officer was waiting for her in his suite below the bridge. Rear Admiral John Marlow was a highly competent, well-regarded sailor who'd served with distinction in the war and had commanded *Britannia* flawlessly for the last two years. This evening, the commanding officer was still in the 'Red Sea rig' of white shirt, black cummerbund and trousers that he had worn at dinner and subsequently, when she and Philip had discussed tomorrow's schedule with him, clustered around the maps that the navigation officer had laid out on the grand piano in the drawing room. Now, Marlow had those maps spread out on the dining table in his quarters. He looked up from them with a grin when she arrived.

'Ma'am! What can I get you? Are you amenable to a glass of port? I have one from Lisbon in '57. Only water? You disappoint me. I gather you had second thoughts about our schedule. I'm at your disposal. We'll be weighing anchor in a couple of hours, and we should be west of Sicily—' he indicated the large island that the Queen always thought of as a football at the toe of Italy's boot '—by dawn. Then the world's your oyster. Or at least, the Med is.'

She gave him a wry smile and a little shake of her head. 'I'm afraid it isn't, John. The plan has changed.'

'We're not going to Sicily?'

'We're not going at all.'

Marlow frowned in polite confusion. Royal plans did not change unless a head of state died, or the Government declared war or sanctions on another country

'Ma'am?'

'I'm waiting for something,' she told him. 'Please don't ask me what – you don't want to know. Only the supply officer has the full story, and please don't ask him either. It should have arrived today, but I'm told he can't get hold of it until midday tomorrow.'

The admiral raised his eyebrows a quarter of an inch, which, from a naval officer to the sovereign, was code for 'Bloody hell!'

'So we'll have to wait here until then,' she added with a shrug. 'Still at anchor. Easy to do, I know, and equally hard to explain. The Duke mustn't know either. I'm afraid he won't be pleased.'

Marlow had a crest of thick, grey hair and a mobile face that could switch from genial amusement to powerful authority in the blink of an eye. As he listened, the frown on his forehead was gradually replaced by an excited crinkling of his laugh lines. Getting anything past the Duke of Edinburgh was a challenge as great as navigating *Britannia* through the narrowest passages in the north coast of Scotland. And the Duke's frustration would be great. For his wife to suggest something to rile him, whatever she was waiting for must be pretty damn significant. Senior officers in the navy loved a challenge. Here was one.

'Did you have something in mind, ma'am?'

'Not at all,' she admitted. 'But I'm glad I've got you in charge, John. You had a busy war. What can keep us in port for over twelve hours? Possibly a little longer, to be on the safe side?'

He was thoughtful for several minutes. The Queen didn't rush him. She poured herself a glass of water from one of his decanters and made herself comfortable in one of his dining chairs. When he spoke, he was slow and measured; he was still thinking.

'I don't think it can be the engines. They're the obvious thing, but they famously don't break down, ma'am, and if they supposedly did, the post-mortem in Portsmouth when we got back would be relentless. I don't think our stokers could survive the interrogation. Alternatively, it's possible that we could require some special piece of equipment or little luxury for you or your household – something that has to be sourced from the mainland. The only trouble is, it might arrive too soon, or too late.'

'I know what you mean,' she said. 'I'd thought about that. We'd have no reason not to set sail as soon as it got here, whatever it was, and if it was held up longer than we really need, I think the Duke might blow a gasket.'

'Alternatively, someone might be suddenly very ill, and need to go ashore . . .'

'It's a thought.'

'Quite difficult to make them so apparently ill we can't treat them in the infirmary here, and yet fool the doctors in Naples when they get there. A heart attack, possibly?'

The Queen felt terrible at the idea of asking one of her yotties to fake a heart attack for a reason that she wouldn't be able to give him. The admiral was less concerned: naval officers would do anything for Her Majesty, up to and including pretending to be almost dead.

'The trouble is, though,' Marlow said, 'however bad it was, we could easily get him ashore by dawn, and then we wouldn't have an excuse to stay here. Do you mind, ma'am? I'm going to ask for coffee. Would you like anything?'

She declined, and the admiral put a quick internal call through to his steward. He paced up and down the room as he thought of solutions and rejected them.

'I'm sorry to do this to you,' she said.

Marlow brushed off the apology. 'You wouldn't ask unless it was vital. I'm trying to think of the last time I was on a ship that was stuck in port for any length of time that wasn't related to engine trouble, supply problems or a collision with a local vessel. The trouble is, the other boats are all behaving beautifully and keeping themselves at a distance. What we really need . . .' He stopped, and a smile spread slowly halfway up his face, where it seemed to hover and pause

'Oh?' the Queen asked. 'You had something?'

'I did, ma'am. Something I remember from Hong Kong. Not us, but another ship. A frightful mess. It did indeed take several hours to resolve and the beauty of it was, above the waterline you wouldn't know there was a problem. It was all below the surface, where frankly anything . . .' He paused again, lost in thought.

'Can I ask,' he said eventually, 'I don't want to press, but is it . . . is it a matter of life and death?'

'It rather is, actually.'

He rested his hands on the mahogany frame of one of the chairs. 'It's just that, if we do this, I'll have to . . . It'll turn into quite an operation, ma'am. We'll have to ask for help from HMS *Decoy*. Appropriately enough.'

'Really?'

Britannia always travelled with at least one warship from the Royal Navy as an escort, with a party of marines on board and also a helicopter, which was essential for ferrying the red boxes backwards and forwards from the mainland. For this trip, the destroyer HMS *Decoy* was currently anchored a little further out.

'What do we need her for?'

'Perhaps it's better if I don't tell *you*, ma'am. Then it can be a nice surprise in the morning. Ah, thank you, Petty Officer.'

Marlow's steward deposited a tray with a pot of piping-hot coffee on the table, and withdrew. The captain poured himself a cup.

'It has the advantage that it's complicated, so outrageous that nobody will question we really mean it, but it's not unduly dangerous. Will that do?'

The Queen thought of her young daughter, tucked up safe at home, and nodded her assent. Anything less seemed doomed to failure of one sort or another.

'I'll need to let the commander know,' he said. 'And a couple of men in the engine room. But they'll keep schtum, don't worry. The captain of *Decoy* served with me on my last frigate; he's a good man who won't ask unnecessary questions. I'll need to have a quiet word with one of his men, explaining what we need fully, but I know the man in question. Needless to say, he'll love it, leap at the chance. There will be expenses, I'm afraid.' Marlow looked at the Queen and shrugged. 'Nothing the navy can't afford. It could be a good training opportunity for all concerned. Leave it with me, ma'am.'

By now, he looked positively energised.

What have I done? the Queen thought.

Chapter 39

One of the many things that made *Britannia* so restful, normally, was that the yotties used hand signals to give instructions instead of shouting, and wore soft-soled shoes on deck, so the royals weren't disturbed in their rest by a crew of two hundred going about their business. The Queen's bedroom was a haven of quiet, until Philip came storming into it through the connecting door into his own, at shortly after six in the morning.

'Wake up, Lilibet. You'll never believe this. We're still in Cagliari! We haven't moved an inch all bloody night!'

'Oh dear,' she said, sitting up. 'What's happened?'

'Some bastard fisherman has snagged his nets on our port side propeller. Or it could be a cable or line of some sort, it's been too dark to tell. I woke up expecting to see a nice expanse of the Med with the coast of Sicily in the distance, but it's the same bloody view as yesterday. I spoke to John Marlow and he's as furious as I am.'

'How awful.' She glanced out of the window. 'And on such a lovely day for sailing, too.'

'Too bloody right. But the damn propeller won't bloody turn however much steam we throw at it, and we're waiting for a diver from *Decoy* to go down and sort it out. Pray to God it's something he can cut with a knife and get us on our way by breakfast.'

'Gosh, I hope so.'

Philip came and sat on the end of her bed. 'Dammit, Cabbage. I don't often get the chance to helm this ship and thought I had two days of it, in good weather, just like the old days.'

His lips clamped together as he looked out at the sky that was turning from pink to blue, flecked with light and fluffy clouds, just like the sort of thing Renaissance painters used to do to indicate heaven. He really had been looking forward to their two days of freedom aboard *Britannia*, and she never failed to forget that if he hadn't married her, he'd have commanded other ships in the navy and had many years doing what he really loved and was good at – rather than following in her wake, always two steps behind, trying to put a thousand strangers at their ease, which had mixed results at the best of times.

The Queen felt awful, and said so.

'Hardly your fault,' he grunted.

She gave him a hopeful smile. 'But we'll have this afternoon and tomorrow before we need to be in Naples.'

'We'll spend half of that chugging backwards and forwards.'

'And Venice,' she added, which was the bit of this trip she was most looking forward to. She dreamed of being a tourist in one of the most romantic cities in the world.

He harrumphed. 'Stuck in a traffic jam on the Grand Canal, with a hundred paparazzi on every bridge, no doubt.'

Oh dear. He was beyond consolation. However, this was ideal for her purposes. The Queen glanced at the wristwatch on her bedside. Five and a half hours until, God willing, Sokolova and the child would be safely gathered in, and she could work out what the hell to do about it.

So, the yacht apparently had a propeller caught on something, did it? She was curious to see what would happen next.

Joan was as astonished as the Duke of Edinburgh to see, on waking, that the yacht was still at anchor. At first, she assumed that something genuinely bad must have caused the delay, but she quickly came to suspect that such fortuitous things didn't happen by accident. Not where Her Majesty was concerned. She began to see yesterday's phone call at the café in a new light.

The talk in the household dining room at breakfast was all about the 'very dishy' navy diver (Lady Sarah's brother had served with him on another ship), who had been borrowed from HMS *Decoy* to go under the waterline and see what was interfering with the propeller.

'How long do they think it will take?' Joan asked.

'No idea,' Hattie Cowell said with a dramatic shrug. 'Possibly hours. Depends what he finds. They're getting a boat ready with one of those blowtorches they use in factories. There's lots of little local boats gathering, too. It's become quite the spectacle.'

Joan was on her way to find Kinnock, the supply officer, when she was buttonholed by Dominic Stonor in one of the passageways.

'The most extraordinary thing!' he said. 'My uncle, Commander Attwell, you know, was on the bridge last night when they found the problem. He tried to get the engineers to restart the propellers and see if they could just blow the thing off, but they wouldn't hear of it. Said it might do even further damage.'

'I'm sure they know what they're doing,' Joan said, distracted.

'I suppose so, but I'd have thought it was worth a try. The Queen'll be livid.'

'I'm sorry, Dominic, I'm needed somewhere,' she said, gesturing vaguely down the passageway. After he let her go, she speed-walked as fast as she could to the operational side of the ship, to find Commander Kinnock.

The supply officer was in his own little office, not much larger than a telephone box, knee-deep in paperwork. He looked round, stony-faced. There were bags under his eyes, and he had the air of a condemned man.

'Oh, it's you,' he grunted. They'd spoken briefly yesterday afternoon, when Joan had updated him on the phone call. 'Does Her Majesty want my resignation yet?'

Joan frowned. 'You are going back, aren't you?' she asked.

'Going where?'

'To the café.'

Kinnock's eyes narrowed. 'Come in and shut the door.'

Joan stood with her back to the wall, taking up the available space. 'She said she'd get there by eleven,' she reminded him.

Kinnock shook his head ruefully. 'We'll have gone by then. This propeller business will be sorted out pretty quickly I imagine. Then we'll be—'

'D'you really think this propeller business is an accident?'

Kinnock goggled at her. '*What?* But . . .'

'I'm on my way to check. But you need to be ready when the time comes. You have an excuse to tell the executive officer, right?'

He was still goggling. 'But who . . . ?'

'Who d'you think?'

'She can't . . .'

'I think she just did.'

He stuttered his words out. 'I-I mean, I can always find an excuse, b-but . . .'

'Just be ready,' Joan said.

He nodded dumbly.

The Queen was working on her boxes when Joan knocked at her sitting room door.

'How's the rescue operation going?' she asked.

Joan curtsied and grinned. 'I've just checked, Your Majesty. They're not having much luck so far.'

'Ah. I didn't think they would be.'

Joan suspicions were confirmed. 'I mean, goodness, ma'am. A destroyer, and a navy diver.'

'The captain thought it through, and this seemed the best way.'

'He knows the story, ma'am?' Joan asked.

'He knows we need a reason still to be here. The thing is, it needs to be so big that most people won't question it, but also small enough that Admiral Marlow can manage it tightly.'

'Does the diver know who asked for the delay?'

'No. And even the captain doesn't know *why*, exactly. But he knows I wouldn't ask if I thought there was any other way. Now, have you seen the supply officer this morning?'

Joan briefly described their meeting, including Kinnock's repeated offer to resign.

'Assure him that he's safe. For now. But tell him we can't wait here forever.' The Queen looked out of the window at the almost cloudless skies. 'Tell him we leave at two. Sooner, of course, if he's back by then. That should give him plenty of time.'

Chapter 40

Prince Philip spent the next few hours on deck and on the bridge, turning increasing shades of purple.

'One bloody cable! Half a day lost! A whole day, at this rate. And we've become free entertainment for half the fishermen and yacht owners in Sardinia.'

The Queen felt terrible for him, but also enormously grateful, which he would never know. It wasn't as if her husband wouldn't have delighted in the truth as much as Rear Admiral Marlow did, or have agreed to keep it secret. He'd have tried valiantly at both. But the trouble was, Philip had sailed round the world with several of these men. They had shared beard growing contests, high seas adventures, visions of the icebergs of Antarctica and many, many drinks and laughs together in the Pacific. They knew him like family, and brilliant though her husband was at many things, inscrutability wasn't one of them. That was more her department. If even one or two people guessed that he was hiding something, it would be round the yacht by teatime.

Instead, his absolute and justifiable frustration was a big distraction from what was really going on. If any sailor paused to think why they hadn't heard all the noises associated with a moving propeller caught on cabling last night, he was soon focused more on the effect on the Duke of Edinburgh, which was vivid and undeniable.

Eleven o'clock rolled by. The band of the Royal Marines put on an impromptu concert on deck for the household and any local Sardinians who'd sailed close enough to watch. As she listened to them play, the Queen pictured Commander Kinnock at the Caffè Genovese and prayed that by now he had taken charge of a scared but safe woman and a little girl.

At twelve o'clock, there was no sign of him, however. He had said he would get a message to Joan when he got back. By one, no message had come.

The Queen's nerves jangled. It had sounded from Sokolova's call to Joan as if getting to Cagliari by eleven might be a stretch, but the scientist originally seemed confident that she could be there for one. With luck, they would be getting into whatever disguise or subterfuge Kinnock had arranged for them, and setting off across the harbour.

Lunch on board with Philip and the captain was a desultory affair. At a quarter to two, she decided enough was enough. Kinnock knew when his deadline was. She put down her knife and fork and said to the admiral beside her, 'John, I do *hope* your marvellous diver can be finished within the next half-hour or so, so we can set sail reasonably soon afterwards. Is that within the realms of possibility?'

'I'll see how he's getting on, ma'am,' Marlow promised. 'These things are notoriously tricky. They can go on forever, or resolve themselves suddenly, out of nowhere.'

*

Ten minutes later, the yacht's fast motorboat delivered Kinnock aboard. Soon afterwards, Joan arrived at the veranda deck, where the Queen was watching the sailors cheer the successful diver from HMS *Decoy*.

Fortunately, they were alone.

'Is everyone safe?' the Queen asked.

'No, ma'am.'

'Oh, God! No sign of them?'

'Actually,' Joan said, 'just as he was about to leave, the person in question rang the bar again and told him she got as far as Naples, but it was swarming with police – in preparation for your visit, ma'am – and she panicked and missed her connection. She and the girl are heading back to Trieste, where she was staying before.'

'Isn't that very dangerous?'

'Probably. It's her best option, as she sees it.'

'What then?' the Queen asked

'I don't know, ma'am. But she gave a contact address, a bookshop in Trieste. She'll check it once a day. She seems to think Kinnock can still sort something out.'

'He can't!'

'No, ma'am. But there's someone who might be able to think of a . . .'

Before they could talk any further, Philip walked up to join them.

'Thank Christ for that! He's cut the bloody cable. Blown it to smithereens, in fact, with a decent length of det cord. I saw the explosion underwater. Oh, hullo, Joan. Bad news from home?'

'Good news, sir, actually,' Joan said. 'I was just telling Her Majesty.'

'And who *is* it?' the Queen asked, as if carrying on a conversation. Which she was.

The royal couple both looked at Joan curiously, though the Queen's curiosity was sharper.

'The head of D Branch at MI5,' Joan said. 'Apparently, he has experience of Italy. He might be able to help.'

'Ah, fought up here during the war, I should imagine,' Philip offered, donning his sunglasses. 'Fascinating what connections the spooks made in those days. Standing them in good stead now, I shouldn't wonder.'

'You might talk to him,' the Queen said to Joan. 'When you can.'

'Thank you, ma'am.'

Joan left them to it. Philip, now that it was over, was already reframing the 'snagged propeller incident' as a nice little anecdote to tell his friends at home. His mood was almost as sunny as it had been dark. He was looking forward to 'driving the boat' this afternoon, and dropping anchor somewhere idyllic this evening.

'That diver johnny deserves a medal, don't you think?' he asked.

The Queen heartily agreed.

Privately, she also reflected that she had just given her APS permission to tell a senior officer in MI5 that *Britannia* had been used in a failed attempt to help a Russian defector, which, if she remembered correctly, was *exactly*, literally *exactly*, what she had originally set out to avoid.

But Joan trusted Major Ross, and he was pretty much the only person who could get them out of the increasingly deep hole the Queen was digging for them. And he might save two lives in the process. He might also give the UK a winning hand of some sort in the space race, but right now, it was the frightened woman and the little girl she couldn't help thinking about.

If you didn't save a life when you could, was that the same as taking one? It had always seemed a very abstract and theoretical concept to her before, but now she was faced with it, the Queen felt she had no choice.

Save a life – two lives, in fact – and face the consequences. It was simple and awful at the same time. She prayed she'd done the right thing, but she knew she couldn't have done anything else. Not with the time pressure they were under.

'. . . wouldn't you say?' Philip asked.

She had no idea what he'd been talking about.

'Quite.'

Chapter 41

For the next twenty-four hours they were at sea, and there was nothing more she could do.

The skies were clear, the little islands off the coast of Sicily were charming, and they stopped for an impromptu lunch on one of them that was quite simply worthy of the gods. The Queen was able to have fresh shellfish, for once, because it looked and smelled exquisite, and she could risk it if she wasn't working. There was white wine that tasted of nectar, and strawberries that were better than the best desserts she'd had in the grandest palaces.

Back aboard *Britannia*, watching Philip on the bridge, she was reminded of her carefree days as a princess and a navy wife in Malta, before her father died. There was a certain ache, given everything that came next. Now, moments like this were fleeting. Still, she was doing what she'd always been trained for, while she had the health and vigour to do it well. She took the opportunity to steel herself for the days ahead.

With Her Majesty's permission, Joan had managed to get a brief message to Hector Ross via the last of the Queen's red boxes, just before the royal yacht finally left Cagliari. It set out Sokolova's initial escape plan, how it had gone wrong, and where she was heading. Joan would have to leave Hector to fill in the gaps.

The message was written fast, and though she avoided giving any names, it wasn't encoded. Sometimes you trusted your secrets to the code itself, and sometimes to the method of transmission. In this case, a sealed envelope marked 'Top secret', from the desk of the sovereign to a senior member of the Security Service, seemed secure enough. Besides, if the message went astray anywhere, it was most likely to be to one of Hector's colleagues at MI5, who could break any code she could devise faster than she could think of it.

Meanwhile, they had four busy days coming up. From the moment *Britannia* docked in Naples, the Queen would be on show. While she was in Rome, the yacht would make her way to Ancona on the east coast of the country, where she would pick the royal party up and take them on to Venice for a day and a night. From there, they would travel by air to Florence, Turin and home.

Joan was disappointed that Hector would have to come up with a plan to save Doctor Sokolova and the girl that didn't involve her. After all, how could she help now, even if she wanted to?

Chapter 42

The official visit schedule that Sir Hugh and Joan had worked on for weeks was laid out in ten-minute increments, from eight in the morning until midnight. By the time *Britannia* docked at Naples, the Queen was dressed and ready for a full day of living in the glare of a thousand flashbulbs. Magazine columnists would dissect every stitch of clothing, while reporters with microphones would try and catch every single word exchanged. Dozens of strangers would be introduced, one after the other. It was hard to have a meaningful conversation with not one but several people so nonplussed they could hardly remember their own names. The Queen had learned how to do it as graciously as she could. This was the job.

In Naples, she was given a twenty-four gun salute, and the streets of the city were so filled with cheering crowds they could hardly hear themselves think.

'Take that, Gagarin,' Philip muttered under his breath, sitting in the back of the state Rolls-Royce beside her.

'I think that if he were here, they'd be cheering for him,' the Queen pointed out.

But today, he wasn't, and the crowds seemed genuinely enthusiastic. Even in Italy, a country that had triumphantly disposed of its own monarchy.

On the presidential train to Rome, she spotted Joan sitting alone in a far corner of the carriage, head bowed over a telegram that she must have received once they docked. The Queen was busy chatting to the dignitaries who surrounded her, but she noticed Joan's expression shift from relief to surprise, to concern and back again. Afterwards, Joan folded the note several times and it seemed to disappear. The Queen had a strong suspicion it was literally up her sleeve.

'Any news from home?' she asked in passing, as they waited together briefly for the red carpet to be put in position on the platform at Ostiense station.

'Oh, just my aunt who's been very unwell, ma'am, as you know,' Joan said. 'My uncle said she's comfortable.'

'That's a relief.'

'Yes, it is. But she still needs help, and he can't persuade her to let him give it. She's always nervous around strangers. He's working on it though.'

'Did he say when he might have news?' the Queen asked – taking an inordinate interest in Joan's relatives, given that she was just about to meet the Italian president.

'He said it might take a couple of days, ma'am.'

'Well, I wish him luck. I'm glad he's looking after her. Is my hat straight?'

'Yes, ma'am.'

Outside, they had finished making the carpet inch-perfect, and the Queen descended the steps, composed and smiling.

Back in Curzon Street, Hector Ross needed all the luck he could get.

Until recently, things had been going well for Hector ever since Miles Urquhart, the Queen's DPS, had delivered some unexpected news about Tracy Thorburn and her link to Sergei Steklyar, the exposed Russian agent runner. Hector's investigations into the Michalowski case had sped up rapidly, with some surprising new discoveries ... And then, along came a note from Joan in Sardinia, and everything became challenging and precarious again.

Joan's note had come out of the blue. Hector had been in Vienna, searching for the missing scientist and the girl, when Madeleine Simon from the office had relayed its contents to him. He wasn't supposed to be there, of course: outside the UK's borders, this was technically a job for MI6. But as Joan knew, his confidence in his fellow British agency was threadbare, to say the least. And anyway, he wanted this prize for himself. He was certain that the missing woman was the 'special' person his contact in London had told him about. He'd worked for it.

Since news of her escape from her minders had leaked through the intelligence community, everyone was looking for Doctor Tatiana Sokolova now. As far as they knew, she was a junior medic from a Russian military hospital outside Moscow. Thanks to his investigation, Hector suspected he was the only one who knew what Sokolova's real secrets were supposed to be. However, the Russians were searching for her desperately, and so all the other agencies had cottoned on to the fact that she was important somehow.

As a result, the Austrian city had been crawling with spies, even more than usual. Hector recognised several people from his war service in Italy, some friendly, some hostile, including two that he had thought were dead. The thing was, they recognised him, too, and if he could tell exactly what their jobs were now, and what they were doing in Vienna, then they could probably do the same for him.

When Joan's note informed him about what had happened in Italy, Hector's first instinct had been to go there. After arriving in Sicily with the Special Raiding Squadron in '43, he had spent a lot of time travelling north on covert missions, blowing things up, making friends and influencing people. Of all the countries in Europe, it was the one he knew best, and it would be much easier to operate if he was on the spot. But right now, the Russians and Americans were working on the assumption that Sokolova had gone west, to Munich. He didn't want to lead them to her by starting a stampede south, and so, reluctantly, he'd returned to London.

The good news was that he'd been able to establish a connection with Sokolova personally, via the contact details she'd given Joan. She was indeed a medic, though she was shy about saying where she'd worked before the military hospital. After her failed expedition as far as Rome, she and the child (her daughter, presumably) had made it back to the safe house Michalowski had originally found for them in Trieste. Their delay in getting to Cagliari was simple: the girl had become feverish on the train through Yugoslavia, and they had needed to rest in Trieste when they first arrived. They got to Rome very late, and panicked when Sokolova thought they were being followed. The same thing happened in Naples. However, now Sokolova put that paranoia down to tiredness. Meanwhile, the girl was still very weak, but the worst was over.

The bad news was that after the trauma of the last few days, they refused to move again, except in the company of Commander Kinnock, or under instruction from Michalowski, using the private codeword between them which Hector didn't know. Hector's own trust issues were significant, but theirs were worse. They were exhausted, traumatised, terrified, and clinging on to the one certainty Michalowski had given them – which was that apart from Pavel himself, Trefor Kinnock was the only person they could rely on. Sokolova had seen in the newspapers that *Britannia* would be in Venice in a few days. It was just round the coast from Trieste. She wanted to wait for him.

If she really held the secret that Hector's contact thought she did, Sokolova would become the most valuable prize of his career. He had hours – or days at most – to save her before one of the other agencies found her, but for a refugee, she was being remarkably uncooperative.

'That's better, isn't it?' Philip said to the Queen that evening in Rome, as a crowd of twenty thousand people stood outside the Quirinal Palace, shouting *'Bella! Viva la regina!'*

'Better than what?' the Queen asked, from the window where she'd been waving.

'Ten years ago, when the cream of society didn't want to know you.'

'Yes, it is a bit,' she admitted. 'I wonder what's doing it. I mean, I knew they'd be welcoming, but this is . . .'

'Ah,' the British ambassador said, from behind them. 'I think I can answer that, ma'am. Obviously there's your personal presence. The young, fragile queen, bravely fulfilling her promise of service to her country . . .'

'Fragile! Ha!' Philip roared. 'They haven't met 'er. Forged steel, I've always said so.'

The ambassador coughed diplomatically. 'And they want to draw a veil over their recent past. They'd like to think we've always been friends as nations. After all, you're here to celebrate a hundred years of nationhood, and the British were the first to recognise Italy as a country after their revolution. It's not a bond that one forgets. They're still grateful.'

'They didn't seem so grateful under Mussolini,' Philip harrumphed.

'Well, no, exactly.'

'But they do now,' the Queen said. 'They've been delightful all day.'

They really had. Not only had they arranged for blue skies, lots of chic-looking men in sleek suits and sunglasses, streets lined with cavalry bristling with gold braid, a visit to the Capitoline Hill and the obligatory trip to a war cemetery . . . But they'd decided that she'd want to spend the afternoon watching horses show jump in the gardens of the Villa Borghese – which obviously, she did – and they were laying on a major race meet for her to watch tomorrow. There would also be opera, which wasn't entirely one's favourite thing, but horses two days running? The Romans really knew the way to a woman's heart.

She should, of course, be worrying about *Britannia*. It had been a very close call in Cagliari, and there was a slim chance that Admiral Marlow would read about the Vienna escape and put two and two together. But she thought it would probably never occur to him that she had been actively trying to aid a Soviet defector. Because it was unthinkable.

And now it was out of her hands entirely. According to Joan, Sokolova and the girl had somehow survived, and she didn't feel responsible for their safety anymore. Hector Ross could take that burden on, thank you very much – she had a soirée of three thousand people to attend, including half the aristocrats who had gone to such efforts not to meet her last time. As she had promised Philip, she would be gracious. They had been so nice to her today, it really wasn't hard.

Chapter 43

The following day was just as rewarding. More crowds, more horses, more streets lined with uniformed soldiers, and dignitaries to meet. There was also another wave of flattering, patronising, newspaper columns about the 'tireless and resolute, if somewhat uncultured Elisabetta', which Dominic Stonor cheerfully relayed to her. As if a love of horses meant one wasn't intimately familiar with Leonardo da Vinci. Which, actually, one was. Or a fan of opera. Which, admittedly, one wasn't, but a jazz concert would have been very nice.

The ten-minute increments ticked by in gloves and hats and changes of clothes, in open-topped car processions and more cheering schoolchildren on the Palatine Hill, in coats and hats, silk and diamanté, banquets and reception lines . . . and all the time the Queen waited for Joan to indicate she had more news from London. And Joan did not.

Meanwhile, *Britannia* sailed round the heel of the boot of Italy and up the east coast towards Ancona.

By the third day of the visit, the Queen was starting to worry again. Not that it was her problem anymore, but . . . she couldn't help it. Once she'd taken on responsibility for the lives of Sokolova and the girl, she couldn't let it go. She wouldn't really rest until she knew they'd found safe harbour, wherever that turned out to be.

Late in the morning, her schedule had two ten-minute admin sessions back-to-back in the Quirinal, for her to deal with her red boxes. Government business didn't pause at home just because she happened to be abroad. Sitting at a borrowed desk, she opened the first box, hoping to find a note slipped in by her APS at the last minute, explaining what the new plan for Sokolova was. But there wasn't one.

What there was, however, was an official update from the director general of MI6, saying that efforts were underway to locate a known Russian defector, a medic and prodigious amateur chess player, who had gone missing in Vienna. Currently, the KGB were working hard to find her. MI6 weren't sure why yet, but they were working on the theory that she must have worked at a secret facility at some point – a nuclear reactor, perhaps, or a missile factory or army base.

They were, were they? So, MI5 and MI6 weren't talking. It was probably for the best, given that an MI6 double agent was on trial at the Old Bailey this very week for betraying several networks of spies across Eastern Europe.

According to the update, the agencies had at first assumed that the defector had headed for West Germany, but now they were starting to wonder if she'd outsmarted everyone and gone in a different direction. Her options from Vienna were limited. The note ended on the optimistic prediction that it wouldn't take long to track her down.

The Queen glanced down her schedule again. She would be in company for the rest of the day, and even in the odd five minutes she'd been granted to herself, Lady Sarah would be with her. Now was the only time she would be alone.

She raced through the rest of the papers, speed-reading, signing everything that needed to be signed and marking just a couple with question marks for her private secretary. Then she called for them to be collected, and Sir Hugh himself arrived. She had five minutes left.

'Everything in order, ma'am?'

'Absolutely, Hugh. I'd just like to see Joan quickly about the Venice arrangements.'

'No need, ma'am. I can pass on any message you might—'

'Thank you, Hugh.'

It was a 'please do as I just asked' thank you, not a 'thank you' thank you. Sir Hugh bowed and withdrew.

Joan appeared a couple of minutes later. She looked drawn.

'No news from your uncle back at home?' the Queen asked.

One never knew if one's allies chose to bug the rooms where one worked. It always paid to be careful.

'There is,' Joan said. She glanced around the room. She was thinking about bugs, too. 'I heard from him last night. But he's stuck.'

'Oh? Why?'

'He needs a woman to help him, ideally. It's hard to find the right one at very short notice. My aunt is being difficult.'

The Queen frowned in surprise. 'Really?'

'Yes, ma'am. She has her reasons.'

'But he can sort it out?'

Joan looked strained. She shook her head. 'I'm sure he will, ma'am. It's just . . .'

This was not the reaction the Queen had been hoping for. She indicated a marbled letter rack on the desk, stacked with paper and envelopes.

'Perhaps you could explain it to me later.'

Joan saw the letter rack and nodded. They'd done this before.

'And by the way,' the Queen added, 'my speech at lunchtime needs a bit of work. Can you give me a new draft before we leave the palace?'

'Of course, ma'am.'

'Thank you, Joan.'

This *was* a thank you, and also a dismissal. It was all they had time for.

As she was getting into the car to drive to her lunchtime event, the Queen noticed a manilla envelope waiting for her on the back seat.

'More work?' Philip said, climbing in beside her.

'Just a little.'

'Anything interesting?'

'Quite possibly,' she said, opening the envelope.

He saw the look on her face. 'It's not to do with Michalowski, is it?'

'Quite possibly.'

He tapped his nose, remembering their conversation from several days ago. 'Mum's the word. I'll leave you to it.'

Attached to the copy of the speech was a note that Joan must have typed just now at lightning speed. It wasn't addressed or signed, and it was as if their conversation had continued where it left off.

> *They are back where they started. She originally said she would only work with K. She has now agreed she will also talk to the woman she spoke to in C, i.e. me. H could get another woman to take my place, but if she fails to see K later, he fears she will not be fully forthcoming. One option presented itself, which is to revert to the original plan but in a new location. It requires either K or me to make the transfer. Short notice means this unlikely. Also obviously unsuitable. H working on further ideas.*

The Queen read it at lightning speed herself, then folded the paper, looked out of the window, and waved automatically at the crowds.

'Everything all right, Lilibet?'

Philip jolted her into the present. The car was several roads ahead of where she expected.

'Gosh, are we nearly there?'

'You've been lost in thought.'

'I suppose I have.'

She folded up the piece of paper further, until it was small enough to fit in a matchbox, and placed it securely in her handbag. She was calculating timings.

the original plan, but in a new location

Oh Lord. *The original plan.* It was back to *Britannia.*

The 'second location' mentioned must be Venice, which was close to Trieste, where Sokolova and the girl were holed up. She and Philip would be joining *Britannia* in Ancona tomorrow. From there, they would reach Venice aboard the royal yacht on the sixth of May, and leave the following day. Today was the fourth. That gave Major Ross forty-eight hours to get Sokolova in position, assuming the 'unsuitable' (and by God it was unsuitable) plan went ahead.

The Queen couldn't believe *Britannia* was back in play. It hadn't crossed her mind that she would ever need to worry about her yacht this way again. But if the revised plan was going to happen at all, it had to be set in motion now. And with every hour that passed, the CIA, KGB and MI6 had more time to track the recalcitrant defector.

Joan's note had referred to 'H', not 'R', which indicated the speed of thought with which she'd typed it. 'Hector', not 'Ross'. It didn't say what the Queen strongly suspected, which was that Major Ross must have asked Joan if she personally would take on the job of this 'transfer', whatever it was. He wasn't in charge of a large spy network, didn't have endless women with appropriate training at his disposal, and Joan hadn't mentioned anyone else. Also, it must have occurred to Ross that whoever undertook the task would therefore know about *Britannia*'s role. The fewer people who did, the better.

Kinnock, of course, was totally ill suited to the task. The man had a James Bond complex, and a poor attitude to risk. Besides, he would be out of contact most of the time while *Britannia* sailed up the coast. Joan didn't need to point this out: the Queen already knew.

So, what the note really said was that Ross had asked Joan if she personally, and *Britannia* more broadly, could help with the rescue after all. And Joan had said no. Hence her strained look in the Quirinal Palace office just now. But the very fact that she'd described what Ross wanted – the Queen knew human nature well enough to be fairly sure of this – meant that on both counts, Joan wanted to say yes.

There was no time to hesitate. Three outcomes presented themselves and Elizabeth reckoned she had about twenty seconds to consider them before her car arrived at its destination.

In the first, Sokolova and the girl stayed where they were, while Ross worked on another plan and the KGB homed in on their location. The Russians were the ones most likely to track their escape route down through Yugoslavia to Italy and it was only a matter of time before they found them.

In the second outcome, the rescue attempt was made from Venice, and was uncovered at some point. *Britannia* would be exposed, but Sokolova and the girl would still make it to safety. The Queen realised she could never return them. It would be diplomatically imperative, but also inhuman. She couldn't in all conscience go to church every Sunday having made that sort of choice.

Or in the third outcome, the rescue attempt succeeded fully, the woman and the girl were safe, and *Britannia* somehow sailed through it all, untouched by scandal.

To leave the scientist to her fate was unthinkable, if the Queen could possibly avoid it. Time was of the essence, she knew that. If they didn't move fast, it was very unlikely Sokolova and the girl would survive. The idea of exposing

Britannia was *awful*, truly awful. But she had already committed to saving those lives if she could. She couldn't imagine herself entertaining fellow heads of state on board one day, or gaily cruising the west coast of Scotland, knowing that she had caused a child to die for the privilege. Such a heavy secret would surely drag one into the depths.

The car drew slowly to a halt. An Italian soldier in full ceremonial regalia stepped forward to open the door.

The third outcome was a stretch, but it was the best of all worlds. In its favour, Major Ross was what they called 'a safe pair of hands'. Joan would no doubt love the work, and *Britannia* would be perfect for the purpose, especially with Admiral Marlow now onside. Michalowski had already died for this end. The Queen might rue it later, but at least those lives wouldn't be on her conscience. Today, she was an optimist.

The car door opened, the paparazzi flashbulbs popped, and a phalanx of government officials prepared to greet her.

The decision was made.

Chapter 44

For a junior military doctor that nobody had heard of, Tatiana Sokolova was sharper than Hector Ross had expected. He didn't mind: it made it easier for him to deal with her in many ways.

From the precarious base of her safe house in Trieste, she still insisted on trusting only Kinnock or 'the woman from the café', whom she had spoken to on the telephone. It would have been easy, surely, to pretend that any woman who showed up was this one, but Sokolova had a plan. All she knew was that this woman had been on board *Britannia*. Her demand was that if the woman was to help, she must be filmed or photographed during coverage of the Queen's visit, wearing a bunch of lily of the valley in her lapel and carrying a rolled up copy of a British newspaper. Then Sokolova could be certain that Hector really was working with the person he said he was.

The sheer outrageousness of this demand was laughable. But Sokolova was Russian – perhaps she assumed that members of the Queen's household could be called upon to dress and carry things at the whim of any member of the intelligence community and stand as close to the monarch as they liked.

The very idea of someone in the private office carrying a newspaper at Hector's request was ridiculous. Ditto, the thought of almost any woman except the Queen's lady-in-waiting getting close enough to her to be in shot. Hector felt as if he was being asked to walk on a high wire and jump through a flaming hoop.

In principle, he didn't like being told what to do by a foreign agent he was, against all protocol, trying to rescue. But he could understand Sokolova's nervousness and she was, in her strange way, trying to be helpful. As he sat in his chair, twiddling a pen in his fingers, he couldn't help marvelling that this particular high wire was one he could walk quite easily. Of all the flaming hoops, this was one he knew how to navigate. He even knew a man at Radiotelevisione italiana who could put it on the news.

Next, *Britannia*. Using the royal yacht was by no means his favourite solution. He had thought through several alternative scenarios, in which he tricked Sokolova into meeting other agents and then forcibly smuggled her out of the country another way, under protest. But how much would she have told him then?

If he could make this one work, though, then surely she would be putty in his hands? She would travel to Venice, as she asked, and she would accept the temporary sanctuary of people he knew and trusted. She would meet Joan herself and, later, Kinnock, as requested. She would be safe. Her confidence would grow. She would tell Hector everything she knew – even things she didn't know she knew, until he and his team fully debriefed her. The identity of the

Chief Engineer, the orchestrator of the space programme, would be the start, but if she had worked at Star City, then what else?

Bizarrely, the image on the news containing Joan, the flowers, the newspaper and the Queen of England first thing tomorrow was the easy part. Now, he had to finish the more challenging task of arranging the escape and making sure that later, Joan – without training – could safely get the most wanted woman in Europe out from under the eyes of the press and the KGB, on the most famous boat in the Adriatic, without anyone noticing.

Wearing ivory lace, ermine and a wall of diamonds, the Queen set out that evening to enjoy another banquet and an evening of Verdi at the opera house. In her honour they had chosen *Falstaff*, in a nod to Shakespeare. She wasn't convinced that the Bard was improved by being translated into Italian and set to music, but one did as one was told.

She was accompanied by Sir Hugh, but meanwhile, Joan, Miles and Dominic had an evening of work ahead of them. The Italian trip was going well, but President Kennedy would be visiting London in a month, and the private office had a thousand details to finalise, and nervous new administration workers to reassure.

When a man from the British Council got a note to Joan asking if they could meet at a bar across the Tiber, she assumed it was a joke, until she got to the post script, where he mentioned that he was 'an old friend of Hector's from his army days', and he looked forward to catching up.

She got her coat and told Dominic and Miles that she would be back as soon as she could.

The bar was in a run-down part of town, the other side of the Garibaldi Bridge. Joan had made sure to pin her hair up tightly and wear a dark silk scarf over it. She slid her trademark pearls into her handbag in the taxi. In Rome, so many women dressed in chic and fashionable outfits that she hoped she wouldn't stand out.

The man waiting for her at a corner table was in his mid-forties: about Hector's age. Dark haired and dark eyed, he could have been English or Italian, but he had a folded copy of *The Times* on the table in front of him, and next to it a very small bunch of flowers, wrapped in brown paper.

'These are for you,' he said, as she sat down. 'I'll explain later. You'll need them tomorrow. I'm Tom, by the way. Can I get you a drink?'

Joan asked for a Bellini and wondered what on earth the flowers could be for.

Tom was charming and relaxed as they drank their cocktails. He was missing two fingers from his right hand, which didn't surprise Joan unduly. The sort of men who knew Hector had often had what the Queen called 'an interesting war'.

They made inconsequential conversation – he, explaining how he worked on encouraging musical and literary exchanges at the British Council, and she, telling him bland incidents from her youth, growing up in Cambridge. Afterwards, he suggested grabbing a meal together. Joan thought of the mountain of work she had to do, but there was no question of refusing. As they strolled towards his proposed restaurant, he told her that there was a note in her jacket pocket, and that she must read it in the privacy of the ladies' lavatory in the restaurant.

In the end, they visited not the place he had mentioned, but one a few doors down. It was getting late, and the streets were half empty. Any couple following them inside would have stood out, but none did.

Joan stood in the tiny lavatory and felt in her pocket. The note – dictated over the telephone, she assumed – was short, friendly and anonymous. It said simply that the writer would have two packages in Venice, organised by his friend Andrea, and would be very grateful if she could pick them up. It mentioned a shop in St Mark's Square that she had never heard of. The last line was the oddest:

Oh, by the way, I honeymooned in Venice. Tom might remember. Give the place my love.

Joan's mind raced. He had them! Or at least, he would have them. Clever, clever, Hector, doing what she'd asked at a moment's notice. Involving her! Trusting her! Thrusting her into the thick of it!

But that note about the honeymoon . . . It soured everything. She happened to know it was true. He'd mentioned it before, apropos his Murano glass ashtray, one evening after much too much whisky. And after he'd seen the look on her face, he'd simply said, 'Yes, well, it was nice at the time,' and never talked of it again.

Joan knew how the marriage had ended. It was his wife's fate to fall in love with the family doctor while he was away fighting, and it had torn Hector apart. Joan knew without a shadow of a doubt that she was the love of his life now, but it still hurt unreasonably hard to think of him being so happy once, with someone else.

The restaurant was small and candlelit, with one elderly waitress and a small menu of dishes she didn't recognise.

'I've ordered for you,' Tom said. 'You'll like it, trust me.'

He poured her red wine from a carafe.

'Everything OK?'

He said it with real concern, and Joan realised she must look conflicted, still. She shook it off.

'Absolutely. I gather you were in Venice with our mutual friend. That must have been lovely,' she said.

Tom's face clouded slightly. 'Er, it was at the time, yes.' He peered at her, clearly trying to work out what she needed to know about his friend's old love life.

'Tell me, did you do anything interesting while you were there?' she asked.

'Well, we stayed in a run-down pensione off the Grand Canal.' He frowned. 'It rained a lot. We visited a couple of galleries . . . You know . . .' His face cleared. 'I suppose the highlight was going to the Locanda Cipriani on the island of Torcello. It's far away from the centre. I suppose you wouldn't know it—'

'Oh I do!' Joan said. 'The Queen's visiting it in a couple of days. She's having lunch there.'

'Is she? Well, she'll love it. It's sort of the middle of nowhere – very rural, relaxed countryside – not what you think of Venice at all, but Arrigo Cipriani knows how to cook. The food will be delicious. It's a special spot. Ernest Hemingway and Charlie Chaplin visited, you know.'

Joan did. She'd done her research. This was what Hector must have been referring to. The island of Torcello was a few miles from Venice, in the middle of the lagoon, and would be shut down to visitors during the royal couple's visit. A safer place than most to 'pick up a couple of packages', if you knew what you were doing – but how, exactly, and when?

'Did our friend say anything else?' she asked.

'Yes,' Tom said. 'Do you have a good memory?'

Joan grinned.

He gave her a six-digit number, which she assumed was a grid reference, and a time the following evening. 'That's all.'

'Do you know Andrea?' she asked.

Tom raised an eyebrow. 'I do. He was with us on that trip. If he's involved, he'll take care of the rest.'

As they came to put on their jackets, after a meal of fried artichokes and fresh pasta, the waitress asked if a small, dark rucksack belonged to either of them. Joan was about to shake her head when Tom smiled in acknowledgement. '*Grazie.*'

He handed it to her as she was about to get into her taxi back to the palace.

'*In bocca al lupo,*' he said. 'It means "in the mouth of the wolf". The Italians say it for luck.'

Joan knew this. '*Crepi il lupo*', she told him with a smile. It meant 'may the wolf die'.

He saluted her with the three remaining fingers of his right hand.

PART FOUR

CHI OSA VINCE*

*Italian for Who Dares Wins, and motto of the Special Raiding Squadron

Chapter 45

The Queen stood at the door of the Quirinal Palace on the morning of the fifth of May, thinking back to her ancestor, Henry VIII. What would he think of her, paying a visit to the pontiff, after everything that he and Thomas Cromwell had done to break from Rome?

As with Henry, the wardrobe told the story. She was wearing a full-length black lace gown and a waist-length black veil, out of respect and tradition; but with them, she wore the ultra-sparkling Kokoshnik tiara, two ropes of pearls and the Order of the Garter, a reminder that she was the head of an independent nation, with an independent church.

Behind her, as the cameras flashed and the TV news cameras rolled, Joan stood next to her lady-in-waiting, wearing a simple blue day coat offset by a corsage of lily of the valley, holding a rolled-up copy of yesterday's *Times*. The Queen took one step to the left, to say something to Prince Philip, and for a moment her APS appeared in the centre of the image. Then she stepped back into the shadows.

Bags and trunks had already been packed and were on their way to the airport, where the Queen would soon join the royal flight to Ancona. In the meantime, she was looking forward to her visit to the Vatican. She'd met the Pope before, as princess. She knew her host would be welcoming, and they'd be surrounded by some of the finest Renaissance art in the world, which – despite what the papers might say – she and Philip would very much appreciate. The Pope's surroundings were even grander than one's own.

Nevertheless, the Queen felt that her sombre clothes reflected her mood. The crowds would see the dazzle of the diamond tiara and the Garter star, but she was a religious person, visiting a holy man. Pope John XXIII was the sort of leader she hoped to be – a moderniser, respectful of religion, a promoter of democracy, a believer in peace. She looked forward to talking to him privately, but she wouldn't go as far as the confessional, of course.

Although, given what her APS was up to this evening, if she did, she'd have an awful lot to get off her chest.

Joan left Rome by train shortly after the royal party left for the Vatican, citing last-minute arrangements in Venice that required her attention. Her early departure hadn't come as a surprise to the Foreign Office or Sir Hugh. While everybody loved the Italians, nobody entirely trusted them. It was nothing personal, just natural scepticism regarding the reliability of anyone not fundamentally British.

It was useful that her absence hadn't been questioned, but Joan's problem was that she *did* trust the Italians. They were, if anything, too hospitable. It would have been natural for her to spend a few hours catching up with her Venetian contacts near St Mark's and on the islands of Murano and

Burano – people she had been liaising with for weeks – but they would want to take her for dinner, and they would be affronted if they weren't allowed to provide her with a bed for the night. She wondered what prestigious hotel or glamorous palazzo they would have chosen. Instead, she needed to be somewhere else entirely, and that would have been impossible to explain.

She arrived at Santa Lucia station at dusk, alone and unannounced, having changed trains – and much else besides – at the railway station in Bologna. Now, the woman who looked out of the window as the train approached its destination, across tracks that seemed to float above the lagoon, wore black hair in tight curls under a cotton scarf, dark cigarette pants under a man's macintosh, and a chequebook bearing the name of Elaine Molloy. Joan's small leather suitcase resided in a left luggage locker in Bologna. 'Elaine' carried the army surplus mountain-climbing rucksack that Tom had given her last night. She felt unburdened, excited and afraid.

Walking out of the terminal, she was struck by the timeless vision of the boats in front of the station, ploughing up and down the choppy Grand Canal with freight and passengers. She could have stopped and stared at it for hours, but that would have to be for another trip. As she merged into to the small crowd queueing for a water bus, Joan didn't bother to look around to see if she was being followed. *If they're good enough to matter, you won't see them doing it*, Hector had once told her. *There will be more than one, taking turns, blending in. They'll look like the ones who have the most right to be there.*

Did the man getting his ticket punched work for the Russians? Or the woman with her baby? Joan felt both ridiculous and fully justified in wondering. Would the KGB really expend so much manpower on one of Her Majesty's bag carriers? But she knew how much was at stake if it all went wrong.

The newspaper kiosk beside the little pier displayed several titles, and the Queen was still the main headline in every one. She would only be in Venice for twenty-six hours, but Joan's contacts had told her the coverage had been feverish for weeks.

The sun was setting and, as she stepped aboard the approaching water bus and fought to stay upright among the passengers by the gangway, a dim pink glow behind the dark grey clouds imperceptibly shifted into lilac, then a colder blue. This was the moment, she realised, when Sandra Pole had seen the body of Michalowski being thrown onto the midden. Joan could imagine Sandra's panic intensifying. It was the witching hour, ethereal and strange.

Away from the station, the waters calmed. There was a gondola, slick and black, so close she could almost touch it. On either side of the Grand Canal, a procession of palazzos looked unreal, like a stage set. Beyond the Rialto Bridge, several bankside restaurants spilled light onto the pavement, so that in the twilight, the water shone like mercury edged in gold.

Joan drank in the view for the space of three stops and then it was time to disappear into the shadows. As she hurried down the first of several lamplit streets, she listened for other footsteps travelling at her rapid pace. By the third turning, there were none.

Working from the detailed map she had memorised in her room in Rome, she made her way quickly northwards, towards the *Fondamente*, as they were called, the quays where ferries left for other islands. She relied on her photographic memory, but even so, she questioned her choice of direction more than once, as little alleys seemed to lead to nowhere, before magically revealing an entrance to a hidden passageway at the last moment. Darkness rapidly invaded the fading twilight. When she was certain she was alone, she looked out for the next sign to announce a little restaurant and ducked inside.

Chapter 46

Meanwhile, *Britannia* set sail for Venice from Ancona, up the east coast. The private secretary and deputy private secretary met outside their cabins, both dressed in immaculate dinner jackets and silk bow ties, ready for a relaxing evening of drinks, good food, cards, and much catching up on gossip from the last three days.

'Ready, Miles?' Sir Hugh asked.

'Absolutely,' Urquhart agreed. 'Let's go.'

The Italian trip had been a great success so far. Rome was home of *la dolce vita* after all, and an ancient line of emperors. Sir Hugh hadn't been sure that the modern, republican Italians would take a fairly straight-laced foreign sovereign to their hearts – but to his great relief, they had done so with brio. They'd treated the Queen not exactly like a movie star, but more a treasured icon they wanted to protect. It was as if she was the sort of leader they now wished they'd had, instead of a general who was ultimately hung upside down from a lamp-post. Straight-laced was good, these days. It was a welcome change after the chaos and tragedy of the war. Well, straight-laced would be able to unwind and relax a bit tonight.

First, he and Miles had some good news to give her. She'd promised Sir Hugh ten minutes in her sitting room before cocktails, and it seemed only right that Miles should come along too, given his key part in the proceedings. All was well as they made their way past the footmen who lined the passageway, to the sound of the navigation officer playing Cole Porter on the piano in the state drawing room.

The Queen sparkled in off-duty rubies and a pink silk cocktail dress. She was drinking a glowing red cocktail in a highball glass, and poured another for each of them from a crystal jug, adding a slice of orange from a small silver tray.

'These are Negronis,' she explained. 'They're made with gin and Campari. Commander Attwell discovered them in Rome.'

Sir Hugh sipped his hesitantly. It was really very red. Normally he loved the whole ritual of traditional gin and tonic with a slice of lemon: it was one of the things that put the Great into Great Britain, wasn't it? But Her Majesty's courtiers were nothing if not flexible.

They all sat down and, at the Queen's invitation, Urquhart lit a cigarette. Sir Hugh relaxed into his armchair, grateful to have full use of his neck and spine again.

'It's about the murder case from the train, ma'am' he said. 'I'm sure you'll be delighted to hear that MI5 have all but wrapped up their investigation into the death of the photographer, Michalowski. It was the Russians, as we suspected. Michalowski was trying to get people out of the Soviet Union, and they didn't like it. I received the report from the head of D Branch this afternoon.'

The Queen smiled. 'How reassuring.'

However, the strain from the last few days in public still showed. She wasn't quite as delighted as Sir Hugh had been expecting.

'You'll be pleased to know that it was Miles here who helped them out.'

'Oh, really?'

The deputy private secretary took a nonchalant drag on his cigarette. He let it burn in an ashtray while he talked. 'I discovered a few days ago, ma'am, before we left for Italy, that there might be a connection between Josiah Thorburn and a Russian agent runner currently in the hands of MI5. Thorburn was the man whose land Michalowski's body was found on. The agent runner, Sergei Steklyar, was someone you might have come across through your equine connections. He was well known in hunting and eventing circles. You might remember him as Bill Douglas.'

The Queen's brow crinkled. 'Bill Douglas? The man with the yellow waistcoats?'

'That's him exactly, ma'am, and I don't know if you saw it in the files a few weeks ago, but he was actually a very successful spy of sorts. Or rather, he organised spy rings in England, providing money, equipment and so on from the Kremlin, and passing secret information back. You might not have noticed – you were busy preparing for India at the time.'

'It rings a bell,' she said.

'Ah. But what you *don't* know, ma'am,' Sir Hugh interjected, 'is that, surprisingly, Steklyar was friends with the rather lovely Tracy Thorburn. Miles found this out at Windsor.'

'Did you, Miles? Well done.'

Sir Hugh sipped his Negroni, which was growing on him, while Miles carried on.

'Tracy's a young eventer, ma'am. A very talented girl, and she took a shine to one of Steklyar's horses. He took a shine to her – in a paternal sort of way – and lent her the horse indefinitely. It turns out he'd been at shooting parties with her father, went to Glyndebourne with her mother, that sort of thing. Not a bosom family friend, but more than a distant acquaintance.'

The Queen frowned. 'But surely he was in the hands of MI5 by the time Michalowski was killed?'

'He was. And this is the interesting thing, ma'am. Steklyar might have masterminded the operation, but he couldn't have carried it out. We – I mean, they – had to find out how he might have arranged the thing with Thorburn if he was incommunicado. The man himself refused to speak. He'd given up so many secrets that this seemed odd at first. Anyway, the head of D Branch wasn't waiting. He changed tack and had young Tracy arrested by Special Branch, and told her family she'd be charged with treason. You see, she was known to have asked some quite detailed questions about Michalowski's movements shortly before he disappeared. It wasn't looking good for her.'

'No, I see what you mean,' the Queen agreed.

Urquhart took another drag on his cigarette.

'After that, it didn't take long for her father to crack.' He leaned back, expansively. 'Three days ago, Thorburn gave himself up and told all. It turned out that he'd been sympathetic to the communist cause for some time, would you believe it? Misplaced sympathies for Bolsheviks, gratitude to Stalin for helping defeat Hitler, and a wilful blindness to the atrocities he's inflicted on countless millions since. He'd done various little jobs for Steklyar, and when the man said he might be going away for a while – he had a sense the CIA might be onto him and we were very lucky to catch him before he ran, ma'am – Thorburn was happy for Steklyar to introduce him to someone else.'

'Oh? Who?' the Queen asked, leaning in. Sir Hugh was pleased at how genuinely absorbed she was.

'Ah, well that's where it gets interesting,' Urquhart said. 'And that's why we're here, really. This new man is a bit of a shady character who goes by the name of Dennis Wilson. An accountant from Oxford, known to the police for a couple of misdemeanours, but what they *didn't* know was that he, too, is a Russian implant. *That* is the secret Steklyar was trying to protect. I forget Wilson's real name. It's in the report that will be in your boxes this evening, ma'am, but I – that is we – wanted to be the first to tell you . . .'

'Of course you did, Miles,' she said.

Urquhart nodded, gratified. 'Where was I? Oh, yes, Wilson. It looks as if he was being trained up to take over from Steklyar. He asked Thorburn for help in tracking Michalowski's movements and Thorburn offered up his pretty daughter to find out the info, which she duly did. Later, when Wilson wanted somewhere to dispose of "unwanted material", far from London, Thorburn didn't ask too many questions.'

Sir Hugh decided Miles had had enough of the limelight. He finished his cocktail and took the stage.

'The Murder Squad had already worked out what probably happened, ma'am. The evidence from the fields was already there. Under questioning, Thorburn admitted he suggested using the pigs on one of the estate farms to take care of . . . whatever it was Wilson needed to dispose of. Then he left the country to give himself an alibi and put his gamekeeper in charge. When it turned out the pigs had gone to market, the gamekeeper told Wilson's men they could use the farm's midden as a temporary hiding place. He thought they were safe to chuck it in amongst the muck and hay, but the royal train came out of nowhere and caught them by surprise. So, they moved the body to the next best place they could think of while they waited for the next batch of pigs. But, before that happened, the police were crawling all over the area, and it was too late. Even then, they thought they were safe because the local inspector is related to Thorburn's housekeeper, but soon afterwards, the Murder Squad got involved from London.'

'Thorburn's admitted to all of this?' the Queen said.

Sir Hugh glanced across at the jug to see if there would be enough Negroni for a little top-up. The Queen noticed, refilling his glass while he talked.

'Major Ross at D Branch has his methods, ma'am. Once Thorburn admitted to doing a favour for Wilson, the rest spewed out of him. Also, he didn't seem too upset about the body, but he was very disappointed in his men. He was keen to share his annoyance at their ineptitude.'

'And Tracy? What about her?'

'Ross made a deal to go easy on her. None of this was her idea. She's playing the innocent and her father's taking the rap. She's very upset that she's lost her horse, I'm told, because the police got wise to the fact that Sirocco belonged to Steklyar, and his possessions have been impounded.'

The Queen's eyes widened at this. Nobody could match her love of horses, but even she seemed to think that Tracy was missing the point.

'Steklyar was doing very well, ma'am, by the sound of things,' Urquhart added. 'The Kremlin had given him some seed capital to set himself up as a businessman with a bit of "oomph", and it turned out he was very good at it. He'd turned a few thousand into well over a million. A proper little capitalist.'

'And Steklyar's successor as an agent-runner . . .' the Queen said, 'Wilson, was it? Has he been arrested?'

She was keeping up remarkably well, Sir Hugh considered. His own thought processes were becoming very slightly frayed at the edges. Where were they? Oh yes, Steklyar's successor. He shook his head.

'No, ma'am, no arrest. MI5 have eyes on Wilson now. They're letting him carry on as normal, and they're confident he'll lead them to all sorts of interesting places. It means not formally arresting Thorburn for the time being, either, so as not to alarm Wilson, but Thorburn has various contacts in the Eastern Bloc, and MI5 think we can use them to our advantage, too.'

The Queen frowned. 'Can we trust him?'

'No,' Sir Hugh said. 'But we can own him. Major Ross comes across as a calm, almost shy sort of chap, but you wouldn't want to get on the wrong side of him. When he scents blood, he's like a shark in the water. He has Thorburn in his power now and the man knows it: he can only do what he's told, or he loses his family, his home, his livelihood, his reputation. That has been made very clear.'

The Queen took a thoughtful sip of her own drink.

'Thank you very much, both of you. I suppose that just leaves the agents who actually murdered Mr Michalowski. I assume they were KGB?'

'They were,' Sir Hugh acknowledged. 'We don't know how the Russians found out about Michalowski's activities in the first place, but somehow, they did. The men who disposed of him worked at the embassy, ma'am. They flew out to Berlin the day after the body was discovered. The Foreign Secretary will be having very stiff words with the ambassador. They won't be coming back.'

She stood up.

'That's been very informative. I'm delighted the information about Tracy Thorburn from Windsor proved so useful.'

'It was nothing, ma'am,' Miles said with a smile. 'We're pleased to be of service.'

'And now MI5 have a new agent runner to keep an eye on, and a new spy to work for them in the shape of Mr Thorburn. How satisfying.'

'Isn't it?' Sir Hugh said. 'It's a relief to have the whole thing wrapped up. I mean, poor Michalowski – sounded like a good chap. Didn't deserve an end like that. But that's the Russians for you. We can put it from our minds now.'

'Yes, I suppose so,' she said, with an odd sort of smile.

Miles grinned. 'And on we go to Venice!'

A footman opened the door to the sound of the piano. The navigation officer was playing Dean Martin, and Sir Hugh hummed along to the tune. Meanwhile, the Queen's odd smile stayed fixed in place.

'So we do.'

Chapter 47

In Venice, Joan looked out over open water. The sky was black now, pierced with occasional stars between the clouds. She was on the last water bus to Murano, heading away from the lights and bustle of the city almost as soon as she had arrived.

The little restaurant had provided a quick and simple dish of rice and peas, or *risi e bisi* as they called it. It was one Hector had made for her many times. She wondered exactly where he'd learned it, and who had taught him how to create the creaminess of the rice, that vivid green of the peas among the grains. No doubt he was pacing up and down the flat in London worrying about her, not entirely trusting her to get it right, wishing he were there instead to do it properly. He had never really seen her at work. He didn't know how quickly she adapted.

To her right, the straight white wall of a small island loomed low against the darkness. This must be San Michele, the cemetery of Venice. Someone had thought the Queen and the Duke might like to visit it on their travels. No doubt it was full of the bones of fascinating public figures, but the royal couple had only one full day here tomorrow, and Joan had politely declined on their behalf.

They had said yes to the island of Murano, though, which lay not far ahead. According to the curator from the Royal Collection who had taught Joan about it, it was the place that all the glass makers had been sent to many centuries ago, when the fires in their furnaces threatened to burn the city's wooden buildings down. They were still working today. The Queen had several antique pieces of Venetian glass in her collection, but Joan's Auntie Eva had a lovely, thick green vase from about ten years ago, which looked like flowing water, caught in the act. And Hector had the striking glass ashtray that seemed to burn with fire from within, bought on honeymoon.

As the ferry approached the island, Joan noticed that it stuck to a course marked by tall wooden posts that jutted from the water, caught occasionally in the beam of a nearby lighthouse. She wondered idly what would happen if the boat strayed outside the channel. This was a place for locals, who knew the lurking dangers and could navigate them. She was glad she wouldn't be alone.

The journey didn't take very long. Standing on dry land after disembarking, she could just about make out the twinkling lights of the city in the distance. Around her, the few passengers quickly abandoned the quay as they hurried off, heads down, to their homes and families.

Joan was struck by how empty it was here. Restaurants were closing their shutters already. Locals were at home. There were no tourists to speak of at this hour. It was hard to imagine that more than five thousand men would be at work here tomorrow, making the coloured glass creations that were shipped around the world. She was fascinated by the process: how did you breathe into glass and make it round, or cylindrical, or a chandelier drop or the shape of a running horse? She wasn't surprised that the Duke, who loved craftsmanship, was keen to see them at it.

But now the workers were at home, the streets were almost empty, and there was an eeriness to the place that seemed to ooze into the water all around. Joan had another mental map to follow and she set off. Murano was much easier to navigate than Venice itself had been. She had only to follow the embankments of the canals, crossing a footbridge as she made her way to the other side of the island. She made it harder for herself by taking footpaths between low industrial buildings, waiting and doubling back, all the while looking for the shadowy figures she'd been told she wouldn't see, even if they were there.

The eeriness persisted as she walked. A low, persistent hum emphasised the night-time quiet, broken by the occasional hiss and crackle. It reminded her of something, and she realised after several minutes of walking that it was the sound of a fire catching in a bombed-out building in the Blitz. The hairs on her arms stood up.

Eventually she reached a small canal opposite a patch of open ground. The wind had whipped up, carrying with it the salty wetness of the lagoon. She found the set of steps leading down to the water that marked the six-digit coordinates that Hector had given her via Tom, and sat down to wait.

Cold, damp air seeped down her neck and up her sleeves. The humming and hissing was overlaid by the irregular sound of choppy waves against the concrete steps, and gusts of wind from across the water. What *was* that hiss? she wondered. And then she realised that while humans slept, the furnaces of Murano didn't. They couldn't be allowed to cool to nothing overnight. According to the curator, they'd recently converted from charcoal to methane gas – a fact to impress the Duke with. Even here, where they'd been working since the thirteenth century, modern technology was changing the world. That would account for the hiss and crackle – but it didn't help her instinctive fear subside.

Joan hugged her arms around her knees and ran through the plan repeatedly, staring out into the mysterious darkness of the lagoon. She'd found an outline of what Hector intended hidden in the lining of the rucksack. Its details were sketchy, requiring the knowledge she already had. The note itself had been written in code on silk, but the rucksack also contained a snapshot of two young women, with '*Betty and Daphne, '57*' written on the back. The women in question were strangers to Joan, but the names were not. She remembered telling Hector about the help that the novelist Daphne du Maurier had given to Queen Elizabeth ('Betty', surely?) on writing her Christmas message four years before. She could still picture the final draft of that speech. It had made a nice, impromptu text code to decipher the silk message.

In eighteen hours, it would all be over. She just had to survive the night.

Joan had almost lost track of the time when a dim chugging sound grew gradually louder, and a slim wooden slipper boat headed towards her with its lights off, before gliding gracefully to a halt just in front of her. The pilot raised his hand. '*Signora.*'

Before she stepped aboard, she had a question from Hector for him. It was like being back in 1943 – but she'd never done this herself before.

'It's an ugly night for being on the water,' she said in Italian.

'Not when the moon appears,' he said in English.

It was the answer Joan was expecting. The pilot held out a hand to help her in, and the boat headed rapidly back into the lagoon.

Grabbing onto her scarf to keep her wig in place, she noticed how the pilot steered a swift but careful course between the marker posts, looking out for other vessels on the water. They were alone, except for stationary fishing boats in the distance. At this speed, it would be impossible for anyone to follow them without being seen. After several minutes, he slowed the motor to a more stately pace. He didn't want to stand out, either. One hand on the wheel, he turned to her.

'*Ciao*, I'm Andrea. You must be Joan. Pleased to meet you. How is Hector? You must tell him he needs to visit us again.'

'I will,' Joan promised. 'He's doing well.'

'I guessed as much, given what we're doing here tonight.'

'What about you?' Joan asked. 'What do you do now?'

'Oh, I'm a farmer and a fisherman,' Andrea said with a shrug.

It was the shrug of a man who spent most of his time neither farming nor fishing. Joan wondered what he really got up to.

'You know our city?' he asked.

'This is my first visit.'

'Not your last, I hope.' He had to raise his voice above the sound of the engine. 'We're going to my cousin's house on Torcello. There are two people waiting to meet you.'

'They're safe?'

Andrea shrugged again. 'For now. They're certainly hungry. Or they were, anyway. They fell on the *salumi* as if they hadn't eaten for a week. The girl is as thin as a twig and doesn't talk. She's still recovering. I saw it in the war.'

'How old is she?' Joan asked.

'About this high,' he said, holding a palm flat at the level of his middle. 'She looks like her mother. There was a problem the other side of the border. The girl was sick, I think. It made them late.'

'Do you know what the journey was like?'

Andrea shook his head. 'Terror, that much is clear.' His lip curled. 'The girl still trembles. They are so proud of their world, those communists, and yet they wrap it in barbed wire to stop their own people leaving. We, we don't mind if our people cross into their side. We know they'll come back.'

Joan thought about border guards on patrol, and they reminded her of what was happening later.

'Hector didn't say exactly how you're going to get us into position,' she told him. 'No one must know we were there . . .'

He held up a hand. 'I understand. They might guess the identity of the lady and the little girl later. I found a solution. Venetian, *furbo*.' He tapped his forehead. 'Intelligent, cunning. We always find a way.'

Ahead, more islands eventually loomed out of the darkness. One of them was built up, like Murano, but smaller, and with more run-down houses. Joan was relieved to see human habitation again amidst the marshland of the lagoon.

'Burano?' she asked.

Andrea nodded. '*Brava*. You've studied the map. The home of the lacemakers. Elisabetta is visiting tomorrow with her 'usband.'

He said it proudly, as if it was a detail that Joan might not know. She realised that Hector wouldn't have explained she was in charge of the details of the Queen's schedule. How *had* he described her? she wondered.

They navigated past Burano, and a new dark mass of land loomed ahead. This one, marked by its huge, soaring bell tower, must be Torcello. At sundown the local *carabinieri* had inspected the place to make sure no uninvited visitors were lurking. They would be back at dawn to lock it down fully against idle visitors and paparazzi, in readiness for the Queen. That left about five hours to get into position.

Joan contemplated the bell tower from the boat. Standing alone, it was square and simple, its only decoration being a row of arched windows near the roof. She marvelled at its height as they approached, because the closer they got, the more the island seemed to have little more to it than grass and trees.

'Who lives here?' she asked, peering into the darkness.

'A few farmers and fishermen,' Andrea explained, 'like me. There are three priests who look after the cathedral next door, and the restaurant owners for the tourists who come here. There's an eccentric scholar who collects stone statues. And my cousin, who likes a quiet life.'

'A cathedral and a tower, just for them?'

He shrugged. 'Torcello was once the capital of the lagoon. When Venice was mud, this was the centre, a thousand years ago. Now it is the edge.'

Far above them, a waning moon appeared in a gap between the clouds. This was the day the Americans had been seeking to follow the Russians by sending a man into space. Had Alan Shepard done it? she wondered. From this spot, in the middle of the dark lagoon, it was impossible to picture.

Andrea steered the craft slowly, quietly, through a channel in the marshland to the east of the island. The bell tower rose high above them to the left. Then the boat rounded a bend, and another, curving channel appeared, running between the island proper and a spur of land to the north. They followed this new channel for a couple of minutes. Joan had just made out the tiled roof of an isolated country villa across the channel from the bell tower, when Andrea cut the engine.

'*Siamo arrivati*. My cousin's house. Let me introduce you to our guests.'

They disembarked. Here on Torcello, unlike Murano, there was no hiss and hum. Beyond the gentle breeze that had whipped up while they were travelling across the lagoon, the place was unnervingly quiet, except for the ever-present slap of small waves against the embankment. The moon cast a ghostly silver light along the brick path through an orchard to the villa. In other circumstances, it would be romantic. Joan wondered if Hector had honeymooned in this very spot. She scolded herself for thinking of it.

Chapter 48

At the villa, Andrea indicated a door that led straight into the kitchen. Inside, three faces, lit by a single lamp, looked up from a scrubbed wooden table. One had luxuriant dark curls, flecked with grey. She was obviously in charge. Joan berated herself for assuming that 'the cousin' was a man. Opposite her, a gaunt, broad-faced woman sat with an exhausted child on her lap. The girl sucked her thumb and clutched a frayed and ragged patchwork dog to her neck, like a comfort blanket. Both had thick, dark hair, cut short, and light eyes. Joan recognised them instantly from the photograph she'd seen in Curzon Street.

'Hello,' she said. 'Doctor Sokolova, my name is Joan. I've come to get you.'

The woman's face dissolved into a wet-cheeked smile.

Introductions were complicated by working out what language to use. Andrea introduced his cousin as Vittoria. Her English wasn't as good as Joan's Italian, so Joan thanked her for her help in Italian, while Vittoria insisted on putting together a plate of food for her new guest. Sokolova's French was better than her English, so she got by in a mixture of the two, accompanied by dramatic hand gestures.

'Tell me about your journey,' Joan said, joining them at the table.

Sokolova shook her head and looked away. '*L'horreur! L'horreur!*'

Joan assumed she wouldn't get much more, after what Andrea had told her, but over coffee, beer and several cigarettes, she warmed up and the story slowly emerged.

It had started ten years ago, when Tatiana Sokolova had been working as a part-time tour guide in her university holidays. Pavel Michalowski was one of the visitors to Moscow, the youngest in his group, and they'd hit it off straightaway. There was supposed to be no fraternisation between the young people, but naturally, there was. She and Pavel had a love of chess in common. They spent as much time together as they could. They promised to stay in touch, and did so, through chess magazines and puzzles, accompanied by letters. Tatiana became a medical researcher, working in the military, while Pavel scraped a living as a photographer's assistant. They got cleverer and more creative as they had more to share, and more to conceal from the censor.

'And the child?' Joan asked, indicating the girl, who by now was asleep on Sokolova's lap. The girl's true paternity had gradually dawned on her as Tatiana spoke.

Tatiana nodded as she stroked her daughter's hair.

'Does she know?'

Tatiana shook her head. 'Maria knows she's my girl, but not who her father is. In my letters, she was always the daughter of a friend. When Pavel asked after her, it was as my friend's little girl. But it was why we stayed in touch.

He always asked, always. He knew what he was.' Her face suddenly clouded. 'I haven't heard from him in weeks. I worry. What has happened?'

Joan sidestepped the question.

'He indicated that you worked at Star City. Is that right?'

'He said that?' Tatiana took a swig of beer and nodded slowly. 'Two years ago. I worked on the . . .' She struggled for the word in English and in French, but it came eventually. 'The centrifuge. My job was to monitor the cosmonauts as they experienced the forces of gravity. I came to know them.'

'And you know who ran the programme, I assume,' Joan said. She knew it wasn't her job to debrief Doctor Sokolova, but equally, something could go wrong at any point. This could be the only chance. However, Tatiana shook her head and waved a finger at Joan.

'I don't discuss this here. Not now. Not with you. Not until Maria and I both see Big Ben.'

Joan smiled at this. 'I'm still amazed that you've got your daughter with you. How did you get her out?'

This was something Sokolova was willing to discuss. As she became more disillusioned, Pavel taught her how to communicate with microdots. The original plan, she said, had been to escape alone, when the chance of the chess tournament in Austria came her way.

'It was a miracle. I had to take it.'

For years, she had been sickened by tales of starvation, murder and repression in the satellite states, in the gulags. She looked around as she spoke, glancing at the darkness through a small gap in the curtains.

'To talk of this . . .' she said, nervously dragging on her cigarette. 'Aloud . . . It is the first time. Excuse me.'

She gave the sleeping girl to Vittoria, and went off to the nearby toilet, where they could hear her retching. On her return, she lit a fresh cigarette. The words came with increasing ease and urgency.

At first, she had lived in hope that Mr Khrushchev would bring about a more open Soviet Union after the death of Stalin, but she sensed resistance to his changes among her countrymen. She didn't think they would last. All the time, she had to lie to her best friends about what she thought and believed. She was losing faith.

'I was losing myself,' she said. 'I was not a worthy mother for my child. I had to do something. I asked Pavel if he could help me, and he told me he had done it before. Somehow, Maria would follow, we would find a way. But when the time came close, I realised I couldn't go without her, not for a second. So I . . .' She hesitated for the first time and looked down. 'I . . . befriended the head of the chess team.'

In the background, Andrea coughed at the word 'befriended'. She looked up again with a thousand-yard stare.

'I said I wanted my girl to have the chance to travel. I think he knew that in my deepest heart, I might want to flee, but he didn't know I had help to do it. For him, it would have seemed impossible, and having Maria with me would make it *more* impossible. He said he would seek permission, and it came two weeks ago. I sent a note to Pavel, telling him, but I never received a reply. Tell me, how is Pavel? I repeat, what happened? Is he alive?'

In her fitful sleep on Vittoria's lap, the girl made a little groan. They all turned to her as Vittoria gently rocked her.

'I gather Maria was sick,' Joan said to Tatiana. 'It made you late for the meeting in Cagliari. What happened?'

'She got sick in Moscow,' Tatiana said. 'I pretended it was nothing. I gave her drugs to calm the fever. She *had* to come with me. I hoped it would go away by the time we got to Vienna, but it was worse. Her temperature was so high she burned. I nursed her on the train, and when she started to hallucinate, I hid her. I gave her so many drugs I wasn't sure she would survive.'

No wonder they had been delayed when they got to Italy. They must both have been utterly drained and exhausted.

'*La povera piccina*,' Vittoria said tenderly, stroking the girl's hair.

'You didn't answer me,' Tatiana said to Joan. Her tone was harsh. 'About Pavel. I ask three times now. He is dead.'

Joan didn't have the heart to lie. She said nothing.

Tatiana resumed the strong, steady gaze that Joan recognised from her photograph. She finished her cigarette without speaking, and ground it into the ashtray at her elbow. Her fingers trembled at first, then stopped.

'He saved us,' she said. 'He knew the risk he took.' She gave the slightest of shrugs.

Andrea raised his left arm and tapped his watch. He took a large, old-fashioned brass key from a dish in the centre of the table and handed it to Joan.

'You're not safe yet. Come on, it's time to go. One thing more . . .'

He raised a finger and indicated to Joan to follow him into the hall. There, he opened the drawer of an old oak dresser and pulled out a small leather satchel, from which he retrieved a pistol. He showed it to her, holding it flat across his palms.

'You know how to use this?'

Joan nodded, with more confidence than she felt. It had been a very long time, but she had gained a fair bit of practice on farms and ranges in the war. If the worst came to the worst, muscle memory would take over. Wouldn't it?

'It's fully loaded. I fired it yesterday. It's in good condition. There's more ammunition in the bag,' he said.

Joan held the gun in her hands briefly, clicking the safety on and off, getting a feel for the magazine release. Then she slipped it back into its satchel, shouldered the strap and nodded that she was ready.

Chapter 49

The journey from the villa to their final destination for the night was short. Andrea carried Maria to an open rowing boat that sat ready beside the sleek slipper boat he had used before. Tatiana climbed in, a large cloth bag strapped to her back containing all she owned, and sat at the stern, with her arm around the girl. Joan sat in the prow, cradling the leather satchel and her rucksack.

It was breezier and cloudier than before. Standing at the oars, Andrea manoeuvred the boat for five minutes along the channel, which formed an S-bend to the north of the island. The bell tower remained ahead and to their left, getting ever closer. Before they drew level with it, without warning, Andrea steered the boat towards what looked like thick vegetation on the bell tower side. At the last moment, a tiny inlet appeared out of nowhere in the moonlight, and he guided them through a waterway so narrow they could have touched the dangling fronds of trees on either side.

Just before they reached a small stone bridge over the waterway, the trees gave way to grass and he pulled in, indicating to Joan to climb out first. She took the boat's painter with her, tying it to a post put there for the purpose, before helping Tatiana and the girl climb out. Maria visibly shivered in the night air, though it wasn't particularly cold. Under her too-small coat, the girl was skin and bone.

Tatiana pointed to the bell tower, now situated about a hundred yards ahead and to their left, across the meadow. Joan nodded. Following the wider channel with the S-bend a bit further would have taken them closer to it, but going overland this way, they were less exposed. They just had to make it to the tower and hide there until morning. It wasn't due to be searched at dawn because, as the key attested, it was usually locked. Life would be more complicated once the royal party arrived, but Joan hoped she could talk her way out of most situations. It helped to know that the Queen herself could back her up, if necessary.

'Come on,' she whispered. 'It's not far.'

Maria stood rigid and sucked her thumb while Tatiana murmured an emotional goodbye to Andrea. Joan waved as he pulled away, turning in a tight circle to return the way they had come. Tatiana grabbed her daughter's hand and, crouching low, they made their way around the edge of the meadow, sticking close to the bushes, while the wind ruffled the tops of the long grasses.

Joan's heightened senses picked up every animal rustle in the short lulls in the wind. From the way Tatiana's head jerked left and right, she sensed the Russian was on high alert. The girl moved silently behind them, as directed. When she looked round, Joan could see the moon reflected in her frightened eyes.

The bell tower sat at the edge of a small complex of ancient buildings with sloping, tiled roofs, which would be part of the royal visit tomorrow. Just beyond it was the cathedral.

It dated back a thousand years, Joan supposed, and she was surprised by its relatively small size: she'd seen larger college chapels in Cambridge. But the tower was dominant, as if its bells had once needed to ring as far as Murano.

As they approached it from the rear, the bushes edging the meadow gave way to a neat, waist-high stone wall that partially enclosed a garden of some sort, and they had to crouch lower still to stay in its shadow. Joan had the tower's door key ready in her hand. Apparently, the entrance was in the wall facing the blank-faced rear of the cathedral. According to Andrea, the lock would be oiled. He was taking no chances.

They had reached the end of the sheltering wall. To their right, a grassy bank ran down to the S-bend channel, lined with a couple of rows of cypress trees that bordered a gravel path between the cathedral and the water. The wind rustled in the branches and the moon cast a patchy light through the clouds.

Joan sensed, rather than heard, a shift in the atmosphere. Something had spooked Maria, who buried her face in her mother's arm. Joan looked around for the cause. Nothing moved.

The tower was ten yards away now. Leading the way, Joan set off for it at a crouch. As soon as she was in the open, she heard a fizz and a loud crack, and at the same time, there was a puff of brick dust in the wall ahead.

Someone was shooting. The bullet had missed her by inches.

Maria screamed and Tatiana froze. Ears ringing, Joan ran back to the girl and threw her bodily to the other side of the garden wall.

Chapter 50

In a moment, everything had changed, and Joan's veins were full of pure adrenaline. At least the low wall beside them offered some protection. After a second's hesitation, Tatiana flew to join them. She threw herself down next to Joan, panting.

'Did he get you?'

Joan shook her head. She couldn't understand why the shooter hadn't fired a second time. She could feel him waiting.

'He must be behind one of those cypress trees, near the water,' she muttered, setting the key down and retrieving the pistol from the satchel at her hip. It had all seemed so theoretical when Andrea handed the gun to her. She wished she had been more honest now, and taken the chance to practise reloading it, at least.

Maria whimpered.

'He knows where we are,' Tatiana whispered through clenched teeth.

'He does. And I doubt he's alone. I'll hold them off while you go to the tower. Run to the back of it, because he hasn't got a clear shot that way.' Joan pointed. 'Then you can go round from that side and let yourselves in while I cover you.

Lock the door behind you.' She handed over the key. 'Do you understand?'

The Russian nodded. Joan released the safety catch on the pistol and got into position on one knee, back to the wall's edge, arm outstretched.

'Go!'

Joan swung round ninety degrees, so her arm was clear of the wall and the gun was pointing at the trees. She let off a shot, while behind her, Tatiana and the girl launched themselves towards the tower. She was about to let off another shot when she realised why the shooter had been stingy with his bullets. The rising wind muffled the sound to an extent, but if someone in a distant home heard rapid gunfire, surely they would investigate? Joan needed to avoid that if she could and so, presumably, did he. He didn't respond straightaway.

It didn't mean that he had given up though.

Joan ran at a crouch a few yards back down the wall, further into the garden. Tatiana and Maria were safely behind the tower's huge bulk by now, and a large cloud was starting to block out the moon. Joan took advantage of what little light there was to check out the garden. It consisted of mown grass, a few low trees and fruit cages, and a rustic tool shed in the middle. She could see a chess game playing out, where she would run behind the tool shed while he ran from the trees towards the cathedral, then moved along its wall towards her, crouching in its shadow. She would be stuck. So instead, she stayed where she was. That way, if he made his move, she'd have a clear shot at him. But then, so would he.

All the time, the wind was rising, and she was listening for the sound of the iron key rattling in its lock. Or the sound of Andrea rowing or running to the rescue. Surely he had heard them and knew what must be happening? But it was possible he had given her the only gun.

The large cloud finally finished covering the moon. A few seconds after the darkness was complete, she heard the dim but distinctive sound of iron on iron. It was possible he hadn't heard it above the wind, and to distract his attention, Joan rose up and let off another covering shot towards the trees, holding her right arm out to the side as far as she could, to disguise where her head was. A shot came back and whistled over her hand. She saw the muzzle flash before she ducked back down, and realised he must be out in the open now, heading straight for her.

There was nothing for it but to pop up and fire again. But before she rose upright, there was another report, louder than before, and this time, it came from behind her. She whipped round, expecting to see another shooter at the tower. If someone was there already, it was over. But instead, Tatiana stood faintly silhouetted against the brick. She must have a weapon of her own – the possibility hadn't crossed Joan's mind – and she had disobeyed Joan's instructions in order to creep round the tower and join the fight. Heavily in shadow, she was almost invisible from a distance. She kept her gun raised, fired again, and Joan heard the man half shout, half groan in shock, before he fell. In the ensuing quiet, the tower door closed. Maria must be inside.

The moving cloud revealed the moon just enough for Joan to see Tatiana shake her head at her. She lifted two fingers. Joan agreed: there would be another one somewhere. These men didn't work alone.

Joan tried to picture what they were up against. Logically, even if a team of KGB agents or local hires had been tracking Joan or Tatiana to Torcello, which they must have done somehow, they still wouldn't know exactly what the plan was. Most people reached the island via a large channel on the other side of it. In order to be waiting here instead, the men must have seen the women leave the villa with Andrea and gone ahead of them, assuming they would head for the square in front of the cathedral, perhaps, which was reachable via moorings near the cypress trees.

It might have come as a shock to see them come via the meadow and head for the tower, and it was the women's bad luck the fallen man had spotted them. It was possible that his partner could still be behind the cypress trees, but from there he would have seen Tatiana's muzzle flashes and shot at her, surely? More likely, he had tried to circle round to surprise them from the other side. By now, he would have had just about enough time to run at speed around the cathedral and the religious buildings attached to it.

If there were three men, they were done for. But the first one had been surprisingly inept for KGB. He was the one on the ground now, after all. So there was hope.

The cloud was passing. Joan motioned to Tatiana to stay in the tower's shadow. She ran towards her and peered round the ancient bricks to get a sense of the land beyond. The key was still in the door. A few yards further on to the right, she could just about make out the curved wall and tiled roof of a buttress-type cathedral building. It seemed a natural place to hide. Ahead was a vegetable garden, and to the left, yet another little channel.

Joan took the opportunity to discard her magazine into the satchel and load a new one. Her training was back with a vengeance, and she thanked God for endless repetition on a variety of weapons in the darkest days of the war. With the weight of the gun in her hand, she could hear her boyfriend's voice telling her to shoot without pity or hesitation. Back then, the Russians were allies and heroes. It was Germans and Italians she had pictured.

She tapped on Tatiana's shoulder.

'This time, go inside,' she instructed in a low voice, against the rising wind.

She ran to the far corner of the tower, beyond the door, and knelt down, heart hammering, pistol at the ready.

Tatiana moved, but so did the cloud, and the tower was suddenly bathed in moonlight. While Tatiana yanked at the door, Joan fired in the direction of the buttress to her right. She had expected to see the flash of a muzzle from beside it, but instead the shot came from her left, near the water channel. It rang in her ears and the bullet was so close she felt it in her hair. Thinking she'd just made a fatal mistake, Joan swung round and saw the second man, kneeling like her, silhouetted in the light. He fired again, and should have killed her with a headshot, but this time, nothing happened. His gun must have jammed. His eyes widened as she pulled her trigger, and her shot propelled him backwards into the water.

She didn't wait to see if he climbed out again, or if there was another one, waiting. Tatiana was inside the tower holding the key, and Joan clambered in after her. They locked the heavy door from the inside.

'Mama!'

Maria had climbed up the winding stairs to a couple of floors above them. They joined her, and kept on going until they reached the top. From the tower's open windows, they had a view of this whole side of the island. They watched as a slipper boat motored very slowly down the S-bend channel to the mooring, and two men in black removed the body from the grass by the cypress trees, carrying him between them as if he were a drunk after a heavy night.

Then it was as if nothing had happened. Dawn came, and with it more boats, carrying police and carabinieri in various uniforms, who prodded and poked in bushes and trees, and peered in the boats at their moorings. Joan watched as a priest accosted them, asking them questions and gesturing at the cathedral. She guessed he had heard the shots, but hadn't dared investigate. The uniformed men shrugged and gesticulated, following him in the direction of the cathedral square.

What they didn't do, was check for bullet casings. After they'd all gone – to guard Torcello's sea approaches, as Joan remembered from her schedule – she slipped out to gather as much spent brass as she could find. She briefly looked for blood in the grass, but it had rained for half an hour just before dawn, and everything looked freshly washed.

Britannia would be arriving in Venice soon. In a few hours, Torcello would be looking its best for Her Majesty. Joan had a lot to tell her.

Chapter 51

For the first time in nearly a week, the Queen was not the lead headline in the papers.

The royal yacht sailed slowly through the lagoon towards St Mark's Square, accompanied by a flotilla of welcoming craft and greeted by a long line of semaphoring sailors along the Venetian shoreline. But the main item on every radio, television set and newsstand was Alan Shepard's successful ascent into the outer atmosphere.

In a perfect world, the Queen would have been happy to let the astronaut hog all the newsprint while she and Philip got on with a quiet little romantic holiday in Venice, unobserved . . . But she was the second headline in all the papers, and the second item on the news. The basin in front of St Mark's was alive with boats of all shapes and sizes, while the square ahead was already packed. Philip had been absolutely right about the crowds. She would simply have to imagine what the city would be like without all of its citizens and several thousand more besides thronging every bridge and quay to see her.

As she left *Britannia* by motorboat, the Queen's first thought was that by the time she came back, the yacht should be harbouring a couple of Russian stowaways. Dear God! If anyone had told her, even three weeks ago, that she would be *hoping* for Russian stowaways, she'd have suggested a rest cure. Today, it was the best-case scenario. If anything had gone wrong last night . . . Well, it wouldn't do to think about that. She had to look cheerful for the packed crowds ahead.

And actually, if any city in the world was going to take your mind off the fact you might just be precipitating the third world war in order to save a woman and a little girl you'd never met, then Venice was the place.

'My God!' Philip said beside her, as they motored across the mouth of the Grand Canal. 'Just look at it! Bloody timeless.'

Indeed, the view looked just like the paintings in her collection from two centuries ago. Over there was the ethereal white marble mass of La Salute. On the canal and in the basin, sailors and gondoliers who manned hundreds of craft wore historical costumes, like a pageant. Across the water was the iconic bell tower of St Mark's basilica, which she recognised from a dozen paintings, and beside it, the Bridge of Sighs.

The mayor and British consul duly greeted, the visit to the bell tower and the golden, glittering basilica duly conducted, the royal couple boarded another motorboat – a local one this time – and took a tour of some of the smaller canals. Every few minutes, the Queen's thoughts strayed to Torcello, and what may or may not have happened yesterday, but Philip and the city demanded most of her attention. Every available space was packed with faces and, everyone, it seemed, was calling out to her. But they were smiling, cheering, shouting '*bella*', and it really was quite difficult not to be charmed – even if, just for *once*, you'd be delighted if they were somewhere else.

The royal itinerary for this part had deliberately been kept secret, so occasionally they passed under a bridge that wasn't crowded. Sometimes there simply wasn't room for people, as ancient houses lined the canal directly. The reflections in the water were mesmerising.

Philip, who had visited as an eager seventeen year-old, pointed out his favourite sights: a trefoil window, an almost-hidden garden, the grand asymmetry of a centuries-old palazzo. Free from the fuss and razzamatazz of St Mark's, he was like a schoolboy again, whipping out his camera to take photographs. She had rarely seen him so happy. And soon, it would be time to cross the lagoon in a very fast boat, which would be the pinnacle of his day, she was sure.

Just as meeting Joan at the other end would probably be hers.

All too soon, they were watching Venice's many bell towers gradually disappear into the hazy distance, while Philip did his best impression of a movie star beside her, gazing out over the bumpy water in fashionable shades. And then the ancient tower of Torcello loomed ahead, a bit like a lighthouse, guiding the way.

Their boat travelled slowly through a channel to the east of the island, then turned into another one with an S-bend to it. The Queen spotted the first house: a villa with a tiled roof to their left, nestling behind an orchard of apple trees. A little further along, they drew up at a quay next to the cathedral and were led down a path flanked by cypress trees to the little square.

This was as close to privacy as the royal couple were going to get – which meant that they were merely accompanied by the Duke and Duchess of Kent, Lady Sarah, a smattering of staff, the mayor, the consul, the ambassador and half a dozen Venetian officials. Still, compared with the thousands in St Mark's Square, it was positively intimate.

Philip had his camera out again, taking pictures of every building.

'Marvellous, isn't it?' he said cheerfully. 'I've never forgotten the atmosphere here. The cathedral's Byzantine, you know. It goes back to the eight hundreds. There's a mosaic of the Last Judgement on the last wall that will blow your mind.'

The Queen nodded. She was scanning the little welcoming party outside for a certain face. And there it was, at the back. Her assistant private secretary. Looking quite smart in a dark dress to hide the fact that it was slightly crumpled. Her bright lipstick and neat red hair only emphasised the pallor of her face. But she seemed unharmed.

'Just a moment,' she said to Philip. 'I need to ask Joan something.'

'Oh, is she here?' he asked, casually. 'I didn't see her on the boat.'

'She came earlier,' she told him, before walking over to greet the group and single Joan out for a little word.

Joan curtsied. 'Your Majesty.'

'Did everything go smoothly?' the Queen asked. 'I know you've been busy.'

'No, ma'am.' Joan's gaze was frank. 'There was some trouble to take care of.'

'Oh dear.' The Queen was a mistress of understatement. Under her light wool jacket, she could feel her heart pounding. 'You were picking up some packages, weren't you . . . ?'

'They'll be safely stowed this afternoon, ma'am.'

'Well, that's a relief. Are you joining us for lunch at Cipriani's?'

'Yes, ma'am.'

'Come *on*, Lilibet,' Philip called. 'Or you'll miss the Last Judgement.'

The Queen, who felt she'd already experienced it, followed him obediently towards the cathedral door.

Chapter 52

The Locanda Cipriani was a low and pretty, rural-looking building just off the square – within easy earshot of, let's say, a pistol fight beside the bell tower. Either they slept very well here, Joan reflected, or they were used to gunshots from night hunters, or they had decided to stay out of other people's business. Whatever it was, nobody made any mention of the night before.

The royal party was entertained to lunch at tables on the terrace, overlooking a neat little garden and beyond it, a minor channel where it was possible – but very unlikely, obviously – for a man who had been shot in the chest to be lying, even now, under the still, calm surface of the water.

Everyone was in a very good mood, delighted by the weather, the setting, the holiday feel of it all. The food was light and delicious, and Joan felt she was probably the only person for whom it turned to ashes in her mouth. She knew that a hungry nine year-old girl nearby had only bread and apples to eat, but there was little she could do about that right now. It could have been much worse.

They lingered on the terrace, smoking, while Philip told stories of his first visit to the island at seventeen, and the mayor of Venice declared the fervent hope that he would often return with his bride. Then, on the way back to the launch to travel to Burano, they encountered a freshly married bride and groom, who laughed and threw some of their confetti at them. Joan saw the Queen smile even more brightly than she normally did.

Her Majesty had relaxed. It was nearly over. Surely nothing could go wrong now?

An hour after the royal party left for the other islands, Torcello had returned to its quiet self. A motor launch drew up to a spare mooring by the cypress trees, barely noticed by anyone, and a naval officer, smartly dressed in a white shirt and trousers, emerged to take charge of two packages that had been left for him by the quay. They were tea chests, accompanied by Her Majesty's assistant private secretary, who had stayed behind to look after them.

When they were safely aboard, Commander Kinnock ordered the yottie at the wheel to set a course in the direction of St Mark's.

'Did it go all right?' he asked Joan, breezily.

'In a manner of speaking.'

She pictured the detailed debrief she would give Hector, later, and Her Majesty, if she asked. Frequently, the vision of her bullet hitting the second man in the chest with such force that it propelled him backwards would come into her head and block out what was in front of her. This must be what it had been like for Sandra on the train, picturing the skipping rope man. There were moments Joan honestly thought it must all have been a dream. She was astonished that her aim had been so sure, after so many years without practice. Although, to be strictly honest, she'd been aiming at his head.

When the launch arrived back at *Britannia*, at anchor in the basin, several sailors had to help Kinnock manoeuvre the tea chests from the boat. Both were unwieldy, particularly the larger one. The yotties were used to it, and did so without complaint, but the executive officer caught them at it and turned on the supply officer, who by now was back on deck with Joan.

'What on earth's going on here?' Attwell demanded. 'How long does it take to retrieve a parcel, Commander Kinnock? You've been gone for nearly two hours.'

'A trip to the islands,' Kinnock said with a winning grin. He turned on the charm. 'They're further than you think.'

'What were you doing out there?'

'He was picking me up,' Joan said, smiling gratefully.

Attwell frowned. It wasn't clear why Joan couldn't have travelled with the rest of the royal party, as she usually did. But she offered no explanation, and he was too polite to ask for one.

'And what's in those tea chests?' he asked, turning back to Kinnock. 'The Master of the Household said he thought you must have gone to Murano to pick up something for the Queen. A gift of some sort. Glass. Is that right?'

'Where do you want them, sir?' one of the sailors asked.

'Down in in the trunk room for now,' Kinnock said breezily. 'Careful with them, won't you? They're fragile.' As the boxes were stacked onto a trolley, they let out a muffled clink.

'So?' Attwell demanded. 'What are they?'

'Special delivery for Her Majesty,' Kinnock explained. 'Plus, I have a contact out there. Let's call it a nice surprise.'

'It had better be a good one.'

Kinnock lowered his voice. 'Of Russian origin.'

Attwell's eyebrows shot up at this. 'Really?'

'I can't speak here. I'll tell you later. Sorry, Commander, I need to go and supervise.'

The tea chests were now being passed along a line of yotties to one of the service passageways that led down to the bowels of the ship.

'Come on, sir,' you can tell us,' the nearest sailor begged, as soon as Attwell was out of earshot. 'We won't breathe a word.'

Kinnock frowned at him. 'Are you sure I can trust you?'

'On my mother's life, sir.'

'Didn't she die last year?'

'On his mother's life, then,' the sailor amended, elbowing his companion.

Kinnock paused and sucked his teeth. 'You have to promise to keep it a secret. On pain of death.'

They nodded.

'I had them sent over specially from Trieste.' He lowered his voice and looked around. 'For the wardroom, later. I got hold of some top-class vodka. It's supposed to be from Finland, but really . . .' He winked.

'Ooh!'

'There's nothing like it, they say. Perfect for one of Mr Bond's martinis.'

'Who's he, sir?'

'A spy. Haven't you read the books?'

'Not yet, sir. Are they good, sir?'

'Not bad. Anyway, not a word, OK? And look after those boxes.'

There was another clink as the tea chests were carefully manhandled down a ladder towards the lower decks.

Chapter 53

Relieved beyond measure that Joan, the doctor and the girl were safe, the Queen thoroughly enjoyed her trip to the lace-makers of Burano, followed by the glass-makers of Murano, where Lady Sarah had previously made a private purchase of two large mirrors on her behalf. The secret to a successful lie was in the details. The Queen refused to be caught out.

Afterwards, the boat ride back to Venice was a quick one. She retired to her bedroom on *Britannia* for a rest, while Philip went up on deck to watch the many sailing boats gadding about in the basin, in celebration of the day.

But after half an hour or so of recuperation, the Queen could bear it no longer. She asked to meet Joan in her sitting room, where her APS updated her in full on everything that had happened the night before.

'They came and took away the bodies?'

'The one that I could see on the grass, ma'am, yes. I don't know what happened to the one in the water. I'm praying he doesn't float up soon. Andrea will keep a lookout.'

'Why didn't he come back to help?'

'He'd been knocked out almost as soon as he left us,' Joan said. 'I spoke to him after you'd gone. He said he was hit with something from the bank and left unconscious in his boat. When the police came, they assumed he was drunk. But he's OK now. Still a bit groggy. Thank God they didn't shoot him. I suppose they didn't want to leave a mess.'

'Who were they, do you think?'

Joan shrugged. 'I assume it must have been a local team, with backup. If they'd been a crack team from Moscow they'd have killed us all, I'm pretty sure.'

'You undersell yourself. You did an exceptional job,' the Queen told her. 'And Sokolova, too. I wonder where she got her gun from.'

'I can only imagine someone in Trieste, ma'am. She can't have had it on the train trip from Vienna.'

'Hmm, I agree. And the girl. Will she be all right, do you think?'

'It's hard to say,' Joan reflected. 'She's frightened now, but she has her mother for comfort.'

'Yes, there's that. Sokolova *is* her mother, then?'

Joan nodded. 'And Michalowski's her father.'

'Ah!' The Queen nodded. 'Yes, of course. And now he won't get to see his daughter.' She felt a tightening in her chest. 'After all that.'

What cruelty the KGB were capable of.

Although, it occurred to her to wonder how they knew well enough what Michalowski was up to in order to kill him – but not enough to identify his old lover and stop her from going to Vienna, or taking the girl with her.

Cruel and incompetent. Which was unlike them, but very, very lucky for all on board today.

'Is there anything else you need, ma'am?' Joan asked.

'Not for now, Joan. You've been busy enough.'

Joan gratefully retired to her cabin for a rest, and the Queen strongly suspected she would sleep the sleep of the dead.

This would be Elizabeth's first and last night in Venice. Dressed in her evening finery with a fur wrap around her shoulders, she watched the sunset reflect against the mouth of the Grand Canal from the comfort of the shelter deck, and knew that it would rank alongside the sunsets in the Western Isles as one of the best she'd ever seen.

Philip joined her, immaculately attired in black tie and bronzed from his hours on deck in the Med earlier, and again this afternoon, on the motor launches.

'Your gondola awaits, Cabbage,' he said.

And indeed, it was true. It turned out that there had been a huge furore, lasting days, over whether the royal couple would set foot in a gondola. The mayor (a motor boat enthusiast) had insisted it wasn't necessary; the gondoliers, incensed, had petitioned that it was. Busy in Rome, and with Joan otherwise occupied, the Queen knew nothing of this. As soon as she found out today, she'd said yes of course to the gondola ride, and now there one was, bobbing on the water, with four gondoliers in their wide straw hats, all dressed in white, ready to guide them down the Grand Canal to their destination.

Tonight, it was the Queen's turn to play host to her hosts. The British consul had originally suggested a formal sit-down dinner at the consulate, but the Queen didn't want this trip to Venice to feel stuffy. She had counter-suggested a stand-up drinks, with a cold collation on the side, so that she and Philip could move amongst the guests and chat. The guest list was packed with all the most interesting people that Sir Hugh, the consul and the British ambassador could think of. And best of all, the consulate overlooked the Grand Canal by the Accademia bridge, so if the chat ever faltered, they could simply admire the view.

Just as Philip had yearned for his free time sailing near Sicily (she still felt guilty about that), the Queen had yearned for this: twinkling lights, reflections on dark water, fascinating people to talk to, gathered gondoliers below, holding lit torches and serenading. And later there would be fireworks . . .

And in the nature of so many things that one looks forward to enormously, after a couple of hours of entertainment, Elizabeth suddenly felt exhausted and a small, ungrateful part of her just wanted to go home.

It wasn't *she* who had been shot at last night, for goodness' sake, but it almost felt as if it was. Just being stared and shouted at by many thousands of people was very tiring. There were all the images of the day in her mind, all fabulous and beautiful, all jostling together. Then there was the deep relief and security of knowing that Tatiana Sokolova and her daughter were safe, the deep sadness at Pavel Michalowski's fate, the mixture of guilt and pride at having endangered her own yacht and saved those precious lives . . . It was all, honestly, a bit much.

Was this an ageing film actor that she had just been introduced to by the ambassador, or an entrepreneur or a musical impresario? Was his wife in floaty pink chiffon and big, baroque pearls Italian, Spanish or South American? She couldn't tell from the accent, and couldn't ask again.

'And where do you live?' she asked, rather desperately. 'On the Grand Canal?'

'Absolutely, ma'am! Well guessed! Almost next door,' the man said, puffing out his chest like a grouse in mating season. 'We like to call it the money-pit palazzo. You passed it this morning on your little tour.'

'Oh, really?' She had passed so many.

'It's the one with the Renaissance façade near the Rialto,' the wife explained.

The Queen thought that description fitted most of the palazzi she'd seen, but she nodded sagely. 'Do tell me all about it.'

The lovely thing about asking questions was that one didn't have to talk while they were answered. Thrilled to be asked, the couple described their home's terrazzo marble floors, damask walls and carved wooden ceilings.

'Did you put those in?' the Queen asked, politely. 'Was that why it was a money pit?'

'Oh no. It was what we had to take out!' the pink-clad wife said. 'For a start, the kitchen was totally illegal.'

How could a kitchen be illegal? But it turned out that, according to this couple, owners of Venetian houses were known to flout planning rules, selling them on to unsuspecting buyers with all sorts of lurking problems requiring permits they did not have, requiring expensive changes or the greasing of bureaucratic palms.

Oh really, the Queen thought. The last thing one needed, on one's only night in Venice, was a rundown of somebody else's property disasters. With four residences to manage at home, she had quite enough of her own. She wished she hadn't asked.

She shifted her evening bag handle from one gloved arm to the other, which was the signal to be rescued, casting a quick eye around the room for Lady Sarah, but her lady-in-waiting was deep in conversation with a diabolically attractive diplomat.

'Of course, we should have known,' the wife was saying. 'The palazzo's cursed. Everybody told us.'

'Cursed? Surely not?'

'Oh yes, all its owners have gone bankrupt or died since the fifteenth century,' the husband said. 'It's like something out of Edgar Allan Poe. We should have pulled out. But they handled us so well.'

The couple exchanged rueful glances.

'How?' the Queen asked. Lady Sarah was heading over at last, but now she needed to know the end of the story.

'Well, it sounds ridiculous,' the husband said, 'but they put the price up. They told us they had another buyer. Then they went completely quiet for six weeks. We thought somebody'd died.'

'Oh?'

'They made us work for it,' the wife pitched in. 'So clever. We had to haggle, and make a lot of calls. We kept thinking we'd lost it. In the end, we put in so much effort that when they finally let us have it, we paid twice what it was worth, permits, curse and all.'

In the gondola with Philip on the way back to *Britannia*, the Queen's mind kept drifting back to that conversation about the palazzo. It seemed very Italian, somehow: great beauty, rich history, a hint of a curse, the heavy hand of bureaucracy. The Venetians seemed to do everything with brio. Even property disasters.

Elizabeth smiled to herself as she and Philip made their way back past the ethereal Salute church, serenaded by a flotilla of gondoliers. It was gently starting to drizzle, so she pulled her wrap around her shoulders, extracted a silk scarf from her handbag and tied it over her hair. All around the basin, the windows of every building blazed with light, and the boats lit the way with torches. It was as if they were in the middle of one of her better Canalettos.

Philip slipped a hand around hers. She squeezed his fingers.

'What are you thinking?' she asked.

'Hmm? Oh, I was just wondering how they get the bloody houses to stay up. Someone said something about stilts, but that can't be the whole story, surely? I should have asked more questions. How could they take the weight? And surely the wood would rot?'

She sighed. And there they were, back to property.

She thought again of the unwary couple who had allowed themselves to be suckered into buying a cursed palazzo that they fully expected to bankrupt them, or worse. And how extraordinary that the suckering had involved making it *difficult* for them to purchase it, not easy. That was very perverse.

Britannia loomed ahead, sleek and familiar, and the sky above suddenly exploded into fireworks. The Queen watched them with delight, but she was thinking how difficult some of the last few days had been for her, too. Those heart-in-mouth moments in Cagliari; waiting to hear from Hector Ross with his plan; worrying about Joan in Torcello – and rightly, as it had turned out. It was only by a miracle that her APS was alive to tell the tale.

Thank God it had worked out in the end. Sokolova and her daughter were safely aboard. Kinnock would take care of them at sea, and Major Ross from MI5 would take over when *Britannia* got back to Portsmouth. The one real tragedy was that Pavel Michalowski wouldn't get to see the woman he loved and the daughter he had made.

The gondoliers slowed their pace, so the royal couple could enjoy the frenzied explosions of light above.

It really *was* a miracle that Joan had survived, the Queen reflected, offering up a quick prayer of thanks to St Mark, whose basilica glittered in the light of the explosions in the sky. After all, Joan was horribly out of practice. If that KGB agent's gun hadn't misfired at the crucial moment . . .

They reached *Britannia* at last, where a platform with a staircase had been set up for her to ascend, and the nearest gondolier reached out a hand to help her. As the wide-bodied craft rocked beneath them, she was glad she had spent so much of her life on boats. With Philip to hold her other hand, she planted her feet carefully and rose.

Why *had* they killed Michalowski? Her overexcited brain wouldn't stop her thoughts from straying.

'Thank you so much,' she said to the gondoliers. 'What a wonderful journey.'

'*Prego, prego, signora. Viva la regina!*'

She beamed at them all.

Yes, but why *had* they? Was it out of sheer cruelty, to deprive the poor man of that moment with his lover? But they didn't know that the defector *was* his lover. If they had, they'd never have let Sokolova travel to Vienna. The Queen stepped across onto the little platform at the waterline where a yottie was ready to reach out and steady her, and pictured that moment of reunion, lost.

Philip followed his wife out of the gondola as the last of the fireworks lit up the sky like a paparazzo's flashbulb. And as the final sparks fizzled in the sky, so the pieces of the puzzle fell into place.

But of course.

After Vienna, the defection had been made *difficult*. And she had made it easy. What fools they'd all been – she herself more than anyone! How perfectly she'd been played.

Chapter 54

Joan was not surprised to be called to the Queen's sitting room the following morning, even though it was someone else's turn to collect the red boxes. It was early, but Her Majesty was already dressed for church. Her personal bags and boxes were being assembled for the lunchtime plane ride to Florence. After twenty-three hours in Venice, and counting, she had very little time left.

Joan sat in one of the chintz armchairs, while the Queen sat across from her on the sofa.

'Is there any news of our passengers?' the Queen asked.

Joan grinned cheerfully.

'They've been made comfortable in the storeroom used for the officers' spare luggage. Commander Kinnock has made sure they won't be disturbed. Maria's looking a bit better after a good night's sleep. Tatiana wants to thank you in person . . . But I told her you would have no idea what she was talking about.'

'Hmm,' the Queen said.

She glanced at her wristwatch. Joan knew they had about six minutes before the consul and the ambassador would be arriving to accompany Her Majesty to church. A look of brief discomfort flitted across the Queen's face, but she squared her shoulders, as if she was the bearer of bad news.

'They were never going to shoot you on Torcello, Joan,' she said.

'But, ma'am . . . they did.' Joan was confused.

'They shot *at* you. They missed.'

'Ma'am?'

'Sokolova is not Sokolova,' the Queen said flatly. 'I'm sorry, but we've been duped, me more than anyone. Moscow wants us to think we've rescued a useful asset. They've made us work for it. Look at us! We're very proud of ourselves.'

'But how . . . ?' Joan began. 'I—Who *is* she, then?'

'I don't know,' the Queen admitted. 'But she isn't the woman Michalowski befriended, and loved, and thought he was getting out of Russia. That's why they killed him. They had to, before the escape succeeded. Because he was the only one who'd have known.'

'B-but . . . She was the woman in the photograph,' Joan faltered. 'The one I saw in London.'

'I realise that. A nice touch. I think they planted that photograph there when they abducted him. Perhaps he'd been sent a different version – one with the real Sokolova. But it was important for you, or someone like you, to see this woman's face, so you would be sure she was the woman he was expecting.'

'But . . .' Joan was still struggling. 'They nearly killed her, ma'am. They've been chasing her since Vienna.'

'No, they haven't,' the Queen countered.

'I don't . . .'

The Queen sighed. 'Last night, I met a couple who told me about the difficulty of buying a palazzo.'

'Ma'am?'

'They moved heaven and earth to buy it, and when they did, they found it was cursed. This was the same idea: make it difficult, so the buyer focuses on the purchase and forgets to question its value. Of course, first, you have to be selling something they want.'

Joan's confusion began to lift. Instantly, she was back in the Caffè Genovese, feeling the tension in every muscle.

'And in our case, ma'am . . . the delay in Cagliari was a ruse? So we wouldn't ever ask ourselves if Sokolova was genuine?'

'I think so. Perhaps not on the first day. I think it's possible that the girl was really ill and that delayed them. They might have thought *Britannia* would go without them and they'd have to use a backup plan. But it didn't. That's when the woman's handlers must have realised that somebody very senior was involved. They decided to make it interesting. Hence your adventures on Torcello yesterday. They created some drama. All the time, they've been delivering her to us on a plate.'

'The picture in the cufflink box,' Joan murmured.

'I'm sorry?'

'There were two pictures in Michalowski's flat. Of interest, I mean. One was the photograph of the woman and the girl that I told you about and the other was hidden in a cufflink box. The women were similar, but not identical. The little photo was obviously precious to him.'

'Sokolova, almost certainly,' the Queen said.

'So, *this* woman, whoever she is . . . she's really a double agent? But why, ma'am? She's Russian. How could she help them? She'd never be allowed anywhere near our state secrets.'

'She doesn't need to be,' the Queen said with a sigh. 'I've been thinking it through all night. Apparently, she had special information about the identity of their Chief Engineer, didn't she? To start with, she could feed our intelligence services whatever misinformation the Russians want us to know. But her real value would be in joining the network of Soviet dissidents in London. She'd be taken to their bosom.'

Joan groaned. 'Especially when they heard all about her daring escape down to Italy, even if she kept the *Britannia* part of it quiet.' She paused in a frown of concentration, wrestling with her memory of two nights ago. Then Joan sighed, too. 'Yes, my adventure on Torcello makes sense, ma'am. Sokolova shoots and someone falls to the ground. It's dark. I can't see a wound, but I assume it's there. When I shoot, my mark has made sure he can fall backwards into the water. The only danger is that I might actually hit him. Who knows if I did?'

The Queen said nothing, but Joan could tell she thought it unlikely.

Joan finished her thought. 'And by morning, the bodies have gone. Do you know what, ma'am? I think the girl knew. Maria started trembling even before the first shot was fired. I think she'd been told there would be a fight.'

'It might have been even more frightening for her, knowing it was coming,' the Queen mused. 'The question is, what do we do with them now? They mustn't go anywhere near the dissident community.'

'Do we return them?'

The Queen shook her head.

'I'm not sanguine about what happens to Russian spies whose missions don't go according to plan. The girl doesn't deserve that. Besides, it's possible that even the so-called Doctor Sokolova is as much a pawn in all of this as anyone. And the stakes are so high.'

'George Blake,' Joan said.

'Precisely.'

Two days ago, Blake had been sentenced in London for his own sordid role in this dangerous game. He'd been given forty-two years for lives lost as the result of the networks he had exposed to the Russians. The life of a spy was as fragile as glass.

'Do you want me to talk to Major Ross?' Joan asked.

'I do. Meanwhile, Commander Kinnock must know nothing. I don't want him to give the game away to Doctor—whoever she is. Needless to say, it's essential she never knows I was involved, helpfully or otherwise.'

'I'll take care of that,' Joan promised.

'And now,' the Queen said, rising, 'I think it's time for church.'

Chapter 55

After visiting Florence and Turin, the royal couple returned home by air. The Queen arrived at Buckingham Palace with particularly tight hugs for her daughter, which Anne didn't understand, but didn't mind.

It was several days before *Britannia* docked at Portsmouth. At customs, the usual formalities were friendly and light. Afterwards, stores and luggage were removed with naval efficiency. The small team of KGB officers lounging at the dock watched with interest as steam trunks and other large boxes were removed. Several were large enough to hold an adult woman, and most could have held a child. Two tea chests in particular were met by a couple of undistinguished-looking men in raincoats and trilbies, who made sure they were separated from the rest and put into a medium-sized, undistinguished van. The van was driven to an undistinguished house on the outskirts of London, where it was parked out of sight, round the back. The Russians were pleased to report to their masters that everything was continuing according to plan.

Apart from one minor hiccup with the girl, which turned out to be a huge strategic stroke of luck, everything had gone like clockwork. What a stupid idea of Michalowski's, to use the royal yacht. Had they been able to intervene to improve his plan, they would have done so. Instead, they simply set out to make it successful, whatever happened. When the little girl slowed everything down, they naturally assumed that *Britannia* would leave Cagliari without the defectors. In that case, they would have arranged for 'Sokolova' to contact Commander Kinnock or the British attaché in Rome some other way. But to their amazement and delight, the royal yacht waited.

They had assumed they were playing chequers with a lowly naval officer. Now, they realised, they were playing chess with someone very important. The top brass in Moscow could hardly contain their joy.

By then, a local team was watching the Caffè Genovese at the port. They saw Kinnock wait, and then have his place taken by another woman, a redhead, who worked for the Queen in some junior administrative capacity. They timed 'Sokolova''s call to perfection, so it arrived just as the redhead was about to leave. It was all about creating tension, despair, panic, hope, relief.

In the days that followed, they refined their new approach. Make them work for it. Say only *Britannia* would do. Make it just possible for another attempt to save her, and the girl, of course. Deliver them to Venice. Then watch them like hawks and make things even more exciting before their eventual 'triumph'. A top team from Budapest was rushed to the Veneto to make it happen. If you want to look mildly but believably incompetent, you need the very best. In the end, they were lucky that one of their men got away with a shoulder graze.

They still didn't know who exactly was masterminding the oh-so-confident British response. It couldn't be Commander Kinnock of the Royal Navy, because he simply wasn't senior enough to have manufactured that overnight stay in Cagliari, or the subsequent assistance offered to 'Sokolova' on Torcello. It was possible, they thought, that Rear Admiral Marlow was working for British intelligence in some capacity. They would certainly keep an eye on him. But their bet was on Miles Urquhart, the Queen's deputy private secretary. He was already known in royal circles to have helped solve a couple of nasty murders a few years ago. He had paid a lot of attention to the disappearance and subsequent discovery of Michalowski. The redhead worked for him. He was on board *Britannia* in Naples, and Kinnock may have confided in him.

Urquhart had obediently 'outwitted' his deadly enemy, and rescued an important dissident from Star City. It was perfect. Perhaps 'Tatiana Sokolova' would be treated to a special reception in Buckingham Palace. She would have so much to tell them when the time was right.

'Sokolova', needless to say, was not in any of the boxes.

She and the girl had been extracted from the yacht days before, in Malta, and put on a military plane to London in the company of Hector Ross and Madeleine Simon. Few words were spoken, no explanations made on landing, no paperwork provided. As far as the ports were concerned, they didn't exist.

While the Russians were busy assuming she was still at sea, Hector had been hard at work creating a new asset. It wasn't gentle or kind, because these things never are. His original plan had been to find out everything she knew about Star City and to use this as leverage with the Americans. However, things had changed.

On landing at Brize Norton, 'Tatiana' had been roughly separated from the girl, whose fate she was not told of, and taken to a facility in Buckinghamshire. There, she was told by Hector himself that a mole in the KGB London station had leaked the identity-swap plan from the start, and his organisation had played along to get her into their hands.

'Why?' she had asked, trembling, terrified, constantly begging for news of Maria, which he withheld.

'Because I'd like you to help us,' he said.

She held out for three sleepless days and nights, but it never really crossed her mind to question whether he knew the truth, or was just guessing. Eventually, she gave up. It was quick, he thought, because she wanted to. It turned out, he was right.

Her name was Valentina, and she had been a friend and colleague of Tatiana Sokolova years before, when they had learned English and played chess together as students. Tatiana had gone on to qualify as a doctor, while Valentina had done further language training and joined the KGB. Her job on this mission was to take her old friend's place and report back whatever she could learn from London. Meanwhile, she was to tell them that a certain Russian general was the secret genius behind their space programme.

He wasn't, although in Valentina's stated opinion, his ego was bigger than the moon. Neither she nor the real Tatiana had ever worked at Star City, so she didn't know the true identity of the Chief Engineer – and she insisted that she wouldn't tell them if she knew. *He* was a hero. A man worth dying for, even now.

What surprised Hector was how bitter and dismissive Valentina was of her handlers, and the way they had treated her old friend. Over days, he questioned her relentlessly on the full story, testing her story for chinks, for signs that she'd been prepared for this interview and was still pretending.

'How is Maria?' she would ask at the beginning of every interrogation. 'Is she safe? Can I see her?'

'You can when you've told me everything I need to know. Now, let's start again.'

Chapter 56

Joan knew what her lover was doing. It was tough, but necessary, for the safety of the dissidents in London, and for all of them.

Maria was being looked after at home by a female Russian speaker from Hector's office. She ate, and slept, and wouldn't be parted from her patchwork dog. But unlike Valentina, the little girl gave nothing away. 'I want my mama,' she would say. 'Who is your mama?' She stuck to the story every time.

'How long does this have to go on for?' Joan asked Hector one Sunday morning, after about a week.

They were going for a drive in the green lanes of Sussex in the beautiful, open-top Austin Healey he had bought himself as a present, after his divorce. Joan was keenly aware of the woman and the girl in their separate places. She knew what it was like for a girl to lose her mother – and it seemed to her that Maria was suffering it twice.

Hector raised a hand from the wheel and pushed a lock of hair from his face.

'Not long now. I think Valentina's given us everything. I'm just making sure.'

'What I don't understand is why the Russians would want to let the girl come to London in the first place. Wasn't she a liability?'

Hector glanced across at her. They were not supposed to be having this conversation, but they had crossed that Rubicon a long time ago. He shrugged.

'They didn't. That was Sokolova's idea. The real Sokolova. She arranged it with Valentina.'

'What? You mean, they talked?'

Hector nodded. 'The KGB arranged for them to be together briefly, so Valentina could learn as much as she needed to about her old friend, and what she'd told Michalowski over the years. As soon as Tatiana understood the plan, she knew she was as good as dead. She realised she could play along, contact Michalowski using the codes they'd worked out, and probably die when Valentina replaced her . . . or she could object and die sooner, and the plan would continue anyway. So, she used the only leverage she had – to be obedient, and to beg Valentina to get her daughter out somehow.'

'They didn't need to kill her,' Joan said. 'We'd never have known about the swap.'

'There's no such thing as "never" in our trade. They don't like loose ends.'

'I should imagine Tatiana's love of Mother Russia was a bit thin at this point.'

'I should think it was,' Hector agreed.

Joan remembered the detail of the 'confession' in the villa on Torcello – the description that the woman she thought of as Sokolova gave about her political fears and disappointments.

Perhaps it had been scripted by the KGB, or perhaps it had been what the real Sokolova thought. Lies could be convincing when they were someone else's true beliefs.

She shuddered. 'But . . . that meant Maria would have to pretend that Valentina was her mother forever.'

Hector's lip curled. 'Yes. They told the girl that she would be doing it as a good communist, but equally, if she ever disobeyed, she would die instantly. No wonder she was in a state of perpetual terror. She knows their plans for her mother, by the way. They gave her some complicated lie, but when she was sick in Trieste, Maria wanted to know if she would join her mother in heaven. She'd been told heaven didn't exist, of course, but someone, somewhere, must have given her a shred of religion to hang on to.'

'What will become of her?' Joan wondered.

Hector shrugged. 'Eventually, she'll need a guardian of some sort. Let me know if you think of anyone suitable. For now, she'll have to live with Valentina, so the Russians think we bought their story.'

He suddenly slammed a hand on the steering wheel. 'I should have seen it from the start. I was an idiot. That padlock on the door in Michalowski's flat. You noticed its incongruity, my darling. So did I. They put it there like a marker, to make sure we didn't miss the treasures inside. At the same time, they inserted the picture of Valentina with Maria, pretending to be Sokolova, but they missed the snapshot of the real Tatiana Sokolova in the cufflink box.'

'I know,' Joan said.

'We knew the women didn't match when we found it, but we didn't make too much of it, because we weren't paying enough attention. We assumed Michalowski had a thousand lovers. We didn't ask ourselves, why this one?'

'He didn't have a picture of his daughter with it,' Joan pointed out. 'Why not?'

'The snap of Tatiana was taken during his visit to Russia,' Hector said. 'I doubt she felt safe sending him one of Maria. It might have looked suspicious . . . until the KGB started giving the instructions. Michalowski thought he was being so careful, but according to Valentina, his relationship was known to the censor's office for years. As soon as the KGB discovered he was behind the failed escape in Berlin last year, they began to wonder how they could use him. His old lover seemed the easiest way.'

'Did he really believe she'd worked at Star City?'

Hector nodded. 'When they took over the correspondence, they claimed she'd been there. I imagine they hoped he'd tell someone like Kinnock, to back up Valentina's story when she arrived. The secret was so big, the prize so huge, we'd be staring at it so hard we wouldn't spot the other little inconsistencies.'

'Like what?'

'Oh, like the fact that they hadn't decently covered their tracks at his flat. I liked to think of them as amateurish, because it suited me. In fact, the idea was for Michalowski to simply disappear, and for me to work out later that the KGB must have made it happen. It was supposed to look as if they'd been searching for information about the escape, but hadn't found it, so we wouldn't be suspicious when it was successful. When I started asking questions sooner than expected, the rumours at the embassy backed it up. I spent weeks thinking they were in a flat panic, when in fact they'd hooked me like a sea trout.'

'They were genuinely amateurish about disposing of the body, though,' Joan pointed out, stroking his arm sympathetically.

'Only just. If it hadn't been for the pigs going to market and the royal train appearing unexpectedly . . .'

'And Sandra Pole looking out of a window . . .'

'Anyway, it explains why there were no signs of torture on him,' Hector grunted. 'They didn't need to question him about anything. They always knew everything.'

He slowed down to go through a village. The bucolic sights of Sussex in early summer were an improbable background for this conversation.

'So, there was no escape to speak of, really,' Joan said.

He barked a short laugh. 'How they must have loved us all descending on Vienna. In reality, Valentina and Maria had been dropped off at the station. The rest was as Michalowski had arranged it. The KGB weren't worried about the workability of his plan because, of course, they could always *make* it work. The one thing Valentina wasn't doing was fleeing from the Russians. If it went wrong, which it probably would, they would just switch to a backup plan – which explains another thing.'

'Oh?'

'Why there weren't any clues about the escape route in the flat,' he said. 'Michalowski was slapdash, but they were reasonably careful. If they had to switch to another plan, they wanted Valentina to be able to say it was Michalowski's all along. If Kinnock hadn't confessed to . . . whoever he confessed to . . . on *Britannia*, I imagine we'd never have known what it was.'

In the stress of the last several days, Joan had forgotten that she'd neglected to tell Hector she'd already known about Cagliari and the twenty-ninth of April. Neither had she mentioned the Queen's involvement. He actually knew a lot less than he thought he did about that side of things. She kept silent.

'And then the girl was genuinely ill,' he said, 'but *Britannia* miraculously waited.'

He described how the Russians must have adapted as they went along.

'Making us work for it,' Joan said grumpily.

'Exactly. Making *me* work for it. And work for it I did. As I say, they reeled me in. No, "Sokolova" couldn't escape quickly and safely, like any sane defector, she had to do it in Venice. Either Kinnock or a woman in the Queen's employ had to be there, which effectively meant using the royal yacht after all. The clock was ticking, I had to make a series of quick decisions. So did you and your taskmaster, whoever he is. We all worked fast, overcoming each obstacle, inserting ourselves more and more urgently into their trap.'

'Until the pièce de résistance on Torcello.'

'Until you, my darling, got shot at by a couple of agents who could easily have accidentally killed you in the dark.' He glanced across with what Joan could only think of as a very soppy look for a man who caught spies for a living.

'That man I shot back at . . .' she said, hastily. 'Does Valentina know if I really got him?'

'Wonderful! Your biggest concern is whether you got a hit. Would that be a good thing, or a bad thing?'

'A good thing, obviously.'

'I love you, Joan McGraw. But I seriously doubt it. The plan was for both operatives to look as if they'd been killed, if possible. How proud of themselves the British would be!'

'So, no bodies in the canal behind the cathedral.'

'No bodies.'

Joan thought back to her fear and pride that night with a shiver of humiliation. She pictured the man theatrically throwing himself backwards into the water. How they must have laughed at her afterwards, over a stiff drink or two, when the operation was over.

'I need more training,' she muttered.

Hector sighed. 'We need to talk about that, but first, I have a question for you. You don't need to answer – I'm merely curious.'

'Oh?'

'Who *was* it who got *Britannia* to stay put in Cagliari for twenty-four hours?'

Joan looked across at him archly. 'Who says it wasn't a snagged propeller?'

'*I* say,' he told her with a grin.

'I'm afraid I couldn't possibly comment.'

Hector frowned, drumming his fingers on the wheel. 'Rumours are, the Russians think it's Miles Urquhart. We all know what to make of that.'

'Do we?' she asked innocently.

'My darling, I've met the man several times now. He could hardly sign his own name on a petition. I used to think it was Sir Hugh Masson, but even the private secretary couldn't hold up *Britannia* in all her pomp. That doesn't leave us many options.'

The penetrating look he gave her was speculative and amused.

Joan sighed. 'I thought you said I didn't need to answer.'

He nodded reluctantly. 'In that case,' he said. 'I've got another question. I've been thinking about it since that night on Torcello. When, as you say, I put you in harm's way with not enough training and a borrowed gun.'

Joan was wary. His soppy gaze was back.

'You only did as I asked,' she pointed out.

'Well, now I have something to ask you.'

They had reached the brow of a hill, where there was a little lay-by. He pulled in, as if the whole thing had been scripted to arrive at this point. The Sussex Downs lay spread out before them like a blanket, under a Wedgwood blue summer sky. Joan stiffened in her seat as he killed the engine and took her hand.

'Will you marry me?' he asked.

Chapter 57

Prince Philip was delighted with his photographs of *Britannia*, Venice and Florence. He spent a happy afternoon arranging the best ones in an album in his study at Windsor.

'What do you think?' he asked. 'I was thinking of showing them to Tony.'

'I'm sure he'd love to see them,' the Queen said brightly.

'But he's a professional. If he showed me the way he drives a frigate I doubt *I'd* be impressed.'

'I think you've done a very good job. Look at all those Venetian windows. Very atmospheric.'

'Thank you, sausage. Of course, the camera helps. I got the one Sandra Pole showed us. On the train, d'you remember?'

'I remember,' the Queen said.

'How's Mrs Pole?' Philip asked. 'I heard the divorce was going through. Having met her, I see Nigel's predicament. Hers, too. Ghastly man. She's well shot of him.'

'She is,' the Queen agreed. 'And I understand she's drinking less. Margaret says she's much more reliable these days.'

'Still, she's hardly lady-in-waiting material. My God!'

'No. Apparently, she's going to invest her money in the theatre. She'll be what they call an angel. She thinks the West End has an exciting future.'

'Does she? The theatre's all people shouting at each other these days, as far as I can see. It'll end in tears.' Philip paused and reflected for a moment. 'I admire her for trying though. It takes balls to hold your head up.'

The Queen wasn't sure about the biology, but she agreed with the sentiment.

Life at the palace was busy as ever, with a packed schedule of summer events and the upcoming Kennedy visit to prepare for. Joan was as punctilious as always, but the Queen noticed her APS was slightly withdrawn – almost melancholic. It was a surprise, after the way things turned out in Italy. The Queen had expected her to be firing on all cylinders.

'Is anything the matter?' she asked, as Joan came to pick up the red boxes one day in late May.

Joan stalled for a while. 'Just a little trouble in Dolphin Square. Nothing I can't handle, ma'am.'

'It's not Major Ross, I hope?'

Joan blushed. 'Yes, ma'am.'

'I imagine he's cross with you for getting shot at.'

Joan looked surprised. 'He is. But he sent me there.'

'And then, having sent you, he worried about you, no doubt.'

Joan's shoulders slumped. 'He did.' They slumped a bit more. 'He decided that he couldn't bear it if anything happened to me, and he had to pretend we weren't . . . weren't . . .'

'That he didn't care for you very much,' the Queen suggested.

Joan nodded glumly. 'He proposed last week.'

The Queen sat back in her study chair. They regarded each other across the rug. It came as no surprise to her that Hector Ross felt this way, but, like Joan, she knew what the consequences would be. Women who got married and were at risk of having babies couldn't possibly stay in busy jobs. Well, one or two did, apparently, but the Queen wasn't sure she'd ever met one. The fact that she *was* one was beside the point. She had a nursery full of staff to take care of the details.

Joan put an absent hand to her pearls, and looked miserable.

'I'm sure that if you said yes, we could find something for you . . . Somewhere in the palace . . .' the Queen muttered vaguely. She plastered on a hopeful smile and knew she wasn't being very helpful.

'Yes, ma'am.'

The Queen wanted to say, 'I'd miss you,' but that sounded too manipulative. Or 'We could make it work out somehow,' but that wasn't true.

'These jobs don't go on forever,' were the words that came out of her mouth.

Hers did, but others didn't. That's what she had been thinking. Could Joan wait a year or two? Or five? Was that too much to ask? The Queen was so very comfortable with her. It *was* too much to ask, so she didn't. Instead, she said, 'How is little Maria getting on, by the way? Do you know?'

Joan's shoulders relaxed a little. 'Quite well, ma'am. Valentina promised her that she would see Big Ben, so we took her to see it strike twelve from Parliament Square.'

'Who's "we"?'

'I took her with Sandra Pole and Henry Coxon, ma'am. They're a bit of an item – or rather, they will be, when the divorce is finalised. They're both thrilled to have a real, live defector in their midst.'

'They don't know the real story, I assume?'

'No, ma'am,' Joan acknowledged. 'They know a little about my involvement, but not yours. Meanwhile, Sandra took Conchita with her on the Big Ben outing, and she and Maria have bonded. Sandra knows the breeder, so she's going to get Maria a dog of her own.'

'Another chihuahua?'

'Maria's thrilled,' Joan said, supressing a smile.

'I wonder . . .'

'Ma'am?'

The Queen had a sudden image, set some time in the future, of a slightly more mature Sandra Pole, liberated from her awful husband and happily settled with Henry Coxon, taking on some responsibility for the motherless girl. After all, it was thanks to Sandra that Maria's father's full story was known, that his proposed escape for her had gone ahead more or less as planned, and that she wouldn't have to lie to everyone about her true mother for the rest of her life – even if she would for a while, until Ross had finished peddling misinformation to the Russians via Valentina. It was a neat little picture, perhaps too symmetrical, but a pleasant daydream anyway.

She brushed it aside. 'Meanwhile, Valentina is cooperating, I hope?'

'Yes, ma'am. MI5 are watching her closely. She won't tell her handlers anything we don't want them to know. And nor will Josiah Thorburn.'

'Two double agents. I hope Major Ross is pleased.'

Joan nodded. 'And there's Mr Wilson, Sergei Steklyar's replacement.'

'Oh yes. I hope he's enjoying tracking his movements too. Major Ross seems to have done rather well out of all of this.'

'He has, rather,' Joan agreed. 'And he's grateful. He knows it wasn't all his own work.'

The Queen had been wondering about this.

'Whose work does he think it was?' she asked.

Joan's grinned widened.

'He told me his theory, which I neither confirmed nor denied, but he's very confident about it. You see, it all comes back to *Britannia*. He's aware that only three people genuinely had the seniority to hold her in port for twenty-four hours, namely you, Prince Philip and the admiral. Hector's met Rear Admiral Marlow, and knows he was abroad in nineteen fifty-seven, when the palace and I last provided unofficial help in solving murders.'

'True,' the Queen acknowledged warily.

'He's convinced my boss in both these matters must be the same person. Marlow's out, so, that only leaves you and

Prince Philip. It couldn't possibly be you, ma'am. Therefore, it has to be the Duke.'

The Queen's lips twitched. 'What a plausible theory.'

'Hector would never want to implicate the Duke in anything, because of the scandal, so he'll say nothing – even to anyone at the office.'

'How very discreet.'

'But he wanted me to pass on his appreciation, if I got the opportunity. He said it's thanks to the Duke's intelligence and quick thinking that Valentina and her handlers didn't get the chance to do any damage.'

'How lovely.'

The Queen wasn't sure whether to be relieved, or slightly disappointed that the director of D Branch wasn't a little bit more perceptive. Was he good enough for Joan?

Perhaps. Eventually.

Chapter 58

The wedding in York Minster was a joyous occasion. Having safely disposed of the Kennedys, the Queen, Prince Philip and the rest of the royal family travelled up by train to attend. Princess Anne was one of the bridesmaids.

After all, the Queen's cousin, the Duke of Kent was getting married. It was a love match with Katharine Worsley – only the second commoner to marry a British prince since the reign of George III. 'How very modern', as the Queen Mother observed. It was hard to imagine such a thing happening in her day – when even she, the daughter of an earl, was judged too lowly by some to marry into the royal family.

Anyway, everyone had a marvellous time and the journey back to London was so raucous that a party guest managed to skewer poor Sir Hugh's foot with one of her stilettos in the semi-royal saloon. The train had to stop briefly at Doncaster so he could be taken to hospital.

'And just when Mr Ward had sorted out his neck,' Miles Urquhart said to Joan with a pious sigh, while he thought about how he'd rearrange the items on the private secretary's desk.

*

Not for the first time that year, the Queen woke up the following morning feeling a little bleary. She was slightly late in joining Philip for breakfast back at the palace, but, most unusually, Philip was even later.

'Too many vodka martinis?' she commiserated.

He shook his head. 'As you know, I was tucked up by midnight. But I couldn't stop reading my novel. Bastard thing kept me awake till half past two.'

'Oh really? What was it?'

'A book called *Call For the Dead*,' he said. 'Sort of whodunnit. Dominic gave it to me.'

'Who's it by?'

Philip frowned and shrugged. 'It has a yellow jacket. Can't remember the chap's name. Very good writer, though. I think we'll see more of him.'

'How nice,' the Queen said.

But whodunnits weren't really her thing, unless they were about horses. She went back to the very interesting article she'd been reading in the *Racing Post*.

Afternotes

There may be points in this book when you have wondered 'Did that happen? Did she make it up?' I've discovered that historical research has been one of the most rewarding aspects of writing these novels. Truth is indeed stranger than fiction.

For example, in this novel, *Britannia* is forced to spend an unexpected twenty-four hours in the port of Cagliari, while the Royal Navy untangles a propeller caught in a cable. This seems the most unlikely thing to happen to the impeccably serene royal yacht. Surely I invented it? But it did happen, as reported in the Italian press at the time. Possibly not for the reasons I give in the book, mind you.

Here are some more research notes and background details that you might enjoy, if you like that sort of thing. As far as I'm aware, nobody ever saw a body being disposed of from the royal train. But if they had done, would we know?

The idea of murder glimpsed from a passing train is cheerfully lifted from Agatha Christie's *4.50 From Paddington*, with a hint of Hitchcock's *The Lady Vanishes* in the female witness who isn't believed. The journey taken by the royal train in this story is one that it regularly made, and the carriages are as accurate as I can make them for the period. The Queen got new carriages as part of her Silver Jubilee celebrations in 1977, but before that, she made do with the mixed bag she inherited from her father, grandfather and great-grandfather, from her own sleeping quarters to the semi-royal saloon. (My own Scottish granny worked for a family in the 1930s who kept several carriages for travelling to London for the summer season.)

Near the spot where the 'skipping-rope man' is spotted, there is a real-life stately home called Shugborough Hall, situated on the edge of the very beautiful protected landscape known as Cannock Chase. I only discovered after writing the book that the Hall itself was partly funded in the eighteenth century by George Anson, 'the father of the British navy – a serendipitous coincidence for a novel that goes on to describe a jewel in the Royal Navy's crown: *HMY Britannia*. Even more serendipitously, Shugborough was lived in by one of the family's descendants, the fifth earl of Litchfield, who as Patrick Litchfield was a very successful photographer in the 1960s, and a good friend of the royals. I wasn't aware of his residence there until I came to write these notes, but if you've read the book, you'll see how neatly he fits.

The agonising discussion of 'the tigers' during dinner on the train is based on events that took place during the royal tour of India and Nepal in 1961. Prince Philip really did 'injure his trigger finger', ensuring that he was unable to shoot the second tiger of the tour in Nepal. He was in a very difficult position, forced to choose between politeness to his hosts and his role in the WWF, which was close to his heart. I believe he did the most diplomatic thing he and his staff could think of, at the time and it shows the tightrope of social expectations the royal couple had to walk throughout their lives. No wonder the Queen chose not to give interviews.

The full story of the photographer Lee Miller and her encounter with Hitler's bathtub in Munich was told to me by Miller's son, Anthony Penrose, when I visited her sublime farmhouse in Sussex, now a museum. The picture was taken on her camera by her fellow photographer, David Scherman, who was Jewish. Both had been among the first to enter the newly-liberated Dachau camp that day. Miller was keen to display objects showing the Fuhrer's kitsch taste in art. The dust from the horrors of the camp is visible on her boots. Only later did they discover the coincidence that it was the day Hitler committed suicide in his bunker.

It is true that Anglican clergymen have a disproportionate love of trains in all their forms, from timetables to model railways. I made it up, then discovered to my delight that it's far more prevalent than I knew.

Some readers may have wondered about 'Mrs Hughes', who helps out Henry Coxon in Chalcot Square. The scene is, of course, invented, but Silvia Plath was married to Ted Hughes and living there at the time.

Sergei Steklyar, the spy-runner, is a fictional character inspired by a man who could have stepped straight out of the pages of John Le Carré or Mick Herron. He was known in London in the 1950s as Gordon Lonsdale, a successful playboy businessman who traded in jukeboxes, slot machines and bubblegum. In fact, he was a Russian called Konon Molody, who had been groomed by Soviet intelligence since childhood. The seed capital for his businesses came from the KGB, and he claimed to have used it to become the first multi-millionaire 'illegal', or sleeper agent. He ran various operations in England, including the infamous Portland Spy Ring, which was exposed in 1961. It's a classic tale of strategic affairs, microdots, hidden radios and dead letter drops. Eventually, Molody was returned to Russia in a spy swap and died in suspicious circumstances, possibly killed by the – ungrateful, I would like to say – KGB.

Both Elizabeth and Philip were interested Yuri Gagarin's achievement as a cosmonaut and glamour as a person. In the summer of 1961, he went on a world tour, but as a Soviet citizen, he was not welcome by the British Government. However, he was invited to the UK by the Foundry Workers Union and the royal couple enthusiastically hosted him to lunch at Buckingham Palace. According to a fellow pilot, 'A pleasant middle aged woman entered the living room, very simply dressed, without jewellery and any traces of makeup – it was the Queen of England.' Lunch was lively, with Gagarin uncertain of aristocratic table etiquette and the Queen, for whom politeness was all, cheerfully encouraging her guests to eat as Gagarin did, while Philip quizzed him about technology. Afterwards, exceptionally, it was Elizabeth who asked to have her picture taken with him.

The 'Chief Designer' and mastermind of the Soviet space programme was Sergei Korolev. His identity was successfully kept secret by the Soviets until after his death following a surgical operation in 1966. Born and educated in Ukraine, Korolev worked on rocket design in Leningrad in the '30s. Under Stalin's Great Purge, he was denounced in 1938 (almost certainly by the man who took his job), tortured in the Lubyanka and imprisoned in the Gulag in Siberia. Despite this treatment and his grudging rehabilitation after the war, he remained one of the Soviet Union's greatest assets. I encountered his story in the Science Museum in London, and he is one of the most fascinating people I've ever read about. While he was in charge, the USSR kept winning important battles in the space race, despite its massively inferior materials and investment. After he died, the USA quickly took over and never looked back. Of course, President Kennedy's support for the moonshot made a huge difference, and Korolev's own moon-launch plans were not going well at the time, but I can't help wondering how the race would have gone if he had survived that operation.

For those interested in the royal family more widely, the baby that Margaret was expecting was Viscount Linley, born in November 1961.

Poor Sir Hugh. The private secretary is fictional, but the skewering of someone's foot by a stiletto heel during the party on the train really happened. And the train did have to stop off at Doncaster to get the victim medical attention. The Queen told that story herself to Sir Robert Goodwill, MP for Scarborough and Whitby, who had lined up to see her in York that day as a boy. How could I not include it?

In the final scene, Prince Philip is reading a novel. Eagle-eyed readers might correctly deduce that it was *Call for the Dead* by a certain John Le Carré. It's the book that got me interested in spy novels when my mother described the plot to me when I was a teenager. Le Carré wrote it while working at MI6, but the success of his third novel two years later enabled him to become a full-time writer. That book, as many readers will know, was *The Spy Who Came In From the Cold*.

SJ Bennett May 2025

Acknowledgements

Once more, thank you to the late Queen Elizabeth II for a life of service, a sense of fun, and for preserving the mystery of the monarchy enough to let me imagine this secret fictional string to her bow.

The series owes its success to Charlie Campbell and Sam Edenborough at Greyhound Literary. I'm also hugely thankful to all the publishers and translators around the world who have helped get this copy into your hands – as well as the booksellers, librarians, friends and family who might have recommended it to you. What a wonderful lot they are.

To my editor, Ben Willis, here is the mystery set on a train that you asked for – except, as you've seen, it's not *entirely* set on a train; there is also quite a lot of yacht. Thanks to everyone on the team at Bonnier, including Nick Stearn and also Iker Ayesteran, for the wonderful covers.

The research for this book covered everything from the life of the canons (men, not guns) at Windsor Castle to the gossip pages of the Italian papers in April, 1961. I have so many people to thank, including Michelle Lovric, Barbara Warburton Giliberti, the staff at the Marciana Library on St Mark's Square in Venice (yes, I researched there and yes, it was as special as you might suppose), Sandra Baker, Lisa Cutts, Charles Howeson, Patrick Kingston for his book on royal trains, the London Library, my friend, the real Tatiana Sokolova, and the organisers of the 'Cosmonauts: Birth of the Space Age' at the Science Museum in 2016, which introduced me to the life of Sergei Korolev, the 'Chief Designer and father of the Soviet Union's success in space. Korolev's life and death, and the secrecy surrounding him, are a fascinating tale in themselves. I only wish I had more space in which to explore it.

In 2024, my life was saved by the very special staff at the Cancer Centre London. There was a pause in the writing of this book while they did their thing, and it owes its existence to their dedication and care.

The Transatlantics kept me going when I wasn't sure, and laughed at the funny bits. I'm lucky to have such a generous critique group. As ever, I must thank my family, who put up with my thousand-yard stares while I am writing, and especially my husband Alex, my first reader and also, in this case, my personal guide to ships and guns. All the good ideas thereon were his, and mistakes are mine.

Last but by no means least, I want to say thank you to you, the reader, for getting this far. If you want to share your own stories of the Queen, or find out more about my research and other writing adventures, then you can sign up to my author newsletter, if you haven't already. You can find it, or contact me directly, via my website: www.sjbennettbooks.com. It's always lovely to hear from you.

If you enjoyed *The Queen Who Came in from the Cold* why not join the S.J. BENNETT READERS' CLUB?

When you sign up you'll receive an exclusive short story featuring the Queen, THE MYSTERY OF THE FABERGÉ EGG – plus Royal Correspondence about the series and access to exclusive material. To join, simply visit bit.ly/SJBennett

Keep reading for a letter from the author . . .

Hello!

Thank you for picking up *The Queen Who Came in from the Cold*.

This is the fifth book in the series, but I hope that each one can be read as a standalone in case it happens to be the one you find on a friend's bookshelf, perhaps, or in the library, or because it had your favourite cover in the shop. I often discover new writers this way. If this is your introduction to the series – welcome!

In the first three books of the series, the Queen is an elderly lady of ninety, using her great experience and hard-won wisdom to solve crimes. The fourth book finds her as a more uncertain woman of thirty, carefully trying to forge her path and balance being a monarch, wife and mother. In *The Queen Who Came in from the Cold*, she's more established, and she knows what she's doing. But yet again, a crucial part of her life is at threat, and she must respond with all her courage, cunning and integrity.

This story started because my editor, Ben, told me he'd love to see a royal mystery set on a train. I was happy to oblige, but I quickly noticed that most mysteries in such settings choose trains because they're a great way of bringing strangers under the same roof for a while. And nobody invited aboard the royal train was ever technically a stranger! Hence my decision to follow Agatha Christie's example from *4.50 from Paddington* and choose a murder seen *from* the train.

Meanwhile, one of my great joys in writing the series is researching the locations and the time period when they're set. 1961 was a year of great change, tension and glamour. I wanted to do justice to the times, and I couldn't resist including the Queen's visit to Italy, where I've spent a lot of time myself, over the years. Hence, the second form of transport in this novel, and the business aboard *Britannia*.

It gave me the chance to research the whistlestop visit to Venice – only thirty-six hours – and to give the Queen's trusty sidekick, Joan, the action scene that she deserved. You can perhaps imagine how much I enjoyed returning to St Mark's Square, and the outlying island of Torcello, for fictional purposes. I'll always look back fondly on the writing of this book. But I haven't finished writing the series yet . . .

If you would like to get updates on this book and future publications, then visit bit.ly/SJBennett where you can sign up to receive Royal Correspondence about the series. It only takes a few moments to join, and there are no catches or costs.

Bonnier Zaffre will keep your data private and confidential, and it will never be passed on to a third party. We won't spam you with loads of emails, and you can unsubscribe any time you want.

And if you would like to get involved in a wider conversation about this book, please consider reviewing *The Queen Who Came in from the Cold* online, or talk about it in real life with friends, family or reader groups. If you've already done so, I send you a heartfelt thank you.

With warmest wishes, S. J. Bennett

www.sjbennettbooks.com

Keep reading for an exclusive extract from the next mystery in the Her Majesty The Queen Investigates series . . .

DEATH ON THE ROYAL YACHT

Coming 2026

Chapter 1

The royal yacht sat peacefully at anchor. Above, the bright morning sky was softened with unthreatening clouds. Ahead, lush green hillsides were dotted with buildings the colours of sugared almonds, topped with pillar-box-red roofs. Around, a busy regatta already filled the harbour, eager white sails flecking the turquoise sea.

'Have you seen the forecast?' Prince Philip asked, sitting back in his wicker chair as he and the Queen finished breakfast in the sun lounge. 'It's bloody.'

'Really? Where?'

'London. Freezing winds, lashing rain . . . It's even wetter than last week, if you can imagine. There's two feet of snow in the Highlands.' He took a sip of coffee.

'Oh dear,' the Queen said, absently, spreading marmalade on the next bite of toast. Actually, she quite liked the idea of snow in the Highlands. And what could you expect in London in February? The younger children would probably enjoy splashing about in their galoshes.

Right now, the weather was doing what it usually did in the West Indies at this time of year – which was to be practically perfect. Elizabeth sighed at the view of St George's

Harbour in Grenada, beyond the veranda deck. Yesterday had been arguably even more idyllic. Twenty-four hours ago, the Royal Yacht *Britannia* had been anchored alongside the palm-fringed beaches of Tobago, where the Queen had been told about thirty times that it was the original desert island of *Robinson Crusoe*. She already knew; it was hard not to.

'Did anyone tell you yesterday that Tobago was the island Defoe had in mind for *Robinson Crusoe*?' Philip asked.

'Once or twice,' she said, drily.

He caught her tone, and grinned. 'As often as they asked if you'd met the Beatles?'

'Actually, for once they didn't. Everyone seemed to know about their visit to the palace last year.'

'Ah.' Philip's lips twitched. 'Let me guess. "What did Paul McCartney say when he got his MBE?" "Did you shake John Lennon's hand?" "Is Ringo as funny as he looks?"'

'Variations on the theme,' she agreed. 'Someone asked me what it was like to meet people who are so famous.'

He roared with laughter. 'Your face, Lilibet! I got asked that, too. I told the woman it was probably a bit like whatever she was feeling right then, meeting me. Except,' he amended, 'she looked rather terrified, so p'rhaps not. And anyway, I've met 'em before. Funny lads, the four of 'em, always larking about. I liked 'em.'

'They were very sweet,' the Queen said, thinking back to last year's medal ceremony. 'Nervous. Keen to do the right thing.'

'I'm not sure they took the whole thing entirely seriously,' Philip said. 'Even at the palace they were giggling and making jokes to each other.'

'Well, isn't that what we do?' she asked. 'Make jokes to each other, I mean? Otherwise, how does one cope?'

Without Philip to let off steam to, she simply couldn't do it, whatever this job entailed. Not do it serenely in public, anyway, with all eyes on your every observation and reaction. Sometimes you had to laugh in private, or you'd go stark, staring mad.

'I hope we're a bit more discreet,' he said. 'And we don't smoke funny substances in the loos, though God knows there are times it'd help.'

She swallowed her toast so hard it made her cough.

'They didn't! They wouldn't! Who told you?'

'I have it on good authority from a Guards officer who went in after them. He recognised the smell. I dread to think how he knew. Didn't ask.' Philip grinned. 'They must have been high as kites . . . The younger generation, God help us all. Mind you, did you hear the steel band at the garden party yesterday, playing their new songs? Very clever, I thought.'

'Was that the Beatles?' she asked. 'Gosh. Yes, *very* clever.'

Elizabeth didn't dare admit that a lot of steel band music – and in the last ten days she had heard a *lot* of steel band music – sounded quite similar to her. But she liked it very much, so it wasn't a problem. If they'd played flügelhorns in the Caribbean on the other hand . . . Well, thank God they didn't.

Philip was still thinking about the garden party on Tobago.

'And that rum punch . . . Fit to blow your head off. Everyone was having a whale of a time.' His brow furrowed momentarily as he drained his cup. 'Except your APS. I saw her looking daggers at Pamela at one point. What's the matter with Joan? She's supposed to be in paradise.'

The Queen grimaced. 'I've no idea.'

Her assistant private secretary was the dependable ex-codebreaker from Bletchley Park, Joan McGraw. Joan had been in the job for nearly a decade, during which she'd seen Her Majesty through several public triumphs and many more private near-disasters. Royal tours like this one were supposed to be the pinnacle of her career, but Elizabeth, too, had noticed Joan looking increasingly uncomfortable on this trip, and positively grumpy yesterday, amidst the palm-tree perfection of Tobago.

'I think Pamela's put Joan's nose out of joint,' Philip observed breezily.

'Oh, no. Joan's far too sensible for that sort of thing.'

'I'm telling you,' he insisted. 'Pamela's a pretty little thing, and she's clever. She's only been your diary secretary for about five minutes, and she's played an absolute blinder so far.'

'Joan was just as impressive last year,' the Queen reminded him.

Traditionally, diary management was one of Joan's roles as APS. Last year's state visit to Germany was the first by a British monarch since before the First World War, so she had been under huge pressure to make the wheels run smoothly. She had used all her language and diplomatic skills to ensure that a very busy tour by train and car, and even the royal yacht itself, had gone without a hitch.

But, loyal though the Queen was to her APS in most things, it turned out that when it came to the West Indies . . . well, the Honourable Pamela Sinclair knew the islands better. She'd arrived at the palace a few months ago to help with filing, but somehow, and the Queen couldn't quite remember how, she'd taken on some of the diary planning for this tour from Joan. It was Pamela who'd devised the more creative highlights of their visits. And her connections were surprisingly good for someone so young. Yesterday, for example, she had produced the perfect open-topped car for the royal couple to tour Tobago. The idea had been to highlight tourism to the island, which badly needed more tourist dollars, after a recent hurricane had played havoc with farms and crops. Joan had been working on a visit to a museum of some sort to make the point, but then Pamela had come up with the drive idea, in a convertible, with the press in hot pursuit, taking pictures at every pretty vantage point. It was a brilliant suggestion, fun to do, and the Queen felt a little bit guilty for preferring it to Joan's, but there it was.

'Pamela's got something, and Joan knows it,' Philip remarked. 'Men are more relaxed about that sort of thing, but when women work together . . . Well, you know . . .'

The Queen did know, and didn't entirely agree. The men who worked for her were not what one would call relaxed when they sensed a potential rival in their midst. Ultra-competitive might be a more accurate description.

'Pamela still has a lot to learn,' she said.

'How old is she? Twenty-four?'

'Twenty-five, I think.'

'Hmph. You were that age when you ascended the throne,' he pointed out. 'You managed alright. And she's a looker. That'll help.'

That much was true. Pamela had legs and lashes like a racehorse, huge eyes, abundant hair, and an overall doll-like attractiveness that men went crazy for these days. She could have been a model, and in fact, the Queen seemed to remember, she briefly had been. To look at her, you'd hardly expect a diplomatic power-house. But Elizabeth felt fairly certain she would do great things one day . . . Assuming she didn't simply marry a rich man and make him an accomplished wife. However, she sensed that Pamela wanted more.

'I'm off,' Philip said, standing up and donning his sunglasses. 'Busy day ahead. I'm going stretch my legs around the decks first. See you later, Cabbage.'

He was right. They were only in Grenada for a day, and there was a lot to do. The Queen swallowed some tea and was about to head for her bedroom to finish getting ready, when a footman opened the door and announced, 'Your assistant private secretary, ma'am.'

Joan McGraw entered the sun lounge from the passageway inside, crinkling her eyes against the light. She was a woman in her mid-forties, in the prime of life. Her red hair was styled into a flip-up bob and her smart summer dress was a turquoise shade that nicely matched the sea. She was always pale, but today, she looked unnaturally so, and there was a sort of unbalanced fizziness to her, the Queen thought, instead of her usual air of calm authority. Something was off.

'What is it?' she asked.

'Your Majesty.' Joan curtsied. For a moment, she looked as if she might faint. 'Pamela Sinclair is dead.'